COWARD'S TRUTH

A Novel of the Heart Eternal

Christian Warren Freed

This is a work of fiction. Names, characters, businesses, places, events, locales, and incidents are either the products of the author's imagination or used in a fictitious manner. Any resemblance to actual persons, living or dead, or actual events is purely coincidental.

Copyright © 2022 by Christian Warren Freed

Cover design by Pop Goes the Pixel
Author Photograph by Anicie Freed

Warfighter Books supports the right to free expression and the value of copyright. The purpose of copyright is to encourage writers and artists to produce creative works that enrich our culture. The scanning, uploading, and distribution of this book without permission is a theft of the author's intellectual property. If you would like permission to use material from the book (other than for review purposes), please contact warfighterbooks@gmail.com. Thank you for your support of the author's rights.

Warfighter Books
Holly Springs, North Carolina 27540
https://www.christianwfreed.com

First Edition: June 2022

Library of Congress Cataloging-in-Publication Data
Name: Freed, Christian Warren, 1973- author.
Title: Coward's Truth: A Novel of the Heart Eternal/ Christian Warren Freed
Description: First Edition | Holly Springs, NC: Warfighter Books, 2022. Identifiers: LCCN 2022904741 | ISBN 9781957326092 (trade paperback) Subjects: Fantasy | Epic Fantasy
Printed in the United States of America

10 9 8 7 6 5 4 3 2 1

ACCLAIM FOR CHRISTIAN WARREN FREED

THE LAZARUS MEN AGENDA

'Reminiscent of Tom Clancy or Stephen King, where you can envision everything happening in an era that don't yet exist but feels as familiar as the room you're reading in at the time.'

'It's a sometimes violent, yet often entertaining, off-world adventure.'

'The author draws us into a world full of conspiracy in which those who have everything want even more because human greed for power is too great.'

HAMMERS IN THE WIND: BOOK I OF THE NORTHERN CRUSADE

'Freed is without a doubt an amazing storyteller. His execution of writing descriptive and full on battle scenes is second to none, the writers ability in that area is unquestionable. He also drags you into the world he has created with ease and panache. I couldn't put it down.'

'Gripping! Hammers in the Wind is an excellent start to a new fantasy series. Christian Warren Freed has created an exciting storyline with credible characters, and an effectively created fantasy world that just draws you in.'

DREAMS OF WINTER
A FORGOTTEN GODS TALE #1

'Dreams of Winter is a strong introduction to a new fantasy series that follows slightly in the footsteps of George R.R. Martin in scope.' Entrada Publishing

"Steven Erickson meets George R.R. Martin!"

"THIS IS IT. If you like fantasy and sci-fi, you must read this series."

LAW OF THE HERETIC:
IMMORTALITY SHATTERED I

'If you're looking for a fun and exciting fantasy adventure, spend a few hours in the Free Lands with the Law of the Heretic.'

WHERE HAVE ALL THE ELVES GONE?

'Sometimes funny and other times a little dark, Where Have The Elves Gone? brings something fresh and new to fantasy mysteries. Whether you want to curl up with a mystery or read more about elves this book has something for everyone. Spend a few hours solving a mystery with a human and a couple of dwarves - you'll be glad you did.'

Other Books by Christian Warren Freed

The Northern Crusade
Hammers in the Wind
Tides of Blood and Steel
A Whisper After Midnight
Empire of Bones
The Madness of Gods and Kings
Even Gods Must Fall

The Histories of Malweir
Armies of the Silver Mage
The Dragon Hunters
Beyond the Edge of Dawn

Forgotten Gods
Dreams of Winter
The Madman on the Rocks
Anguish Once Possessed
Through Darkness Besieged
Under Tattered Banners
A Time For Tyrants*

Where Have All the Elves Gone?
One of Our Elves is Missing*
Tomorrow's Demise: The Extinction Campaign
Tomorrow's Demise: Salvation
Coward's Truth
The Lazarus Men
Repercussions: A Lazarus Men Agenda*
Daedalus Unbound: A Lazarus Men Agenda*

A Long Way From Home+

Immortality Shattered
Law of the Heretic
The Bitter War of Always

Land of Wicked Shadows
Storm Upon the Dawn

War Priests of Andrak Saga
The Children of Never

SO, You Want to Write a Book? +
SO, You Wrote a Book. Now What? +

*Forthcoming   + Nonfiction

A thought…

This one was a wild ride. Difficult to compress and explain. Sort of like your favorite coffee, bourbon, or cigar. There are hints of this and that in here and, much like those three vices, you might not notice them, but you will know if you like it or not.

Let's take example from the modern world. In the Heart Eternal we have elements of the Syrian Civil War with 'peacekeeping' armies, tribes similar to the Afghan mountain region, and the chaos of old demons and gods just trying to get by. Did I mention the squad of space marines stranded in the desert?

Hopefully you enjoy reading this one as much as I did writing it. Don't fret, we'll return soon to the Heart Eternal with the sequel: Down Dark Roads Best Forgotten.

See you in the pages.

PROLOGUE

Hohn popped up from his bunk, confused. Klaxons blared throughout the ship, warning of impending peril. The *Acheron* rocked, throwing him and the others in the troop bay to the cold deck. Curses and snarls added to the growing confusion. Flood lights sprang on, bathing the barracks of the transport in unnatural brightness. The deck lurched beneath them. Hohn watched as packs and other equipment started sliding.

Years of experience focused his mind. Metal groaned deep within the *Acheron's* bowels. He smelled fire. Melting wires. Hohn snatched his blouse from the bunk post and went to work. "On your feet, people! We're under attack!"

Soldiers stirred. Hohn zipped the front of his blouse and reached for his boots, catching them after they began to slide away. One hundred men and women, the rest of his company, struggled to do the same. Packs were shouldered. Weapons grabbed. Hohn wasn't the only one barking orders. Other squad leaders and platoon sergeants were struggling to maintain order, while desperate to understand the situation.

"Sergeant Hohn! I want everyone to the drop ships. The *Acheron* is breaking apart," a thin, blue skinned lieutenant announced upon entering the bay.

Genius. A real krakking genius. "Yes, sir! You heard the El-Tee. Ruck up and move out. Squad leaders maintain positive control of your troops."

The klaxons blared louder, pausing as the ship's captain, his gravelly voice the product of a lifetime of smoking, said, "All hands, abandon ship. This is the Captain speaking. Abandon ship."

Time was running out. Panic threatened to rob him of reason. Hohn wasn't in the navy. He was a ground pounder, figuring it would be best to fall six feet to the dirt than out of the sky or get blasted apart in the forever of space. The *Acheron* was one of thirty troop transports taking his division to the R-n-R world of Kandron after a brutal seven-month campaign. The enemy had other plans.

Hohn's fingers curled around the familiar plastic of his rifle after he buckled his body armor. He'd learned early in his career that the best way to avoid damaging thoughts was to put the needs of subordinates first. As long as he had men and women who looked up to him, he had purpose. Frightened faces looked back at him. Three of the lights burst, darkening specific parts of the bay in a shower of sparks and glass. They weren't going to make it to the drop ships unless he acted fast.

"Sarge, what do we do?" a nervous private shouted. More heads turned in his direction.

Hohn winced at the term, for he despised being called sarge. That was a battle for another time. "Collect up everything you can and head for your ships. Squad leaders, if the way becomes blocked, I want everyone in the nearest escape pods. Understand?"

Chimes of 'Yes, sergeant', echoed back. He nodded. *Good.* "Move out!"

Soldiers began filing out, where raw chaos greeted them. Crewmembers rushed down the once pristine corridors, desperate to escape. Lost was any thought of duty. Fear for their lives forced them onward as the *Acheron* burned around them. Screams of panic could be heard and it was all Hohn could do to swallow his own fears.

He snatched the same private who'd asked the question as he was shuffling through the door. "We're going to make it. Remember your training and listen to your squad leader."

Comforted by the lie, the soldier nodded and hurried off. Hohn watched as the rest of the company went by. He did a quick sweep to ensure no one had been left behind before joining the others. The *Acheron* shuddered under his boots, reverberating deep into his bones. He'd seen starships break apart before. Unimaginable horror as crews were sucked into the vacuum to die without a sound. There was no worse way to go, in his estimation.

Drawing a deep breath, Hohn entered the corridor and headed to the loading bays. He tried not to think about what went wrong but the thoughts grew stronger the farther his feet carried him. Did the enemy strike? A warhead might have detonated from one of the ammo bays. The possibilities were endless, and none of them mattered. Yellow lights flashed down the length of the corridor. He barely noticed when the klaxons stopped. Men and women shouted and cried out.

Hohn caught snippets of conversation. Phrases otherwise meaningless. A bulkhead collapse on C Deck. Friends were spaced. Fires raged unchecked in the engine room. The bridge was sealed off and nothing rescuers attempted could open the doors. None of it was good. He'd already suspected the ship was almost dead. Necessary systems were beginning to shut down and it was only a matter of time before the critical ones followed. If the bay doors couldn't open …

He let the thought fade. Thinking of death held no place in a soldier's mind. Of the many things a soldier could control, death remained untouchable. Variables dominated the battlefield. Worrying about death was as pointless as dreaming of home in the middle of a firefight. Better men than he had lost that fight, prompting him to vow to never think about what can't be controlled. A promise. He'd made a promise. *See to your soldiers and the rest will sort itself.*

The *Acheron* pitched hard to starboard, throwing his shoulder into the wall. Cursing, he shoved off and picked up the pace. It wouldn't be long before the entire ship broke apart and he had no desire to drift across the void for eternity. The loading bays were too far off. He wasn't going to make it in time. The situation demanded change. Hohn started collecting the soldiers nearby and directing them to the closest life pod bank.

Each pod held ten, with enough rations and water to last one week. Army pods also contained basic ammunition loads and first aid kits. Everything a squad needed to stay on its feet until a rescue party arrived. Several had already launched. Featureless grey doors slammed shut in their place. Hohn found the first empty one and started shoving people inside. Once filled, he slammed the side of his fist into the securing button. Doors shut, and the pod launched.

A quick head count left him with eight others. They hurried inside, leaving him alone. Hohn was about to enter when movement drew his attention. A female crew member in standard black uniform was running his way. The orange glow of flames raced behind her. He was faced with the difficult decision of saving almost a full squad or trying to save one more. Professionalism took over.

"Hurry up! We've got room for one more!" he shouted over the rising noise of the *Acheron* disintegrating.

Flames reflected in his eyes. She was still thirty meters away and flames were catching up. She wasn't going to make it. Hohn closed his eyes and whispered a prayer as the initial wall of fire lit her backside. Her screams cut off as he closed the life pod doors and collapsed in one of the empty couches. Automatic safety belts slid down his shoulders and across his waist, locking him in place as the pod launched.

Hohn's head struck the cushion behind him. He wanted to cry, but emotions were for the weak. The others would look to him for strength. Experience taught him the only time for a leader to show weakness or emotion was alone, in the heartless comforts of the sleeping bag when no one was watching. Unable to stand what he thought was accusatory looks, Hohn turned his head to peer out the tiny porthole. He wished he hadn't.

The final ruination of the *Acheron* played out before him. Flames erupted in massive balls of exploding gas, only to snuff out an instant later. Bodies drifted away. He saw the bridge explode with more fury than an assault division could muster. A drop ship, caught in the blast, disintegrated as building sized pieces of shrapnel sliced through it. *All those people.*

A glimpse of a planet, nothing more than a split second, showed him a large giant of swirling greens, blues, and browns. Not Kandron. *So where are …* Debris struck the life pod, jarring his head into a computer console to the right. Hohn blacked out before finishing the thought.

PART ONE

THE HEART ETERNAL

ONE

Ghendis Ghadanaban was once a city of wonder. An oasis where the cultured and civilized flocked to impart their knowledge and culture upon the world. A city so fair, it was ruled by a genesis of gods, one at a time. Golden towers speared into the heavens, desperate in the pursuit of wealth and knowledge. People of every culture were welcomed with open arms, for the gods were benevolent. Kingdoms dispatched emissaries with longstanding embassies to treat with the ruling body. It was meant to be a golden time. Ghendis Ghadanaban represented everything good about the world.

Once, but no more.

Today, the sprawling streets contained thousands of refugees, for the kingdom was locked in a years-long civil war. Once sparkling streets were cluttered with detritus. The stench of filth permeated entire districts, no matter how hard the Prefecture attempted to maintain some semblance of order. Yet despite the gripping turmoil, the city endured. It became stronger. Its light brighter. Citizens and refugees began to refer to it as the Heart Eternal, for not even the violence of war was strong enough to eclipse the light of hope.

Sandis Vartan sipped from the small glass cup. Hot turang, he'd discovered, was the best thing to take off the night's chill. The caffeinated properties of the drink were widely discussed and bickered over. Sandis heard none of it. His elevated position among the clergy precluded him from the restrictions of the masses. Pursed lips filled with cracks only age brought, touched the glass and he sucked the hot liquid into his mouth. A wry smile crossed his face as he imagined the scolding his mother would have given, if she were still alive. It was a daily ritual.

A platter of fresh fruits and pastries sat off to his right, dominating nearly half of the marble table, prompting him to wonder how much his staff thought he ate. By their estimations, he should be well over four hundred pounds. Not at all representative of his slender, almost painfully thin frame. Frowning, Sandis ignored the food and finished his drink while gazing out across the city.

White birds drifted in flocks over the terra cotta tiled rooftops of the wealthy. Beyond, almost obscured in the morning haze, stretched the rest of the city. It was his duty to patrol the streets and bring the word of the god king to new arrivals and those suffering from lack of faith. He didn't understand their worry, for the god king was kind and benevolent. No ill came to Ghendis Ghadanaban during his reign.

Sandis knew the truth of matters. That the current ruler was the forty-seventh of his line. Each ruled over the course of several mortal lifetimes, enriching the city and residents beyond measure. Sandis enjoyed the comforts of that knowledge, even while struggling with understanding how anyone could dispute otherwise. Yet they did. Heralds and criers began popping up more often as throngs of new people arrived. One of the problems with the world, he'd determined long ago, was that people tended to bring their belief structure with them after fleeing a land where those beliefs failed.

Slippered feet hurrying down the pillar lined corridors disturbed his few moments of daily tranquility. Sandis turned to face the linen curtains acting as his doors, drink in hand. He didn't wait long. Two men, boys really, entered without observing protocol. He spied the strain, the unmitigated stress in their eyes, and began to fret. They were breathing hard and were red-faced with worry.

"You had best explain yourselves," he said, with a rasping voice. Sandis was a generous man, but not one to encourage disrespect.

"First Prophet," the smaller of the two said with a deep bow. "You must come quick. Omoraum Dala'gharis is dead."

The glass slipped from his hand to shatter in a thousand pieces at his feet.

Aldon Cay ran for his life. The sounds of pursuit edged closer, thundering down the empty, winding alley. His pockets were heavy, laden with jewels lifted from one of the newer merchants in Ghendis Ghadanaban. They weighed him down. Slowed him. Aldon had spent years working the overcrowded streets, enjoying the constant influx of arrivals as the Eleboran Civil War entered its fifth year.

Distant battles and tales of death didn't interest him. He'd seen none of it, for no one wanted to provoke the ire of the god king. Grinning as only a foolish youth might, Aldon ducked down a side alley and ran on. The Prefects weren't easily fooled. They knew this city better than any. Catching a meager thief was barely worth their effort. Aldon wasn't willing to make it easy for them, valuing his neck more than a handful of baubles—even if they would feed his family for weeks and pay for the medicine his mother needed.

His linen pants brushed against dirt stained walls. The loose-fitting vest that had become his signature look, billowed back the faster he ran. Aldon never doubted he was going to escape. The Prefecture may own the streets, but there was another world, a hidden world, few ventured to explore. He knew it well, and along with a small group of like minds, used it to his advantage. He only needed to reach the hidden entrance.

"You there, halt!" a deep voice bellowed.

A sword was drawn. Rifles were unslung and cocked. Aldon felt his chest constrict. He was fast, but not fast enough to outrun a wall of bullets. He skidded to a halt and started raising his hands. Boots crunched the loose gravel. Aldon winced, expecting the blow to the back of his head. It never fell. Instead, he was surrounded and confronted by the squad officer holding a parchment.

"Why did you run?" the prefect asked. His pale grey eyes searched Aldon for signs of duplicity. "Are you afraid of those assigned to protect you?"

Confused, Aldon didn't know what to say. His mouth opened and closed several times, while his mind struggled to catch up. Certain the prefects were baiting him to admit his crime, he decided the best option was to remain silent. He shook his head, fervently hoping they didn't kill him.

Eyebrow arched with doubt, the prefect clicked his tongue on the roof of his mouth. "Where are you going in such a hurry?"

"Home, sir," Aldon replied with honesty.

"After curfew? You know children are not allowed on the streets after dark."

Aldon swallowed his rising fear. "My apologies, sir, but I was let out of work late. I ran because I knew I was in violation."

The prefect sized him up, deciding Aldon wasn't a threat. A quick hand motion and the others lowered their weapons. "Where do you work?"

"For Master Hean, sir," Aldon answered. It wasn't necessarily a lie, for he did the occasional odd job for the owner of the Arax Trade Company. Not only was it the largest and most powerful trader in Ghendis Ghadanaban,

Hean employed so many, there was no way to verify if Aldon was among them.

The prefect scowled but stepped back. "Very well. Best get home before something bad happens. There's been a murder."

He threw the comment in the hopes of catching Aldon in a lie, a last goad to glean the truth. Aldon gawked in genuine surprise. He was close to the wealthy district, where the rich and powerful resided. For a murder to have been committed here bode ill for the rest of the city, and for amateur pickpockets trying to scratch out a living. The Heart Eternal was the paragon of peace, a beacon others across the world attempted to emulate. Murders did not occur here.

Aldon imagined the flash of a blade coming from the dark and hot blood pouring down his chest. The ignorant trappings of youth prevented him from thinking long on death. The prospect seemed so far away, anything else would be a waste of time. Aldon shook the image off and focused on the man before him.

"Yes, sir. Without delay!" he said with enthusiasm. Aldon had no desire to meet the killer, nor could he press his luck. He was, after all, a thief in possession of a wealth of jewels.

"Go on, now. And don't let me catch you out again or it's the iron bars for you," the Prefect growled.

Aldon ran off, heading straight for home instead of the White Crow where he could unload the jewels for money. The prefects moved on, desperate to catch the killer before he could strike again. Important things were about to collide in Ghendis Ghadanaban. There was no room for chaos.

Ask anyone and they would say the White Crow was a landmark feature of the Heart Eternal. Patrons came from every district to enjoy the spirits, and for those brave enough to take the chance, food. It wasn't uncommon to find elites sitting beside the downtrodden at the long, lacquered bar. Prefects and politicians drank with day laborers and dock workers. Any pretense of cast was left at the door. Look hard enough and one might find the uniforms of all three armies currently surrounding the city among the crowds, though they were tolerated with a measure of mistrust. The kingdom may be locked in civil war, but the Heart Eternal was separate. Different.

First Prophet of the god king Sandis Vartan slipped into the Crow. Abandoning his vestments for common clothes, he ignored the crowds and went for his usual table. Sandis wasn't surprised to find it already occupied. It always was. Perhaps the only reason he found to come this far across the city was the man sitting with his back to the wall, facing the entirety of the room.

"You're late," he accused after Sandis sat.

Ignoring the comment, Sandis gestured for the nearest server. "My usual, please."

The server smiled and wormed through the crowds.

"Don't you get tired of this, Relghel?" he asked.

Relghel Gorgal grinned, his wide face showing two rows of impossibly white teeth. "What else is there for me to do? I've no tongue for politics or chaos. No, my friend, drinking suits me nicely."

Laughter broke out from a group of Mordai armsmen several tables away. Heads turned but looked away after deciding it wasn't worth the effort. The White Crow welcomed all.

Sandis drummed his fingers, impatient with the usual banter. "You know what happened?"

"I heard. A shame. What are you going to do now?" Relghel asked, before draining his mug and belching.

Wincing, Sandis failed to see how his friend didn't place much emphasis on recent events. "There has never been a murder of this nature. Not in forty-six previous rules. We have entered unprecedented territory."

"And with emissaries from the warring factions set to meet soon. Ill timing," Relghel added. "Sandis, at some point you are going to have to accept that not all matters are controllable, and that even gods die."

A dangerous avenue just opened. One Sandis wasn't ready to travel down. He regarded his friend for a long moment, taking in the lines of impossible age creasing his face. The time-worn bronzed skin on the backs of his hairless hands. He wondered what sights Relghel had witnessed over the ages and became sorrowed that he would never have the experience. Mortality was frightening when the trappings of society were peeled away.

"Do you know who did it?" Relghel spared him the conflict of probing deeper.

"No. There are no clues either."

"Truly?" Relghel was surprised. "What of the Scarlet? Were they questioned?"

Sandis smiled as the server placed a small glass of amber liquid before him and another mug of beer for Relghel. Alcohol was a rare pleasure forbidden to the Prophets. "Under what authority? They answer only to the god king."

"And he is dead."

Sandis raised his glass in salute. "Long live the king."

Word had yet to get out, thanks to great effort on his part, but that wouldn't last long. Rumors had a way of reaching the farthest corners of the city, especially when efforts were enacted to prevent such. Relghel mimicked him but remained silent.

"Where do you go from here? Omoraum is the last in line. Another will not be ready for generations," Relghel said, his voice conspiratorially low. Drunkard and closet nihilist, he enjoyed prodding Sandis with irresistible barbs.

"Honestly, I don't know," Sandis admitted. There was one option available, but Relghel abandoned that life long ago.

TWO

Twin ranks of scarlet-clad guards lined the short hallway. Each was fully armored and bore a seven-foot glaive. Faces were concealed behind chitinous face masks. If not for the wings growing from their backs, Sandis might have thought they were human. He marched past them without so much as a glance. The Scarlet were many things, conversationalists not among them. Placing his palm over his heart in tribute to the god king, Sandis entered the royal apartments.

Three others greeted him. The first was a slender woman of middle age and elegance. Overseer Larris ran Ghendis Ghadanaban with as much compassion as any leader might. She was well-liked among the general population and well-regarded among the ruling members. The sternness of her face offered little hope of a pleasant conversation.

At her side stood Tega Ig, Master of the Prefecture. His barrel chest looked ridiculously out of place among the smaller members in attendance. Sandis respected the man, but reserved trust. Tega had only been in power for a few months. Not enough time to have his quality judged. Perhaps, Sandis surmised, this debacle would prove his allegiance.

The third person came as slight surprise. Verian was the Lord of the Scarlet and the god king's right hand. No one knew the origins of the Scarlet, though Sandis suspected they were of a lesser race related to the gods. How else to explain the naturally occurring wings and faint glow surrounding them? He didn't trust Tega Ig, but he and Verian had never seen eye to eye. The Scarlet thought themselves above the Prophets, and many in the Prophets felt the opposite.

"At last, now we can begin," Verian said with undisguised disdain. Feathers ruffled over his shoulders.

Sandis feigned bowing. "Yes, let us. Have you discovered anything, Master Ig?"

Tega glanced at the Scarlet, choosing to ignore the insult. "Nothing. My people have scoured every inch of the palace. Whoever did this was thorough."

Yes, every inch these pretentious bastards allowed you to. "Truly? It is my experience that no crime is perfect. Was there nothing to be found in here?"

We ... ah, were not permitted to search the god king's private chambers," Tega's face blushed.

"That is an internal matter and you know it, Sandis," Verian immediately defended. "The Scarlet is responsible for all matters that occur behind these doors."

"That would imply that it was entirely due to your negligence that resulted in his death," Sandis quipped back.

"Gentlemen," Larris said with golden voice, as she stepped between them. "Arguing amongst ourselves is pointless. There is a killer at large and we must combine our efforts to ensure he is caught. All agencies must work together, if we are to accomplish this before word spreads. We cannot risk losing the people on the eve of the most important meeting of this long war. The question we should be asking is where to begin."

Sandis approved. Larris, once again, proved her worth by outmaneuvering very worthy adversaries. "Whoever did this, obviously has no fear of reprisal, along with intimate knowledge none of us possess. Do we know how he was killed?"

The words stuck in his throat. How does one kill a god? So alien was the concept, Sandis found difficulty in accepting the god king was truly gone. Never in the history of their rule had a god been slain by mortals. This was an unprecedented moment, without having any alternate plans in place to counter the disaster. The First Prophet, like the others before him, was left in a void and unsure how to proceed.

"It was poison," Verian confirmed, though his voice bore the weight of reluctance.

How does one poison a god? Sandis had his suspicions, but without evidence, there seemed little point in voicing them. "That certainly narrows down the list of potential assassins."

"Not enough to matter," Tega replied. He folded his arms, straining to cross his massive chest. "Thousands work in the palace. Even more have some sort of indirect access. We could be searching for years without result."

"I venture that we do not have that long," Larris cooed. Hard lines framed her face, presenting a formidable visage they rarely witnessed. "This matter must be resolved within the next few weeks or we stand to lose everything. Knowledge of the god king's death will signal an end of all this city stands for."

"Will the Scarlet assist with maintaining order throughout the city?" Tega asked.

Verian's scowl was slight enough to go unnoticed. "No. We are the sworn protectors of the god kings, not hirelings to do mortal bidding."

"You may not have a choice," Sandis countered. The Scarlet's failure to protect their master might have damned them all. He was about to say more, before Verian could snap back, when a hint of movement behind one of the wall size curtains drew his attention. "What is…"

The attack came swiftly. More than a score of figures burst from concealment from around the chamber.

A fetid reek preceded them. Sandis stared in horror, as walking corpses ambled closer, intent on ripping them apart. Rotted flesh sloughed off bone and muscle. Drops of liquified sinew and blood spattered the pristine marble. Feet dragged. Others slapped the floor with unmitigated fury.

"Waerga!" Verian hissed, as he brought his glaive up.

Sandis withdrew, mouth filling with bile. Twice in two days, his mind recoiled with shock. No plausible explanation for the undead being in the god king's apartments, the First Prophet felt the walls of his carefully constructed world shrinking. Death had come for them all and he was ill equipped to defend himself. He wasn't alone, a sidelong glance showed Overseer Larris fade to the rear of their group. Rumors circulated that she was once a formidable fighter worth her weight in salt. Even if that were true, Sandis doubted her skillset covered fighting the undead. Wisely, they let the warriors assume the lead.

Never in his six decades had he witnessed one of the Scarlet in action. Their full battle fury was both inspiring and horrifying. Verian's flowing robes swirled around him in endless pageantry, as his glaive slashed and speared through the undead. Bodies fell sliced in half. Others crumpled under their own weight to stain the floor in pools of viscera. Eight were incapacitated before Sandis remembered to breathe.

Not to be outdone, Tega Ig barreled into the foe with the force of a sledge hammer. The war bar in his right hand, his favorite weapon, crushed skulls and snapped arms. Three undead slammed into him, knocking him to the floor, where they fell upon him. Tega rolled, losing his grip on the weapon. He roared, proud and defiant. Raw strength pushed his arms clear enough for him to grab two heads. Tega slammed them together. The force of the blow shattered their skulls, dripping bone and brain matter on his face and chest.

Sandis heard a shout, cutoff and strained, from behind and turned to see an undead lurch for Larris. Her skill and grace echoed in the fluidity of her movements. Unencumbered by loose clothing, she danced around the creature, striking blows with open hands. A wrist broke, the hand hanging limp. She slashed across it's throat and the head tilted over to rest on its shoulder. Debilitated, the undead was open to her assault. Her movements were precise, unrelenting. Sandis marveled at the speed with which she carried out her attack. The undead was rendered immobile at her feet in moments, allowing her to stamp down with her right foot. The corpse twitched once and lay still.

The Scarlet guarding the hall entered four abreast. They charged into the few remaining undead and reaped a terrible toll. Golden steel rose and fell without mercy. Undead fell without scratching the Scarlet's armor. The battle was over in less than a minute. Gore painted the floor in dark stains. Never again would the god king's quarters be unsullied.

"Someone get me a towel!" Tega roared as he reclaimed his weapon. Blood coated his lower jaw and chest.

Verian planted himself in the center of the killing ground, eyes scanning the chamber. "Fan and out and search every inch of these rooms. I want no more surprises!"

"Clearly this matter is unresolved," Sandis offered.

Tega placed a finger over his right nostril and blew hard. Chunks of gore flew out. Wiping his fingers on an unstained part of his blouse, the Master Prefect seconded, "Clearly."

"This should not have occurred. We are beset by enemies," Larris said, as she flattened her robes.

"Lord, the floor is clear."

Verian dismissed the Scarlet with a clipped salute, and waiting for them to leave, addressed his companions. "I have changed my mind. The Waerga should not have been in these sacred rooms. You may have the assistance of the Scarlet in your efforts."

"What else do we need?" Tega asked the group.

Sandis coughed. "A Reclamator."

Larris immediately agreed. "Very well, I shall summon the Guild. We must be prepared for follow up attacks. This does not feel over. Contingency plans must be drawn up. Word of this cannot get out to the general population. The last thing this city needs is to become part of the war. Am I clear?"

Though none outranked the others, her ability to take charge in the absence of the god king was undisputed. Their gathering ended when she spun and hurried back to her offices. Sandis watched until she was gone from sight, impressed with her demeanor. Ghendis Ghadanaban would have need of such strength in the uncertainty ahead.

"Will someone get me a gods damned towel!" Tega repeated to no one in particular.

The Heart Eternal held many secrets. Some were known by all but never mentioned. Others belonged to a select few with the tenacity to discover their power. Clandestine organizations arose among the underworld, for those who held knowledge, held power. The city ran on power. All under the noses of the agencies in charge. Efforts were undertaken to stamp several of the more violent offenders out, while others proved useful. The Reclamator Guild was foremost in that regard.

Soloists, Reclamators roamed the darkest recesses of the city in search of what shouldn't exist. People shied away when one walked by. Some placed their palms over their hearts in prayer, for it was unnatural for the dead to walk again. Few in number, the Guild maintained high standards that came with a hefty price.

Night had fallen over the Heart Eternal. Whispers of ill tidings were already circulating. Fear rose. Doors were locked. Windows shuttered. Prefect patrols increased, the curfew going from the mid of night, to dusk for all but the necessary. Gathering halls and taverns shut their doors for the night to all but the foolish who chose to spend the entirety of the long dark drinking their fears away.

Tula Gish ignored it all. Her dark leathers blended her with the night, and those quietly forgotten paths and alleys sane folk ignored. A weapons belt was filled with numerous blades and stabbing instruments. Twin swords were crossed over her back. The staff in her hands was carved from ironwood and capped with steel. Despite the weight of her boots, Tula moved with stealth.

A slender beam of moonlight brightened the passage before her, showing her a glimpse of her prey. Tula knelt, gloved fingers touching the small puddle at her feet. Blood. The undead was somewhere ahead and it had taken a victim. Her sense of urgency propelled her forward. That any should suffer the nightmares of being torn apart by a creature that should have been in the ground was unimaginable.

She reached behind to draw one of her swords when the sounds of scuffling feet rose. Heart quickening, Tula rounded a corner and found the undead. It was hunched over, back to her, devouring what remained of a young woman. Without a sound, Tula charged and took the undead's head. A look at the victim's remains showed there was no salvation. She blew out the frustration of having let another fall to the abominations and withdrew a small vial from the inside pocket in her jacket. Bright blue-green liquid spilled over the body. Tula offered a prayer as the body melted.

"What'll it be, Tula?"

Her smile brightened the dour mood settling over her. Eamon Brisk, proprietor and bartender of the White Crow knew her, and a great many of his patrons by name, providing a comforting environment to escape the troubles of the day. Tula slumped into an empty seat at the bar, resisting the urge to lay her head down.

"Turang, no sugar," she replied.

The bags under her eyes, unnaturally dark for such fair skin, worried him. "You do not look well. Perhaps that is why you ask for such a foul drink. No sugar! One might as well drink sewer water."

She failed to prevent the laugh from escaping. Eamon was many things to many people. A father figure to the ones who'd grown up without one. A sage ear with a keen sense of picking up on the slightest nuance. Folks valued his contributions to their lives. There weren't many in the Heart Eternal who did not know the name Eamon Brisk.

"You know I don't drink alcohol, Eamon," she teased.

His grin stretched from ear to ear. "One tries. How goes the hunt?"

Tula sighed. "Three more. There was a time when finding one in a night was a big deal. I feel like we are failing the people."

He placed a fatherly, time worn hand over hers. "Some dangers should remain unknown. You perform a grand service."

The doors opened before she replied. Heads turned to see three prefects march in. They ignored the crowds, locking eyes on the black, leather clad Reclamator. Her mind raced through recent events, wondering if she had broken any laws or regulations. Privilege of position allowed her much more leniency than the common citizen, but there were times when that wasn't enough.

"Tula Gish," it came out a statement, not a question.

"You already know that, or you wouldn't be here," she said.

Eamon threw the dish towel over his shoulder and scowled at the interruption. "See here, what's the meaning of this?"

"No disrespect, Eamon, we didn't come here to start trouble with you," he glanced back at the hulking figure rising from a seat by the door, "or Baradoon. This Reclamator has been summoned to the Overseer's offices," the prefect sergeant said.

"What are the charges?" the bartender pressed.

The prefects glanced at each other. "No charges. She is requested to attend a matter of the highest importance."

Tula almost laughed. Her life had taken her down many unforeseen paths, this was not one even considered. She always imagined that her time was ending when the prefects came for her. Destiny proved otherwise. She allowed them to lead her away, careful to walk behind them to avoid the illusion of being arrested. Tula was a proud woman. Let the crowds see what true power was like.

THREE

Imperator Thrakus tapped his charcoal pencil on the map covering the mahogany table in the center of his tent, eyes screwed in concentration. Icons of different units spread across the map, all centered around Ghendis Ghadanaban. He cared little for the city or its hundred thousand inhabitants. Streams of refugees were pouring in from embattled parts of the kingdom, and despite his orders to turn them away, continued entering the city. Useless individuals with frightened women and children and military aged males unwilling to fight for their homes. They could all serve as collateral damage in his view. He was here for one specific purpose.

Elements of the Mordai army were stationed on the eastern flank, several thousand meters from the city's outer ring. Why he was tasked with leading an assault division into Eleboran was beyond his level of inquiry. Orders were dispatched and he performed them without question. A shrewd man, Thrakus viewed lives in terms of numbers. Only his soldiers were important. All others could rot.

Facing him was a conglomeration of militia from the rebel tribes. Thousands of bitter warriors whose specialty was mountain fighting. Their disagreements with the Eleboran government, perhaps rightly based over perceived unjust laws, sparked a civil war that had seen far too many deaths to be termed efficient. Thrakus took pleasure in well executed plans but viewed the waste of life darkly.

He'd been deployed to Eleboran for almost two years and was ready to go home. They were accomplishing nothing. Compounding his issues, two additional kingdoms had sent soldiers to assist in peacekeeping efforts. None of them made much of a difference when it came to ending the civil war, for Eleboran controlled the board. Thrakus was trapped in a delicate game and his hands were tied.

Frustrated, he tossed the pencil down and went outside. Life in the field wasn't bad. All his needs were cared for and no one was shooting directly at him. As long as supply trains continued to bring replacements, weapons, ammunition, and food, he could remain here indefinitely. Fortunately, the Vizier had other ideas. Wheels were turning. A plan in motion. It had already begun.

Thrakus winced as sunlight struck his eyes. He despised the kingdom of Eleboran for its infernal climate. It was always too hot and seldom rained. Vegetation was sparse, providing little natural cover or relief from the blistering sun. So unlike the plush fields of his home. A ring of guards surrounded his tents. Each was hand selected, providing him with total security. They saluted as he walked past.

Thrakus was a supreme tactician. A veteran of several wars. His keen sense of operational strategy led his kingdom to victory on numerous occasions. The situation in Eleboran was unlike any he had participated in, presenting new challenges his clinical mindset began tackling the moment he learned of his deployment. Hands clasped behind his back, the Imperator marched with authority. A pair of brown clad guards walked a pace behind. He gestured them to wait outside of the Alchemist's tent and proceeded to enter. There was much to discuss and the day was still young.

"Imperator, we have been expecting you," a painfully thin man, old and frail, greeted.

"Senior Alchemist Horrick, what have you to report?" Thrakus always felt wrong within these tents, as if his stomach soured at the thought of what they did for the kingdom of Mordai.

Horrick motioned and one of the assistants hurried to him with a half nude man at his side. Dressed only in white linen pants, the man was shaved bald and wore a tight leather collar. Both his eyes had been taken, as well as half his tongue. The alchemists insisted he was deaf, as were all symbiote hosts the kingdom used. The unnatural was never meant for exploration, regardless of how useful a tool it represented.

"Word has come from the Citadel," Horrick said. He hobbled on a crooked cane to stand beside the symbiote before producing a golden jewel he attached to the man's throat.

The symbiote spasmed. Fists clenched and Thrakus was sure the man was going to break his spine. Golden light poured from his nose, mouth and empty eye sockets. The deep, resonating voice trembled the sand at his feet. "Imperator Thrakus, have your efforts commenced?"

Thrakus bowed at the sound of the Vizier's voice. "It has, my lord. My contacts report the deed was accomplished two nights ago."

"Interesting; I have not yet heard of this. Are you certain the god king is dead?"

Was he? The ruling council of Ghendis Ghadanaban were either going through great pains to prevent word from escaping or his contacts had lied. Either possibility remained viable. "To the best of my knowledge, Omoraum Dala'gharis is no more. The city is without a true leader."

"If true, they will hold no sway over the upcoming summit," the Vizier theorized. "Now is the hour to press. You may enact the second part of your assignment. Unleash chaos on Eleboran."

Horrick snatched the jewel away and the symbiote slumped to his knees. Steam issued from his head. "All goes according to plan?"

Disgusted with the abuse of flesh and soul, Thrakus resisted the urge to place a pistol shot between the alchemist's eyes. "For now. Do not summon me again unless the Vizier commands."

"As you will, Imperator."

Ah, Ghendis Ghadanaban. Shining jewel in a dour world. What brightness lifts spirits and provides hope to so many. Abbas Doza grew up hearing stories of the Heart Eternal and its fabled god king rulers. Forty-seven if one counted, though he found the notion absurd. Why would a god bother handling mortal affairs? During his years roaming the city, he had never seen evidence of any gods, or the Scarlet guardians. Some facades, he decided, were designed to keep the population in check.

He found work at the turning of manhood with one of the smaller assassin guilds and proved an astute learner. Not bad for a farm boy from the middle of nowhere, who had only killed animals for food. Abbas applied his new talents with fervor, quickly gaining a reputation as true professional. Demand soared as minor nobles' houses continued an ages old game of political positioning and power. Not once did Abbas pause to consider the implications of his job, and his cost rose with each job. Killing was easier when he viewed his targets in terms of coin.

His last assignment worried him, frightened him, if truth be told. Abbas made it a point of pride to never pass on an offer. That pride took him down dark and winding paths he worried he might never recover from. Keeping his mind occupied, and off the topic, meant indulging in extremes. So it was he found himself in the corner of the White Crow ready to lose his recent earnings.

Baradoon tossed three silver coins into the pot. "You're thinking too hard, Abbas. Men like that lose fast."

Abbas waved him off. Every glimmer of light reflecting off the coins reminded him of the flick of a blade. "Mind your hand, big man. I'm in no mood for banter this night."

His deep chuckle shook the table. At seven feet tall and close to four hundred pounds of muscle, Baradoon was almost as well-known as Eamon Brisk. Few were foolish enough to cross the man, and for good reason. Eamon took him from an Eleboran prison island some years back, after he'd been arrested for murdering three men with his hands. The White Crow was in good hands, while the giant stood watch.

"Hear that, boys? Abbas wants to give us his money."

Laughter circled the table.

"How's that different from any other night?" a young blonde-haired man asked, while twirling his moustache.

"He seems more determined this time," the guardian snorted.

Abbas glowered at him. "You talk too much, my friend."

"Comes with the job. Are you going to fold?"

A fourth look at his cards and he was convinced. Abbas tossed them down. "I need a drink."

"Something bothering you good?" Baradoon guessed.

Where do I begin? If anyone knew what I did, the whole city would be after my head. "More than you will ever guess, my friend."

"Is it the undead? Folk say they have been seen all over the city. Even in the wealthy districts," his blonde friend, a rogue named Raismus, said. "You haven't seen one?"

"No, at least not yet," Abbas admitted. "Nor do I want to. There is only so much my mind can take before it snaps."

"What are you prattling about? We've never heard you talk like this," Baradoon scoffed.

"He's spooked," Raismus seconded. He matched the giant's bet and raised.

Baradoon scowled and reevaluated his cards.

"I think I need to get out of the city for a while," Abbas divulged. Since completing his last job, it was all he could think about. Powerful forces were gathering and he wanted to be as far away as possible before the storm broke. *Damned Mordaians, I should have walked away when I had the chance.*

The game continued in silence, though his thoughts were focused on fleeing. Should anyone learn of his involvement, his head would be on a spike over the Western Gate. It was time to abandon the life of luxury he once enjoyed and leave Ghendis Ghadanaban, for not every glittering tower was covered with gold.

Nights were inexplicably cold in the low desert. The heavy cloud cover prevented the moonlight from reaching the ground, prompting the theory that it would also prevent heat from leaving quickly. Experts were seldom correct. Any soldier knew that. One of the first things learned was how to read and predict the weather. For Sergeant Hohn and his squad, trapped on an alien world they still didn't understand, it became critical.

Hohn shivered beneath his poncho. From a water world, he hated sand. A quick look at his wrist chrono showed there was two hours before dawn. The perfect time for their work. Night vision built into his helmet clicked over, showing him the world below. Dispersed boulders and scrub brush lay in patternless formations. This close to the mountains, Hohn found the landscape almost as inhospitable as the weather.

The squad was emplaced on a rocky outcropping halfway down the mountain slope, spread out at five-meter intervals. One in three slept, for it was unrealistic to expect them all to spend the night fully alert. Ambushes were a learned skill and seldom occurred when planned for. The government soldiers of Eleboran were more than willing to ensure his people remained trained.

Hohn found employment with the mountain tribes once it became obvious a rescue wasn't forthcoming. So many of his company remained missing and he feared them dead. A shame seeing as how they'd earned the respite after a grueling campaign. Instead of recovering, his survivors were embroiled in a civil war. He'd always believed there was no rest for the weary. If this night's work was any indication, that adage would prove true.

"Movement."

The quiet voice rang over the helmet's intercom. Hohn didn't see anything. "Where?"

"Ten o'clock at five hundred meters."

Hohn adjusted his line of sight and picked up the first ranks of a government company heading their way. Rifles were shouldered and the outlying pickets weren't paying attention. Computers in his helmet counted thirty soldiers afoot and the officer on horseback. One understrength platoon. Hohn was almost insulted. His squad was more than a match for any local force twice that size, but he recognized the government boys would be able to overpower the militia forces.

"Wait until they are within fifty meters. I got the officer," he ordered. "Maintain fire discipline. No unnecessary firing."

No one replied. They didn't need to. Each had been through the routine too many times. He felt weapons being readied on either side and focused on the scene below. The targets marched closer. The stamp of their boots echoing across the canyon. He was amazed at their audacity. Any unit should be more cautious when in the middle of enemy territory. It would aid in their downfall.

Hohn drew a slow, measured breath and sighted his rifle. Metric gauges flashed across his helmet's visor. Fifty meters. The tip of his index finger gently squeezed the trigger. A bolt of red-orange energy flashed across the distance, followed by nine others. Ten soldiers dropped, and the slaughter commenced. Hohn knew it wasn't fair. Some might not consider it ethical. After all, this world lacked energy weapons. His ideations of fair evaporated as the ambush continued.

The battle lasted less than a minute. All thirty soldiers were down, leaving Hohn with the unenviable task of sending people down to treat wounds and take prisoners. Those who weren't going to make it, would be left with water and given sedatives to help ease their passing. He wasn't a murderer and the thought of one of his people bleeding out in the forgotten night rankled his sense of professionalism. Rising from his concealed position, Hohn slung his weapon and issued the orders.

"Might as well catch that horse, if you can," he added, as soldiers started heading down. They'd done enough walking since joining the militia. Even a horse was better than fresh callouses.

"They make it easy, don't they?" Tine said, after stopping beside him.

Hohn's second in command was short for a soldier, but his raptor-like appearance presented a formidable facade. They'd served together for the better part of five years and had almost become friends.

He shook his head in wonder. "I sometimes wish they didn't."

Hohn would never admit it aloud, but he almost wished his squad had found a way to link up with other survivors and had gone off to a secluded part of the world to await rescue. That dream felt almost foolish after seven months. The cold reality was they were trapped.

"Anyone get hit?" Hohn asked, knowing the answer.

Tine's grin was visible in the dark night. "Come on, sergeant. We haven't lost a man yet to these back-world armies."

"Doesn't mean we won't at some point. We're running low on ammunition and medical supplies," Hohn said. "Our advantage won't last forever."

"Meaning we need to use it while we can," Tine countered. "I'll go see to their wounded. It's not right for a man to die thirsty."

Hohn nodded and was again alone. Leadership had many virtues but being set apart from the rest of the soldiers was almost painful. There were strict fraternization policies in the army, but they weren't in the army anymore. Not really. Hohn and his squad were castaways in a hostile environment. Soon, the lines would blur and then the krakking world would explode. A growl in his stomach reminded him he hadn't eaten since midday. The life of a soldier.

FOUR

"I wish you wouldn't wander the streets so carelessly, Aldon," his mother chided. The worry on her face expressed by a sour frown.

His father, more even-tempered, sat in a worn chair in the far corner where he could always see her bed. Pipe smoke filled the tiny room. Each coped differently. His gaze flitted from his wife of thirty years, to his son. They looked so alike, leading him to question if he was indeed the father. *Too late now. Boy's been raised right by me. Let another try to claim him.*

Blushing despite having undergone the same ritual every few days, Aldon lowered his head. "Ma, it's not that bad. Prefects are going around trying to keep people scared. Something's going on we're not supposed to know about."

"Been saying it for years," his father added. "Those in power only keep their power by miring the rest of us in ignorance. Bah! Undead they say. I ain't never seen one and don't expect to. Ghendis Ghadanaban is the most respected city in the world. Just look at them armies fighting around us. If things were as bad as the Prefecture tells us, we'd be occupied by now!"

"You hush, Jorrus! Don't go scaring the boy any. The war will get to us in good time, if it's meant to," his mother scolded.

"I said I was all right, Ma. There's no need for worry," Aldon felt outnumbered, lost in the conversation between elders. He used to wonder if they'd ever tire of the game, but long years passed without change, leading him to believe it had been happening long before he was born. Without a wife of his own, Aldon imagined all relationships were this complicated. "Besides, I got enough to pay for everything we need for the next month."

Her gaze shifted to Jorrus. Unprecedented sorrow filled them suddenly. "Don't."

Jorrus, unable to maintain control of his emotions any longer, shoved to his feet. "Boy, you and I need to speak. Follow me."

"Jorrus, please. He's not ready," she protested before succumbing to a coughing fit.

"Boy's nearly twenty years. That's plenty enough," Jorrus said and left the room.

Aldon gave his mother a worried look before following. The rest of their small home was dark. Built into the side of a five story tenement, there was just enough space for two bedrooms and a multipurpose area used for eating and gathering. Aldon had grown accustomed to living this way, though there was no joy in it. His clothes were threadbare and patched, sometimes patches placed over existing patches.

"Sit," Jorrus gestured to an empty chair at their table and rummaged through the cupboard. He joined Aldon with a pair of wooden cups and a half-empty bottle of amber liquid. Pouring two cups, he shoved one toward his son.

"She's dying, isn't she?" Aldon asked, the only explanation possible after so many hidden meanings in his father's actions.

Jorrus drank deep and poured another. He paused, the cup an inch from his lips. "I wish there was more we could do, but the apothecary doesn't know what else to do. The disease has got ... gotten too far."

"Nothing? The god king must be able to help. He has to!" Aldon protested.

Jorrus shook his head. "It's too late for that, son. I … I figured you should know. Best we can do is make her life as comfortable as possible before her time. Can you do that with me?"

Emotions collided in his young heart. Anger. Fear. Anguish. Aldon fought back the tears. His tongue lacked the strength to say the words his father needed to hear. Lost the courage to be there in this dark hour. With his father away in the government army for a large chunk of his youth, Aldon's mother had been the one constant in his life. Now he was losing her and there was nothing for it. He emptied his cup, the liquid burning down his throat, and stormed from the house. Jorrus watched the door close behind him and drank.

Aldon ran until his legs tired. The liquor continued burning until it forced him to stop and vomit against a grime covered wall. He felt lost, like his tiny place in the world was being ripped away, leaving him with naught. It wasn't fair! Tears filled his eyes, spilling down his cheeks in unchecked streams. Unable to control it, Aldon slid to his knees and wailed. Some nights were cold and dark, even in the Heart Eternal.

He didn't know how long he sat there in the filth and muck. At least until the tears dried up and his chest burned from the effort. His hands trembled and stung. Aldon looked down to find his nails had dug gashes in his palms. The pain was almost welcomed, for it stole his mind away from the nightmares at home.

Aldon paused, suddenly conscious of the immaturity of his actions. Raw emotions took over and forced him to flee, but why? Nothing he did was going to change the facts. His mother was dying. His father already on the path to staying in his cups. And he ran. Ever the scared little boy too afraid to stand up to his bullies. How life was doomed to repeat itself was almost a cruel mockery of where he saw his life going. Shame overwhelmed him. It was time to go home.

He pushed off the wall, wiping his hands on his pants. A rumble in his stomach reminded him he hadn't eaten since early in the day. Suddenly eager to be home, Aldon took those frightened, fateful steps back to confront his fears. He made it three steps before the shadow detached itself from the wall and barred the way.

Aldon froze, unsure how to proceed. His expertise lay in picking pockets and disappearing in the crowd after. Aldon wasn't strong, or very brave. He made up for it with a quick wit. The shadow enlarged until it blocked the entire street. Aldon took a step back. The shadow mocked him. He peered closer. Shadows swirled, unaffected by the moonlight. New fear inspired him to run. This was not natural.

He turned to flee. The shadow was faster. It rustled over the gap between them in the blink of an eye. Wisps of darkness swirled, lashing out to grip Aldon by the arms and legs, turning the boy back to it. Aldon fought but his strength fled in a moment of sheer terror. He was turned until he was face to face with the looming shadows.

Infinite darkness stared back at him, swallowing his gaze in a sea of endless night. Aldon opened his mouth to scream. The shadow clutched tighter and funneled down his throat. Unconsciousness claimed him, and he knew nothing more. Oh yes, the night was filled with many secrets. Some were never meant to be learned.

The Arax Trading Company was the most used and well-known business in Ghendis Ghadanaban. With envoys riding to a dozen neighboring kingdoms, even as far as across the ocean, it held a reputation of never having missed a delivery. Hean built the company from nothing and it now rivaled the royal coffers in terms of wealth and power. It still wasn't enough.

Hean was a cowardly man. Overweight and foul of temper, he drove his employees with an iron rod. Many were hard-bitten men with no families or kingdoms to beckon. They protected caravans and took care of work best done in the deep night. Hean wasn't naturally violent. He merely wanted more. Fear drove him to excess, for he knew that death was stalking him and it would not be long before his carcass was left to rot in the ground. His every whim was determined not to allow that day to come.

The wagon rolled up to the graveyard sometime before dawn. Three men jumped down, snatching tools before heading among the tombstones. Hean climbed down, slowed by a sudden fit of gout. He grabbed the lantern from the post beside him and hobbled after his people. There was work to be done ere the sun rose.

They went past rows of graves, stopping only at one covered in fresh dug soil. Hean's eyes lit. "This one. Quickly. The Prefects will be here soon."

Shovels set to dirt and the digging commenced. Hean watched, snaking his tongue to lick the corners of his mouth as the hole deepened. A thunk announced they'd reached the wooden coffin. True children of the desert were wrapped in fresh linen and left to return to the ground. It wasn't until outlanders arrived with their vastly different customs that coffins started being used. He frowned on the custom but wasn't one to judge. His family long participated in burning their corpses and letting the ash drift across the winds. Hean was different, for he had no aspirations to meet the other side of life.

"Hurry!" Hean urged.

"You want this whole box?" a one-eyed woman with close cropped grey hair asked. Her tone suggested they weren't willing to go that far for a handful of coin.

Hean resisted the urge to strike her. It wouldn't do to be seen hitting his employees. Besides, there were other ways to ensure rigid discipline. "Pry the coffin open and take the body. Fill it back in so as not to arouse suspicion."

They did as told. The two men carried the wrapped body to the wagon, leaving her to finish filling the grave. A rotten stench permeated the air, prompting complaints and curses. The work was unnatural, not to mention illegal. If the prefects arrived, they were all bound for the gallows. Hean, at least, would be beheaded in front of a private audience. The others would be mocked and scorned, even as their bodies spasmed while the rope choked tighter.

"Go back and help her," Hean hissed once the body was loaded. He climbed onto the wagon and extinguished the lantern.

Soon, all three returned, tossed their shovels in the back, and joined their master. The wagon rolled away, back to where Hean felt secure enough to conduct his true business. An odd air was settling over the Heart Eternal and he didn't know what might follow. They had arrived at a crossroads. Of that Hean was certain. Which way the winds blew next remained obscured, as if some power was trying to keep the city from seeing the truth. The wagon rumbled on, creaking down cobblestone streets.

The night was both friend and nightmare to all creatures, from the lowest rat scurrying through sewers and trash heaps, to the highest diplomat asleep in lofty towers capped in golden crowns. The most famous city in the world beheld many wonders. Some were meant to be seen. Others were best forgotten, if the witness knew what was best.

Abbas Doza had never been afraid of the dark. He found the obscurity of darkness welcoming, giving him free reign to pursue his targets with impunity. Guilded assassins were overlooked by the Prefecture, believing they performed valuable services for the city and her citizens. In return, Guild Masters provided the city coffers with a small percentage of the total take. Simplistic, the system served everyone well. Except for those who were contracted to die.

His earlier thoughts of fleeing Ghendis Ghadanaban dissolved. Abbas's last job wasn't sanctioned, running the risk of him being labeled a criminal. The potential for arrest rose, but he knew where to lay low. Some parts of the city went unpatrolled. He had a well-developed support network who'd prove more than willing to provide him with cover. A man like Abbas took pride in being a step ahead.

Pocket full of meager winnings, Abbas moved purposefully through the winding streets of the market district. Empty stalls, linen walls blowing softly in the night wind, stared back at his passing. Wagons emptied of ware choked the side alleys. Trays of turang glasses, cleaned from the day's excesses, were piled beside pitchers and serving trays. Fires were extinguished, though merchants and cooks would return well before sunrise to begin baking breads and roasting meats for the new day.

Abbas was surprised when five men emerged to surround him before he exited the merchant district. He knew he shouldn't have been. Nothing ever seemed to work the way he planned it. The assassin stopped in midstride and readied. Loose throwing knives were positioned around his waist, concealed by the knee length leather jacket he was fond of wearing. Other weapons were strapped to different areas. All compact and capable of being thrown. He'd never been a sword or axe man and the thought of unworldly powers soured him. It was the blade or nothing for Abbas Doza.

"Figured we'd find you skulking through here."

Abbas squinted, barely able to make out Ninean Foul's scarred face. Henchwoman for the Guild Masters and loyal to a fault. The others would belong to Foul and more than capable of killing him without breaking a sweat.

"That you, Foul? I've done nothing wrong," Abbas called. "You've got nothing on me."

"Don't we?" Foul snapped and spat a mouthful of tabba juice. "Word is you done a bad thing, Abbas. The Master don't look kindly on freelancing."

"I did what I was contracted for," Abbas defended. There was no point in denying his indulgences. "You'd have done the same. No questions."

Foul shrugged. "Not my problem. I come here to do a job. Don't suppose you coming peaceful?"

He tensed. "You know I can't do that. Not without knowing the charges."

Breaking into laughter, Foul cast her head back. "Charges are usurpation 'gainst the Guild. You can come easy or we can convince you."

"I've always been a slow learner," Abbas replied and braced for the beating.

The enforcers moved in blurs. Abbas threw a short dagger at Foul and crouched as he spun to strike the first attacker with a boot to the ribs. The enforcer fell and Abbas threw a second blade. This was knocked aside in a shower of sparks. An elbow caught him in the back of the head, knocking spittle out. Stunned, Abbas was unable to recover before his legs were swept out. He hit the cobblestones with all his weight and was pinned.

"Don't kill him! Bosses want him alive for questioning," Foul ordered.

Ropes were looped around his wrists and ankles. An extra one around his neck for good measure. Abbas struggled, knowing his efforts would only draw the ropes tighter. Perhaps it might be better to die here than face a tribunal. Foul loomed over him, teeth stained black from years of chewing tabba leaves. Some of it dripped onto Abbas' cheek.

"Just remember, you had this coming," Foul said.

The last thing Abbas saw was a meaty fist come down to crash into his face.

FIVE

First Prophet Sandis Varian was in a foul mood. Every effort to discover the killer proved fruitless. Teams of prefects and the Scarlet scoured every part of the god king's palace. They found nothing. His one solace was in no additional undead being found. A plague of that proportion would devastate the upcoming peace efforts and the kingdom needed a respite from the revulsions of war. Mind trapped in overlapping circles of impossibility, Sandis struggled to understand the far-reaching implications of recent events.

Forty-six successive reigns without major incident. The why and how of deicide occurring during his tenure was not only improbable, but deceptively simplistic. Sandis felt decades weigh him down. Age catching up, his position was no longer fulfilling. Unless he managed to find the killer, his legacy would forever be tarnished. If the city continued to stand.

Word was already beginning to circulate. It wouldn't be long before every street murmured what happened. He prayed they succeeded soon, else the city would devolve into chaos. There'd be no chance for peace talks with the city under martial law. Years of bloodshed would continue until naught remained of once proud Eleboran. His sigh was strained, tired from long, sleepless nights.

His palanquin arrived, borne by six brutish creatures. Each had diluted grey skin with odd tufts of hair sprouting from various places on their exposed backs. Tusks jutted from their lower jaws. Flat faces and tiny, recessed eyes stared dumbly as Sandis entered. The origins of the Mascantii were lost to time, though Sandis suspected sorcery had been involved—turning hapless creatures into a mockery of humanity. Regardless, they'd served the people of Ghendis Ghadanaban for generations. He shuddered at the thought of what they might do, if they decided to cast aside their servitude.

The lead Mascantii grunted and the palanquin was hefted to their shoulders. Sandis clutched the cushions to keep from being jostled and settled in for the short ride to the city Overseer's offices. It was a trek he'd made far too many times recently. One that was beginning to feel pointless. Without additional information, Sandis found their meetings as little more than the voicing of grievances. Larris wasn't deceitful, at least he didn't believe so, but neither was she counted among his top allies.

The ride was mercifully short, preventing his mind from wandering too far. His Mascantii bowed in genuine respect and carried the palanquin away, as Sandis entered the building. The echo of his sandals slapping across the gold veined marble tiles would have been considered offensive in his building but here it seemed appropriate. Prefects hurried about their daily chores, oppressive in their black uniforms.

Sandis failed to understand the concept of rule by force. Born a peaceful man, he dedicated his life to the service of the god king. A void now existed, and he was clueless how to fill it. Mortality suddenly took on new urgency. A pair of functionaries awaited him outside Larris's offices. They parted the curtains to allow him entry.

"First Prophet, good morning," Larris almost sang.

He smiled, for her golden voice could raise the dourest spirits. "Overseer, it is indeed a good morning, if soured by our current predicament. Have you made any progress?"

"Alas, no. The matter is proving more difficult to solve. My people are exhausting all resources, mostly in aid to the Prefecture," Larris replied.

Sandis took the proffered seat. "Lord Verian's promise?"

"The Scarlet can't go marching through the city at random. Imagine how others would respond to seeing giant, winged men with grudges." She shook her head, locks of hair sweeping across her shoulders. "We are in a tight position."

He held out his hands. "What more can be done? The resources at our disposal are not infinite. I fear the war has robbed us of the ability to adequately deal with this."

"It's not as if we can send to the government for assistance. This city is the only thing preventing the kingdom from disintegrating. If we fall, this part of the world will drown in the blood of a million sons and fathers." Larris frowned, frustrations boiling over. "The timing of the assassination leads me to believe it was premeditated. Calculated."

"What are you saying?" he asked, afraid to know the answer he already suspected.

Larris gave a deadpan look. "That the god king's assassination was committed to keep the kingdom at war."

The implications frightened him. "If such is true, the other three kingdoms already have the city planted with agents and are actively undermining our efforts."

"Which one has the most to gain?" Larris asked. "I fear the answer is not forthcoming and there is little time to flush out the culprits."

Sandis leaned back in the chair, shoulders slumped in defeat. His service was to a god, not the prevention of political intrigues. Retirement beckoned, thrusting bribes to secure his full attention. "This is not the only reason you summoned me."

"Very astute, First Prophet. No, indeed. We have discovered a certain path that was previously unimaginable."

"Certain paths?" he questioned. It wasn't unheard of for the Overseer's offices to expand their power in the name of maintaining control.

Larris cleared her throat. "I have sent contacts to the Assassin Guild."

"Assassins!" he sputtered. "What happened to the Reclamators? Were they not our primary outsourcing?"

"They are, but this is not the time to hedge our leads," Larris said. "The Reclamator should be here within the hour. I am told she is one of their best."

"That does not absolve the sequester of the assassins. They are honorless people, Larris," he scolded. "We cannot trust them."

She raised a placating hand. "I know what you are thinking, for I have spent many hours deliberating the same."

"Who is to say the assassins weren't responsible for Omoraum's murder?" Sandis asked. "We could be inviting disaster within our ranks. It was a foolish move."

"Perhaps, but it is too early to tell," Larris said. "In the meantime, it would be best to focus our efforts on the Reclamator."

"What is it you suspect, Larris? As uncommon as the undead are, they are certainly not the thing of myth we should be overly concerned about," Sandis pressed.

She paused, as if unsure how to proceed. Her appreciation for the First Prophet was documented and she bore no animosity toward him or his office. Still, some matters—especially of state—were best conducted internally. Larris studied his eyes, searching for any sign of betrayal. All she found was unconditional loyalty. A rare quality in these tumultuous times.

"I need you to follow me. It is time I showed you the caves," she relented.

Caves? Sandis knew many secrets but had never heard of any cave system under the city. The founders designed the ruling branches to work separate but together, so as not to compromise their individuality. Whatever secrets he knew were not shared by the Overseer or the Prefecture. Until now, it had proven a failproof system.

They exited her official offices through a sliding panel behind her desk. Larris paused to light two torches, handing one to him, before hurrying down the spiraling stairs. Sandis observed his surroundings, suspicious that the path was meticulously clean. Not a cobweb or speck of sand accompanied their descent. *Secrets in use. What does she know? Am I being led into a trap?* Down they went, until the air turned cool and his torch burned low. What he discovered went beyond anything his imagination could conjure.

Relghel Gorgal seldom left the White Crow. Centuries of traveling the world culminated with near total satisfaction of curiosity. Relghel retired from public life almost as quickly as he'd fled his destiny, thus altering the course of god kings forever. He no longer gave the matter thought, for it had happened so long ago, few mentioned it, and then only in scholarly debate. His opinion mattered little. Let them speak, for his days were infinite.

Few knew his truth, and he liked it that way. There was little good that might come from the general population knowing he had turned his back on the succession of god kings. Some would try to eliminate him. Others attempt to turn him to their bidding. Relghel avoided it all by occupying a regular table in the most famous tavern in the city. After all, who paid attention to a drunk old man with more stories than sense?

Eamon Brisk was one of the few who knew Relghel's sad story. Sworn to secrecy, the portly owner funneled drinks, along with room and board, to the sorrowful fallen god. Business was good enough, he didn't worry about the loss. He figured it fair collateral for the wealth of stories Relghel was prone to share.

The midday crowd hadn't funneled in yet, giving Eamon and his people time to clean and prepare the Crow. Wiping down the bar, Eamon slapped the rag over his shoulder and ambled over to Relghel's table. Baradoon watched with little interest from his place by the door. The giant long thought about what it would be like to fight a god, even a fallen one like Relghel. He chuckled before looking away.

"Bit early for the cups, even for you," Eamon gestured to the half empty bottle of wine.

Relghel gave him a look of time holding no meaning. "Join me?"

"You know I don't drink," Eamon teased but took the proffered seat. "I assume you've heard the rumors circulating?"

"It is an interesting time to be alive," Relghel confirmed.

"It won't be too long before they come for you," Eamon added. "You're deemed too valuable by the Hall of Prophets."

"What use am I? The days of my ascension are nothing more than blurred memory," the fallen god said. "My time was three thousand years ago."

His tone was flat, missing the jovialness many were accustomed to. A hollow spot lingered behind the depth of his almost pale eyes. Regret? Eamon didn't want to find out. He couldn't imagine the weight Relghel bore. Or the guilt.

"That doesn't mean they won't come. I'm surprised your friend hasn't shown up again," Eamon referred to Sandis Vartan. It was no secret the First Prophet enjoyed drinking and conversing with the fallen god.

"I imagine he is quite busy," Relghel said. "Between you and me, there is no successor chosen. Omoraum's time was not supposed to end for another seven hundred years."

The admission stunned Eamon. Immersed in the true heart of Ghendis Ghadanaban, the bartender seldom bothered with the political aspects involved in running the city. Let those in power be in power. That was his view. He claimed nothing on the morality of leadership, nor was it his part to ensure laws were just and fair. Eamon tended to all walks of life, giving them a place to come and forget their worries, if just for a few drinks at a time.

"I think your life is about to change again, my friend," Eamon said after some deliberation. *And not in ways you wish it.*

Tula had never seen the interior of the Prefecture. Her business kept her in the darkness, where people didn't want to look. She was fine with that. Work of her nature was meant to be conducted without witnesses. The human mind could withstand a great many traumas, but she found reality stretched to the limit when it came to the undead. The natural order of things, when threatened by abnormality, was to retreat and defend. She, and the other Reclamators, were the counter offense meant to restore order.

The prefects hadn't explained why she'd been summoned, or in what capacity. Tula didn't care. Her work was at last being recognized, and for that, she was grateful. The opportunity to further serve her city and kingdom was always welcomed. She was the third generation in her small family who'd donned the uniform. A point of pride evident in the way she carried herself through the streets. Some chose to slump, to walk with heads down, as if ashamed of their work. Tula looked everyone in the eye, daring them to approach.

Her haughty attitude didn't sit well in the Prefecture. Eyes glared with open disdain, for her work was frowned upon by the rightful enforcers. Tula ignored them, even as the knowledge burned deep within. She did what came naturally, as did these others. The hypocritical nature of powerful organizations often ground others beneath its wheels. She would be no different, if she failed to stand for herself.

Escorts left her at the edge of a training field and bade her wait. Tula frowned, but held her tongue. The open field was surrounded by small buildings, barracks and offices. So unlike her Guild, who met in shadows with faces cowled. Two ranks of ten prefects entered and began loosening up. A severe woman followed and began barking orders.

They took opposite sides of the field, wooden swords in hand. Tula admired their discipline, if not their fervor. She recognized them for what they were; a weaponized branch of the ruling body, capable of turning the law to suit their purposes. Good men and bad worked among their ranks. She'd witnessed their indiscretions numerous times but wisely kept the matters private. Raising concerns drew attention.

"On my command!" the woman, a sergeant, barked.

Prefects tensed, crouching in attack position. Winds dropped down from the rooftops to swirl among the dried grass. Tula caught a glimpse of the sergeant's missing ear as her hair danced up. Puckered scars lined her neck, curling around the base of her skull. The Reclamator didn't understand how anyone might endure such.

"Attack!"

Ranks clashed with terrible fury. The prefects weren't soldiers, but with the war continuing to rage across the kingdom, militarization became a necessary act. Peace was fragile in the best of times. It didn't take much to imagine hordes of enemy soldiers flooding the city streets in conquest. She wondered how much of a fight the prefects would be able to withstand before being overwhelmed.

"This way," a sharp voice called from over her shoulder.

Tula gave the training drills a final look before following her escort. She failed to see the sergeant glaring back at her. Escorts led her into the labyrinthine halls of the main Prefecture headquarters. Orderlies and menials shuffled about, ignoring her. She was taken into a small room on the second floor and told to wait. Tula feigned a smile as the door closed, leaving her alone in a room with two chairs separated by a small table. A pitcher of water sat in the middle.

She'd just poured a glass and sat down, when the door opened and Tega Ig entered. The Lord of the Prefecture was an imposing man of ill temper and it showed in the deep scowl he bore. She tensed, preparing for a fight, though there was little she might accomplish against such a beast.

"Reclamator Tula Gish," he ground out, his baritone rumbling across the chamber. "You have been temporarily reassigned to the Prefecture."

SIX

The winds of war swirled over Eleboran unchecked and unopposed. Enemy armies clashed in the desert, the mountains, and across grassy plains. Whole villages were brought to ruin and forgotten as flesh striped skeletons wasted away where they'd fallen. Units from three kingdoms took defensive positions across the kingdom but lacked mandate to prevent the war from continuing. Locked in the center of the insanity, Ghendis Ghadanaban.

Why the war started was lost to time and dulled memory. Tribal leaders swore it was the kingdom's central government who overstepped their bounds by demanding increased tariffs. They abandoned their villages and fled deep into the mountains, where winter often held sway. Soldiers who pursued learned the error of their ways. Mountain warfare was unnatural to flatlanders, and the tribes were masters of the hills.

Militias formed, and the war deepened, until an unending cycle of violence was born. The kingdoms of Mordai, Uruth, and Hyborlad deployed army divisions to quell the storm but with severe restrictions. Without being able to fully engage, nor risk firing on each other, those divisions became insurmountable roadblocks.

Hohn was no stranger to the politics of war, even if they often failed to make sense. What he missed was the operational support of a massive military machine to rely on. Artillery, armor, air cover. He had nothing here and didn't even know what planet he was on. The locals were not forthcoming with the information either, for they believed their world to be the only one in existence. Narrow and problematic, but manageable.

Living in caves, away from cities and major population centers felt wrong, but Hohn and his soldiers had grown used to it, viewing their ordeal as just another extended campaign. War, when it boiled down, was the same no matter where. He sat on a rock lip jutting over the cave mouth, watching the sunset. It was an old habit.

"They killed the prisoners."

Hohn sighed without looking back at Tine. His second in command was a quality sounding board, with almost as much experience. Should anything happen to Hohn, the squad was in good hands.

"Both of them?" he asked.

Tine sat beside him. "Without thinking about it. Once it became clear neither were going to talk, they had their throats slit. Bodies were taken down to the fire pit."

"Wouldn't do to leave a trail for the enemy to find," Hohn said. He'd witnessed barbarism before and it always turned his stomach. The army he came from had laws, especially regarding prisoners of war.

Tine looked around for the guards he knew were warding the cave. Their camouflage was good enough to avoid detection. "What have we gotten ourselves mixed up in?"

"The truth? I don't know. At first, I thought we were doing the right thing by helping these hill tribes." He shook his head and tossed a pebble. "Now? The more we work with them, the more I'm beginning to think they're animals."

"Tribes have always had a hard life, more so when a fancy government gets involved," Tine countered. His early life was spent in a hunter-gatherer tribal setting. "Folks with more powerful toys come in thinking they have the right to take what they want. It's the folks who aren't as advanced that always lose."

"Name me one hunter-gatherer society that outlasted any invading force," Hohn said with sadness. He caught Tine's shoulders stiffen. "Sorry. I'm just getting tired of this war."

"It's not the war we wanted," Tine began.

Hohn grinned and dropped his head. "It's the one we got."

"Only show in town. Malach wants to see us."

The tribal leader was veteran of many campaigns. A wily man of many odd talents. It was rumored he could see the souls of the departed walking among the living. Hohn didn't believe any of that but wasn't foolish enough to discount it in front of the fighters. He also didn't care to meet with a man who'd ordered the ruthless murders of prisoners.

They found him seated before a large fire deep in the cave. Several of his chieftains surrounded him in their usual pattern. All were weather scarred men of bronze skin and thin hair. Their hard looks glared at the foreign soldiers. It was a nightly ritual. Their heads were wrapped in colorful scarves, a contrast to their otherwise morbid attire of grey, brown, and black.

Hohn ignored them and took his place. "Gentlemen. What news from the front?"

"That is none of your concern, outlander," Malach replied. His hawkish nose was curled at the tip. The result of having been broken too many times. "We have received word that the enemy is preparing a new campaign."

So, they're finally coming for you. "How long do we have?"

"Days. We are marshalling all tribes for this offensive," Malach said.

Hohn doubted the intelligence of this but knew better than to voice his concerns. "Where do you want my people?"

Technically, they were mercenaries. Working for food, a place to rest their heads, and a small sum of promised money when the war ended. Hohn knew better than to demand payment. The tribes were savage fighters who'd just as easily cut his tongue from his head than deal with foreigners.

A snicker came from several chieftains. Malach ignored them. "It is time to send your people away. I have a special task for you."

Krak. "I'm listening."

"You will accompany Delag and his warriors down to the foothills. There, you will ambush the approaching soldiers."

Hohn was no fool. "A sacrifice. To buy you time to gather the rest of the tribes. That's suicide."

"It is the will of the gods," Malach retorted. "Who are we to argue otherwise? Do you shirk from this duty, Hohn of the stars?"

Tine's growl was low, only heard by Hohn. "No, I figure we have enough ammunition left for one good fight. After that, its black powder rifles. How many soldiers do you figure are coming?"

"Several thousand."

The answer chilled him. So many. There was little chance of a reinforced company holding off what amounted to a division, even with their advanced weaponry. He sensed the attitude of those around him. They wanted Hohn to walk away. Any justification for removing the dishonor they represented to other, worthier, participants in the great campaign. He refused to give them the satisfaction.

"When do we depart?" he asked in defiance.

"At dawn. It is best this way," Malach said. "Go with our blessing and serve us well. We shall talk more upon your return."

The soldiers walked away, back to the others in their secluded part of the cave. Hohn wasn't surprised by the dismissal, but the manner in which it was delivered. He hadn't expected to be crossed. Too many militia filled the cave system. The fight would be brutal and Hohn failed to find a positive outcome. He carried the news to his people, expecting them to share his views. Every leader comes to understand regret, he theorized. It was figuring out how to overcome those feelings that determined good from bad.

How much time passed, Aldon didn't know. The last thing he recalled was being smothered by a large shadow. Pain and death should have followed, but he still lived. His mind was clouded, as if filled with too much. Aldon eventually awoke in his bed, tired and head pounding. His chest ached, almost as if it had been stretched open. Taunting images ran through his mind, robbing him of the tranquility most his age took comfort in.

Dawn had broken, and judging from the heat funneling through the windows, it was close to midday. He sat up and regretted the sudden movement. Aldon struggled to understand why he was still alive, and in his bed. Bare feet touched the cool tile floor. Dizzy, he reached for the water his parents insisted he keep beside the bed. The liquid felt cool and produced similar effects throughout his body.

He staggered into the common room. His father was gone, but the stench of a hard night's drinking lingered. Aldon looked in on his mother, who appeared sound asleep. Rather than wake her, he watched her sleep.

The rise and fall of her chest comforted him, a subtle reminder she still lived. Satisfied, he let her be. One foot in front of the other, Aldon returned to the streets. His mind was in a fog. Actions uncontrolled.

Aldon wound through the streets in search of solace. He found only noise, crowded streets, and the oppressive heat summer produced. Foreign sensations assaulted him, threatening to rob the strength from his legs. Why? The city had been his home for almost twenty years. There was nothing in it to make him uncomfortable before. He shook his head in the hopes of clearing his mind.

His course took him through the markets, where he bumped and careened off people. Aldon's eyes were lowered, focusing on each footstep. His stomach growled, and penniless, he looked for an easy mark to take a meal. Fruit vendors competed with bread makers. Cartloads of fresh vegetables brought in from the farmlands made his mouth water. None would miss a handful of figs. An apple. Aldon slowed and moved on his target.

Women dressed in brightly colored robes paraded through the crowds offering water to the thirsty. Aldon waited until a pair passed and dipped his hand into the bin of figs. He made it a step before the cry of thief was raised. Aldon ran, but the way was choked with many people. Escape was impossible.

Where panic should have resided, only serenity was found. Aldon pushed his way through the crowds of confused bystanders. They parted as if cast aside by a mighty gust of wind. Ignoring this newfound strength, he started to run faster. Just a few more meters until the market ended and the open streets began. He was almost free.

"You there! Stop in the name of the Prefecture!"

Aldon ran faster, pushing his muscles to exhaustion. He should have felt tired. Should have been doubled over with burning lungs. Instead he was filled with energy. Invigorated. It was a feeling unlike any in his young experience. He broke into laughter. Rounding a corner, the young thief skidded to a halt. The way was blocked by two full squads of black clad prefects. Spears were lowered in a menacing wall. Swords drawn. The heavy stomp of boots closing around him warned the way behind was blocked as well. He was trapped.

"I should have known you'd prove trouble," the squad sergeant said as he advanced.

Aldon winced, for they recognized each other from the other night. Once was ill fortune. Twice a habit. He knew nothing he said would walk him out of trouble. The prefects were generally fair but had little tolerance for thievery. Another came forward bearing a heavy pair of rusted iron manacles.

"Have you weapons, boy?" the sergeant asked.

Aldon opened his mouth to speak, but instead of words, golden light streamed forth. A cosmic scream followed, driving the prefects to their knees while desperately covering their ears. Some failed, their eardrums ruptured. Others were forced to look away lest they become blind from the light. If Aldon knew their plight, he failed to recognize it. The boy titled his head back and endless moments of pain and rage escaped his body.

Only the sergeant remained unscathed. He crawled low under the light, coming up behind Aldon. Flipping his short sword around, he aimed the hilt and swung. The blow caught him on the back of his head. Light vanished. Darkness rose. When he next awoke, he was bound and in a windowless room. Aldon was frightened, mostly of opening his eyes and discovering the wicked light remained.

The air was damp. Moist. Heightened senses picked up the sound of water dripping down a crease on the far, unseen wall. The weight of chains prevented him from lifting his arms. His head ached with an impossible pounding, deep within the skull. Perhaps worst of all, was the gaping hole in his memory. The last thing he remembered was being hungry and trying to grab a handful of fruit. Everything after swirled in a dark haze, as if he'd been watching from outside his own body. The first spark of terror awakened.

The door unlocked and was pushed open. Aldon caught his first glimpse of his prison. It was an empty cell, void of furniture or trappings. A pail for waste was off to his right. Food and water to his left. Chains were snaked through rings bolted in the rock wall. He wondered who his tormentors thought he was, what strength he might possess. Three figures entered and he was no longer alone.

"What is your name?" a woman asked. Her golden voice stirred his heart.

Aldon, wincing from the sudden bright light, replied, "Aldon Cay."

"I wonder," she said in return, head cocked.

An elderly man in rich green robes glided into the room and halted a step away from Aldon. A bag of tools was in his right hand. He laid them out with methodical precision before returning to Aldon. His wizened face studied the boy. "Do not move, Aldon Cay. This will not hurt, if you follow my instructions."

He was poked and prodded. His mouth opened, and torchlight shoved down his throat. The old man stumbled back, for he had seen the golden light buried deep within Aldon's chest. Falling to his knees, he placed his palm over his chest in prayer and bowed his head. Turning, he fled back to where his companions waited.

"It is unmistakable," he said, his voice shaking. "The spark is within him."

"Impossible," Sandis replied. "How could this boy hold the spark?"

The old man shook his head. "I do not pretend to understand the way of the god kings. What I do know, is that he has been chosen."

"You are not mistaken?" Larris seconded. Doubt, however debilitating, was a powerful motivator and she was willing to give in to it.

"Positive. This boy must not be harmed. Nor can we allow him to be set loose."

Sandis cast a cautious glance to the Overseer. "We are taking an awful risk on this. What happens if this spark is proven to be a lie?"

"That, First Prophet, is a risk I am willing to take." She turned to the prefects behind them. "Have him cleaned up. I want those chains removed. Bring torches and bedding. He is to remain in this cave until we can fully ascertain the truth of the matter."

They rushed to obey. Larris looked at Sandis. "If what the Truthsayer suspects is true, we might have the answer we have been searching for."

SEVEN

Days blended together with disturbing regularity, the longer a soldier spends on campaign. Combat is horrifying. A deed no sane person should ever wish to indulge in. Worse, the space between battles when sheer boredom threatens. Morale and the will of the army waiver, teetering on the edge of dissolution before violent action calls all those harrowed souls to return. On those rare occasions, soldiers can vent months of pent up frustrations and unleash the full fury of their training.

The village of Khurget was small. Massive, sand stained tents formed twin circles on one side of the drying riverbed. What had been intended for greatness was diluted, abandoned by the winds of fate. Only a handful of weary sentries were awake when the raiders stormed through. Government soldiers on horseback, bearing torches and black powder weapons. They burned every tent. Slaughtered every resident. Those fortunate enough, died in their sleep, never understanding the evil being perpetrated upon them. Once finished, the raiders hurried away and were lost to the morning sun.

Ten leagues to the east sat the village of Gruek. They were awake when the government company rode into their one road town. Wooden homes lined the street, for Gruek was built in a harsher climate. Lacking cause for concern, the citizens greeted the soldiers with open arms and friendly waves, for they were loyal to Eleboran. The elder body came out to formally accept the soldiers and were slaughtered for their troubles. Like Khurget, they were slaughtered to the last. Unlike their distant neighbors, they were forced to watch as their world burned down around them. A seven year old girl was the last to die, her body staked in the open road as a warning.

Several other villages and towns suffered similarly. Always government troops moving in, killing, and riding away. They left but a handful of survivors to tell the tales of their deeds to the arriving units from Hyborlad and Uruth. Military leaders began to fear a new campaign was beginning. One that would end with the genocide of the entire kingdom. Reports were collected and sent back to commanding officers. Concerns grew. Whatever storm approached, the combined peacekeeping armies were woefully understrength and ill-prepared to deal with it.

Behind it all waited Imperator Thrakus. The instigator of so much suffering, he watched as his campaign of terror spread. Chaos gripped the kingdom. He knew that a battered people could only withstand so much before they broke. Time was on his side.

They sat around a plain wooden table. Important men and women ignorant of the kingdom's plight. Ghendis Ghadanaban had been wounded, perhaps mortally, but somehow found a way to recover. Even as whispers of the slain god king continued to spread. Even as panic rose in subtle levels. Even as hope waned. Salvation was possible.

The rustle of wings broke the strange silence gripping the table. They were all accustomed to being around the Scarlet, but to be trapped in a room thus was most unnatural. Verian, arms folded, wore a look of doubt. He'd served five god kings, never once failing them until now. The assassination was taken personally, for he was the guardian of gods. Exile was the only option left for him and his cadre of Scarlet. They could never return to the mountain halls of Rhorrmere again. There was no redemption. No peace of mind. He and his cadre would spend eternity in defeat.

"There is no precedent," Verian told them. "Forty-six god kings have been born and died, but never before their time. There is no one trained to take Lord Dala'gharis's place. It is too soon and nothing this body decides is capable of altering that fact."

"What truths are you hiding from us?" Tega asked. The Master of the Prefecture long suspected Verian of concealing many truths. While the general populace didn't need to concern themselves with the trappings of immortals, Tega decided it imperative they each understood the other's truths.

Verian bristled, unused to being questioned. "Those matters belong to the Scarlet, and the gods. We have never once answered to a mortal and you will not be the first. I like you, but do not push me."

Rebuked, Tega sat back in his chair and scowled.

"Bickering amongst ourselves is pointless, gentlemen," Overseer Larris said. "I believe we must accept this cruel twist of fate and proceed. We cannot do that without the full cooperation and support of the Scarlet."

"What would you have me do, Larris?" Verian asked. Desperation crept into the edges of his tone.

"There must be something in the ancient scrolls. I refuse to believe we are powerless to advance the next ascension." She cast a look to Sandis for support. "First Prophet? What does the Order of Prophets say?"

Sandis chose his words carefully, eager not to offend any party while struggling to understand what he'd seen firsthand. "I know what I saw, but I do not comprehend it. Yet. The Truthsayer confirms the divine spark is within that boy. How or why, I cannot speculate.

Officially, the order has no stance other than the need to have the spark transferred before it is too late."

"I assume there is a known way to make this happen?" she pressed.

"If there is, I am unaware of it," he admitted.

"Bringing us back to our false starting point," Tega chimed in. "Unless our winged friend here cares to tell us how gods are made?"

"That is not for mortal ears," Verian said. He refused to look any of them in the eye.

"So there is a way?" Tula Gish interrupted.

She'd felt awkward joining this group of austere leaders, for it had never been her place. Tula was proud but lacked the skillset to deal with high ranking superiors. She felt out of place after only an hour. Her one strength, in this setting, was her lack of patience for game playing. She preferred a straightforward conversation, her superiors often claiming she was direct to a fault. Thus far, it had served her well.

"Perhaps," Verian relented after they all stared at her. Approval lingered in his eyes. Audacity was a mortal trait. One he often felt jealous of. "You are wise, Tula Gish of the Reclamator Guild. No mortal is meant to know the ways of the gods."

"It doesn't sound like they are asking about them," Tula countered. "More like they just want to know what to do next."

The Lord of the Scarlet unfolded his arms, placing his wide palms flat on the dusty table. "Yes. There is a way, but I must see this boy first. You may accompany me, Reclamator."

Sandis failed to grasp the significance of the turn of events. Verian was an oddity few had interactions with, himself included. The Scarlet kept to themselves. Alone in their golden towers, where he imagined they perched like birds at the end of a long day. Amusing as the thought was, Sandis often wondered what happened behind those closed doors.

"What of the undead? For them to have been within the god king's sanctum speaks of dire events and a powerful enemy we are not prepared to combat. Surely the Reclamator would be better spent warding the palace?" Sandis questioned.

"My name is Tula, First Prophet," she refrained from snarling. "Tula Gish. You sent for me, not the other way around."

Rebuked, he presented a stern face with tight lipped smile. "Of course."

"Are we finished?" Verian asked. "I would like to see the boy now."

The Scarlet didn't wait. He rose, and gesturing Tula follow, headed down to the caves. The others were left behind to stew. A quiet showman, Verian enjoyed bringing his companions to the edge of anger, where madness and reason intersected.

"A most infuriating creature," Sandis said under his breath.

Tega Ig snorted his amusement.

Bound and gagged, Abbas had been tied to a wooden X and left on display in the center of the Guild floor. Assassins and functionaries walked by without looking directly at him. He was their reminder to obey the rules. To not cause waves or work outside the lines. The Guild was licensed by the city and the kingdom. Breaking those laws was akin to suicide.

The Guild Masters arrived after a day. Their faces were hidden behind featureless masks, suggesting anonymity among the masses. Hands folded into robe sleeves so not an inch of flesh was exposed, the three masters marched through the gathering to stand before Abbas. All others knelt in deference. A chime sounded and the assassins rose as one and stood facing the accused.

Abbas squinted at the masters with his one good eye. The other had been swollen shut by Foul's fist in the market. He coughed, a line of blood laced spittle spilling down his chin and staining his tunic. Once proud, Abbas Doza saw death standing before him in silent judgment. His actions were inexcusable and perpetuated by greed and selfishness. He raised his head, the only act of defiance left to him.

"Abbas Doza. The time for your atonement has arrived."

Another chime sounded. The masters stepped closer.

"State your crimes."

He wanted to laugh, not at the proceedings, for he held them in veneration. No, he wanted to laugh at the audacity with which he'd willingly gone against the Guild. There was but one god in Ghendis Ghadanaban. He spoke through cracked lips. The sound of his parched voice alien to his ears.

"I admit to taking contract with entities outside of Guild regulations," he said.

Heads bowed. No one spoke, for there was no need. Assassins were singular beings. Those who knew Abbas held their tongues, for to claim kinship with the condemned meant sharing similar fates.

"You willingly disobeyed the law, thus putting all of us in jeopardy. There is but one penalty for this crime. Death."

"Is there no inquiry?" Abbas asked. He expected to die, but like any true artist, wanted a platform for his work to be seen.

The masters stood motionless. How they conversed with each other was a great mystery. One Abbas never figured out. There was a bond each held, allowing them to speak without words. A convenient tool to prevent being overheard.

"What do you wish to tell us, condemned?"

"Yes, speak."

"Speak of your crime."

His head began to pound as the psychic vibrations lacing their words slammed into him. Oh, how he wanted to tell them the glories of his deeds. How he slipped through the most vaunted security in the world to conduct his business. But the words did not come. Try as he wanted, Abbas could only meet them with what little defiance he had left.

"Silence is admission of guilt."

"Yes. He must die."

"There is no tolerance for this behavior. An example must be made, so others do not follow."

Abbas let his head fall. There it was, played out before the members of the Guild. Death without full confession. He reasoned the masters were somehow responsible for keeping him silent. Weakened, the only thing he could do was wait for the end.

"The condemned is to remain here for all to bear witness for the sum of three days. At which time he shall be removed from existence."

The chime ended the tribunal. Assassins knelt until the masters returned to their cryptic haunts and then filed off to their business. Head down, Abbas failed to see one woman stare at him a moment too long. Then, she too, was gone. His fate was sealed and not one of them would ever know the magnitude of his greatness. After all, how many could say they had killed a god?

The door opened again, and despite not having suffered any abuses or mistreatment, Aldon flinched away from both light and intruders. He'd barely eaten or touched his water. Lack of social contact left him wary. How much time passed since his capture was unknown. The rational part of his mind suggested it had been only a few hours. A day at most.

Aldon's mind felt stretched. He saw through his hands when lifting them up to his face, as if they were little more than a pale curtain of flesh. A stranger in his own body. Lack of understanding perpetuated the madness, threatening to rip apart the fragile constructs of his young age. He wanted it to end.

"You are he?"

Aldon jerked back in shock. The man before him was tall, powerfully built, and he had a pair of wings poking up behind his back. Levels of impossibility raced through his inexperienced mind. Opening his mouth to speak, Aldon felt raw power gush forth. Golden light returned and his mind retreated to dark corners, while another, parasitic entity took control.

Verian dropped to his knees, head bowed. His pulse quickened, for he never imagined the slain capable of returning. His doubts forced him down to the caves. Perhaps to spite the others and their blind naivety. Those petty emotions washed away, delivering him back to a position of dominance he'd enjoyed just a week before. Tula remained a step behind him.

"You should show respect," he half growled and whispered.

She frowned, dismissing the boy with golden light pouring from his eyes. "For what? A child?"

"That is no mere child," the Lord of the Scarlet said.

"What is he supposed to be?" she asked.

Verian raised his head. "That golden light is the essence of the god king. We are saved."

Tula bore her doubts. The incredible was a daily occurrence in Ghendis Ghadanaban. She'd seen more than her share returning the dead to the grave. To be confronted by a being supposedly holding the slain god king, a mere child, was more than her mind was able to process.

"What proof is there?" she asked.

Verian closed his mouth, the thoughts changing on his tongue. There was no precedence for this, leaving him uncertain. It was an unusual sensation. One capable of robbing him of his senses when he needed them most. The golden glow evaporated. Aldon crumbled to the floor. Tula was at his side and helping him to his bed. She hardly noticed Verian lifting Aldon and setting him down.

"Is he dead?" Tula asked.

She was getting tired of asking questions and not being answered. Working outside of the Reclamator Guild wasn't her first choice, nor was she comfortable with it, but orders were meant to be obeyed. Tula admired the Scarlet for their unwavering devotion, even if it turned them into obstinate fools too proud to see the truth around them.

"He lives, for the essence will not allow him to die. He has been chosen," Verian replied.

Why can't anyone say what they mean?
"Meaning?"

"We must return to the others. There is much to discuss."

He left without waiting. Verian's life took on new purpose. The prospect of avoiding failure, and the potential consequences that followed, inspired his weighted footsteps. Cursing under her breath, Tula stormed after. She was determined not to be the outcast any longer.

EIGHT

Seldom a time was the White Crow void of life. Patrons old and new flocked through the silver doors with regularity, much to Eamon Brisk's approval. The staff complained from the lack of breaks throughout the day. He laughed their worries off, citing their families would prosper from their efforts. But for the few moments between meals, the White Crow saw more traffic than the god king's palace.

Clandestine moments were best conducted when many people were around, at least in the First Prophet's mind. Dinner service was just ended and the drinking crowds were beginning to funnel in. Sandis ignored them. His focus was on his elder companion of too many odd moments. The fallen god was oblivious to whatever laments tortured the prophet and already on his third mug of honeyed ale.

"You worry too much for a being who lives but a few decades," Relghel scoffed. "Relax, Sandis. There is more to life than fret."

"Agreed, but that does not change what is happening. I know you turned from this path many lifetimes ago but that does not change the fact that this city stands upon an uncharted precipice. We need your help," Sandis said.

An unconcerned hand waved him off. "Sandis, what more is there for me to do? I am shunned. Banned from the place of my birth. My realm consists of what you see before you. Nothing more."

"Omoraum is not dead."

The revelation stunned them both. Sandis couldn't believe the audacity with which he'd cast the declaration upon the table. Relghel tried to imagine the how of it. Silence dominated the space between them. Each calculated where the other meant to strike next. A game of sorts. Strategy had always been a favorite of Sandis's. Verbal sparring sharpened his mind in preparation for the long hours spent listening to petitions and complaints. So few bothered to offer praise where it was due.

"That is … difficult to believe. You saw the body," Relghel replied.

Sandis nodded. "Not long before it dissolved into a flood of bright light."

"Golden light befitting the gods," Relghel finished.

Sandis poured another measure of liquor. Raising his glass, he studied the warm colors, while swirling it around. "The same golden light we have found in a boy."

The fallen god blinked. "That cannot be. He is mortal. The transfer would have obliterated him."

"You, of all people, should not underestimate the powers of the gods," Sandis chided. "We are in undocumented territory. Nothing I found in the archives of the previous forty-six detailed anything remotely close to this event."

"Which has led you back to me," Relghel concluded. "I do not have the answers you seek, Sandis. I don't suppose any in this city does."

Sandis frowned. "Not good enough, old friend. You are more qualified to provide answers than any other. Give me something. Anything I can take back to the others. We must not allow the light to die."

"His essence was transferred before the body returned to Rhorrmere. This should not have happened." The fallen god sighed and reached for his mug. Moments like this made him dislike his inability to get drunk.

"But it has. Verian confirmed as much."

Relghel snorted. "That cock. He's fretting over his last few days on this world. Those Scarlet are nothing but trouble, for the god kings and this city."

"All that aside," Sandis ignored the ingrained animosity the fallen god bore, "what if there is a measure of truth in this? What if the god king's essence has been transferred to someone?"

"The succession of kings would continue."

"How?" It couldn't be that easy. Sandis struggled to see how an untrained child could become king.

Relghel relaxed into the soft, well-worn cushions of his chair and clasped his hands behind his head. Calloused fingertips poked through his hair. "There is a way. No mortal can hold a god's essence for long. He must be taken to the halls of Rhorrmere. Only there can the transfer be completed."

"This boy will die," Sandis said.

"If not handled quickly, yes."

"What aren't you telling me, Relghel?" the First Prophet asked. He'd always been suspicious of the fallen god. One does not turn away from destiny without severe flaws. Dark secrets lingered in Relghel's past. Sandis only hoped those secrets never emerged to threaten Ghendis Ghadanaban.

"What you seek is not as easy as you assume. Yes, a process exists that will keep the line of kings, but it is not convenient. Perhaps most of all for those chosen to go to the temple. If this boy can reach the mountain in time, you will save the city."

Sandis left the White Crow with more questions than answers. Relghel was especially difficult, though if by chance or design, remained to be seen. There were many holes in the fallen god's explanation, but he had the basic plan. Rhorrmere. The future revolved around keeping a boy alive long enough to resurrect a god. There was never a dull day in the Heart Eternal.

Electricity cackled and sparked throughout the circular room. Functionaries in floor length leather dusters and thick framed googles scurried about equipment no other living beings in Ghendis Ghadanaban had ever seen. Cables ran between two spires. Massive orbs sat atop each, wreathed in blue and purple lines of lightning. Between was a long metal table. A corpse lay atop it.

Hean stood against the wall, hands clasped with giddy excitement. He'd performed this ritual numerous times. Each ended in utter failure. His confidence remained high, for he knew that eventually the secret would be unlocked. Unending life would become his. A power to rival the god kings in their golden palaces. The future would be his alone.

Already wealthy beyond mortal measure, Hean's vision of expansion for the Arax Trading Company would encircle the world. Kings and queens would bow before him. Until he discovered the secret, it was just a vision. Hean grew increasingly frustrated with each failure. A hint of insanity swirled just out of reach. The sweet beckon seduced him.

"Raise the power!" he squealed.

A man in a hood shuffled through the madness to crank the lever. Power hummed, vibrating the ground. A shower of sparks washed over him, melting parts of his clothing. Hean covered his eyes, peering through slightly parted fingers. Electricity gathered in the orbs and funneled down to the body. Sparks rained. The stench of burned flesh and hair filled the room.

One of the power cables melted and burst into flames. The machines shut down with a strained hum. A row of three glass canisters filled with amniotic fluids boiled over to splash on the rubber floor. Hean watched as his efforts dissolved in spectacular disarray. A tear formed but he refused to allow it to drop. This was a moment he'd undergone far too many times. People hurried to salvage what they could of the equipment, themselves well versed in the drill.

Soon silence filled the room. Hean was no fool. He'd constructed this lair far beneath the city streets, where only the rats and ghosts of yesterday dwelled. There was no chance of being overheard or discovered. Not even by the dubious Reclamators. He'd planned well, though without the right formula, his efforts were pointless. Hean clenched his fists in rage. Then he spied the momentous.

The sheet concealing the body twitched. He squinted through the cloud of haze filling the room. Could it be? His heart beat an extra beat. Anticipation, the promise of forever, made him lick his lips. After so long. The sheet moved again and he took a step closer. A hand slid out to dangle. Hean studied it, hoping against hope. The index finger curled and straightened. Twice. Hean was almost at the table.

The body popped up. The sheet fell away to reveal a hideous figure, scarred and tormented. Empty eyes turned his way, focusing on him with accusation. Any hopes of success disappeared. Hean backpedaled to escape what always followed. His slipper caught on a cable and he fell. The undead fell off the table and crawled toward him, as if it knew who was responsible for ripping it from the long sleep.

Panic made Hean flail about, but no matter how he tried, he couldn't get off his back. His eyes widened. The undead was almost upon him, when a pair of men tackled it away. Another hurried over to help Hean to his feet and see him to safety. The undead fought in silence. Outnumbered, it was forced back toward a trapdoor on the far side of the table. One of the men was bitten. A finger dropped in a spray of blood. His scream turned to grunts, for the men Hean hired to guard his caravans were among the toughest in the kingdom.

Hean could only watch as they dropped the undead down through the trapdoor. It fell without a sound, cast into the sewers where it would rise again to trouble some distant part of the population. The caravan master cared little about that. The Reclamator Guild was established to see to such arcane needs.

"Master, are you injured?" a guard asked, as he brushed the dust and residue from Hean.

He was pushed away. The sting of yet another defeat burned deeply, forcing his thoughts inward. He'd missed a vital step. Calculations were off, skewing the paths between life and death. Hean began to pace, a finger tapping his chin in thought.

"Eh? Yes, I'm fine," he said, almost forgetting the question. A groan of pain, stifled to prevent everyone from hearing, drew his attention. His eyes narrowed in search of the culprit. "Who made that noise?"

Guards and functionaries looked around confused. One man, one who helped remove the undead, shied away. The man beside him spotted the blood. His eyes widened, the whites almost glowing in the charged air. Hean inched closer. His hand dropped to the dagger at his hip.

"It's just a scratch. Nothing more," the guard protested. Every man in the room knew what happened to those who came in contact with the undead. "I'll be fine."

"Kill him," Hean ordered.

"No, wait!"

The sword plunged through his neck, angling down to pierce his heart. Dead before he hit the ground, the guard's last sights were of the trapdoor opening and the gaping chasm swallowing him. Hean snorted his disapproval and stormed off. His mind raced through possibilities and what it would take to finally achieve his dreams. First, he needed another fresh corpse. There was always work to be done in the Heart Eternal.

One thousand leagues away, far from the lights and glory of Ghendis Ghadanaban, where civilization advanced unlike any other place in the world, stood a mountain range as old as time itself. Broken crags cast in perpetual shadow rose high into the sky. A mockery of all that was holy. No life grew here, for it was a place of the dead. Caves large and small connected deep with tunnels where light never penetrated. Foul clouds kept the range in utter darkness.

Humanity shunned the area long ago after learning the bitter truth. How many died before that truth spread was lost to history. The stories spread, but time diminished them to legend and then rumor. A few brave souls ventured back, eager to explore the darkness of the forgotten. They became lost. Twisted ruination of flesh and soul. Enough came to form a tribe. Violence dominated their lives.

Deep in the bowels of the world, far below the cannibalistic tribes of regressed humans, deeper than the oldest tunnels, was a chamber of unadulterated darkness. Only once had the chamber been visited, and that so long ago, none living knew where to find records of the event. Millenia of hatred, vitriol, and evil coalesced within. Consciousness sought to escape, to break free from the binding which imprisoned it so long ago.

The ground trembled, vibrating with a sonic hum stretching across realms. A spark turned to flame. The unexpected light offended the dark. Shadows rebelled, swirling in an assault on the light. A hush of wind followed, as the shadow funneled down onto the orb of light. Stone and rock broke from the ceiling to crash around the titanic battle. Chasms ripped the ground. The soul of the world was laid bare. A fingerling of power, unimaginable with grace and fury.

Whether shadow or light won remained unclear. The light absorbed shadow until they bonded to form a singular being. Ageless essence crackled like molten lava boiling down the face of a volcano. That shapeless form coalesced into a humanoid figure. Muscles bulged, burst, and reformed. Hate filled eyes burned deep. Light and shadow. Beginning and end.

Each step taken was pain. The rage of countless eons gave birth to a primal scream as memory returned. It knew why it was trapped within the world. That reality translated to unmitigated suffering. Wrongs had been committed. Wrongs in need of retribution. The being became aware. It had a name. Razazel. Eldritch powers filled his body. He stormed through the cavern with a singular goal in mind.

Razazel reached the far wall and halted. He could go no further. Throwing both hands out, he unleashed a wave of energy the world had not seen since its creation. Stone and rock melted. The power burrowed through the mountains and Razazel followed. When at last he emerged from darkness, emotions threatened to overcome him. He didn't remember sunlight. The taste of air. The feel of dew kissed grass or the caress of wind across his face.

His body solidified. Larger, stronger than any mortal. Fresh air burned his lungs as his heart beat harder.

Razazel took in the bleak surroundings with odd familiarity. His arrival drew the attention of the local tribe. They poured from their huts and caves to witness the creature they'd worshipped for generations. He studied them, sniffing their weakness. Razazel broke into a grin, toothy and venomous, and stormed down into their ranks. The slaughter was furious and not a man survived.

Drenched in the blood of his minions, Razazel cast his head back and roared at the heavens. Born again with renewed purpose, he knew what he needed to do and where he needed to go. Far away to the west was the object of his obsession. Ghendis Ghadanaban. The Heart Eternal. Scene of his worst crime and his place for retribution. He began to walk.

NINE

Aches spread throughout his body. The leather cords binding him to the wooden frame were tight, cutting circulation. His hands and feet turned purple. Hooded, he could not see his surroundings, though he knew them well. Pain from the beating he'd taken at the hands of Foul and others, mingled with the sharp twitch of broken bones. Each time he coughed, blood spilled forth. Abbas Doza was ready to die.

It was in cruel torment the Guild Masters left him on display. Their sense of showmanship was appalling by design, for great lengths were taken to ensure further acts of sedition were not considered. The shadow organization was as ruthless as it was efficient. Abbas had no qualms with that. Assassins were violent men and women with little moral regard. He'd demonstrated that by accepting the contract to kill the god king.

Ambition got the better of him. The offer too much to refuse. Why the foreigner chose him, and why he accepted, were incomplete mysteries with far reaching effects. Abbas cared nothing for the needs of the city. Ghendis Ghadanaban was no paradise of virtue for a man of his talents. The promise of immortality proved too much, despite the anonymity that came with the job. His greed placed him in opposition to the Guild.

He supposed being captured by his own people was better than if the Prefecture arrested him. No doubt they were searching every part of the city. Reputation preceded them. The prefects had the propensity for ruthlessness of their own. Should he be handed over to them, his suffering would be prolonged before a public execution. Death, Abbas mused, wouldn't be so bad right now.

His tongue was swollen from lack of water. His eyes itched. The hood segregating him from the rest of the world smelled of rotted flesh and urine. A parade of mistakes flashed in his mind. Where had it all turned? He'd grown up in a wealthy family with loving parents. His siblings all got along and he'd been happy, but never content. Abbas was the child who wanted more. Desires turned him astray, seducing him to dimly lit paths the sane seldom trod. It wasn't long before the Guild called and he was forced to prove himself. Abbas never looked back, until now.

Movement caught his attention, disturbing the misery of lament. He remained still. The rustle of cloth. The soft tread of a slipper. The chamber could be full, for all Abbas knew. Perhaps the time of his execution had arrived. A final moment of reckoning before the shroud of forever darkness claimed him. He didn't know whether to laugh or cry.

The blade sliced through his leg bonds first. Abbas lacked the strength to kick. Feeling lost in feet and legs, he slumped. The left arm popped free, followed closely by the right. Strong hands prevented him from falling. He was dragged away. Needles of new pain lanced through his limbs, as blood began to flow. Abbas wanted to scream.

"Quiet and quit struggling or we'll be discovered," a feminine voice ground in his ear.

Abbas bit down on his pain and did his best. He wasn't being executed. He was being saved. Where they went, he did not know. The hood remained in place. He lost track of time. Step after step until he was thoroughly lost. The pain became too much. Unconsciousness swarmed him and Abbas knew no more.

He awoke some time later. The hood was removed, cast to the floor. Abbas blinked rapidly, trying to focus but the brightness of the candlelight stung. Soft cushions tempted his body to give in, to return to much needed slumber. A pitcher of water and a plate of fruits sat on a small table beside the bed. What little else of the room he could see, was bare. Abbas tried to speak but his tongue remained too large for his mouth.

"Be calm, Abbas Doza," the same woman said. "You are safe for the time being."

Abbas failed to prevent the yawn from sending fresh waves of pain through his body. He looked upon his savior for the first time but didn't recognize her. "Why?" was all he managed.

She brought the glass of water to his lips. "Slowly."

"Why?" he asked again.

She gave him a quizzical look. Her features were sharp, angular. The faintest hint of amber speckled her brown eyes. Long black hair was tied back in a tail, producing a severe look others might find intimidating. It was the scar under her chin that drew his attention. Abbas felt as if he should know her, but the memory remained blurred.

"What you did was wrong. You cast aside all we stand for, and for what? Vain glory? Do you truly believe you will be remembered for your deeds? We work in anonymity. For the public to recognize our names or faces is to fail. Your actions threaten to bring down the Guild."

Abbas rolled his eyes. "That isn't much of a reason."

"The Guild Masters were wrong in their judgment. You should have been given a trial before they executed you," she stated. Her matter of fact tone left nothing to his imagination.

She wasn't helping him out of friendship. This was for justice, for others that might follow in his footsteps. Honor among murderers. He wanted to laugh. The Guild struggled with the pretense of fitting in, of being a legitimate organization in the city's eyes. They were fools. Assassins were little more than paid killers most people had the good sense to avoid or ignore.

"You should have left me. I am guilty."

"Of course, you are. Don't be a fool. It was the way in which they determined your fate that does not sit well with me," she replied. "You will be safe here. At least long enough to recover your strength. After that, you must leave the city."

He studied her a moment. There was the possibility of this being a trap. That she was implementing some scheme the masters found amusing. Abbas was in no position to act. Speaking inspired fresh pain, threatening to overwhelm him.

"Thank you," he managed.

"Don't thank me yet. You may still die before this is finished," she said and then left him.

Alone in his misery, Abbas Doza reflected on the past and his failing moment of selfishness that seemed to have damned him.

Sergeant Hohn's stomach growled. Again. The forced pace of their march down from the mountains was as much of a strain as any his squad encountered during their different deployments. Feet ached. Blisters formed and boots rubbed flesh raw. It was all part of the infantry lifestyle he'd long come to terms with. Army life was not easy, nor should it be, in his opinion, as it helped create strength, while weeding out weakness. He chose to ignore that his unit was meant to be on R-n-R.

They moved from sunup to sundown, covering more ground than he was used to. Shoulder muscles ached from the pack straps digging deep. His undergarments were soaked through with sweat. White rings of salt had formed in various places on his uniform. Hohn knew the others suffered similarly, but like good soldiers, weren't going to complain so he might hear it. One of the first things a soldier learned was how to properly complain. He admired their tenacity, and discretion.

The hill tribes were sturdy people. Rugged and built for bad terrain. They handled the march with equal stoicism. Their grim demeanor and utter silence might have frightened others, but Hohn was experienced. He also recognized their ferocity in battle. Hardened by war, the tribesmen knew their business. He guessed they wouldn't hesitate to turn against his ten soldiers, placing Hohn in an unenviable position.

The sun was dipping below the far mountaintops when Delag finally called a halt. Men and women collapsed where they stood. Hohn knew the real misery began after the body stopped moving. He urged his soldiers to form a perimeter and establish a small camp within the larger camp before sitting down. Tribesmen glared at them, wondering why the foreign soldiers did not relax when afforded the opportunity.

Hohn figured they'd covered well over twenty-five miles, but without access to Delag's thoughts, didn't know how much further they needed to go before engaging the enemy. Dropping his pack, he placed Tine in charge of the squad and went in search of the tribal captain. He kept his rifle in both hands. No matter how long he spent among the tribesmen, Hohn refused to succumb to trust.

"Your people did well today," Delag said without looking at him.

The mountain warrior stared at the fledgling fire at his feet. Hohn would have cautioned against giving their position away, but the tribes were set on their ways. It was one of his first lessons on this alien culture. He took it as a positive, for there would be no fires if the government units were near.

"What happens next?" Hohn asked.

A professional, he was unaccustomed to wasting time with small talk. Lives were in the balance, and though it had been over six months since their stranding, he intended on ensuring everyone stayed alive long enough to be rescued. He watched Delag and the junior officers clustered around him for signs of duplicity. He wouldn't be the first sergeant caught unawares.

"Rest," Delag looked up. Reflections of firelight lent him a maniacal gleam. "We move again at the mid of night. Eat. Drink. Sleep while you may. My people will stand watch."

Understanding he'd been dismissed, Hohn turned on his heels and marched off with chin out and back straight. He'd be damned if Delag saw him slink away like a beaten dog. No one questioned him when he returned to the small circle his people had established. Hohn slumped down beside his pack and tugged off his boots.

"I take it we're all happy friends?" Tine asked. He watched Hohn rub his aching feet and felt the urge to do the same.

Hohn closed his eyes and tilted his head back to drink in the last rays of sunlight. "Do you get the impression we're not wanted here?"

Tine laughed. "Every day. These people are backwards, compared to where we come from. They're scared of us but need us to help their cause. I don't envy their position."

"Their position?" Hohn's eyebrow raised.

"You know what I mean. Our weapons and armor are more sophisticated than everything this planet has to offer. They know we can kill them a hundred different ways, even like this."

"Your point is?" Hohn asked. It was a conversation they'd had numerous times since joining the war effort. Tine's take continued to evolve with each telling and Hohn was curious to see where the junior noncommissioned officer was taking it.

"My point is, these people are afraid of us, Sergeant. Can you imagine being in their position? Unsure who we're fighting for?" Tine asked.

He had a point. Everyone seemed to have better weapons and equipment than the tribes. Malach and his people had been harassed, murdered, and hunted for generations. Entire bloodlines were erased. Fighting was all the survivors knew. All they had, lest they too, be removed from existence.

"That doesn't work for me, Tine," Hohn replied after some thought. "Malach can't get rid of us, not without killing us. He can't risk us signing with the Eleboran government. These people may be fighters, but they need us. Even if they won't admit it. All I'm asking for is some insight to their plans. We can't be effective if we're continually treated like children."

Tine refused to argue. He sat beside the former platoon sergeant. "Any idea when they expect to start the fight?"

"We're moving again at midnight, if that helps. Delag is more closed lipped than Malach. My guess is the government column is barreling straight for us and we'll be in the storm before midday," Hohn theorized.

"Krak," Tine said. "I'll go tell the squad. Any special instructions?"

"One in three can bed down. I want eyes around our happy little circle all night. Tine, ensure everyone gets some shut eye and something to eat," Hohn ordered.

"Sergeant," he replied and left.

Hohn glanced around the camp, hoping to find signs of the tribesmen's intent. Delag was a cunning, shrewd man, but not one for long speeches. The man had spent the better part of ten years fighting, making him a formidable warrior. His men had been with him for almost as long. The weak were gone, weeded out at the beginning of their fight. It was the same in every army he supposed. The sun sank out of sight and the cold set in.

Explosions ripped the ground around them. Hohn's squad was prone, using a slight rise for natural cover. Enemy soldiers marched at them while cannons fired overhead. Delag's people took the brunt of the indirect fire. Bodies could be seen through the acrid haze and black smoke. A terrible waste of life. Others charged forward to prepare firing lines.

Hohn let them go. They were the distraction. Black powder weapons were new to him. An impossible demonstration of past chaos. Waiting until the lines formed and committed, Hohn ordered his people to shift left and flank the approaching army. Thousands of government forces, a full regiment, was arrayed below them. There was no way to find victory, not even with Hohn's energy weapons.

"No one fire until those lines are fully engaged," the order passed through their helmet intercoms. "Aim for the officers and noncoms first. Cut off the head and we might delay the inevitable."

He'd issued contingency orders to collapse and retreat away from the tribesmen, should the battle turn ill. Unconcerned with their ability to follow orders, Hohn activated his helmet's targeting systems. Red icons flashed, marking senior leadership among the ranks. The officers rode horses, making them instant targets. He had vague knowledge of local ranks and chose his targets carefully.

The front two ranks of government soldiers halted. The first kneeled and readied to fire. The second remained standing and repeated the move. Curiously for Hohn and his squad, they did not fire until Delag's militia followed suit. *Why these people are so intent on killing each other so politely, is beyond me.* He amplified the audio sensors and waited.

"Front rank … ready!"

The government soldiers placed eyes to sights and took aim. A slight breeze kicked up, blowing artillery smoke across the field. Hohn watched, his heart quickening. He'd been in numerous battles, but to watch one unfold was a new experience. The militia copied them, but instead of waiting, opened fire. Chaos erupted.

Bodies dropped. Stunned, the government ranks were slow to recover. Delag's militia fired again. Hohn knew the advantage was temporary. The government returned fire. Screams rose from both sides as the dying continued. Soldiers frantically reloaded. Any composure they had before the battle began, was lost after seeing friends and comrades fall. Mangled bodies littered the ground. Some dead, others missing limbs.

Seeing opportunity, Hohn gave the order. Flashes of energy sped across the space between him and the enemy. The first to die was the commanding officer. He slumped in the saddle and slipped to the ground. Blossoms of red mist blew out his back. Others followed and the leadership chain evaporated. Off guard, the government ranks looked about, waiting for orders. The militia took advantage of the confusion and fired a second volley. Leaderless, the better disciplined soldiers broke.

Hohn ordered his squad to displace. They dashed across the uneven terrain. Weapons and armor rattled. Dust puffed up with each boot step, as they hurried to alternate positions among a stand of eight-foot cactus and scrub brush. Tamura, the squad's heavy weapons specialist, dropped the bipod of her weapon and slammed into the sand beside Hohn. He'd always thought she was a bit too zealous with her job and it showed through her perpetual grin.

Their new targets were the enemy cannons. As long as they held the advantage of artillery support, there was no way Delag's fighters could break the lines. Hohn hated going against cannon crews. Their uncanny speed to turn the guns on new targets with devastating effects stole many friends from him. The rest of the squad spread out to prevent enemy gunners from wiping them out with one shot.

Closing his eyes, Hohn ordered Tamura to open fire. The bark of the heavy machine gun thundered across the field. Bolts of energy sliced into man and machine without discretion. Limbs were severed. A cannon tube melted from superheated energy. Tine and the other sniper, a sickly looking man who called himself Iruut, eliminated anyone who appeared to take charge.

Their diversion worked and Delag's lines were able to advance. The government soldiers had never encountered such firepower and were ill prepared to counter it. The battle lasted another hour before bugles blew the call to retire. Shouting curses and triumph, the militia raised their rifles to the air defiantly. Hohn watched the final moments unfold and considered removing the enemy commander. Horse and rider disappeared behind a small hill, preventing him from making the decision. He let his helmet plop into the sand. The battle was over.

"Anyone hit?" he asked without moving.

A string of negatives came back. Once again, they'd pulled through. He wondered how much longer their luck would last. With their ammunition running out, the advantage Malach clung to was coming to an end. That was a problem for another time. Right now, he was just glad to be alive.

"Keep your positions. I don't want any surprises while the militia is still in the open."

TEN

Alone in his chambers high atop the tallest spire, Lord Verian sat cross legged in the center of an arcane symbol from older times. With four points oriented to the cardinal directions, the Lord of the Scarlet was situated in the exact center. Eyes closed, he placed his hands on his knees, palms up. This was the one place he could stretch his wings without judgment. A haven among an ocean of mortals, who either despised or loved him, based on preconceived notions.

The Lord of the Scarlet often felt disconnected with those whose lives began and ended in a space of heartbeats. He wondered why the god kings were so interested in humans, for they were filled with strife and held an uncanny affinity for violence. They were a stain upon the world, yet one with whom he was forced to coexist. Times, he reflected, were changing faster than he was able to keep pace with. The death of Omoraum Dala'gharis signaled the ending of all he had known. Verian knew humans were responsible for the death. A betrayal of unparalleled proportion.

He vowed to discover the killer. To expose whatever cult was responsible for ending the line of god kings. It was his one solace. A final chance for redemption, for his judgment would be harsh when he returned to Rhorrmere. His kind was unforgiving. Reprisal for his failure would be severe, perhaps life ending. Verian accepted that. The cost of his incompetence. The rest of the Scarlet would be spared, or so he believed.

But the summons home had not been issued, leaving him free to pursue his justice. Eyes closed, Verian cleared his mind. A void formed. That subtle darkness blinking away at the edge of reality. It was there he looked. Deep within the wells of the soul where the undefined dwells. A sliver drew his attention. Verian reached out, grasping it before it disappeared. Regret filled him. All the pain and confusion the god king felt as he lay dying unfolded, funneling into the Scarlet. Verian let go, for his will was lacking.

Questions arose. Too many to answer in the killer's mortal lifetime. Verian stopped breathing and allowed his mind to cool. How did the perpetrator know what would kill a god? The combination of poisons was unknown to mortal minds, leaving Verian to suspect a larger conspiracy. All sorts of nefarious beings were known to inhabit the seedier parts of the city, but none were known by the authorities. Meaning an external influence was at work.

The logical step forward was to question the Assassin Guild. Verian failed to understand why that hive of villainy was allowed to exist. Men and women lacking morality were a pox on society, though they remained outside of his jurisdiction. The Scarlet were bonded protectors of the god kings, leaving the city to the whims of the Overseer. Larris was a strong woman but filled with flaws. Any move against the Guild would have to be approved by her. It was a thin supposition, but the strongest lead he had. Satisfied with a beginning, the Lord of the Scarlet rose. There was much to be done.

Deep underground, beneath the bowels of Ghendis Ghadanaban and forgotten by all but the current Overseer, sat the caves. A rudimentary series of former prisons, where only the worst offenders were housed. Secrets from generations past remained. They clung to the walls like ghosts. Tula felt them as she walked down corridors long abandoned. Of them all, she was the only one of the group—a new initiate among the upper echelons of power—who felt comfortable. Shadows and obscurity were her boon companions.

The Scarlet on guard tipped her head to Tula and stepped aside. Tula failed to keep her grin from showing. She, like the rest of the city, had only heard rumors of the winged god king protectors. Being so close to one, much less speaking on a near level field with their lord, was more than anyone could ask, though she was sure Verian failed to see it her way. He was cold, standoffish. There was subtle lethality in his demeanor and it left her chilled.

Tula slipped past the Scarlet and into the freshly appointed cave. She found Aldon seated at the edge of his bed. Slippered feet swung idly, reminding her of a child without worry. Tula almost envied him but stopped when she remembered why she was here. Holding the essence of a god king was not enviable. Madness lurked behind his eyes. She watched it grow and felt only sorrow. The innocent always suffered most.

"Hello, Aldon. Do you remember me?" she greeted.

The boy ignored her. His eyes focused on the swing of his feet. Tula didn't blame him. She doubted her mind would be able to rationalize what had happened. Nor would she be strong enough to shoulder the burden. Years of guilt weighed heavily on her shoulders. She'd killed, regardless of the justification. Pushing strings of greasy hair out of her face, Tula crouched before him.

"My name is Tula. I'd like to speak with you, if you don't mind," she said. "This is a difficult time. For all of us. The city has undergone a change and you are a large part of it. I don't know if you understand this, but you hold the future of us all within you."

Aldon glanced up. The soft innocence in his eyes was almost pleading. As if silently screaming to be free of the burden. "What is happening to me?"

"I wish I knew, but this is all beyond me, Aldon," Tula smiled. "What have the others told you?"

"Nothing," he mumbled. "Something about the god king, but I don't understand. I'm scared, Tula."

She wanted to tell him it was going to be fine. To lie. She couldn't. Tula had grown up surrounded by lies and vowed to never treat another the same. She placed a hand on Aldon's knee.

"We must all play our parts, Aldon. That is the game of life."

"What will happen to me?" he asked.

"That is what more important people than I are trying to decide. I came to see what we can do for you in the meantime. It cannot be easy down here," she said.

His eyes teared. "How is my mother?"

"Your mother?" she asked.

He nodded. "She … she is dying."

Caught off guard, Tula studied him. For one so young and innocent, he exuded the weight of ages. Tula slipped onto the bed beside him and listened as he told the whole story. When it ended, tears spilled freely down her cheeks.

"Calm yourself, Tega. This is a complicated matter, not something one of your prefects can solve by bashing a head in," Sandis scowled.

Tega Ig, face bright red, shook a meaty fist at the First Prophet. "I am calm, you popinjay. The whole palace would know, if I wasn't."

Sandis privately enjoyed prodding the head of the Prefecture. There was simple genius in enraging a man who might easily tear the world apart. The First Prophet ignored the insult, figuring it to be little more than vented frustration. Since the god king's death, Ghendis Ghadanaban had entered a surreal military state. Armed patrols increased. Curfews were enforced with unprecedented authority.

The stop measures worked to limited effect. Panic continued to spread but without the rioting Sandis feared. There'd never been an effective way to keep the news from getting out. Bad word traveled faster. The consensus of fear was, from what his prophets had been able to collect, the city was now in jeopardy of becoming engaged in the years old civil war. Already a haven for refugees and those seeking to escape the destruction, Ghendis Ghadanaban was wide open to the same prejudices the rest of the kingdom suffered.

"Then perhaps you should sit before you wear your sandals out," Sandis chided.

Tega spread his arms. "Where is he? We are wasting valuable time, Sandis. Time the killer goes deeper underground, or out of the city."

"He will be here when he is ready."

One did not summon the Lord of the Scarlet. As close to godhood as possible, the winged protectors answered only to the god king. Verian was now unchained, free to do as he pleased before his reckoning on Rhorrmere. A sliver of Sandis' thoughts trembled at the thought of the Scarlet loosed. The damage might well be unrecoverable from. He almost felt as if he were drowning. The idea amused him, sparking old childhood memories of his one visit to the ocean.

"Not good enough. Brilliant ideas are meaningless without action," Tega continued. "As long as we sit within this room and talk, there is nothing getting accomplished."

Larris cleared her throat. "We have the essence of the god king, Tega. We have hope."

"Hope?" he snorted. "More words. What is hope without decisive action? Yes, the essence of the god king remains, trapped in a boy locked deep beneath these halls. How far will that hope take this city when war arrives?"

"The kingdom has been at war for five years. We have not," Sandis countered. "Your fears are unwarranted."

He shot him a withering glare. "Are they? Until a few days ago, none of us could have imagined deicide."

The veil of beige linen curtains parted as Verian strode in, the vision of vengeance made manifest. Authority flowed like his brilliant robes behind him. He regarded his companions, not as equals, but as subordinates. He was above them all and it was time the city came to understand that.

"What steps have been taken to find the killer?" he asked, foregoing the customary greetings.

Tega bristled, assuming the question was directed at him and implying an inability to accomplish the task. "You already know the steps, Verian. You were here when we established them. How much more can you expect?"

"Everything," he said with a deadpan look.

"What then are your mighty Scarlet doing? I've heard no word of progress from your end," Tega fired back. His cheeks darkened. "Don't come late to this gathering casting accusations. We do not work for you."

"This bickering is pointless," Larris interrupted. "Our primary focus must be in securing the transition of the god king's essence to a new host. To do that, we must work together. Lord Verian, have you discovered a path forward?"

Disturbed with being dismissed, Verian ruffled his wings. "There is a way, but it will not be easy."

"Salvation seldom is, from my experience," Sandis said.

"Perhaps," Verian replied. "We must get the boy to Rhorrmere. Only there, on that most venerable mountain, will we find the means to salvage the god king and continue the line of succession."

"Your mythical homeland is not on any map I have seen," Tega said. "How do we get to a place we have no knowledge of?"

"That is my concern," Verian said. "Rhorrmere exists and every Scarlet knows how to return home."

"The question is who will go. We cannot afford to send you, Verian," Larris said.

"I will detail one of my best," Verian confirmed. He had no intention of leaving the city. Not until the murderer was in chains and waiting to be cut to little pieces. Vengeance demanded retribution and he was the instrument of justice.

"One Scarlet is not enough to ensure the safety of our people," Sandis added. "Others must go. The boy needs counsel as much as security."

"Humans are not permitted to enter Rhorrmere," Verian said.

"They do not need to enter, Verian. It is enough to escort young Aldon to the mountain, where your Scarlet can finish the process," Sandis replied.

Verian paused. His confidence in the others remained slim, but they were worthy of their positions. Chosen for a reason. He relented. "That is acceptable. Though the number must be small."

"It must be, if they are to slip through the war undetected," Tega theorized. "Not to mention the soldiers of the occupiers. They've all but established a blockade around us."

None denied that truth. The kingdoms of Mordai, Uruth, and Hyborlad were quick to send forces to encircle Ghendis Ghadanaban, while keeping the civil war from entering. Both government and militia forces remained in the desert and mountains. The potential for widening the conflict to the surrounding kingdoms remained high and the king of Eleboran was loath to lose any more than he already had.

"I will send a prophet to keep Aldon sane. His mind is already fragile and ready to break," Sandis said.

"A detail of prefects will go along for additional protection," Tega said.

"What am I to do during this expedition?" Tula interrupted. Frustrated with having been summoned to attend their incessant squabbling, the Reclamator was becoming less sure of her role. "It is clear you have no further need of my services."

"Not precisely true, Tula," Sandis said. "The potential of enemy agents learning of our quest is high. It is not inconceivable that the assassin may send additional undead to finish the job. We need you most of all."

Suspicion aroused, Tula regarded him through veiled eyes. She'd been through enough during her time as a Reclamator to know when something wasn't being said. Sandis presented himself as a harmless old man, but the truth was closer to a venomous snake. He was up to some undecided ploy and calling him on it was a mistake. Tula sat back in her chair and remained silent.

Verian interrupted. His patience with them come to an end. "Time is of the essence. We must get the boy to Rhorrmere."

"Why the rush?" Tega asked.

"There are older, more sinister powers in the world who would seek to seize the opportunity presented," Verian replied.

Larris felt a chill down her spine. This was a conversation for a different time, when she could get the Lord of the Scarlet alone and he was more apt to talk. She shifted focus back to the task at hand. "I believe this meeting is at an end. Go and summon your people. The quest will depart in two days' time. With luck and faith, they will deliver us unto salvation before the peace delegations arrive."

They filed out, no small talk among them. Each was considered powerful yet relied on the others to present a full force of leadership the rest of the kingdom of Eleboran could never attain. Tula was the last to go, having decided to wait until she and Larris were alone. New developments with Aldon prompted concerns and she remained distrusting of Sandis.

"Tula, what bothers you?" Larris asked.

Tula wanted to smile at the soothing tones of her golden voice. "The boy spoke with me, just as you believed."

"Did he now? What did our new friend have to say?" she asked.

Tula glanced over her shoulder, wary of prying ears lurking behind the curtains. She told Larris what she needed to know about Aldon Cay and the compounded miseries besieging him. The two women sat in silence for long moments after. It wasn't until Tula left that Larris grasped the first inklings of a plan. The peace talks were happening before the next full moon. She had little time to save their world.

ELEVEN

"I pray we are doing the right thing," Sandis said after finishing the last swallow of honeyed ale.

Rhelgel nodded his head absently, his mind racing through abstract possibilities. "The future is not set. Only the past. You speak as if you have limitless choices."

"I know I don't. That's the problem. Since the situation was first brought to my attention I have felt powerless," Sandis admitted. "There is more at work here than we understand."

The fallen god kept his counsel. Some matters were not meant for human ears. Rhelgel felt mired by human interaction, almost to the point of longing for a path he'd shunned several lifetimes ago. Had he elected to receive godhood, Rhelgel would already be gone. His time spent and his essence departed from the world. It was an odd fantasy, for his desire to turn his back on leadership and succumb to the pleasures of the flesh, was what placed him in his current position. Ghendis Ghadanaban was a city of wonder, filled with dreams and nightmares of equal measure. A vice for his weak soul.

He enjoyed his conversations with Sandis, though they'd turned dark since the god king's murder. The human mind was inherently weak, incapable of finding purchase when confronted with matters beyond the realm of reality. He'd witnessed several of the best succumb before coming to understand their mortality. Protecting Sandis was more than personal choice. It was an extended kindness.

Frustrated by the lack of response, Sandis curled his upper lip. A stench drifted across his face just then. One of death. Of rotted flesh. He shifted to scan the half empty room. Baradoon sat on his stool by the door, oblivious to trouble. Eamon Brisk chatted with a pair of merchants from beyond the desert. No one was reacting similarly, prompting Sandis to question his senses. The attack came so fast, he barely managed to react.

Undead rushed from the hall leading to the back storerooms. Always silent, the only sign of their arrival was the unnatural smells wafting from their decaying bodies. Three of the creatures entered the main room and headed for the First Prophet. Sandis felt true fear, stronger than the engagement in the god king's quarters. Without protection, he prepared to die.

Fast as the undead were, Rhelgel was faster. The fallen god jumped up from his chair, knocking mugs of ale and his chair over. The splash of beer hitting the floor was oddly loud, even as he drew an ancient sword that sparked blue flame when exposed to the air. He wheeled on the undead and swung. Two heads sailed across the bar. Bodies tumbled in a heap of wasted flesh. The third managed to avoid decapitation and struck Rhelgel. The fallen god winced as unnatural claws raked his ribs.

"Rhelgel!" Sandis shouted, broken from his daze. Fumbling in his robes, the First Prophet grasped the grip of his pistol and drew the weapon.

No marksman, he'd taken to carrying the weapon after the recent attack on his life. Fear was a powerful motivator, one he hoped would extend his life to natural termination. He watched as Rhelgel slowed, trading blows with what had been a young woman. Blood wept from the wounds on his side and his grimace threatened to break teeth. Sandis waved the pistol but could not get a clear shot.

"Rhelgel, move!" he shouted.

The fallen god sidestepped his opponent. The report of the pistol thundered. Smoke and noise filled the room. Patrons fled. Eamon clamped his hands over his ears. Baradoon rose and charged into the battle. It was too late. Sandis waved smoke from his face and was rewarded with watching the undead collapse. Adrenalin coursed and he couldn't stand still. The First Prophet rushed to Rhelgel's side, after watching him all but collapse into the nearest chair. Eamon followed, wet rags in hand.

The fallen god snatched the bottle of liquor, abandoned, from the table and drank deeply. A belch followed, making Sandis gag. "That … was more than I wanted. Good fun eh, my friend?"

Fun? Sandis had had enough of near death experiences. Thoughts of retirement, of abandoning public life to a family village nestled among fields of grapevines, beckoned. He saw Rhelgel's wounds and wondered who the undead had come for. Him or the fallen god? Too many events were happening to be coincidence. What was clear, was whoever was responsible for killing the god king, wasn't done. A reaping was coming to Ghendis Ghadanaban and the city might never be the same.

Falon Ruel watched her trainees drill with reserved enthusiasm. She was one of the best sergeants in the Prefecture. Training instructor was a highly sought after position, one recognized by a career of quality performance. Less than two in ten who applied were deemed good enough. Falon was beside herself on the day Tega Ig summoned her to offer the job. Unlike most of her peers, Falon never applied. Never took the time away from her squad and their responsibilities to look at anything for herself. She owed her life to this city and aimed to spend the best days repaying that kindness.

"Again!" she barked, her voice stern as only a sergeants could be, when the training cadre failed to meet her standards.

They formed ranks and readied rattans. Complainers and whiners had been weeded out. Those remaining knew better than to voice opinions of disagreement. Falon was fair and impartial but suffered from quick anger and the ability to act on it. It took only one broken arm before the others fell in line. She'd expected reprimand of some sort, but command was silent. Falon took that as approval and drove her cadre harder.

They were drenched in sweat, some were panting. Hawk-like eyes absorbed every movement. Each mistake amplified in her eyes. They worked through the drills until the sun dipped below the cityscape and still she kept them moving. Times were changing. The city was no longer as safe as it had been less than a week earlier. Falon imagined a pressing need for increased patrols and manpower. Her job, as she saw it, was to provide a stable environment, free from war and strife, where families could continue to raise their children. Falon did not consider herself a hero. She was merely a guardian.

"Stop!"

Falon stormed to the center of the field, while the cadre hurried back into ranks. "Sloppy. Imprecise. Your movements will get you killed, or worse, get your squad mates killed. This is unacceptable. Cadet Badir, front and center."

A slender trainee with sun kissed skin from the deep desert tribes obeyed, facing her. His chest heaved from exertion, while his eyes remained wary, almost hesitant. The rattan was loose in his hand. Falon extended her arm and a cadet rushed to fill her empty hand with a rattan.

"Much is required of you, if you are going to perform your jobs to standard. Darkness encroaches this great city, endangering us all. To fall in the line of duty is admirable. To fall due to your lack of skill or understanding, is a crime against your bloodline," she ground out. Closing her eyes, Falon told the man before her, "Begin."

He hesitated, unsure of her intent. Reluctance gave way after he caught the hungry glares from his cohort. He swung, aiming to strike her neck. Falon stepped back, tilting aside to avoid the blow. Momentum took him off balance and she lashed out. Her rattan slapped the man in his exposed ribs with a loud thwack. Eyes still closed, she resumed her original position, while affording him the opportunity to reset.

"Again."

Angered, he went low, only to raise his swing. Falon, dropped the tip and blocked the side swipe. Faster than he could react, she stepped in and chopped her free hand across his throat. He fell, dropping the rattan to instinctively clutch his throat. She spun and brought her rattan down diagonally where it lightly touched his exposed neck. Demonstration complete, she helped him up and tossed the rattan back to the cadet.

"Take nothing for granted. No, we are not soldiers. Nor are we expected to go to battle as such. That does not preclude the necessity for absorbing as much skill and knowledge as possible. Events are changing and we must either change to adapt or fall. You have two minutes for water."

They broke ranks. Falon wished times were different and the need for severity diminished, but she feared the death of the god king was the beginning of the end of all she knew. The future was uncertain for the first time in history and the city was ripe for the taking.

"Sergeant Ruel."

She stiffened at the sound of the stern voice breaking across the training grounds. Falon spun and went to attention as Captain Oban entered. "Yes, sir."

"You are to come with me," he said. "Corporal Haslem will assume the rest of your duties."

She regarded the smaller man partially hidden behind Oban. Haslem was capable, in a diminished capacity. Without a choice, Falon left the training grounds. The stares of her training cadre burned into her back.

Falon waited until they were out of earshot before asking, "Sir, may I ask what this is about?"

"You are being reassigned, Sergeant." His reply was cold, flat.

"I am losing my post?" she asked. Her mind struggled to sort through the conflicting reasons.

"This comes from Tega Ig himself. It seems they have a special mission for you," Oban said, his voice conspiratorially low.

She knew better than to ask. Prefecture command was laced with myriad levels of secrets she wasn't meant to learn. Content to bide her time, Falon walked in step with her commanding officer. Their boots stomped down the corridor with haunting authority.

Despite suffering a string of setbacks that might otherwise break a poorer man, Hean continued his studies, all while increasing the size of his coffers, as his caravans stretched across the neighboring kingdoms. His empire was every bit as powerful as the major ruling bodies, though lacking the authority. Hean didn't mind lacking the trappings of station. He was a free man, operating within the constraints of the city's strained laws, answerable only to the Overseer. The situation could not have been better.

He sat on his third-floor balcony, smoking a hand rolled cigar of aged tabba leaves. A decanter of Alsaean red wine sat beside him, half empty. The imported wine was considered one of the best in this part of the world. A delicacy only the richest could afford. As the importer, he managed to slip a case of bottles off the inventory before reaching the customs station with each caravan returning from the tropical kingdom.

The luxuries of his life were plenty. They meant nothing, if he was not able to find a way to enhance his lifespan. Years of searching were spawned by a visit to the Uppala Mountains far to the east. Hidden among the snow-covered peaks was a monastery filled with men claiming to have unlocked the secrets of life everlasting. He spent months trying to get them to elaborate, to give him their secrets, but the monks were reluctant to trust an outsider.

The idea of living forever filled him with euphoric glee. That such was possible, if not likely, gave his life new purpose. A new direction to expand his empire. Hean became obsessed with the idea, until his mind twisted. Ever a prude man, his greatest concern was leaving behind his fortune to be devoured by hungry masses grown fat on greed. To live forever was to keep it for himself.

At last unable to contain his compulsion, Hean ordered his bodyguards to break into the monastery's hidden library and steal every text they could find. Free reign to kill whoever was foolish enough to get in their way, the guards ransacked the room as well as what they thought to be a treasury. A handful of bodies marked their passing. Hean cared nothing for the monk's private treasures. His mind was focused on the books. That hidden knowledge he was never meant to learn.

Hean swirled the wine around his glass, blowing out a cloud of blue-white smoke. The texts were below, but he lacked the skills necessary to enact them. He was close, so very close. Contacts outside the city, as well as within, assisted him, though they knew it not. His web stretched wide, catching a great many. It was only a matter of time before he caught the right person.

The sun was setting, an angry red orb casting shadows across the city. He felt no affection for Ghendis Ghadanaban. It may have been a city of wonders, but to him, it was merely home. A place to lay his head when the day allowed. Hean stared across the golden domes and spires capped with statues. His mind was trapped in a cycle of loss. The need to unlock the secrets and live forever, propelled him to the borders of madness.

"Master," a thin voice called.

Hean scowled at the disturbance. "What?"

"Word has come from the Overseer's offices that you need to hear."

Frustrated, Hean swallowed the last of his wine, as if it held no more value than water, and faced his servant. "Speak, Igli."

Igli swallowed. His nerves amped, just as they were with each visit. "The god king is not dead. His soul is trapped within a boy. They are taking him to the god mountain of Rhorrmere to attempt to revive the god king."

"Are you certain of this?" Hean asked.

"The message was quite clear," Igli replied.

Hean grew giddy. Every life he'd used thus far was inadequate for the transformation process. If he managed to get his hands on the boy carrying the god king inside him, there should be enough residual life energy to accomplish his desires. A plan hatched. Hean's grin prompted Igli to step back. He dismissed the servant with a casual gesture. There was much to plan. If the expedition was already formed, it would not be long before it departed for the south.

TWELVE

The battle lasted long into the evening. Delag's militia were hard pressed to retreat to the safety of the mountains. A trail of bodies lay in their wake. The government army kept up their relentless assault. Any gains the militia made at the start were wiped out through attrition and poor tactics. Panic ensued to the point they were ready to break. Dour warriors with a lifetime of experience were being slaughtered under a hail of cannon fire and better trained marksmen.

Hohn felt the tide shift and was powerless to do anything about it. All his suggestions were met with disdain, for even after delivering them a major victory, he and his squad were viewed as outsiders and potential enemy agents. The mountain tribes trusted no one. Hohn suspected this was part of Malach's grand design. The militia general was as wily as he was deceptive. There seemed little concealment in a plan aimed at weeding the off-worlders out of his army.

Strong winds blowing in heralded the coming night. Without the assistance of night vision, the local armies were forced—mostly—to retire until the dawn. Hohn and his people continued to operate throughout much of the night but were finding less success as the enemy became aware of their presence. Fight an opponent long enough and they begin to adapt. Hohn wasn't willing to risk any lives frivolously, regardless of what Delag insisted.

He waited until nightfall to take his squad out of the militia camp. Reasoning suggested they'd be safer away from Delag. The militia leader was ruthless but inexperienced where he needed it most. Arrogance prevented him from accepting foreign counsel. Hohn reckoned that was going to prove their undoing. He had seen it before. Too many times. A cocky officer fresh from the academy thinking his way was the only way. If he did not lead his people into slaughter, he'd usually find a way to get himself killed. Hohn chuckled. The military had a way of weeding out poor leaders.

They hunkered down in a small group of boulders, using the stones for natural cover. Hohn established the perimeter and assigned sectors of fire. Paired off, the squad decided who would go to sleep and who stood watch. Sometime after midnight, he would take the first raid out. Their most recent string of attacks never made it beyond the second row of sentries. He doubted they would find any substantial success this night.

"You need to rest," Tine said, offering him a cup of steaming turang.

Hohn winced, having come to almost despise the local drink. Without access to the stores aboard ship, he was bereft of his favored kaf. He took the cup. "How can I, when we're this close to being obliterated?"

"Makes you wonder if we chose the right side, doesn't it?" Tine said. He was almost glib.

"Damned war," Hohn said.

"Damned war," Tine echoed.

Taking a sip, the platoon sergeant wanted to gag. "I swear you're getting worse at making this. Are you sure you used the right leaves?"

"There was some green stuff I added. How bad could it be?" Tine asked.

"Tastes like skrag," Hohn chuckled.

Tine nodded and drank from his mug. "Almost makes you think its time to pull out and find another employer."

"It does start to feel that way," Hohn agreed. "Won't be long now before they turn on us."

Resentment was spreading through the militia survivors. Scores of comrades had fallen, yet not one of Hohn's squad. The offense grew. Proud men, they almost demanded equal misery. Delag had never liked Hohn. That much was no secret. It prompted the sergeant to devise a secondary scheme to fall back on should it come to outright betrayal.

"Get some sleep," Tine urged. "I'll take care of this."

Hohn relented. Exhaustion forcing his hand. They had been in a running gunfight for the last three days and it was taking a heavy toll on their minds and bodies. A soldier only had so much to give. "Wake me in a little. I'm leading tonight's raid."

"Happy hunting," Tine said.

Hohn passed out a moment after his head touched the pack beneath.

They gathered under the morning light. Five men and women in prefect uniforms, rigid and crisp, stood off to one side. A Scarlet with hands folded inside the sleeves of his robes looked down upon them all. Easily a foot taller than the biggest, he was large and powerful. Beside him stood a slender man in bland beige clothes designed to be discreet. His nervous fret was echoed through them all, for none had ever dreamed of undertaking a quest of this nature. A score of Mascantii waited beside wagons of supplies. They were the muscle needed to get the expedition to its destination. Their thick grey skin was tough enough to keep from burning under the desert sun and they were made for endurance.

A chime sounded and they all turned to face the arched doorway. Overseer Larris entered first, as was befitting. She bore unparalleled grace, appearing to glide rather than walk. On one side walked the First Prophet. His demeanor was cold, yet hopeful. To her right marched Tega Ig. The Master of the Prefecture was a bear of man, imposing in his boiled leather armor and cape. Behind them came Tula and her charge. Aldon Cay stared wide-eyed as he entered the area. Comprehension remained just out of reach, for none in recorded history had ever born the weight he now carried within his soul. Verian, Lord of the Scarlet, strode a step behind. His gaze was hawkish, wary of another attack.

Larris waited for them to move into place before addressing the expedition. "You have been selected for this special purpose because of your merit, your courage, and your willingness to give all to this great city and those within the walls. No medals await your return. No parades or grand fanfare. You depart in anonymity, under the cover of night. No one will ever know you have departed, for to do so is an invitation to disaster.

"Within this young man rests the essence of the god king. Your task is to escort him to Rhorrmere, where the Scarlet will assist in transferring the essence to a new host, thus bringing rebirth to our lord and master. The way will not be easy. Many dangers await, though I cannot foretell where or in what form," she paused. "We are provided the rare opportunity to change our fate. To return the god king and squash the dissent gripping our streets.

"You are all that stands between this city and total ruin. I cannot stress the importance of what you are about to attempt. Some of you may not return. Others will be irrevocably changed by this ordeal. There are no promises. No guarantees of safety. There is also no shame if you wish to back out. I will order no one to depart, unless you understand and agree. The choice is yours.

Friends, will you attempt to save Ghendis Ghadanaban and all within?"

Uncomfortable silence hung on the air between them, as if the winds of opportunity were blowing and the quest was about to fail before departing. A prefect stirred as nerves caught up with him. The stark realization of what they were trying to accomplish proved daunting to all but the strongest hearts. Larris saw their sudden indecision lurking deep within their eyes. Raw emotion tugged at her. She began to fret.

Falon Ruel broke the tension in one simple move. She strode to the center of the area and planted her feet shoulder width apart. "I will do all I can to ensure this mission meets success, Overseer. You have my oath."

Others joined her. All the prefects formed a near perfect line behind her. The Scarlet was a heartbeat behind, for he was given no choice. This quest was his to perform and he was the only one who could gain access to the temple. Larris watched as the reluctant prophet joined them. She was most worried about Sandis' choice. Surely there were others within his ranks more capable of enduring a journey of some distance requiring hearty moral fortitude?

Movement at her side drew her attention. She nodded approvingly as Tula escorted Aldon to the center of the questers. All pieces were in place. The city would stand or fall on their shoulders. Larris was too conservative to feel safe, however, for much could still go wrong. Stray thoughts crept in. The assassin was still unaccounted for. None of their efforts provided tangible results, thus leaving everything mired in uncertainty.

She stirred after realizing all eyes were on her, waiting for those last words of encouragement to send them off to mythic lands beyond the desert. Larris, emboldened, yet still gripped with quiet fear, raised her arms, palms open. "Thank you all. There are no words I can say that accurately explain the emotions colliding within my heart. You are the very best this city has to offer. I am confident you will succeed. Go now, with all our blessings. Return swiftly and in peace. Return our god king."

Sandis stepped forward. "This way, if you will."

He led the procession through abandoned halls, down beneath the ground level and deeper into the palace complex. No one spoke. There was nothing to say. The time for deeds had arrived. Reaching an iron door, Sandis waited until the last gathered in a small cobweb filled entry chamber. It was meant as an escape route for the city leaders in the event of capitulation. Never could any of them have imagined using it as a means for beginning a clandestine operation.

"Your Mascantii caravan will meet you at the Gholid Oasis," he said. "While there is no designated leader, I expect Sergeant Ruel to maintain operational command until you reach Rhorrmere. From there, Caestellom will take the boy into the temple. Go with our blessings. You are our only hope."

Ruel saluted and turned the wheel unlocking the door. She drew a small breath, held it, and pushed the door open. Cool breeze rushed in, tickling their exposed flesh and turning their sweat cold. Knowing the significance of taking the first step, Ruel did not hesitate. Moonlight was weak, as the orb was still rising above the horizon. Stepping to the side, she waited as the others filed out, one by one.

Sandis sidled away to allow them easy egress. He smiled and offered humble words to each of them, only reaching out to take Tula by the forearm when she passed. He leaned close, so she was the only one who could hear him. "Watch your back. These may be allies but the chance of betrayal remains. Take no chances with the boy. He is our only hope."

The door closed behind her. An unsuspecting city lay behind, oblivious to efforts being undertaken on their behalf. Half a city away, Eamon Brisk drank a toast with Relghel. The fallen god was uncharacteristically morose. A madman with delusions of grandeur nursed thoughts of obtaining what man was never meant to hold. Wheels were in motion to secure his bid for immortality. Hidden from the men and women eager to end his life, Abbas Doza nursed his wounds with plots of vengeance filling his heart. High above, below the lower edge of clouds pushing through, Lord Verian hovered. He was a vision of salvation, inspiring the handful of men and women trying to preserve the Heart Eternal.

Night deepened and the city slept.

PART TWO

A PLACE CALLED HOME

THIRTEEN

There are many secrets in the world. Terrible and inspiring. Mankind was never meant to learn many of them, for they stemmed from before the first dawn. Ancient nightmares locked away in the forgotten places of the world where men seldom trod. Hatred left to rot and fester, while the sun blessed the world with warmth. Only a few remembered these places, for knowledge unused is often forgotten. A pity. It is the unexpected danger that often wields the worst damage.

Razazel was ancient, older than most of time. Freed from his prison, he stalked across the face of the world in search of key allies who had fallen in his defense. Old wrongs demanded correction. Hooved feet left impossible tracks across grasslands, mountains, and deserts. Determined, Razazel strode to the center of a fetid swamp. The stench produced memories. He was in the right place. Death permeated the ground, turning the water black.

Razazel ignored the muck and marched to the center of the swamp. The god kings, thinking they had outsmarted their eternal enemy, did not know he knew the location of his faithful Orpheliac. His defenders. His champions. This was the first. A lethal creature with the ability to kill from distance and melt into the night. Razazel halted. He cocked his head, spiraled horns straining his neck muscles.

The great enemy closed his eyes and brought his open palms to the water surface. Water boiled and spat. Muck flew into the trees, covering his upper chest with filth. Razazel muttered words no mortal ear had heard in forty-seven millennia. The swamp erupted. Water and mud blowing up around him. An impossibly black mass arose. Swirling shadows prevented the eye from focusing. A behemoth, the monster stood silent before its master.

Razazel grinned, wicked fangs poking through the flesh of his upper lip. "Waujulx. My old friend."

"Razazel." The speech was slurred, as if time conspired to rob Waujulx of speech and thought.

"It is time to finish the work we began."

The mournful wail spread wide across the swamp. Birds dropped from the sky. Small animals and insects fell dead into the sucking waters. Walking death had returned to the world, bringing vengeance in a war against the light.

The quarters of the First Prophet were lavishly appointed, far exceeding the current occupant's tastes. Sandis was a man of simple taste but tradition prevented him from reappointing the rooms. Artefacts dating back thousands of years decorated the outer rooms and halls leading to his private offices. Those, he conceded, were better decorated for his needs. Modest furniture framed a small desk where he wrote long into the night. Shelves of books and scrolls filled one wall.

Sandis took comfort here, away from the forced issues of the city. Here, in this solitary oasis where he was free to speak his innermost thoughts, the First Prophet recharged his energy and prepared to face new challenges. Ones he wasn't prepared to deal with. Uncertainty threatened to paralyze him. The god king's death changed everything, shattering the false constructs of a world he once took for granted. Worst of all, Sandis felt lost.

Omoraum was just the beginning. The recent attack in the White Crow left him bereft of confidence, when the city needed him most. He grew convinced the murderer wanted him dead. Cut the head from the beast and the beast dies. The city would be mired in bureaucracy without spiritual leadership to steady hearts and minds. Sandis refused to allow the continued devolution of his beloved home.

Worn fingernails drummed across the teak table, a gift from some ruler or another long before his time. Age and care preserved the wood, though it bore the scars of numerous First Prophets. Pitchers of water and warm ale, an imported delight he had taken a liking to, sat on a small serving table to his right. Empty glasses flanked them, for he lacked any thirst. His thoughts were focused on the handful of men and women marching off into the southern desert, to the great unknown.

Part of him was jealous. An odd sensation, considering what they were attempting. It was the lure of exploration, of finding a holy part of the world he doubted existed. Much of faith was built around trust that myths and legends bore a measure of truth. Sandis struggled with this during his early years as a prophet. The rational part of his mind refused to accept a faraway mountain as the home of the god kings. None of his research unlocked any secrets. Progression through the ranks failed to deliver the answers his mind knew must exist. Ultimately, Sandis accepted Rhorrmere as fact, embracing the concept with open arms.

That did not negate his concerns for the expedition. Pious, Sandis was forced to accept the fate of the city was beyond his influence. It was a strange sensation he had not come to terms with. He closed his tired eyes, the lines around the corners amplified from his lack of sleep. A small price to pay for vigilance. The rhythm of his heartbeat soothed him. Sandis was a man of simple comforts, reminiscent of his simple beginnings.

"You mortals are an odd sort."

Verian's voice disturbed him. The harsh tone sounded condescending, though Sandis had come to expect nothing less from the Lord of the Scarlet. "We are not blessed with the gifts of eternal life as you, Verian."

The Scarlet dropped to the balcony floor, folding his wings back and placing his cloak where it belonged. Night was deep. What there was of the moon was pale, almost dull, as if it knew the god king was no longer alive. Vigil on the quest complete, Verian flew to Sandis's quarters.

"You do not drink?" he asked, after noticing the empty glasses turned upside down.

Sandis smiled. "No. There is much on my mind that I fear would be lost, if I found my way to the bottom of my cups. Is the quest on its way?"

"They linked up with the Mascantii not long ago," Verian confirmed.

A nod. "How long will it take to reach Rhorrmere?"

"Provided there are no unforeseen distractions? Two weeks. It is a straightforward path, yet not easy, as Larris hinted. This journey will change them, Sandis. If they manage to succeed."

The tone unsettled Sandis. Thoughts of failure were not conducive to keeping hope alive. "What aren't you telling me?"

Verian puffed out the apprehension he entered the room with. "Ever have you been able to read my thoughts. You are the first, you know? Three millennia among your kind and not one has been able to accomplish half of what you have. Impressive really."

"Verian, you are stalling," Sandis chided.

"Very well. I sense danger, though I know not from where," the Lord of the Scarlet replied. "It feels muted, as if I am being blocked. The quest is in jeopardy."

"That is hardly a new development. First, they will need to clear the camps of our humble occupiers. Then comes the battle lines between the militia and J'hquar's forces. Whatever dangers you claim, lurk upon the path they follow. I would not trade with any of them," Sandis said.

Verian saw the lie but kept his tongue. "The matter is out of our hands. We must now turn our efforts to finding the killer."

"Perhaps it is time to reach out to the Guild," Sandis suggested.

"Possible, but their absurd code of honor will keep them silent."

Sandis tapped his fingers on the table. "The use of force is not out of the question. You know I have long believed that guild had no place in this city. Removing them will lift the dark cloud consuming us for too long."

"Say the word. I will deploy my Scarlet Guard. The matter will be ended within a day," Verian said. He'd been itching to be let off the leash since this matter began. Frustrations compounded daily, rendering him ineffective.

"Let us send an emissary first," Sandis replied. The less bloodshed, the better, for everyone. He'd read the histories of the great assassin purge of seventeen centuries ago. The harvest of lives was inexcusable, and he did not wish to repeat the nightmare.

"Inaction may prove our damnation, Sandis. Do not let this matter linger too long. I will give you the remainder of the week. After that …" he rose. Having said his peace, Verian went back to the balcony and launched into the night sky.

Sandis watched him go, thoughts a swirl. He decided he needed a drink after all. There were too many alpha type egos loose in the city, each threatening to subsume the others, while leaving Ghendis Ghadanaban exposed. Golden liquid filled his glass.

They marched across the eastern desert. Ranks of men and women in resplendent tan armor and uniforms. Sunlight glinted from polished spear tips. The weapons were ceremonial, for most of the civilized kingdoms had been using gunpowder weapons for at least a generation. Still, there was something to be said for the old ways. Rank after rank carried on. They were in high spirits, for their long deployment was coming to an end. This final task was appointed out of respect for their service to the kingdom of Uruth.

Few kingdoms in the world were as proud of their military as the Uruthi. Grand parades were thrown to the conquering heroes. Fetes and celebrations raged across their capital cities, all honoring their soldiers. Even in defeat, were they celebrated. It was no easy task to serve one's kingdom. To blindly sign their lives away at the whim of a ruler they would never meet. Less than one percent of the population volunteered for military service. A testament to the courage and iron in their spines. Uruth was but one kingdom among hundreds, but its legacy was world renown.

At the center of the procession was a richly appointed wagon bearing the Uruth ambassador to Eleboran. The long-awaited peace talks were approaching, making it imperative to reach Ghendis Ghadanaban in time. Ambassador Ytel had been groomed for the position, fully understanding what needed to be done. To present a powerful image, he was to reach the Heart Eternal first, thus establishing dominance in the coming peace talks.

They were within a day of the city. One hundred men and women, the best of a kingdom. Pride kept them motivated through oppressive heat and freezing nights. Several villages and small towns waved and cheered their passing, for it suggested the end of a war that had gone on for far too long. Thousands were dead, and if rumors were true, many more were being slaughtered to the north.

Ytel dozed in his wagon. His wagon had every comfort of home. Layers of thick pillows covered the floor. A chest of ice, rare for the deep desert, was nestled among platters of fruit, dried meat, and cheese. Scrolls and a few books decorated the center of the wagon, most concerning the internal political landscape of Eleboran. They'd put him to sleep more than once.

A pragmatic man, Ytel lacked interest in his assignment. The kingdom of Eleboran was an unstable situation at best, the beginning of the end at worst. The only decent part of the kingdom was the independent city of Ghendis Ghadanaban. A prize every king and vizier in the region coveted. Ytel cared little for any of it. His thoughts centered on his lake house estate where he planned to spend the remainder of his days. After this final task.

Ytel awoke as the wagon jerked to a stop. Cursing, he demanded an explanation. Screams answered. Gunfire shattered the midday calm. Men and women fell dead or wounded. His men and women. Soldiers who'd earned the right to return home to friends and families. Stunned, Ytel fumbled for his pistol, as his mind struggled to comprehend what was happening. Nervous fingers dropped the weapon, where he had difficulty finding it. Heart hammering, the ambassador tried to force the screams out of his mind, lest insanity grip him too tight.

The door panel slid open to reveal a panicked man. "Ambassador, we are bei…"

The man pitched forward, blood splashing over his shoulders to strike Ytel's pillows. He was dead before slumping to the ground. Ytel felt warm wetness run down his leg. Sounds of battle died down, fading altogether. Boots closed around the wagon. Every sound amplified, Ytel prayed. Never a violent man, the ambassador of Uruth knew his time had come. With the peace summit only weeks away, he understood a universal truth few with sheltered lives ever discovered. Good men die for no reason. Peace was a lie. Mankind was destined to destroy itself.

Shadows fell over the wagon. Ytel drew a deep breath, forcing courage where little was to be found. People in his position were prized, their political collateral high. A sliver of hope refused to fade, for there was every chance of being captured and ransomed off. He heard soldiers come closer. Instead of the faces of men he assumed were his captors, he stared at the cold metal barrels of several rifles. Ytel started to beg. Gunfire roared.

FOURTEEN

Time held no meaning. Days blended into night with flawless perfection, while Abbas Doza remained mired in near darkness. Rare moments when food and water were brought to him by his mystery savior were his only interaction with the rest of the city. Candles burned low, flickering until they died. Left alone to the wickedness burrowed deep in his mind, Abbas thought of revenge.

The Guild betrayed him. His death was meant as a lesson of inspiration to the others. A reminder that betraying the Guild was not tolerated. He, like the others, were minor pawns in a greater game beyond the scope of their imagination. Abbas lay in his bed, body healing, while his mind continued to stray. Suddenly, unbidden, he longed for companionship. Abbas was social, for an assassin, though he preferred a select group. Anything to free him from the isolation of madness.

Wishes, it seemed, were granted on whim. The door cracked, lantern light flooding the chamber. Abbas threw an arm over his face to protect from the intrusion. His trained ears picked up two sets of boots entering. The assassin expected to be discovered and dragged back to Guild headquarters, where his humiliation would be complete. They'd come for him sooner than he'd anticipated.

"Put your arm down, fool. No one is here to hurt you," his rescuer said.

Abbas complied, though with reservations. Wounded as he was, Abbas doubted he'd be able to fend off any attackers. "When are you going to tell me your name? I don't like playing games."

"Obstinate bastard isn't he?" a familiar voice asked.

Abbas squinted, the brightness preventing him from seeing the others clearly. "Merrick? Is that you?"

"I couldn't stay away when I heard you were turned into a cutting board," Merrick grinned. "You do have a way of pissing people off."

"I do what I must," Abbas said.

His rescuer coughed, diverting attention back to her. "Touching, but the time has come for you to leave. It is no longer safe. The Guild has dispatched kill teams. Your remaining time is limited and I will not be held accountable for any of this."

"Accountable? I don't know who you are!" Abbas shouted. He regretted the decision as fresh pain rippled across his ribs.

The responding slap on his injured ribs rolled his eyes back. "I told you that was not important. You can no longer stay here. Your friend will see you to another safehouse."

Glaring at her through tear filled eyes, Abbas added her to the growing list of those who'd wronged him. "Where in this city is safe? You know the Guild."

"They will stop at nothing to find you and make you an example," she replied.

"Which is why you are dumping me off. Why go through the trouble of saving me at all?" he asked.

She paused. Not from the severity in his tone, but from the accusations lacing it. "My reasons are my own. All you need to know is that you still draw breath. Use that to your advantage, while you still can. Regardless, you are no longer my problem."

Merrick stepped in before the matter turned sour. "Come now, Abbas, let's get you somewhere the Guild won't touch you."

The battered assassin barked a laugh. "There's no such place in the city. They have eyes everywhere."

"Not where we have in mind," the woman said.

Abbas paused, considering his options. His body remained sore, preventing him from walking away on his own. The hindrance was enough to make him reconsider his life choices. An animal in his position would die. The woman continued to perplex him. She wasn't an ally, nor was she ready to collect the bounty on him. Leaving him where? He didn't know. The only thing he did know, was that staying here was no longer safe.

"What's the bounty up to?" he asked. Abbas locked eyes on his rescuer, searching for answers neither was ready to give.

"Twenty thousand," she replied.

He balked. The Guild wanted him dead. With a price that high, every killer in the city would be after him. Abbas added time to his growing list of enemies. "So much …"

"This is not the time for puffing your chest out. You need to leave. Now," she said. Arms folded across her chest, her fingers curled around the dagger hilt attached to her forearm.

Abbas grunted as he struggled to rise. Body rebelling, the assassin accepted Merrick's help. His knees were weak from too many bedridden days. Darkness swirled around the edges of his vision before he fought them off. Abbas allowed Merrick to take his body weight, no longer having the fight.

"So, where are we going?" he asked.

Merrick glanced at the woman. "Somewhere the Guild will never think to look."

A touch of madness sparked deep within the folds of his mind. Tantalizing fragments of images and thoughts threatening to carry him beyond the walls of reality and into the unknown, undreamt. Lacquer gathered beneath his fingernails, the product of excessive drumming on his office desk. Hean sat in darkness, fearful of spying his reflection in one of the many mirrors decorating his walls. Vain, the merchant was once fond of his appearance. Obsession with finding a cure for death altered that.

Ever desirous of knowledge, Hean dedicated years of his life in the pursuit of becoming more than his mortal frame allowed. A whisper and a rumor ran through certain sects in Ghendis Ghadanaban. They spoke of how the god kings were selected. Hean had never been interested in the untouchable rulers, at least not until the last had been murdered. If a god king could be killed, what chance did a mere man have?

Each day death marched closer. He felt it. His body slowed. His mind hesitated, where once it was crisp. The merchant's obsession with death suddenly became his potential salvation. If only he could unlock the secrets. To do so, he needed information that was unavailable to the masses of common citizens. He extended his networks, burrowing deep into previously off limits establishments.

Spies within the offices of the Overseer and the Prophets confirmed an expedition had departed under the cover of night and was heading south. Hean spent hours pouring over maps, desperate to learn the expedition's destination. Desert sands stretched for twenty leagues before giving way to gentle hills and scrub grasses. A wide river, followed by a vast expanse of flatlands came next, nestling against a nameless mountain range. Frowning, Hean failed to find any logical destination.

"Valir!" he barked.

Curtains parted as his right-hand man entered. Large and with more muscles than a normal man might otherwise need, Valir stormed in. His beard stretched down past his neck, thick and deep crimson. A head of equally crimson hair wreathed his shoulders, lending him an appearance of a dangerous, wild man. A boiled leather jerkin did little to hide his immense strength. He halted a meter from the desk, feet shoulder width apart.

Hean appraised his most trusted servant with enthusiasm. Few men in his employ encouraged him as much as the giant from the far north. Where he came from remained obscured, for Valir had no tongue. It was Hean's experience that only a serious crime resulted in such deformation. He cared not, for a man's sins were his own to bear. All that mattered was Valir the Tongueless was a loyal servant.

"I have a task for you. A small group of travelers has departed Ghendis Ghadanaban and are heading south. Follow them. Track their movements and determine where they are going. Do not fail me in this," Hean ordered.

The severity of his tone left little room for imagination. Ever the business man, Hean left much of the task ambiguous, in the hopes that Valir would exercise initiative. Others would go, leaving the Tongueless in charge. Hean envisioned all manner of calamity erupting once both parties met in their inevitable collision. Too much was at stake to accept defeat, however, for though he could not confirm it, Hean suspected the expedition had something to do with the god king.

Valir offered a clipped nod and stormed away. Heavy bootsteps were almost insulting to Hean's delicate ears. He appreciated the vigor with which Valir approached his work, even while knowing that it might not be enough this time. Too much was at stake. Contingencies needed to be emplaced. Hean resumed drumming his nails as plans within plans came to life. It was past time he left the security of his offices and made a visit to the one person in the city capable of guiding him in the right direction. His only question was if she would agree to see him.

Night stretched on. Impenetrable darkness gradually giving way to slender tendrils of light. Jackals stalked the dunes, running parallel to the small group of adventurers braving the night. Far to the southeast lay the encampment of Hyborlad. Pickets would be set, but they were far enough away that not a sound would be heard. Sergeant Ruel had no concerns about them. Her confidence in her people, despite being saddled with a child and ghoul catcher, was complete.

The Gholid Oasis was near and she estimated there was just enough darkness left to reach it undetected. They'd been walking through the night and suffered from blisters, sore feet, and shoulders burning from the weight of their packs, despite stopping numerous times during their trek. Falon grew agitated, for she knew more could go wrong than not. Compounding her misgivings was the fact she did not know where they were going other than south. The general direction awakened latent fears, failure most among them.

With dawn creeping across the horizon, Falon led the others into the swaying palms of the Gholid Oasis. She paused at the edge, sending her prefects in first to secure the area. Nomads and other desert dwellers tended to use the oasis for less than savory purposes. Losing her charge this close to Ghendis Ghadanaban was akin to committing suicide. The all clear whistle reached her not long after and she sent the others in, choosing to be last.

Her eyes tracked the hobbling boy with the spirit of the god king. Though she doubted the accuracy of his tale, Falon had given her word to see the boy to his final destination. She tried to get a closer look in his eyes, hoping to see the golden spark First Prophet Sandis confirmed, so that her fears might be allayed. There was nothing. Just the dull brown look of a typical boy. Deflated, Falon followed him into the oasis.

Several Mascantii milled around a string of hobbled camels and a pair of wagons stacked with enough supplies to see them to Rhorrmere. Theoretically, Falon was told they had more than was necessary. The representative of the Scarlet, Caestellom, was taciturn, unwilling to share his thoughts or knowledge with the others, leaving Falon working through a string of scenarios based on guessing. That ill feeling in her stomach strengthened.

Admitting her weariness, Falon dropped her pack and slumped down beside it. Water lapped against the shore nearby in soothing tones that reminded her of simpler times. She almost gave in to lament, to that unfettered quality capable of driving her to ruin. Resistance won out and Falon was able to refocus her attention to the mission. The others moved around her, ignoring the rigid sergeant with purposeful stride and iron constitution. She didn't mind. Aside from her prefects, the others were inconsequential. Even then, all that truly mattered was seeing Aldon Cay to Rhorrmere. Everyone else, herself included, was expendable.

Deciding she needed to do something, Falon stifled a yawn and went to confront the Scarlet. Unlike the others, Caestellom remained on his feet. Large wings of purest white stretched out behind him, for he was no longer concerned with being viewed as he really was. Verian's orders were that no Scarlet was to show his true self among the common people of Ghendis Ghadanaban. Here, the rules were fragmented, if not wholly ignored.

"You wish to speak with me," he asked.

Falon cursed, halting in midstride. He faced away from her, prompting her to reconsider what she thought she knew. Unwilling to back away, she dug her heels in and spoke her mind. "Where are we going?"

The angelic figure remained still, as if pondering his response. Wind scurried through, blowing his long hair across his shoulders. Caestellom remained staring at the last moments of starlight. "The mountain of the gods."

She clenched her jaw. "I understand that, but unless you are going to share more than general direction, you handicap us all."

"Irrelevant. All that matters is that boy," he replied. His tone left no room for doubt. "We continue south until I say to turn. I realize this is difficult for you, Sergeant, but there are some matters humanity is not meant to know. While I hold no endearment for any of you, I am dedicated to seeing my Lord returned. That should suffice for you."

"Should it? I wonder why I am uncomforted by your words," she retorted.

"You worry about matters far above your station," the Scarlet said. He folded his wings, tucking them down beneath his flowing red cape and turned to face her. "How old are you?"

Taken aback, Falon's gaze narrowed. "What relevance does that hold?"

"I have walked this world for seven hundred and forty-eight years and now I find my days dwindling. Like all with whom I serve, I will be summoned to Rhorrmere to face judgment if this quest fails. My failure will end with my death. Whatever troubles you think you are facing are insignificant in the scheme of time. For the time being, know that I take my charge seriously and will do all within my ability to see we reach the mountain."

She watched him walk past and into the fading night. Any hope of finding answers was lost to the whims of failed conversation that only served to muddle her thoughts more. Falon felt additional weight fall upon her shoulders, as new confusion settled in. The world, she'd determined, had devolved to madness.

"Twenty-three," she said to the dark.

FIFTEEN

"Sergeant, the wagons are loaded. We are ready to depart."

Tula's head perked up. She'd been dozing on and off since arriving early in the morning. Unaccustomed to sleeping outdoors, the Reclamator found rest difficult. From the ceaseless assaults of various bugs, to the deep croaking of frogs hidden in the water, the oasis conspired to keep her awake.

The morning sun was rising higher, bathing the desert in an oppressive heat she'd almost forgotten. Tula yawned and stretched some of the soreness from her body. Odd hours and less than desirable work kept her in shape but there was nothing compared to marching through the night across loose sand with excessive weight on her back. She already wanted to go home, but the boy kept her around. Whatever troubles she might envision, Aldon was going through the unimaginable.

Her heart wept for the boy. His predicament was unwanted and damning. Tula's years of hunting undead in the forgotten parts of the city left her encased in a hardened shell, but Aldon's fate tugged at her emotions. No one deserved such cruelty, even if it should have been an honor to contain the essence of the god king. Tula laced her boots and rose. At least today would be on camel back.

"Good morning, Tula," Aldon said with a smile.

She returned the gesture, feeling genuine warmth with the boy. "Good morning. How did you sleep?"

"I wish I could say in a bed, but the sand was more comfortable," he replied.

Not for me. "I'm glad you were able to rest. How do you feel today?"

He paused, as he struggled to put thoughts to word. First Prophet Sandis assured him that no one in the history of Ghendis Ghadanaban had ever endured what he was, making the experience unique. Relating any of that to the others was proving difficult. "Well enough, I suppose. Has there been any word on my mother, Tula?"

She frowned. "No, but that does not mean word is not coming. We left the city without anyone knowing. Trust to this group. They will see us through."

"I wish I shared your confidence," he said and lowered his head.

Tula placed a tender hand upon his shoulder, wishing she felt as confident as she projected. "This is a wide and wonderful world, Aldon Cay. While I don't profess to understand much of it, I do have hope and that is enough."

On impulse, Aldon wrapped his arms around her and hugged tightly. She stood for a moment, unsure how to respond. She was an only child and had no surviving family. Emotions came hard for her, though Tula was experiencing an uncomfortable stirring in her heart. Aldon wasn't much younger than her, but his need pushed her to the edge.

"Mount up! We need to ride," Falon's harsh voice cut the scene.

Tula whispered a silent thank you, as she and Aldon headed for their rides. The Reclamator eased into the saddle, while Aldon climbed aboard one of the Mascantii wagons. He shied away from the grey giants, fearful at their appearance and stature. Tula broke into a grin, for she had once suffered similar misgivings toward the species. A look around showed only the Scarlet remained on his feet. She found it curious but knew the rumors surrounding the winged guardians.

Falon edged to the front of the column and waved them forward. Camels snorted. Wagons groaned as wheels struggled to find purchase in the sand. The quest to save the god king was begun. South. They headed south.

Meone wiped his pale forehead for the thousandth time. The rag was already drenched, as were his prophet robes. Rivers of sweat ran down his legs to pool in his sandals. Miserable, he lamented being chosen for the quest. That the First Prophet knew his name came as a shock, for he was a minor player in the order. Meone had only been a ranked prophet for two seasons, nowhere long enough to make him an expert on anything. Whatever reason Sandis decided to send him, remained mired in shadow and self-doubt.

Underdeveloped muscles ached from the long march from the city to the oasis. He longed for his bed and clean sheets. Meone knew his worth and it was wasted in the field. Lamenting his situation, the prophet tried to find a comfortable position on the unforgiving wooden bench. All he got was splinters for the effort.

"You should not be here."

The obvious retort died on his lips when he saw who was addressing him. Falon Ruel was as unforgiving as the bench but far more dangerous. Angering her this early in the quest was akin to asking for banishment. Meone swallowed his misery and accepted her comment. He was the first to admit he was out of his element. Acknowledging that in front of his companions was another matter.

Falon edged her camel closer to the wagon. "Have you ever been outside of the city?"

"I was born in Sawaldi," he answered. Her look prompted more. "A small village about two days west of Ghendis Ghadanaban. We used to ride to the city for supplies and to trade. My mother ran a market stall in both places."

"You are not answering my question, Prophet," she pressed. Operational control meant she needed to know the capabilities of each of her companions, strengths and weaknesses. Trust would come later, if at all.

"This is my first actual assignment," he exhaled. The admission left him with buoyed spirits. A veil of secrets fell away, offering fresh courage.

Falon nodded, expecting so. "I do not profess to know where we are going precisely, but this is not our typical operating environment. Do not fret, Meone. We are in this together and only through combining our skillsets will we succeed. The First Prophet chose you for a reason. Though it may not be obvious to you, or me, I have faith in him."

"Thank you, Sergeant Ruel," he said. Genuine relief lifted his tone.

She nodded again and urged her mount forward. Meone slid across the bench, trying to find a spot where each bump wouldn't drive the splinters deeper. They had far to go. Much farther than any of them might guess.

Valir the Tongueless hated the desert sun with unmatched aggression. Exposed for too long, which was to say not long at all, his pale complexion burned and blistered. The heat radiating off his skin often left him drowsy, sluggish. He missed the snow-covered mountains and endless winter nights. The cold soothed him, the heat drew anger. Valir often regretted the decision bringing him south, despite its necessity. Revenge often left a man with little choice.

The one aspect of Eleboran that made him feel at home was the endless array of warring tribes. There were many along his path who required a quick chop of the axe. He chuckled at the thought of bringing resolution to those in need. Valir appreciated a good fight. No stranger to violence, the giant from the frozen north brought his special brand of justice to the desert with ruthless passion.

He dug his heels into the flanks of his moorvaan, spurring it faster. The moorvaan was as close to a monster as any nightmare conjured from the north. Twice as big as a draft ox, the creature was part cat and part lizard. Claws the length of his forearms dug into the loose sands as it charged over an endless sea of dunes. One moment the moorvaan had skin of darkest night, the next it looked like sand. Intelligent and an apex predator from the deep desert, the beast was first tamed by roaming tribes seeking a new life. Valir didn't care, didn't know why he bothered to learn the fact, aside from an appreciation for strength and power.

The rest of his detail languished behind on slower camels. Valir was terrified of the beast, but who was he going to tell? Many things amused him these days. He attributed that to having his tongue cut from his mouth. His gods abandoned him that day, leaving him to the whims of mere mortals. The insult remained, though Valir tried making the most of it. Ever a man who loved to laugh, even while splitting heads with his beloved axe, he could barely produce a distorted chortle that often sickened those who overhead it.

It seemed an act of fate that Hean took him in, making him the merchant's chief enforcer. Few desert men had his size or strength. Valir was a natural, ending disputes with a glare. When Hean ordered him into the desert, in search of a band of travelers lacking description, Valir didn't hesitate. It was his privilege to perform such for the man who'd given him renewed purpose, despite the hated sun and oppressive heat. He didn't know who he was looking for, or why, only that he would know them when he came upon them. Until then, Valir the Tongueless rode the sand dunes, a beast among monsters.

Turmoil gripped the kingdom of Eleboran. Between numerous villages being eradicated without reason and the murdered envoy from Uruth, the population was scared. No one had taken credit for either action and no word had been issued by the central government. Half the kingdom believed the mountain tribesmen had taken the war to a new extreme, while the rest stood behind King J'hquar. Without resolve, the situation worsened daily. Ripe with fear, the kingdom threatened to tear itself apart.

Imperator Thrakus sat within the comforts of his field tent drinking from a carafe of spiced wine, a personal favorite brought from Mordai. He was one of the few alive who knew the truth of matters. That he was the architect of such fear and chaos. Long had his Vizier desired control of the Heart Eternal, but with the god king in place, there seemed little opportunity to exert any force. Thrakus would have loved to take credit for the assassination, but it was a combination of agents and turncoats within the city's senior leadership who sponsored his chance to place Mordai at its rightful place among the great kingdoms.

Knowing his manipulations dictated the fates of a great many lives, all from the quiet shadows no one thought to look, Thrakus delighted in the chaos. His was a life of constant yearning. The promise of more lured him to greater acts outlawed by civilized societies. A man of humble beginnings, he clawed and fought his way through the ranks. Already one of the highest-ranking soldiers in Mordai, Thrakus wanted more. His efforts won him the validation of the Vizier, bringing the promise of rule over Ghendis Ghadanaban, once the city was captured.

A great many details needed to be carried out before he gained domination. Thrakus needed to end the civil war and return peace to the kingdom, all in his name and deed. Doing so was more difficult than it seemed. The government was determined to eradicate the mountain tribes. While admiring their zealous efforts, Thrakus found the notion ridiculous, if not impossible to achieve.

Pondering how he would approach the issue, Thrakus drank deeply. A knock disrupted him, prompting what amounted to a near permanent scowl he attributed to the harsh desert climate. "What?"

"Imperator, my apologies but we have the prisoner you requested."

The dark mood lifted from his features. Thrakus became almost giddy. It had been too long since he last enjoyed the sweet sounds of torture. "Bring him in."

The tent flaps parted, and a trio of guards entered. They bore a haggard, bloody man between them, depositing him roughly on the ground. He moaned and remained still. Thrakus watched the man with disdain. Men of stature must always maintain an air of dignity, regardless of the situation. He rose, coming to stand a few feet away, despite the warning displayed in his guard's stances.

"Get up, this is no way to present yourself," Thrakus chided.

His prisoner groaned and stared him in the eye. "Perhaps you should have told your men not to attack me so ruthlessly."

"Ytel, that you draw breath is at my whim. Consider yourself fortunate I was in a giving mood when my people found you," he replied.

"Found me? Your soldiers hunted us down and murdered some of the best soldiers in Uruth," Ytel spat. Blood and spittle flew from his broken teeth.

Thrakus waved his concern off. "A necessary act of war."

"When did Mordai and Uruth go to war? We are allies, last I looked."

"Cautious allies at best. This kingdom is ripping itself apart. I intend on being the sole power standing when the dust settles. Removing your delegation from the board advances my cause," Thrakus explained.

"My people are dead."

"As you will soon be, if you continue irritating me," the Imperator growled. "Do not mistake my allowing you to live for charity. I care not whether you live or die, Ytel. You are a tool. A useful instrument that will be discarded the moment I no longer need you."

Ytel hung his head and tried to laugh. The sound choked in his throat. "Kill me already. Send me to my ancestors, so that I may be finished with your idiotic rantings."

Thrakus crouched before him. Madness lingered in his eyes. Hateful specks of light inspiring panic. "Death will meet you soon enough, have no doubt of that. What happens between now and then, remains to be seen. Get him out of my sight."

Ytel was pulled to his feet and dragged away. Thrakus waited until they were at his door before calling, "See that our guest does not die. Not yet. I have something very important in store for him."

The guards departed, leaving him alone again to contemplate the future. Angered with the encounter,

Thrakus decided he needed to speak with the senior alchemist, Horrick. The Vizier needed to be apprised of the situation before he proceeded. Eleboran was a powder keg, ready to explode. The time had come to request fresh troops. It was time for war.

SIXTEEN

Explosions tore the ground around him, throwing Hohn to the ground in a hail of rock and sand. Black smoke drifted over the space, separating his squad from the government cannon battery seeking to destroy them. Burning pain lanced the back of his right arm. Ears ringing, he rose to his knees. Grime covered his face and neck, thickened by a healthy stream of dried blood caking the side of his face. Several militiamen were down around him. Their lifeless eyes staring up at the cloud filled sky. Hohn spat a mouthful of blood and dirt. He looked around and saw Tine shouting at him wordlessly.

"What?" he shouted back. Hohn winced, drumming echoed in his skull. Another salvo of cannon fire landed a hundred meters beyond his position.

Tine crawled near. "Are you hit?"

The words were strained but Hohn was able to make them out. He shook his head, stopping halfway through, when his vision swooned. "Just some shrapnel. Where the krek did those cannons come from?"

"I don't know, but they're doing a number on the militia. We lost nine already."

"We need to clear the ambush zone before we're all dead," Hohn shouted.

Tine helped him to his feet and they ran. Modern cannons were no match for well trained infantry, especially ones trained in space combat. That didn't preclude them from being deadly accurate in an ambush. No amount of body armor was capable of withstanding a near direct hit. Exposed in the open as they were, Hohn's unit was asking to be killed.

They regrouped with the rest of the squad behind a stand of thorn trees. Slender trunks wouldn't do much to shield them from incoming fire, though the drooping branches concealed them from spotters well enough. It wasn't much but it was enough. A handful of militia were scattered among the boles. Hohn took stock. Not enough to mount a full-scale assault, but they might serve as a worthy distraction.

"You men listen up," he barked. Heads snapped his way. "We're going to take out those cannons. I need you to lay down covering fire from this stand."

They milled about, confused and disoriented from the sudden barrage. Tine stepped in, his natural mistrust evident in his tone. "On line, now! Spread five meters apart. Stay low and maintain good fire discipline. This ends now."

They moved, more afraid of the small corporal than the enemy guns. Rifles were loaded. The militiamen crawled forward to get line of fire on the enemy. Hohn and Tine watched with muted interest. In the few months they'd been marooned, neither noncom was impressed with the fighting capability of their counterparts. Savage, hard warriors, they lacked almost all concept of tactics and strategy. Handicapped, Hohn had no other choice but to use them as fodder.

"You ready for this?" Hohn asked.

Tine barred his fangs. "No, but that has never stopped us before."

"Every day's a good day to die," Hohn replied.

The squad slipped to a small trench, concealing them from the observers and cannoneers. Tine took point, forcing Hohn back to the center of their column. Edging as close as possible without giving away their positions, Hohn ordered a halt. Until now, his helmet was clipped to his utility belt, robbing him of the heads up displays he'd grown reliant on over his time in service. The smell and feel of combat was unlike any other sensation he'd experienced. Matters were too dangerous to continue, forcing him to clamp the helmet on.

Comfortable again, he peered beyond the various statistics scrolling across his faceplate to take in the enemy emplacements. Three cannons were on line, unleashing fire on the militia positions. A fourth was held back, prepared to cover each flank. The crew, he noted, were focused on the firing line, ignoring their battle positions and providing Hohn's squad an assault point. He swallowed the lump in his throat, an increasing dilemma he'd discovered the longer he served among the militia.

Sporadic gunfire erupted from the thorn trees. Puffs of dust kicked up around the cannons. Not a round struck true, however. Hohn wondered how any of the militia managed to survive this long, being that bad at shooting. The diversion was set and the chrono was ticking down.

"Move," he commed.

The squad bounded forward in three to five second rushes, using natural terrain for cover. Teams of five covered the ground quickly and without notice. Smoke obscured most of the battlefield. Twenty meters out, Hohn ordered them to open fire. At speed, there was little the enemy could do to react. The reserve cannon crew was cut down in moments. Tine rushed forward, thermal grenade flying from his hand.

Fire intensified on the militia position. Trees and bodies were torn apart, the detritus cast away like unwanted wreckage upon a distant shore. Some of the government soldiers began to notice the assault, which had now flanked them. Those not involved with operating the cannons picked up rifles to counterattack. It wasn't enough. The squad removed the threat and swept through the firing position. Rifle fire continued to come down from the trees, some narrowly missing Hohn's people.

"Order those idiots to stop firing!" he shouted at Tine.

A blue flag was raised. Hohn frowned at the primitive tactic, but it was the only way to communicate at distance. The firing slowed and then stopped. Satisfied, Hohn scanned the field, searching for survivors. Experience showed that the militia would murder survivors outright. An unconscionable crime where Hohn came from. The best way to avoid the situation was to destroy the remaining cannons and ammunition and move on before Delag sent his people to secure the area. Though the militia needed the firepower, Hohn wasn't willing to let men be slaughtered for no good reason.

A fire team spread out to secure the perimeter, while Tine went about rigging the cannons for detonation. Hohn ordered the five survivors brought to a central location. The squad medic treated wounds as best he could, while a small kit of water and rations was collected. Explosions rocked the firing battery shortly after. Ten alien soldiers in unmatched armor loped back to where a handful of militiamen remained in waiting. The battle was over.

The Heart Eternal remained a place of wonder, regardless of the intricate wheels of doubt running through the population. Streams of refugees continued to pour in to the city, though slowed by increased military action and doubt fostered among the smaller villages and towns, for Ghendis Ghadanaban remained the most secure location in the kingdom. Prefect patrols were increased in the hopes of preventing additional assassinations. Criers and prophets were dispatched throughout the city, proclaiming peace was at hand. The ebb and flow of emotions continued to reap a toll.

Eamon Brisk cared little for the mood of the people. He was a businessman who'd spent the last few days recovering from the attack in his common room. New furniture was built. Fresh stocks of alcohol brought in. Baradoon hadn't taken time off since the attack, wrongly believing it was his lapse in security that was responsible for so much damage. No amount of convincing otherwise worked. Eamon left him to his post, knowing the White Crow was safe again.

He slapped a clean rag over his shoulder and headed to the table occupied by Relghel. Despite being closed for two days, the Crow continued to serve the fallen god. Eamon pulled out the chair opposite and sat. He was tired, ready to walk away for a few weeks before returning to the daily grind. There was but so much a man in his position could stand before fatigue overwhelmed him. His body already ached, his mind struggled to focus from lack of sleep and food. Relghel saw this, too.

"You do not look well, Eamon. You should drink."

Eamon snorted, their conversation already held a thousand times. "You know I don't drink, Relghel. Wouldn't be right for business."

"These are trying times," the fallen god replied.

Eamon nodded, his mind already moved on to other matters. "What have you heard from the palaces?"

Relghel paused, mouth open and trapped between thoughts. "A delicate question with indelicate implications. The higher powers running this city do not often include me in their considerations."

"Nonsense. How many times has the First Prophet come to speak with you?" Eamon countered.

"At least he has the manners to drink with me," Relghel said.

Eamon continued. "Some might think you yet have a hand in ruling Ghendis Ghadanaban and that your will secretly guides policy."

Relghel's expression darkened. His mood changed, reflecting the severity of the accusation. Eamon was searching for something, an answer Relghel wasn't willing, or able, to deliver. "What is it you really want, my friend? You have known me for years. When have I ever been more than what you see before you?"

Eamon knew better. Appearances of being a drunken old man fooled most of the crowds, but a select few recognized the truth. Relghel, despite having turned his back on the city generations before Eamon was born, was a force to be reckoned with. Coaxing information out of him was next to impossible, but worth the effort. The front doors kicked open before he could speak again.

Heads snapped around. Baradoon was on his feet a heartbeat later, meaty fists balled and ready to strike. Already wary from the previous assault, neither he nor Eamon were ready to concede the Crow to another round of destruction without a fight. Three newcomers stumbled in and stopped short when they found the hostile welcome. Eamon went to them. He recognized Abbas, rather what was left of him, and Merrick as well. The woman he had never seen before.

"Tough night for a stroll?" he asked.

Abbas tried to laugh and only doubled over in pain.

Merrick helped him to the nearest chair. "It hurts to laugh, Eamon." Baradoon's shadow fell over them, prompting him to glance up at the giant of a man. "There's no need for that, Baradoon. We didn't come here looking for trouble."

"No, it seems trouble has already found you. My question is, how close behind you is it?" Eamon asked. A gesture with his head sent Baradoon back to his post by the door.

"Too close," Abbas replied.

Eamon knew better than to ask, for men like Abbas kept to the shadows. He suspected, but had not been able to confirm, Abbas's dealings with the Assassin Guild. Having a man like that in his establishment presented problems, especially if his suspicions were true. "He needs to see a surgeon. I've got nothing here that can heal him."

"That is not possible," the woman said. Her tone left no room for debate.

Cornered, Eamon scratched his jaw. Abbas was most likely a fugitive, placing everyone in jeopardy. The guild was ruthless and would stop at nothing to finish their tasks. His saving grace stemmed from having Relghel in house. Given recent events, even that was not insurance enough. *Yet what choice do I have? Abbas is a friend, of sorts. I can't cast him aside, only to watch him die. At least not until he's healed.*

"Very well," Eamon said. "Follow me. There is a private room where he can heal. After that …"

"I'll worry about that when it comes," Abbas said.

Eamon gestured them to follow. He cast a backward glance to Baradoon. "See that no one enters."

Time was an interesting concept. Life moved on. The sun and moons swirled around the world without care or delay. Time, Sandis decided, was a mortal construct meant to give people drive, to hold them accountable, and to be a steady reminder that each must find an end, often before they were ready for it. Time, Sandis thought, was his enemy.

He'd lived a long and interesting life, filled with trials and tribulations that might have broken lesser men. From an innocuous childhood on the streets, Sandis carved out a name for himself in his teens. He performed odd jobs for dignitaries and religious leaders for many years, even a stint in a small mercenary group that ranged as far east as the salt flatlands. He had no regrets. Every experience strengthened his mind and body.

It wasn't until he was presented with the option of becoming a prophet, that his life irrevocably changed. Rising through the ranks, Sandis learned secrets few others were afforded. He gained clarity on the god kings and their eternal rule over Ghendis Ghadanaban. How the people had come to rely on the monarch and his prophets for stability and security. His desire to learn, to grow, continued deep into his career, until it turned into obsession.

Sandis knew there were secrets being withheld, even from his lofty position. It became a steady irritant he could not escape. Obsession easily turns to imbalance, where even the most rational person might succumb. He was no exception. Deals were made in the night. Whispered promises of what might be. His greed strengthened, until it became a dominating force. First Prophet Sandis was a man of wealth and power, but it wasn't enough.

The sudden knock upon his private study door jarred him. Locked in darkness, Sandis' heart quickened. Fear of discovery made him act. He took the heavy fabric and wrapped the half-naked woman in it. Her empty eye sockets stared back, as they had the day she'd been delivered. It did not take much imagination to think what would happen if anyone discovered his truth. He exited the small chamber tucked away in the walls and smoothed down his robes.

"What is it this time?" he demanded, angered over being interrupted.

"Overseer Larris is here to see you, First Prophet."

Consumed with his recent task, Sandis almost forgot their meeting—one he requested. "Very well. Send her in."

He had time for a second look to ensure the door to his private chamber was invisible to the naked eye before taking his place at his desk. In those few moments he waited on Larris, Sandis wondered what the Overseer would say if she discovered he was in direct communication with the Vizier of Mordai.

SEVENTEEN

Nerves collided with raw emotions. The streets felt narrower, as if each building was about to collapse. Claustrophobic tendencies ran deep in Hean. A common fear many clung to, but seldom allowed to manifest in ridiculous proportions. The practical portion of his mind knew there was little to fear, even with considering his current scheming. The world ground out a blistering pace when caught unprepared, which was where Hean was beginning to feel.

A storm brewed in the southern desert, forcing high winds carrying a wall of sand toward the city. Harsh grains slapped Hean across the face and hands, choking the alleys and main avenues. Still manageable, Hean knew the power of sandstorms and offered silent prayer to the gods that the city was spared. Whatever affected the city would also delay his people from gaining on the quest south. A delay he could ill afford if the deal he was about to attempt failed.

Normally a confident man, Hean felt out of sorts with his decision. With Valir the Tongueless already departed, he was bereft of his greatest asset. Naked but for a handful of lesser guards he would not have trusted with more than tasting his food for poison, the merchant hurried through the Heart Eternal without sparing a glance sideways. Those who recognized him called out but were ignored. Others shuffled out of his way, lest they incur his wrath. So fixated were his thoughts on the coming meeting, Hean ignored them all.

That the Lady Duema agreed to see him at all came as a surprise. They traveled in different circles. Entertaining opposite clientele, without interfering with each other. A small penance for going ignored by what he knew to be a powerful presence in the city's underworld. Duema was rumored to be many things, forgiving not among them. Hean had one chance to plead his case and win her over. Others who had gone before were never seen again. Not one to believe in magic, the merchant felt uneasiness growing in the pit of his stomach. What if the whispers were true?

He came upon her shop before he was ready. A quaint building nestled between multiple story tenements housing hundreds. Breath short, though from the exertion of walking so far or from his growing nerves, Hean was unsure. He took in the flowers decorating the windows, the alabaster furniture placed just right on either side of the door. All aspects of a cottage somewhere far from here. If not for the severity of it, Hean might have found the notion ridiculous.

He drew a deep, steadying breath before laying a sweaty palm on the door handle and entering. The smell of incense and myrrh assaulted him the moment he stepped within, slapping his senses profanely. Nose scrunched so as not to sneeze, Hean's merchant instincts took over. Shelves were filled with jars of herbs and dried flowers. Many contained items he lacked any knowledge over, proving her informal title of collector of rare antiquities. Baskets of reddish-grey brick were stacked against the far wall.

Vines of bright yellow flowers, fragrant and foreign, decorated three of the four wooden pillars stationed around the main room. Altogether a pleasant, if odd place, he decided. Hean clasped his hands behind back and tried to block the collision of sensations threatening to overwhelm him. Jars of liquid drew his attention. Within each was a small animal, fermented and preserved, though for reasons he failed to fathom.

"They come from the mountains of the Desolblie, far to the east," a woman's voice sang to him. "Never seen this far west, however. A shame, for the potential to grow is nestled within their bones."

"Lady Duema," Hean said.

He offered a half, clumsy bow as he took her in. Lithe and middle aged, Duema had dark, coppery skin and even darker hair tied up behind her. Emerald eyes looked down the length of her hawkish nose, judging him. He caught the edges of a few lines around her eyes and backs of her hands, signs that without, she would have appeared a young woman half her age. Perhaps she had much to teach a tired, old man.

"Merchant Hean," she replied. Duema did not move, instead planting her feet shoulder width apart and folding her arms across her chest.

Confused, Hean decided to respect her and wait for her to continue. Awkward silence settled over them. She in no hurry. He apprehensive. Duema was not known for her lethality, though Hean harbored little doubt over her skills in martial arts, should it come to that.

"You wished to speak with me, Hean. I did not summon you to stand before me like a doddering child," she chided.

Stunned, Hean found difficulty stringing coherent thoughts together. A bead of sweat dripped off the corner of his left eye, splashing his collar. "Forgive me, Lady, but this hardly seems the place for conversations of the sort I wish to conduct."

"You may speak freely. There is no risk of discovery in my shop," she replied.

Wiping his palms over the loose-fitting trousers, Hean felt compelled to speak his deepest thoughts. How much time passed in the telling was unknown. His throat was sore from the effort but the admittance felt like a great weight lifting. Duema listened, cocking her head at interesting points but not interrupting. This guilt, a crime unspeakable to most, was meant for one man. Any relief Hean felt was short lived, for Duema's only reaction was to glide her tongue over her bottom lip in thought.

Say something, damn it. The silence was explosive, burrowing concern deep in the recesses of his mind. Hean started to think coming to her was a mistake.

"That ... is a tale best left untold," she said, interrupting his thoughts. "Many have sought to achieve immortality. None have ever succeeded, indeed, meeting the very fate they sought to avoid. You tread dark paths, merchant. I will not help you."

Confused, Hean sputtered, "But I ..."

"You what? Thought that coming to me would miraculously solve your problems? That I was the answer to your foul designs?" Duema snorted. She seemed to grow large as shadows clustered around her. Hean cowered, unable to prevent his fear from rising. "There is darkness in your heart, merchant. I will have no part in watching it grow. Do not seek me out again."

A burst of light. The crash of thunder in his ears. When he opened his eyes she was gone. a thin puff of smoke in her place. Magic indeed. Hean stood in place, gathering his thoughts, while his heart slowed. There was real danger in clandestine meetings with Duema, as well as other characters, even he was hesitant to seek out. Angering her might end his pursuit and life. Deciding cowardice was not without merit, Hean hurried away. The sensation of being watched followed.

Duema stared out from the lone second story window facing the street. Her lips were pursed in thought. Men like Hean were a disease, but he was different. She couldn't figure out why, and that intrigued her. A voyager of several lifetimes, Duema pondered what might happen should she decide to get involved. Certainly the undoing of creation was prevalent. The reason she removed so many others who'd come before him. The world, after all, was ripe with possibilities.

Foot in front of foot. Stride after stride. The tiny band plunged farther from the cold comforts of Ghendis Ghadanaban. The Heart Eternal was already several leagues away, a fading memory as the reality of their situation settled in. Winds pelted them with sand, forcing all but the Mascantii to cover their faces with scarves. Falon Ruel and her prefects ranged ahead of the main wagons. While not in enemy territory, she was unwilling to take unnecessary risks.

They moved as fast as their camels could plod without increasing dehydration or exhaustion. A cautious woman, Falon planned every aspect of their trek. Roving patrols from Mordai and Uruth ranged the southern desert, making their crossing perilous. No occupying force had the right or authority to halt an emissary of the god king, but with rising incidents of violence being reported, it was only a matter of time. The central government was losing control daily. The war was going ill.

Cresting a dune, Falon motioned for the others to halt. Parched, she drank a mouthful of warm water and stared across the desert. Endless dunes stretched as far as her eye could see and beyond. A subtle reminder of how finite humanity was. She glanced back to the others, satisfied to see them gathered in the valley between dunes. There was little chance of being caught unawares by bandits, especially in the midst of Mordai controlled territory. However ruthless the black clad warriors seemed, they were effective beyond measure. Caravans were reporting record success rates with rising profits because of it. She decided that was further proof not everything was as it seemed.

    Her gaze swept across the ever-changing dunes. It was a release. A way to remember the old ways. Falon found solace this far from civilization and its trappings. There was no urgency, no sense of always being watched. It was absolute freedom. This mission prevented her from returning to that fragile tranquility, for no greater task could ever be laid upon her shoulders. She whistled shrilly for the nearest prefect to attend her position.

    The wagons were clustered together defensively, though no threat had been discerned. The Mascantii were capable beings who knew their business. None living in Ghendis Ghadanaban knew their origins, though many rumors swirled among the elites. Falon ignored them all, for the truth mattered not. They were useful servants and wily fighters when it came to blows. The safety of the god king demanded no less.

    Halting her camel beside the main supply wagon, Falon slid from the saddle and stretched. Her entire body ached from long hours on the move. It had been too long since she was last forced to ride so long. The vertebrae along her spine popped, causing her to groan. Falon stretched her legs, feeling the burn as her body remembered its true form, and went in search of Tula.

    The Reclamator went against everything she had been raised to believe in. There was no room in the world of the living for animated corpses or the oddities collected to hunt them down. Stains upon the Heart Eternal in her eyes. She found Tula leaning against the second wagon with her eyes closed. Sweat ran down Tula's cheeks, stained from the grime layering upon her. The desert was harsh.

"How is the boy?" Falon asked. Her tone left little room for banter. She was a sergeant in the Prefecture and not prone to wasted conversation.

Tula's eyes remained closed. "Well enough. He goes through fits of consciousness and being subsumed by the god king. I do not envy him."

"It is not our place to approve or envy. Aldon Cay is the future of our city," Falon replied. "It is on our shoulders to see him to the mountain of the gods."

Tula opened her eyes, staring hard at her counterpart. There was no chance of becoming friends. She knew that and had no qualms with it. Falon was a hard-bitten woman whose trials were unlike Tula's. Not every disagreement was capable of finding resolution.

"You are a true believer, aren't you?" she asked.

Offended, Falon stiffened. "You are not? The god kings have ruled our city in peace for forty-seven thousand years."

"Where has that left us now?" Tula gestured toward the wagon bed where Aldon lay sleeping. Soft winds tousled the tan fabric covering the bed. "That boy is all that is left of the entire line of god kings. How could a divine immortal allow himself to be assassinated? The chances of such feel small."

"Clearly events are unfolding that remain beyond our realm of consciousness," she bristled. "It is not our place to question what happens or why. We must carry on and maintain our way of life regardless."

"Even when that life is intent on collapsing? This is not a black and white matter, Falon. We are lost in a sea of grey."

Falon paused, considering the implications of Tula's words. Until now she'd never questioned the will of the gods. They just were. Those fortunate enough to work among the city's higher echelons were considered blessed. There was no questioning. No debate. The god kings had always resided in Ghendis Ghadanaban. Who was she to argue their authority?

Only the answer was no longer clear. Tula was right in assuming the matter was not as clear cut as the First Prophet suggested, loath as she was to admit. Her distaste for the Reclamator threatened to prevent her from accepting the truth. Falon was many things, a fool not among them. She checked her thoughts, unsure how best to proceed.

Tula softened her stance. "Falon, I am not suggesting the rule of the god kings is defunct."

"What are you saying?" Falon pressed.

"That we are caught in a game beyond our count. There is more at work than we know. It frightens me."

Chills travelled up Falon's spine at the admission. Fear was the enemy of every warrior, just as much as it was a boon companion. She seldom considered herself a soldier. Prefects were different in that they were meant to keep the peace, while armies raged across the kingdom. Few in number, she and the others were overwhelmed by increasing amounts of refugees. Being selected to escort the god king's essence was the highest honor.

Faced with the realization they might be out of their element, Falon resigned to the fact they might be stalked by enemies of the Heart Eternal. The prospect was unnerving. She traced obscure patterns over the pommel of her sword with gloved fingers, lost in thought. Confronting Tula was now pointless. It was the Scarlet with whom she needed to speak.

"Thank you for your candor, Reclamator," she said and excused herself.

Tula watched her for a moment before closing her eyes and leaning back against the wagon. It was a long trek to Rhorrmere. Succumbing to conflict with each other would only set them back, and in an extreme circumstance, lead to chaos and failure.

EIGHTEEN

There are secret places in the world. Areas so dangerous that they are best left forgotten. Man, in ignorance, often turns a blind eye to what he does not wish to confront, for it is easier to ignore what we don't like than to strike forth to meet it head on. Fear of the unknown can grip a society to the point of immobility.

Rumors swirled around the great stone formations of Dhae southeast of Ghendis Ghadanaban. Generations of locals avoided the location, citing obscure legends of monsters or worse stalking the muck. Whatever truths lay behind those legends were forgotten by all but a handful. A convenience for modern times.

The demon Razazel stalked the darkness, plunging deeper into the impossible rows of stones of Dhae. He left no sign of passing. No disturbed footprints. No puff of kicked up dust. Yellow eyes glowed in the closed in space, for the stones rose so high, they blocked out most of the light. The air had a permanent reek to it from animals and other less fortunate creatures trapped within. Razazel ignored it all, for he was intent on his prize.

He swept through the maze and came upon a large circle. The ground was black, rotted. How long had it been since he last stood upon this spot? Memories failed to form. Countless centuries of imprisonment robbed him of many faculties he once took for granted. The price of his betrayal. Razazel strode to the center of the circle and placed a palm on the ground. Dirt and sand melted, burrowing a growing hole deep into the soul of the world. Razazel stepped back, lest he be sucked in and forgotten once again. Phosphorescent green light flared with each footstep. Satisfied he was clear, he turned and waited.

A putrid stench burst from the ground. It was the culmination of millions of deaths. Hands followed. Distorted and broken. Razazel grinned, his fangs bared, as the creature pulled itself from what was meant to be eternal imprisonment. He watched with trepidation, for he never imagined his disciples would survive their torments. Saiatuterum was the most fickle of the three. Her feathered body reminded him of great predators that no longer walked the face of the world. Hatred pulsed from her dead eyes, as she emerged from the hole and stood before him.

"Razazel," Saiatuterum said and bowed. The crown running down her head was sharpened bone capable of slicing a human body in two.

"Destiny calls once again," he replied.

Her feathers ruffled. "The god king is dead?"

"Dead enough. Go to Rhorrmere and await my instructions. Our hour of ascension is at hand. This world will soon be ours, just as I promised so long ago."

"It had better be," she said and burst into flight.

Decayed feathers drifted down around him, a reminder that their window of opportunity was limited. Two down, Razazel stalked off in search of the last of his Orpheliam. The time was quickly approaching for him to gain a throne wrongfully stolen so long ago.

The desert slowly began to give ground. Endless waves of dunes diminished until the ground flattened. Oppressive heat remained, drenching the questors in sweat and grime. White rings of salt stained their clothes. Falon spied the first hints of scrub brush and rocky terrain without relief. They were but a short way through their quest. If what Caestellom suggested was correct, it was still many dayss to the mountain of Rhorrmere. Much too long for things to go wrong.

"Bring the wagons up," she ordered the nearest prefect. "And have the Reclamator come forward."

Tula was her last choice, but with the Scarlet refusing to participate any more than watching the boy, her options were limited. The Prophet Meone was useless in her estimation. Why Sandis decided on him was lost on Falon. Quests were meant for stronger people. She'd trade Meone for any one of the Mascantii. Fretting over the limitations placed upon her, the sergeant could only look forward to the next phase of their quest.

Suspicious of being called forward, Tula arrived a moment later. She felt no admiration or companionship with Falon. They were too different to ever get along. "What is happening?"

The prefect answered without looking at Tula. "We are going to scout ahead. There must be a road along our track."

"We are in the middle of nowhere," Tula replied. She'd studied maps of their path enough to know civilization was spread thin the farther south they went. "Chances of stumbling upon a road are slim."

"Nevertheless, we must attempt to find one," Falon reinforced. "You will come with me."

Tula pursed her lips. Her eyes narrowed. "Why me? You have a detail of prefects for that job. I should remain with Aldon."

"The boy will be well watched over," Falon answered. "He has the prefects and a Scarlet to ward him should any danger befall."

"Planning on returning alone?" Tula muttered, as she resigned to her fate.

Falon urged her camel forward with a grunt and the duo hurried across the last few patches of sand.

Neither spoke, each lost in thought. Tula remained a step behind, just enough to give warning should Falon strike. Paranoia threatened to set in. It was not an unreasonable perception induced by days of smothering heat and limited water intake. Neither woman had ever ridden this far from Ghendis Ghadanaban and their minds were assaulted by questions of what if.

Exiting the desert, they found no wind blowing, nor was there any visible water source. Disappointed, they kept on. Concerns of dwindling supplies were still days off, for they had packed the wagons well. That did not prevent discouragement from creeping in.

"I think I might prefer the desert," Tula said, taking in the sweeping emptiness stretched before them.

"Seeing the route on maps is far different from experiencing it firsthand," Falon agreed.

"You have been this far south before?"

A slight shake of the head was her answer, confirming Tula's suspicions that Falon was just as out of her element as the others. Thunder rumbled across the land. Looking skyward, Tula found the sky pale and blue, without a cloud in sight. Another rumble echoed from the same distance. One of the horses skittered and attempted to turn around.

"A storm?" Tula asked.

Three quick rumbles sparked Falon. "That is not thunder."

"Care to enlighten me?"

Falon gripped her reins tighter and prepared to advance. "Let us find out."

Disturbed with being casually dismissed, Tula hurried to catch up. The prefect rode with confidence she didn't feel. Though she would never admit it, Falon was gripped with indecision. Nothing on their journey had gone the way she envisioned when being assigned with this task. The Scarlet, who should have been her greatest asset, was closed off and taciturn. The prophet was a pointless addition. Her prefects did as ordered but failed to provide companionship enough for her wandering mind. She wanted a check, a balance to verify if her orders were the right ones. Only the Reclamator offered any resistance and she would rather slice her tongue than seek counsel from Tula.

Fresh sounds drew their attention. Smaller, rapid cracks interspersed with ongoing booms. Seeing a slow rise ahead, they slipped from their saddles and tethered their camels to the nearest trees large enough to keep them from breaking free. The women drew sidearms and made the short crawl up to the crest. Suspicions confirmed, they watched a battle play out in the valley below.

Soldiers in black formed orderly ranks, and supported by cannon fire, advanced on what appeared to be government soldiers of Eleboran. Falon held her breath, unsure of what she was witnessing. Her knowledge of the war was limited to local sources, but she failed to recall any instance of Mordai fighting the kingdom.

"I thought the other kingdoms were here to keep the peace?" Tula voiced what Falon felt. "Why are they attacking our own forces?"

Bodies littered the ground. Most were from Eleboran. Clouds of smoke, thick and black, dominated the sky above. Cannons belched flames, their shells detonating among the government ranks with devastating accuracy. Arms and legs, ripped from bodies, flew through the air to land with wet thumps. Less than a score of Eleboran's soldiers remained when the white flag of surrender was raised. Undeterred, the commander of the Mordai ordered his soldiers to surround the enemy, where they promptly relieved them of weapons and executed every last one.

Horrified, Tula and Falon backed away before wandering eyes turned in their direction. Unable to speak, they hurried to their mounts. Neither spoke on their return to camp. How could either accurately translate what they'd just witnessed, when neither were experienced in the nightmare of combat? Chewing the inside of her cheek in the vain attempt at calming her rising nerves, Falon worried over which direction the Mordai moved. Suddenly, running into an aggressive force, while attempting to sneak out of the kingdom, was a very real threat. Whatever messages being delivered in Ghendis Ghadanaban, Falon was now sure they were nowhere near the reality of the situation surrounding the Heart Eternal.

Valir the Tongueless despised the desert sun. His fair skin, already freckled from exposure, was burning, despite being swathed under layers of robes and linens. Longing for the winter nights of his homeland, Valir continued his trek through the last stretches of the southern desert. Nothing prevented him from turning around to make the long trip home. Nothing but his word. A man of honor, Valir had given his bond to Hean and promised to follow orders without question and through fruition. A daunting task under most circumstances.

The others in his group hung back, for they were fearful of the silent man with a permanent scowl. Known for his decided lack of patience, and good humor, Valir had little issue enforcing Hean's will. Confident to the point of arrogance, he led the tired group through the desert and upon the scene of great slaughter. Bringing his moorvaan to a skidding halt, Valir studied the battlefield.

The smell of death clung to the air in thick miasma. Flies swarmed in their thousands. Vultures, spring foxes, and other opportunists picked around the edges, wary of the intruders. Valir knew the sight well. He was born in battle, cut from his mother's womb, and spent a lifetime honing the craft of violence. Squinting in the bright sunlight, Valir counted the bodies, noticing that all wore the uniform of Eleboran. Whoever was responsible for this slaughter was smart enough to remove all evidence before retiring. His pulse quickened, thirsting for the thrill of a good fight.

"So many," a dark skinned man known only as Zeen muttered.

A second man vomited. Valir glanced over his shoulder with a menacing glare. The warning clear. Angered by the lack of respect for the dead, Valir gestured them remain behind, while he rode down into the center of the field. Rodents scurried away, lest they be trampled under. Vultures picked their heads up, studying him to decide whether he was a threat to their meal or not. He ignored them.

Reining the moorvaan in, Valir finished his count. One hundred and three. Proud, brave soldiers who'd given their lives without hesitation. He dismounted and spied the row of bodies, neatly laid out. These soldiers were not killed in battle but executed after. Anger filled his heart, for this was no way to die. A white flag lay not far away, trampled under the boots of many and stained with blood. Kneeling, he reached for the flag but stopped short.

A glitter in the mud caught his eye. He snatched that instead. Brushing the mud away with a thumb, he recognized the sigil of a Mordai officer. Valir's instincts took over and he scanned the area around him, wary of a trap. Mordai's involvement complicated everything. Not only was his path ahead no longer safe, he was forced to worry about the unexpected prospect of war coming to

Ghendis Ghadanaban in his absence. Fate, he decided, was fickle indeed. A renewed sense of urgency propelled him into the saddle and back to the others. Time was now their foe.

NINETEEN

"How long are we going to let him stay here?"

Eamon wiped the strain from his eyes and saw Baradoon in a new light. The giant of a man was one of the best hired muscles in the city but was never known for a deep sense of intellect. Surprised by the depth of thought, Eamon began wondering how long it would be before Baradoon decided he was being underpaid.

"As long as he needs, my friend," Eamon replied.

Baradoon folded his arms, muscles bulging on his neck and arms, and gave Eamon a disapproving look. "The Assassin Guild is trouble. It won't be long before they think to come here."

Eamon held out his empty hands. "The price of being famous. We've seen our share of misadventures over the years. This should be no different."

"I signed up with you to get out of doing that sort of thing," Baradoon brooded.

"What more can I do? Abbas was brought here seeking aid. Do you expect me to turn him away, while he stands at death's door?"

"I expect you to put the Crow first."

Eamon broke into a cautious smile. "I am. This establishment is nothing without our patrons. Abbas may be a paid killer, but he has been a friend for years now. What reputation would besiege me if I began turning away friends in their hour of need?"

Eyes narrowing at what he viewed as double speak. Baradoon licked the corner of his lips. "I don't like this, Eamon. He will bring trouble."

"There seems to be no shortage of that these days. An ill wind blows through our streets." Seeing he wasn't making an impact, Eamon relented. "If this bothers you so much, I give you freedom to act as you see fit."

Interest brightened his eyes. Baradoon unfolded his arms and clapped Eamon on the shoulder, almost knocking him to his knees. "Sure thing, boss."

Eamon watched him stalk off, wondering what obscure thoughts were going through his head. Some things, he decided, were best left unasked. Men like Baradoon were as rare as they were dangerous. Eamon knew of his violent past. He also knew that men of violence seldom forgot what made them that way. *Best to be careful until this blows over. The last thing I need is the Crow wrecked again.*

Merrick closed the door and slumped down into the chair beside the only bed in the room. Stained and covered in dust, he sneezed when a cloud of brown reached his nose. Whatever issues he suffered from were minor compared to the plight of his friend. Abbas Doza was asleep, recovering from the most severe wounds. How the man managed to survive the guild beatings was testament to his inner fire. Merrick doubted he'd have fared so well.

Caring for his friend, which in itself was a loose term, for assassins were solitary creatures by nature and prone to mistrust, went against his instincts. Retribution would be swift, should the guild discover his involvement. They lived in a world without outside jurisdiction, operating in the blind spots allowed by the offices of the Overseer. Merrick was low on the list, but he'd placed a large target on his back by agreeing to help Abbas.

Compounding his rising misery was the conversation he happened to overhear in the common room between Eamon and Baradoon. While he trusted

Eamon, to an extent, the bigger man was an issue in need of resolution. Should Baradoon decide to take matters in his hands and evict them, there was little Merrick could do to stop him.

The temptation to cut his losses and run emerged from the recesses of his mind. Self-preservation ever a matter of value, Merrick considered his options with guarded interest. Abbas stirred, drawing Merrick's attention. The candle beside the bed flickered. It was the middle of the day, but he decided not to risk unwarranted discovery. The guild was ruthless and it wouldn't be much longer before their hounds were on the trail.

"You need to wake up," Merrick said. "The longer we stay here the more prone we are to attack and I can't defend both of us."

Abbas did not stir. Merrick sighed. The walls felt close, as if attempting to smother the fight out of him. Never a strong man, he struggled with conflicting emotions. If he left now, no one would be the wiser and his involvement in this affair remained anonymous. Doing so left one of his only friends exposed. Merrick huffed out the breath filling his lungs and rubbed his eyes.

He was tired. Life as a fugitive was exhausting. A stiff drink was the cure he needed, but one he could ill afford. Options limited, Merrick resigned to sitting watch, while Abbas recovered enough to take off on his own. He was already gaining strength. Bruises appeared less dark and redness and swelling had gone down across his body. It was the broken bones that prevented Abbas from walking into the shadows and disappearing forever. Until they healed …

Merrick swung his legs down and drew his snub nosed pistol with his left hand and a dirk in his right. Footsteps echoed down the hall. Soft, almost quiet enough to go unnoticed. Experience kept his mind clear, his heart paced. They'd found him quicker than he'd imagined and were brazen enough to ignore the neutrality Eamon Brisk was known for. He drew a bead on the door and waited, all while hoping whoever approached was heading for a different room. Luck was never his friend.

The footsteps stopped outside his door. A puff of dust seeped under his door. Merrick tensed, finger hovering over the trigger. Instead of bursting inward as he expected, there came a soft knock. He paused. No assassin would bother with formalities, unless they sought to catch him off guard. Regardless, he was trapped within a tight room, with no other exit and an unknown opponent blocking escape.

"Enter." His voice cracked, despite being unafraid.

The knob turned. The door pushed inward. A shadow fell over him. Merrick held his breath and raised his pistol. The feel of iron cooled his finger. He was about to fire when the shadows parted to reveal Baradoon.

"Damn it, Baradoon! Next time announce yourself. I almost shot you," he barked and released the pressure on the hammer.

Baradoon squinted at the pistol, unimpressed. "With that? You would have made me mad, Merrick."

"What do you want?"

"To talk," the big man answered.

Merrick felt his stomach clench. This was it. Judgment day. Eamon's enforcer had come to give Abbas over to the guild and free the Crow from the threat of violence. Merrick thought of firing a quick shot and lunging in to stab Baradoon in the throat.

"You're not going to turn us over to the guild, Baradoon," he said. "I'll die first."

"Why is everyone in a hurry to die nowadays?" Baradoon asked. "I'm not giving you to those murderers, Merrick. They are not nice people."

Merrick paused. He had to know Abbas was one of them, didn't he? "I heard you and Eamon talking. Why else would you be here?"

"I thought we was friends?" Baradoon questioned. A look of genuine disappointment soured his face.

Merrick finally holstered his weapons. There was no malice in Baradoon's tone. "We are, which is why I was concerned after hearing you tell Eamon how you thought we needed to leave the Crow. Words have meaning, my friend."

"I never said I was going to kill you, and I stand by my opinion. You two need to leave. Soon," he said.

"What do you propose? Who knows we are here?"

"No one, so far as I know," Baradoon said. "Won't last long though. More than one person of the shady sort has been seen here since we had that … incident a few days ago."

The how and why of an attack by the undead was lost on Merrick. Eamon had done a good enough job concealing it from the general population, that few knew it occurred. Tensions were rising across the city as the peace conference among the kingdoms loomed. Merrick suspected small crimes would rise as well, making the streets dangerous. Engulfed in chaos, it might prove easier escaping unseen.

"Why are you here, Baradoon?" he repeated.

"To help."

"What are you ladies blathering about?" Abbas asked. His voice was raw, dehydrated.

They turned in unison to see him glaring at them, as if angered at having his sleep disturbed.

"Trouble is brewing, Eamon. The attack by the undead was just the beginning. Without the god king to protect us, this city is ripe for the powers of chaos. It is only a matter of time before we become embroiled in a greater conflict."

Eamon mulled Relghel's words. There was much to decipher, and as usual, he suspected the fallen god knew more than he was willing to divulge. The attack on the First Prophet was no accident, nor was it coincidence. Whoever killed the god king was attempting to remove the heads of power in Ghendis Ghadanaban, immobilizing the greatest champion of peace on the continent.

"The city is neutral. We do not hold allegiance to Eleboran or any other," he protested.

"You say that like it matters. Put yourself in a different frame of mind, Eamon," Relghel replied. "True, we are not beholden to any kingdom, nor does any land outside of the city proper belong to the Heart Eternal, but there is unimaginable power contained within these walls. Freedom is a most precious gift. One all others covet. The lure of such will often drive a man to levels of depravity, if just to catch a glimpse."

Deflated, Eamon wanted to walk away and forget the conversation. Dealing with a being thousands of years old was infuriating. "Speak plainly, Relghel. If only this once."

Relghel grinned. His stained teeth dull. "Enemies gather around us, prepared to ride the head of the storm through our gates. We have already witnessed the opening salvos. Omoraum was the first. The assault on the First Prophet, the second."

"They could have come for you," Eamon offered.

"What am I but a failed experiment from a forgotten time? No, there is no profit to be had by taking my head, else I would have died long ago. Cut the heads off and this city falls to whoever wants it most."

"That's not enough. Who is coming for us?" Eamon pressed.

Relghel, content with what he'd said, leaned back in his chair and drank deeply from his mug.

Frustrated, Eamon stormed off. He'd had enough games. Whatever secrets Relghel decided to keep not only had the potential to cause great harm to everyone Eamon cared for but a great many more promised to become victims in a game being played levels above his comprehension. He needed to speak with someone who might take appropriate action. That gave him but one option. It was time to get word to Sandis Vartan. The First Prophet would know what to do. Relghel watched him stalk off, saddened by knowing that a carefully constructed world of neutrality was once more about to come crashing down. Humanity never learned.

They discovered the body shortly after sunrise, when the mists still clung to the streets. A trio of feral cats sat beside it, licking and nibbling on the fingertips. The patrol cordoned off the street, forcing back growing crowds of onlookers and gawkers. Murder was raw in the Heart Eternal, for the city prided itself on being a haven for all in need of a home. By late afternoon, many of those who'd come to see their first corpse had gone home or about their day. The fascination evaporated much like the mist.

Tega Ig pushed through the crowds with ease. His immense size was unrelenting when moving. When at last he came upon the scene, he was not disappointed. The prefects had done well and the body was covered by a grey blanket.

"Let me see," Tega ordered.

A woman bent and pulled the blanket back.

"Shit," he muttered as the green robes of a truthsayer were revealed. The implications spoke ill of the future. "Any idea who did this?"

"No, sir," she replied. "But the wounds are not human. It looks as if she had her throat torn out and shoved into her mouth."

"Why would anyone want to kill a truthsayer?"

She remained silent.

Fists balled, Tega punched his thigh. "I want everyone questioned. Everyone. This wasn't murder. This was much worse. We cannot afford to have another execution. Find the killer and bring him before me. Am I understood?"

"Yes, sir!" she said.

There was nothing left for him to do. Recover teams would collect the corpse and notify the Overseer. Being independent, truthsayers did not fall under any jurisdiction. Their rarity made them sought out commodities among the ruling elites and common folk alike. Public outrage was sure to follow once word spread. Tega wanted to bellow his frustrations. This was another setback at precisely the wrong time. Delegations from Mordai, Uruth, and Hyborlad were approaching the city. Any continued disturbances threatened to end peace talks before they began. The civil war would continue, leaving Ghendis Ghadanaban a lonely island in the middle of a sea of war.

"I know who did this," a soft voice carried over the crowd.

Tega scanned faces before settling on a wizened old woman who had seen better days. Lines covered her face and hands, buried under a layer of grime. Stringy black hair struck through with grey dangled over her shoulders and across her stained clothes. Homeless, most likely a refugee, Tega assumed, for he refused to believe anyone organic to the Heart Eternal lived in such squalor.

"Let her through," he ordered. "I wish to speak with her."

The prefect nearest the woman parted the cordon, allowing her to meet with the Master of the Prefecture. Tega walked down the nearest alley in the hopes of their conversation remaining private and placed his fists upon his hips. He measured her gait, discouraged by the pronounced limp in her right leg. The stench wafting off her confirmed she hadn't bathed in a long time. He wondered how anyone would let their lives devolve to this point.

"Speak plainly. Who murdered the truthsayer?" he demanded.

She licked her lips, cracked as they were. "T'was one of the winged ones. I saw him with my own eyes."

"You can prove this?" Tega asked. Winged ones meant the Scarlet. If what she said was true, life in the Heart Eternal was about to get much worse.

"I saw what I saw," she replied.

He wondered if she did. Experience taught him that people tended to see what they wanted or had ulterior motives. Another day he might have dismissed the woman, but circumstances were far from normal. Tega ground his teeth, while sorting through the various angles she might have. He knew it was a waste of time for he had an obligation to get to the truth. Murders, he'd learned, were like a virus. Once the first occurred, others followed. He needed to end this now, before worse happened.

"Corporal, escort this woman back to headquarters and do it quietly. I don't want the whole city knowing about it. Am I clear?" he ordered.

"Yes, sir."

"Good. Move out."

He waited until the woman was shuffled out of sight before ordering the scene cleaned up. Life in Ghendis Ghadanaban threatened to get more hectic, casting him deeper into an already foul mood.

TWENTY

"Sergeant, wake up."

Hohn growled, angered over losing what little sleep he allotted himself during their time in the field. Years of experience did little to temper his fiery attitude after a miserable night. His body was always sore, filled with aches in too many places. He didn't need to open his eyes to know it was still late.

"This better be important, Tine," he snapped.

The smaller corporal crouched nearby. It was a ritual they'd adopted since before crashing several months ago. "Would I wake you otherwise?"

"Depends on what mood you're in," Hohn replied.

Rolling out of his sleeping bag, Hohn tugged his boots on and crawled to his feet. He wasn't as young as he used to be and his bladder proved it. Hohn waved Tine away while he went to relieve himself.

"Now, what is so important you interrupted my dream? A very nice dream with a pair of lovely women, I might add," he asked.

Tine extended the datapad in his right hand. "This. I picked up a ping not long ago. Took me a minute but I was able to triangulate the location down to one hundred meters."

"What is it?" Hohn asked. The stream of data provided little information he could use.

"Looks like a vehicle drop pod," Tine said.

An eyebrow arched. "One of ours?"

"Yes."

He handed the datapad back. "How? We've been on world for three months. How is it possible we're just now learning about this?"

Thoughts of how different their lives would have been if they'd had transportation from the onset marred his vision. No mountain tribes. No civil war.

"I don't know, looks like we were out of range," Tine said. "Do you know what this means? We don't have to walk anymore."

"We're infantry, we're supposed to walk," Hohn said. He couldn't keep the grin from spreading. "What it also means is we might not be the only survivors from the *Acheron*. There could be debris spread across the planet. Now that we have a vehicle, we can start looking."

"If it works," Tine countered.

The possibility of malfunction during the drop was high, despite their surviving. Any vehicle might be flattened beyond repair. The last thing Hohn wanted was to get his squad's hopes up. They'd been through enough, more than any commanding officer might ask, during their time on world and he feared ill news might finally break them. One thing was clear though. Staying with the militia wasn't a viable option any longer.

"How far is the signature?" he asked.

Tine checked the pad. "A few days. Getting there won't be much of a problem, except for the militia."

Hohn had had enough of Delag and the militia. Next to useless as soldiers, they were more inhuman than some of the more civilized people he'd fought against. Savages, they knew how to fight as individuals and were as fierce as any combatant. Working together was a weakness and it had hounded them since leaving Malach. Over half of Delag's force lay dead on a host of battlefields stretching back to the mountains.

Tensions were already high between the groups. Hohn and Tine stopped several fights before they got out of control. It was only a matter of time before someone snapped and blood was drawn. Given time, Hohn's squad would slaughter the militia, but he doubted Delag would give him that. Betrayal was already in motion.

"We need to leave," he said.

"The question is, do we leave under cover of darkness or try to reason with Delag? Either way, I don't think they will take kindly to us abandoning them," Tine said.

Hohn folded his arms. "They only care about our weapons. I don't give a krak what they think. It's time we took back our lives."

They knew the civil war was a dead end. Malach's tribes wouldn't be able to hold out against a better equipped and disciplined government army indefinitely. The situation deteriorated rapidly, despite his efforts otherwise. Hohn suspected Delag had orders to eliminate the squad the moment opportunity arose.

"We'll need to get a head start. They know this terrain better and have the advantage of horses," Tine countered.

"An easy fix. How far away do you suppose those government boys are?" Hohn asked.

"I can launch a drone and find out," Tine said.

"Do it."

The ability to track enemy units across multiple battlefields remained a secret to the militias. Hohn wasn't willing to divulge all his tricks, lest his usefulness expire. He watched Tine punch in several keys on the pad and raise his right hand. A small drone, black and angular, lifted from the vambrace on silent motors to disappear into the night. With it went their hopes of freedom, and if luck continued to hold, a way out of their exile.

Home was a powerful word.

Several hours and great distance later, Hohn and his squad were moving with speed. They headed for the camped government soldiers, hoping to lure the militia into making a fatal mistake. Leaving camp hadn't been difficult. They incapacitated the guards and ran the horses off. Tine argued for taking the horses but Hohn ruled against it. Once they gained the vehicle the horses would have been left on their own. He wasn't willing to gamble their lives, even if they were animals.

They huddled under a stand of thorn trees after spotting the government picket line. Gambling on Delag being close behind, Hohn waited. The squad formed a tight circle with interlacing sectors of fire. Night vision dominance provided a clear battleground. It was one advantage Hohn needn't worry about losing, for their equipment was both battery and solar powered. The batteries died long ago.

"I hope you're right," Tine whispered. "We're caught in a bad way if Delag stumbles on us too soon."

Hohn stared off into the night. His mind was elsewhere. "Locals don't like fighting at night. You know that. I'm betting they stick to that."

Or we're dead otherwise. He glanced at the chrono built into the lower corner of his visor. It was an old habit developed over years of experience. A former commander called it a nervous tick. Hohn saw it as a mental exercise preventing him from losing his mind in those tumultuous moments waiting for a battle to start.

There were no clouds in the sky, showing him an endless blanket of stars. Out there, one tiny prick in the countless myriad, was his home. Their home. A world far from this backwards planet they were stranded on. The more time spent here, the less he dreamed of home. This was life. This was reality. Hohn watched the stars with passive interest. There had been a time he found majesty among the stars. A sensation akin to godhood. Constant campaigning stole that notion, robbing him of innocence. Bitter, hardened beyond measure, Sergeant Hohn cared nothing for the stars.

"Sergeant, movement. Two hundred meters out."

Snapping back to reality, Hohn enhanced scanning. His helmet sensors picked up a dozen bodies heading in his direction. A dozen more followed. Then more. He calculated just under two hundred angry men searching the night for his squad. Hohn imagined Delag used his desertion to form a tale of betrayal to the others. Most followed without question, for they had never found a common denominator to bridge the gap. The militias were comprised of backwards thinking mountain tribes, incapable of seeing a different point of view. It was but a matter of time before Delag exercised his orders and slaughtered the squad.

"Guns up. No one fires unless I command it," Hohn ordered.

The soft click of weapons training on the approaching targets drifted back to him. They were heavily outnumbered, reducing the chances of them escaping unscathed, but it was a gamble Hohn felt they had to take. Only by getting both sides to attack each other would he find enough time to reach the vehicles. The tribesmen kept coming. He crouched down, risking a glance back at the government camp. All remained quiet.

If circumstances were different, Hohn might have been impressed with the tribesmen. They stalked across the open terrain like wraiths, silent and intent on killing. One hundred meters. His finger curled over the trigger and he took aim. His heart began to pound despite years of experience. Hohn supposed that was a good sign. No one should ever get used to violence on this level.

"Tine, do you have your targets locked?" he asked.

"Roger that. It's a long shot but I can make it."

Fifty meters.

"Do it. Everyone else stand by," Hohn ordered.

The thump of a magnetic grenade launching from the under barrel of Tine's weapon was barely audible. It took a handful of seconds before the hand sized grenade locked on to the nearest cannon, attached itself, and detonated. A ball of flame and shrapnel billowed in the night. Men screamed. Chaos erupted as the government camp came to life.

Hohn grinned. "Now. All guns engage."

Energy weapons lanced deep blue from the position. Tribesmen dropped. Tine launched a string of grenades into the government camp. Soon rifle fire began to range into the night. Government infantry formed ranks. The militia, thinking their enemy had accepted the traitor squad into their ranks, shifted targets and engaged the government troops.

"Cease fire!" Hohn barked. "Displace. Fall back in teams to the rendezvous. Comms silent. Now."

Tine left in the first group. The corporal would lead the others to a secure location far enough away from the firefight to prevent being detected. Hohn, after much arguing, would be the last to leave. The egress didn't take long. Bounding in twenty meter intervals, the squad retreated to safety. Curiosity delayed Hohn, for he grew interested in how the firefight was going to play out. Everyone dying was the ideal situation, and if not that, at least Delag and his lieutenants. Removing them reduced his chances of being caught.

Bodies littered the ground on both sides. A waste of life. Even with night vision there was next to no chance to spot Delag. Hohn abandoned his quest and retreated with the others. They consolidated, where he did a quick head count. Ten soldiers weren't an unmanageable number, but there were multiple factors adding difficulty.

"All present," Tine announced. His helmet was off, strapped to his utility belt. "What are your orders?"

Hohn had given the issue much thought during his sprint. "We dig in here for a bit to rest up. I want us on the road before dawn."

"You're not concerned about being hunted?"

"No. They were giving each other enough grief to forget about us for the time being. We have time, though how much remains to be seen," Hohn said. "I figure we have time for a little rest."

At this point, he was willing to take anything. The trek south to the vehicle promised to be taxing. Any reprieve available was worth the risk. He was asleep the moment he slumped down.

"Ytel, the moment has come for you to prove your worth," Thrakus said.

It took great effort to keep from gloating over his captive. The ambassador of Uruth remained silent, with his head hung low. The fight had left him.

"Come now, what is this? You have been treated well," Thrakus said. "No one has laid a finger on you. My people fed you, gave you water. Even let you relieve yourself from time to time. What more can a prisoner ask?"

Refusing to lift his head, Ytel said, "You have violated one of the sacred laws of these lands, Thrakus. No envoy on a mission of peace is to be assaulted. The kingdoms all agreed to this. You betray Mordai."

"Betray? No. I am bringing glory to my lands. Glory your pathetic little mind is incapable of understanding." He stormed off before jerking to a halt and spinning back around. Anger distorted his features. "Why is genius always mocked for simplicity? Those who cannot fathom true greatness, are doomed to die forgotten. You, my friend, will not suffer that distinction."

Ytel raised his head. Red streaked eyes glared at Thrakus. "What do you mean?"

"Why ruin the surprise?" Thrakus asked. Madness flared in the empty parts of his eyes. He addressed the guards standing on both sides of the ambassador. "Bring him."

They dragged Ytel, weakened from the trauma of his capture, to the alchemists' tents. His knees trembled as realization crept in. Thrakus was mad.

"You've brought me a present, I see," Senior Alchemist Horrick snickered.

There was a time Thrakus viewed the alchemists in disdain. Thoughts of home and leaving the political morass of Eleboran forever were almost gone, lost among his awakened dreams of conquest. The Vizier gave him full confidence and jurisdiction to enact Mordai's plans. A closely guarded secret unknown to all until recently. Thrakus now knew the catalyst for this change was the assassination of the god king of Ghendis Ghadanaban. Now, fully committed, Imperator Thrakus dreamed of becoming a god in his own right.

Ytel fought but wasn't strong enough to break free. The alchemist tapped his fingertips together with glee. Thrakus stepped aside, still uncomfortable with the unorthodox methods the alchemists used. Useful tools, they were an embarrassment to all the fighting men and women. He folded his arms and experienced a moment of doubt as Ytel was handed over for conversion. Regardless of serving a different purpose for an opposing kingdom, Thrakus felt pity. No one of station deserved this fate.

"How long will this take? Our ambassador needs to be in Ghendis Ghadanaban in two days," Thrakus said. "I want him ready for the transformation by the time we reach the city. There is no room for error, Alchemist."

"Before sunrise," Horrick answered.

Satisfied, and with a twisted stomach, Thrakus left the tent. He had no interest in hearing Ytel's screams.

TWENTY-ONE

The Heart Eternal was ripe with rumor and trepidation. A thousand different stories spread through the city like fires on the far eastern savannas. Tensions rose as encounters with the undead doubled. Reports of the Scarlet patrolling the night, stealing people from their homes prompted many to lock their doors and windows. The Prefecture was swamped with incidents of theft and violence on levels never seen. The city was ready to erupt.

First Prophet Sandis stared down on his home from his balcony. This high up, the scents of morning were lost. He remembered the pleasing sensation of fresh baked bread and roasting meat, but that was long enough, the memory was dimmed. Time jaded him. He'd grown bitter in his older years. The city no longer offered the promise it once lured him with. He felt … trapped.

Wrapped in linen robes of the softest white, Sandis was already sweating. Unopposed by clouds, the sun beat down with unrelenting fury. He hated the sun and the heat. Ghendis Ghadanaban was close enough to the desert to absorb much of the punishment meant for the endless sea of dunes. Heat wrinkled his skin, bronzing him to an unhealthy shade. White lines creased his arms and face, exposed wrinkles where the sun did not shine. Spots began appearing some years ago. Time conspired against him as well.

Tired of looking at the endless rows of houses and buildings, markets and shops, Sandis retired to his office. Meetings filled his day, almost making him regret waking. The longer he served in his position, the more he came to frown upon others. Slumping into his chair, with the cushions long conformed to fit him just right, Sandis stumbled upon a realization.

Enemies abounded, more than any of the others running the city understood, and he had been attempting everything on his own. The efforts robbed his strength and increased his worry to unprecedented levels. Sandis decided he'd been approaching the problem all wrong. Surely others would be receptive to his designs. The notion amused him. Men, he learned long ago, were easily corrupted.

But who to seek out? Every person who came to mind could turn him over to the Prefecture to enhance their individual situations. No doubt Tega Ig would relish the opportunity to put him under the torturer's implements. Sandis discounted anyone in the Prefecture. They were disturbingly aggressive and suffered little tolerance of the office of Prophets.

He poured a small glass of turang, spooning several cubes of sugar into the hot liquid. Sandis enjoyed watching the grains dissolve. It reminded him of simpler times now lost. The clink of his spoon stirring his drink was soothing and he needed calm more than any other time in his life. Recent events weighed heavily on his mind. Sandis knew the risk of accepting the Vizier of Mordai's gifts, but that did little to assuage the guilt gnawing at him.

Sandis drank the turang too fast and it burned his throat. The tool hidden in his closet—he still wasn't sure what the official term was for the men and women enslaved to act as long range communication machines—plagued him with guilt. How much longer could he keep his affair with Mordai secret? Every day brought him closer to the latest peace conference and exposure. The only factor preventing him from breaking free of his predicament was his lack of knowledge of the Vizier's driving motivations.

Wincing from the scalding liquid trailing down his throat, Sandis slammed the glass on the table and decided he needed wiser counsel than the infuriating anonymity of his own thoughts. Weekly rendezvouses with the fallen god were now limited, for he suspected Relghel had a hand in the assault in the White Crow. There was a duplicitous nature to the fallen god inspiring suspicion. Finding solace with Larris was likewise out of the question. His options were constricted by the immorality of his desires.

Sandis threw on his robes of office and struck out. There was much to be accomplished before the sun set and even after. The office of the First Prophet was overburdened on the slowest day. As he strode down marble tiled corridors, his mind raced over who he could discuss the future with. No matter how hard he tried, his thoughts returned to the approaching Mordai envoy. Power was a lonely trap.

Hean drank. He drank to forget his failures. Drank to wallow in the misery of immortality dangling just out of reach, while time conspired against him. Most of all, he drank to the future ever out of his grasp. Temptations tormented him to no end, while whispering promises of glory no mortal had ever achieved. The entire cycle proved infuriating. The glass of Alsean red wine went down smoothly, as it always did when the burden of his desires proved too strong.

The tiny room he chose to inhabit had no windows and a single door. It was close to his secret laboratory, where experiments both wicked and dark, were conducted. A travesty against the laws of nature, but he needed to know if immortality was achievable. That the god kings and their winged protectors were the only beings deemed worthy of never ending life galled him, driving him to deepening wells of concentration.

Dozens of corpses had been taken to the lab, where they were ultimately discarded and transformed into the undead. He wanted to laugh at the private amusement of being responsible for a growing epidemic the Reclamators were struggling with. No doubt Tega Ig and his pompous prefects would lop his head off if they discovered this offending truth. How many more corpses would come to roam the streets remained to be seen, though he placed much hope in Valir's mission south. The Tongueless was his favorite employee. An irascible man with little time for foolishness. If anyone could steal the secrets of the god kings, it was he.

There'd been a time when the idea of bringing the dead back to life appalled him, for Hean was once a pious man. His endeavors, aside from getting wealthy off a healthy trade empire, was to serve the god king in the best way possible. Greed never set in, unlike most of his competitors, but he came to understand that the direction his life took was not enough. He wanted more.

The catalyst came one night he was nearly trampled beneath a team of moorvaan. The driver was drunk and not paying attention. Death was inevitable. He recalled watching those massive hooves raise above his head, poised to crush him, and cringed years later. It was then Hean decided that there must be another way. A path across the void between life and death, where a man might live forever. It became a noble quest.

Footsteps coming down the hall stopped him from pouring another glass of wine. It was time. A new caravan was arriving from Mordai and Hean was expected to meet them at the warehouses. Tedious under the best conditions, it was part of the job. He was out the door before the expected knock and in his carriage. The city was always crowded, an irritation intensified by the onrush of refugees trying to escape the war. Leadership among the ruling class saw little use for the masses, but Hean was an opportunist. Men and women in search of a better life were willing to work for a fair wage. He had need of quality people to expand his business.

He stared at them in passing, curious to find another asset as strong as Valir proved. Lost in thought, Hean arrived at his complex of warehouses where he found his foreman, a dour woman name Xev, waiting with her signature scowl. She was tremendous with numbers and accountability, but he would never trust her enough to learn his darkest secret.

"You are late," anger laced her words.

Hean dismounted the carriage and brushed his clothes off. The vest alone cost more than a month's wages for most people. Crimson and lavender, he found the color scheme enhanced his portly image. "Yes, yes, Xev. Business is not a precise act. This is not the army."

Her disapproving look was answer enough. "Fortunate for you, the caravan is delayed. I assume the drivers had difficulty pushing through army lines. These are foul times."

"Indeed, but there is profit to be had for all if we look in the right shadows. War is a business unlike any other," Hean said. "We have already tripled our holdings since entering into agreements with each of the neighboring kingdoms. The influx of refugees guarantees our continued success."

"Profit from the poor is not honorable," Xev scolded.

"Perhaps not, but it is easier than supplying weapons of war to the various armies occupying Eleboran," he countered. "War is a nasty affair, Xev. We want no part of it. The suffering of others is enough to assuage our troubled conscience and line our pockets in the process. Everyone wins."

"You are a strange man," she replied and led him out of the mid afternoon heat.

Dockworkers and lower functionaries filled the main building. Storage room was being made for the incoming goods. Wagons were loaded with supplies to be delivered to the various refugee centers and marketplaces scattered through Ghendis Ghadanaban. Profits out and profits in. Hean remained in awe of his staff. Spies reported lesser operations conducted by his competition. They were in it purely for the wealth, seldom taking a moment to think on their actions. A critical failing in his estimation.

Merchants already carried a foul name among the ruling class. He intended to keep his name from their lips, unless it was to bestow glory. The people loved him, those who knew him. Hean built a careful image among the masses, for it was their combined strength that kept him in business. Sure, plenty of greedy men and women lined the path, many getting rich off him, but his intentions were pure. The people always came first. A lesson learned from his father when he was but a boy.

The caravan pulled in some time later. Drivers and guards were covered in sweat and dust, wearing haggard, almost defeated looks. It was the same every time. Hean had gone on a few trips during his early days at his father's insistence. The takeaways remained with him now, strengthening his understanding, leadership, and purpose. He went to greet the caravan master and then each crew as they climbed down from the massive wagons.

Each of his wagons were two stories high and carried six. Four guards to protect against bandits or rovers, a driver and one alternate. Four moorvaan pulled one wagon. They were the only beasts capable. Crimson and purple fabric covered the sides and roof, a declaration of ownership, recognized in several kingdoms. Hammocks were strung in each, offering sleeping space for those off duty. A small kitchen with ample water supply was located in the back by the driver deck, along with a portable toilet. Stopping every time someone needed to relieve themselves was not cost effective.

Having performed his duties, Hean was about to return to the office. The caravan master stopped him. Unexpected, for Hean seldom entertained in depth conversations after the welcoming ceremony, he paused. None of the others seemed to notice or were wise enough not to get caught, if they did.

"I have a special item for you," he said.

Hean grew suspicious. There was no word from any envoy or contact warning him to expect anything noteworthy. "From whom?"

"His name is Imperator Thrakus."

The regional Mordai commander. Interesting. "I do not believe I have had the pleasure."

"That is not the term I would use. He is a shrewd man with veiled purpose," the caravan master said.

"Why then reach out to me?" Hean asked.

"He did not say, but there is a chest in my wagon meant only for your eyes."

"Curious," was all Hean said. He weighed the options, realizing they were already constricted. Either he accepted custody of the chest and the contents within or he left them. There was not much of a choice at all. "Very well, show me this chest."

The winged Scarlet rose from the shadows in the crook between two of the taller warehouses. Unimpressed with the speed and efficiency the dockworkers unloaded Hean's wagons, he was more concerned with the chest of bone unloaded from the first wagon. Such creations had not been seen in Ghendis Ghadanaban in centuries. He flew back to his Lord to deliver the news.

"You are certain of this?" Verian asked, after hearing the full report.

"I am. It was one of the three boxes of Quaudag."

"That name has not been spoken in this city in a very long time," Verian said.

And for good reason. Quaudag was a necromancer who terrorized the kingdom three thousand years earlier. His experiments ruined countless lives. Some attributed the rise of the undead to his foul work. Verian knew the truth was lost to time, for it was well before his tenure as Lord of the Scarlet. Regardless of the circumstance, the resurfacing of one of the boxes bode ill for the world.

"And this Hean is a willing participant?" he asked.

"Unclear. He was not expecting the delivery and appeared hesitant to accept it."

"That does not free him of any wrongdoing. The city is a powder keg, ready to explode. Larris is convinced the war is getting closer and there seems little to be done about establishing a lasting peace. Neither side is willing to talk. Villains and agents of our enemies will soon attempt to infiltrate the city, if they haven't already. The death of Omoraum Dala'gharis has weakened us."

Verian began to pace. The feathers on his wings ruffled, disturbed by the collision of opposing thoughts. No matter how hard he tried to find a clear path, his thoughts returned to an ancient hatred once thought defeated. Razazel.

"Something disturbs you, Lord?" the Scarlet asked.

"More than that I should say. I have a task for you, Loywel."

"Anything."

"Assemble three others and go to the Dark Mountains," Verian ordered.

Loywel recoiled in shock. "You think the demon has escaped his prison?"

"I need to find out," Verian replied. "We are vulnerable, at least until Caestellom gets that boy to Rhorrmere. Funny, isn't it? How all our hopes rely on a young mortal boy with no concept of what he bears. The world is a cruel place. Leave as soon as you can. If Razazel is free, we will need all the time possible to prepare. Ever has the demon wanted to seize this city. We are all that stands in his way."

"Your will," Loywel said with a bow.

He left the Lord of the Scarlet mired in self-doubt, for the world had grown dark indeed and the threat of worse promised to bring pain on too many levels.

TWENTY-TWO

Three days passed before one of the prefects returned to the wagons with news of a road. The desert was leagues away, already a forgotten hardship. Mascantii wagon drivers pushed their charges through low hills and rocky terrain. Caestellom insisted Rhorrmere was many weeks away, forcing the quest to travel faster. Roving patrols of Mordai soldiers added new urgency to an already fragile expedition.

Falon Ruel wiped the blood from her hands on the grass and looked at her handiwork. The hare was small, almost too young to be harvested, but supplies were running low. They needed to find a town to resupply. She proceeded to clean and dress the hare, burying the offal to prevent scavengers from swarming the camp. Dusk was settling, and with it, the prospect of another lonely night in the middle of nowhere. At least the fresh meat would break up the monotony of travel rations.

She handed the hare over to the Mascantii cook, who accepted it without comment. Brutish creatures, the Mascantii were not known for conversation. Only the prefects acknowledged her return. The rest were either too absorbed in their own thoughts or disinclined to find camaraderie with her. Falon didn't mind. They were so different in their personal lives and endeavors, she found it difficult to accept them as a cohesive group. Should trouble find them, that might prove their undoing.

She recognized her role in the disparity. Any commander was expected to see to the welfare of the group, despite personal differences. The animosity between her and Tula remained high and she wasn't sure she wanted to cut it. Reclamators provided a service to

Ghendis Ghadanaban but at an expense Falon found no justification in. The dead were never meant to walk. A problem growing worse, the longer the city remained without a god king. Falon knew her issue came from Tula herself, not the work she performed.

Drawing a deep breath, Falon headed to the back of wagon Aldon rode. As expected, Tula was not far away. "Reclamator, how is the boy?"

Stifling a yawn, Tula tucked the dagger she'd been sharpening back into the sheath. "Less of himself. Every day the god king's essence strengthens."

"He is dying?" Falon asked.

"In a manner. The closer we get to Rhorrmere, the more I see a noticeable difference. He is not the same Aldon that left Ghendis Ghadanaban," Tula said.

Concern burrowed in the grime covering her face. Lines deepened. Red streaks filled the whites of her eyes, marring the crystalline blue. Their time on the road, compounded with the knowledge she was far beyond the limits of any comfort zone, conspired to weaken her resolve when Tula needed it most.

"A sacrifice beyond our control," Falon grunted. She struggled understanding what Aldon was enduring, so foreign the idea. Working for the Prefecture evoked a multitude of emotions, empathic understanding, not one of them. Still, she needed to ensure Aldon reached the god mountain unharmed.

"Have you no compassion?" Tula fired at her. "This boy is suffering a fate far worse than any we might conjure."

"Compassion is wasted here. We have one task and I will accomplish it to the best of my ability," Falon retorted. "His fate is beyond my reach. What will be, will be. Perhaps you should look closer at your own frailties. They might be your undoing."

Falon stormed off, tired and irritated with the conversation, leaving Tula wondering what the future held. Discouraged from being segregated from the others, the Reclamator wanted to return to the city and her quiet job. Why she was chosen to report to Overseer Larris remained unknown, while becoming an irritant she struggled to ignore.

Tula blew out the breath she was holding and climbed aboard the wagon. Talking with Aldon relieved her troubles, if barely. He was losing more of himself to the god king daily. She feared there would not be any left by the time they reached Rhorrmere. The journey was far from perilous, despite the ranging patrols of various kingdoms and the looming threat of being embroiled in the wide ranging civil war. At least she had that much to keep her mind off the troubles of the moment.

She pulled aside the flap covering the rear and saw Aldon staring back. Instead of his normal smile, for seeing her was as much of a highlight for him as for her, his eyes were sallow and laced with fear. Tula's heart sank. She already devoted too much time avoiding the difficult conversations with Aldon. Seeing him distraught, left her feeling guilty.

"Aldon, what's wrong?" she asked and settled in beside him, adjusting the pillows to provide better support for her aching back.

The boy reached over to hug her. "I am afraid, Tula."

"Nonsense. There is nothing to fear. We are on track and on schedule, at least according to Prefect Falon. We should be at Rhorrmere in the next …" Tula struggled with the desire to speak the truth. To tell Aldon that, while she didn't know precisely what was going to happen at the god mountain, he was going to be irrevocably transformed into a being far beyond mortal comprehension.

Aldon nestled into her shoulder. "No. I heard what Falon said. The others won't speak with me. Not even the one with wings."

That surprised Tula. She expected Caestellom to bond with the boy, teaching him the ways of what was expected. For the Scarlet to abandon Aldon, and the rest of the quest in the process, proved troubling. Deep rooted suspicions ingrained against the upper, ruling class, invoked misgivings among many of the lower classes, Tula included. Ghendis Ghadanaban was a city of wonders and opportunity, but much was restricted against the wrong people.

"Falon is a driven woman with a heavy task. Do not place much weight in her tone. She is doing what she believes is right for you and the group," Tula said. She hoped her tone was convincing enough to prevent additional concerns from arising. Having Aldon mistrust most of the quest led down the road to damnation. One faulty link would break the chain.

Aldon's shoulders remained tense, as if carrying the weight of an entire civilization was driving him to the ground. "Tula, no one understands. I … I am afraid. There is another being in my head. He speaks to me, telling me all is going to be all right, but I don't believe him."

"He speaks to you?" she asked.

Aldon nodded.

"What does he say?"

"He tells me of his past and what will come. It is so confusing. I don't understand most of it, but I do know that I will not be me after we find Rhorrmere."

She felt his suffering, as her blouse grew wet from his tears. Heartbroken, Tula was torn. Taking the information to Falon and the others was the responsible thing to do. The lack of cohesion among the group prevented her from doing so. She felt like an island, forgotten and alone in the loneliest corner of the world. Indecision gripped her.

"Aldon, I ..." she fell silent. Unsure what to say, nothing felt useful or consoling.

He lifted off her and hung his head. "Tula, this being is taking over. Every day he grows stronger, while my memories fade." Tears flowed freely. "I just want to see my mother again. I don't even know if she is still alive."

"Your mother? The First Prophet said he was going to find out and see to your parents," Tula said after some thought.

"She is dying, Tula, and I won't be there for her before the end," Aldon fell silent.

Tula squeezed him hard, funneling her sympathies into the move. Aldon was a special young man and it pained her that there was nothing in her power that might remove his fears. A lingering hand on his knee and Tula left. There was nothing left for her to do.

"Tula," he called before she slipped behind the flap. "I want to go home."

So do I. She left.

Falon jerked awake. Her hand reached for the pistol beside her bedroll.

"No," a stern voice warned.

Her blurred vision cleared to show the Scarlet, Caestellom looming over her. She surmised he had awakened her. But why? "What's going on?"

Darkness surrounded them, though the first fingers of brightening sky began to appear. "We are being hunted."

"Hunted?" she blurted. "By whom?"

"Soldiers," he replied. His tone suggested there was more he was unwilling to share.

Falon suspected the Scarlet took to flight during the long hours of the night, while most of the others were asleep. His ability to fly provided unquestionable advantage. Now she knew he could also see in the dark. She filed that bit of information away in the event she might need it later.

"Whose soldiers? This is no time for secrets, Caestellom," she chided.

The Scarlet helped her up. "Mordai, from what I can tell. Their uniforms blend well with the night. They are headed this direction and should be here within the hour."

Falon struggled to comprehend the why of it. Mordai was not their enemy, nor should there be any reason for a patrol this far south. They were already in the deepest reaches of Eleboran, about to cross into the Uruth outer lands. The Vizier had grown bold to send soldiers wherever he pleased.

"You are certain they know we are here?" she asked.

"They are heading directly toward us. Bayonets are fixed and rifles unslung," he confirmed. "We are going to be engaged in battle, if we do not move now."

"We must rouse the others," Falon said. The last thing they needed was an entanglement with a foreign power. Her jurisdiction ended at the city limits, though her authority came from the Overseer. A meaningless fact, all things considered. Ghendis Ghadanaban was a singular entity that happened to be within the kingdom of Eleboran.

"I will return to the soldiers. Should they get too close, I will distract them," Caestellom said. His matter of fact tone left no room for further discussion. He was airborne before she could comment.

Falon watched him until he was but a speck lost in the darkness. "Typical."

She hurried to wake the others as quietly as possible. Mascantii porters packed the few belongings taken from the wagons during camp. The expedition was ready to move within minutes. Not for the first time, Falon regretted having only a handful of prefects. The overall lack of combat power placed them at a disadvantage. Depending on how many Mordai soldiers were approaching, the quest to Rhorrmere might end far too soon.

"Why are they doing this? We should have soldiers with us," Meone complained, as he rode by her.

"The Overseer could not foresee conflict with armed bodies of soldiers, Prophet Meone," she snapped. "Do not be so fast to judge the actions of others. There is much we do not know."

Rebuked, the prophet continued riding.

Night died with quiet fanfare. Adrenalin forced the quest deeper south, desperate to escape the Mordai aggressors. No soldiers among them, Falon decreed noise discipline was paramount to success. Sound traveled farther at night, a fact not lost on any of them after the first few days. The less noise made, presented better odds for success. Falon needed all the luck she could muster at this point.

They hurried on to the symphony of wagon wheels and groaning beasts. The moorvaan were used to strenuous work but had grown accustomed to recuperating at night. Falon feared their strength might begin to lag the longer this went on. Nothing for it, they kept moving long after the sun came up.

Dawn greeted them without incident, but Falon kept the same pace. Resting now spelled disaster. During their flight, she struggled to understand why Mordai soldiers were tracking them. None of the obvious reasons made sense and only one chilled her enough to inspire fear. Falon kept her thoughts private, unsure even as her mind cemented. The possibility of the Mordai attacking them remained, yet she wanted to believe that any issue would be solved by a simple explanation. There was no logical reason for any military intervention.

So why am I suddenly afraid? The urge to flee arose, inspiring her to abandon her charge and return to the city where life made sense. Honor prevented her from doing so. She'd given her word to Tega Ig and the ruling council. Anything less was admission of cowardice. Falon never considered herself strong. She could bend but had never been pushed to the breaking point. This quest was already taking her well beyond her comfort zone. Doubts rose with each step forward, threatening to paralyze her. Falon tried to shake the feeling off, but it never went far.

They rode for half the day before Caestellom returned with dire news. The Mordai were continuing on pace, tracking the tiny band from Ghendis Ghadanaban. It would not be long before they were overtaken. Panic arose among the group, for they were ill prepared to fight a battle.

"Quiet," Falon urged. "This will serve us no good. Caestellom, are you certain they hunt us?"

"Yes," was all he said.

She had hoped otherwise. That this might be an error of judgment. "We cannot outrun them. Nor can we meet them in a direct engagement."

"Our mission is to reach Rhorrmere, not fight a war," Meone chimed in.

Falon ignored him, recognizing a weakness greater than her own. "We must look for a place to hide. To get far enough out of their way that they will pass us by."

"Hiding won't solve the issue, Falon," Tula said. She watched the prefects bristle, as if offended that anyone would differ in opinion from their sergeant.

Hands on her hips, Falon wheeled on her. "What do you propose? We meet the Mordai with smiles and open arms? The Scarlet says they come to fight. We cannot defeat an entire company of trained infantry."

"We should at least learn what they want. It is possible they believe we are an enemy force," Tula countered.

"This is not their territory, nor their kingdom," Falon replied. "They have no jurisdiction this far south. Reasoning with their commander is pointless."

"How do you know unless you try?"

Falon opened her mouth and quickly shut it. The bitter retort died on her tongue. One wrong move ended the quest and the Heart Eternal. She wished there was another selected to lead the group. Too much was being thrown at her and she did not know which way to turn next.

"We keep riding. The Mordai are not our enemies, nor are they allies. We should avoid all contact until we reach Rhorrmere. The fewer who know, the easier our task becomes."

She led them on. Farther south. Closer to Rhorrmere. Caestellom stood behind, watching the small wagon train ramble on. The scowl on his face went unseen.

TWENTY-THREE

The open markets of Ghendis Ghadanaban were renowned for their quality and diverse range of goods. Merchants from across the kingdoms brought their wares to the Heart Eternal to gain maximum price and exposure. Silks of every color fluttered in the breeze, rifling through the streets. Birds of prey sat hooded in a dozen stalls. Exotic birds from far distant lands. The aroma of roasting meats and fresh baked breads mingled with spices and incense to create a heady environment.

Merrick strolled from vendor to vendor, searching for the best buy for his coin. Merchants outnumbered the buyers, prompting a price war. Finding what he wanted wasn't difficult but getting it at cost took more effort. He was moving past the food stalls and into the artisan area where metal and wood goods were sold, when a burly hand landed on his shoulder and arrested his movements.

"Where are you going, Merrick?"

He closed his eyes at the sound. She was the last person he needed or wanted to see. "Ninean. To what do I owe this interruption?"

Guild enforcer and arguably one of the meanest women in Ghendis Ghadanaban, Ninean Foul wore a dark, brooding look. He assumed it was her natural state, for he failed to recall ever seeing her smile. The scars on her knuckles, from years of inspired beatings, rose above her hand enough to draw his attention.

"I'm looking for Abbas. Word is you are close to him," she growled.

"Haven't seen him," Merrick replied. "Last I heard, your friends took him."

Ninean removed her hand from his shoulder and made a show of cracking her knuckles. "I'm not here to play games, Merrick."

"Neither am I. There's a fellow somewhere around here that sells the best sweet meats. Can't remember his name."

"I'm serious, Merrick. Don't cross the Guild on this one. Abbas is wanted for breaking sanctions," Ninean said. "Anyone caught with him will suffer the same fate. It would be a shame if that pretty blond hair got ruined over a fool like Abbas."

Merrick swallowed. "Like I said, haven't seen him. I'll be sure to pass the word around for you though. Wouldn't do to have a fugitive roaming the streets like that. Murderers and all."

"I'll be seeing you, Merrick," Ninean threatened. "Real soon."

He offered his best smile and waved. "Enjoy your day, Ninean."

Only when she was out of sight did he breathe normally again. People like Ninean Foul frightened him more than he was willing to admit. Precisely the reason the Guild hired her, he surmised. Appetite ruined, Merrick continued toward the smiths. Leaving the market now would evoke suspicion, for he was certain Ninean had other eyes watching him. The best thing he could do was act as if nothing was out of place. He began to whistle as he walked. The day was too nice to spend mired in suffering.

Merrick returned to the room at the White Crow to find Abbas going through a series of painful stretches. The assassin was wobbly, looking as if he was ready to fall. Merrick supposed that was expected. A lesser man might never have recovered this far. He watched his friend out of the corner of his eye, as he closed the door and set the small bag of supplies down. Aside from a loaf of dark bread and a wedge of yellow cheese, Merrick brought a bottle of spiced wine from the northern kingdoms, a rare vintage this far south.

He slid a second sack off his shoulder and onto the bed. Within was a pair of short swords, some daggers, and a belt of throwing knives. Merrick had never used them before but figured Abbas had plenty of experience. Killing wasn't one of his better traits. In fact, Merrick avoided it most of the time. He found solving disagreements much easier without the need for bloodshed.

"You're late," Abbas commented. He was covered in a sheen of sweat. The rise and fall of his chest was fast, strained from too many days of inactivity.

Merrick pulled the lone chair out and sat. "I had an unexpected visitor. Foul is looking for you. I get the feeling the Guild is about to put a price on your head."

"If they haven't already," Abbas grunted. "Damn. I was hoping for more time."

"We don't get to choose," Merrick said and snatched a fig from the tray beside the bed. "What do you want to do?"

Killing Ninean Foul wasn't an option he cared to exercise, though it would bring a measure of satisfaction. Abbas was no fool. Understrength and still feeling abused, the assassin knew keeping his head down was the most viable chance for surviving long enough to get revenge on the Guild.

Abbas grabbed a towel and wiped his face. "We're not ready to fight back, not yet. Even with Baradoon, the Guild would win. Not to mention Eamon becoming irate at us for wasting his favorite muscle."

"So we run," Merrick concluded.

"Did Ninean lead on she knew anything?" Abbas asked.

"Nothing in words, though I suspect she knows something. She was fishing," Merrick said. "What about the woman who brought you here?"

"I don't even know her name," Abbas replied. He paused, trying to place her voice. The slightest hint of familiarity teased him, but no more. "There is the possibility the Guild finds her and makes her talk."

"Nothing we can do about that, if we don't know who she is," Merrick said. "This is damned frustrating. We are trapped like rats in a maze."

"This is not what I had in mind when I was approached to help you. We need to find a way out of this mess that doesn't end with our necks in a noose."

Abbas feigned a smile. He tossed the towel aside. "Give me a little more time. Once I am back to form, we act."

"You're still serious about bringing the Guild down?" Merrick asked.

"Everyone responsible for what they did to me," Abbas confirmed.

Merrick whistled. The Prefecture was going to be a busy place in the coming days. Now might be a good time to look for a place outside of the city. Life in Ghendis Ghadanaban was about to turn violent.

Hohn was impressed. His small squad, who had never been forced to march on foot for extended distances, covered the ground between the war zone and the downed vehicles in impressive time, while dodging any further patrols. The militia led by Delag and the government soldiers fought a pitched battle long into that first night, providing the perfect opportunity for escape. Hohn figured they were hours away before anyone remembered the deserters. Not a bad start to winning their freedom back.

They reached the source of the electronic ping without difficulty several days later. Nerves tightened in his stomach. Hohn was a pessimistic man at heart. It was his experience whatever could go wrong, usually did. Those apprehensions rose the closer they got to the vehicles. He hoped for the best, that one would be serviceable enough to get them far away from the civil war of Eleboran. That one had a working transmitter, and a friendly ship might be passing through the system, was too much to ask for.

Hohn was the last to the position. Some of the squad busied establishing a defensive perimeter, while Tine and the one quasi engineer rushed to the trio of vehicles. Hohn was just as eager to see if they had found a way home but refused to show it. The last thing any of them needed was to succumb to false hope. He slid his pack off and stretched. The soreness spreading through his body refused to dissipate, forcing him to walk with a slight hobble and a perpetual sour expression.

"Tine, what do you got?" he called after coming alongside a reconnaissance jeep. The vehicle was tilted on its side and covered with rock and sand. Not a good sign.

The diminutive corporal poked his head through the passenger hatch. His look said enough. "Nothing here. The drive is shot. My guess is it shattered on impact."

"The buffer bags didn't deploy?" Hohn asked.

"Not a one," Tine shook his head.

Hohn grimaced. "What about the others?"

"I haven't checked them yet," Tine admitted.

He scrambled out of the vehicle, dusting his trousers off after hitting the ground. The day was warm. Much warmer than the mountain region they were now accustomed to. Sweat already ran down Hohn's back, his uniform clinging to the flesh, prompting him to reevaluate his position on the weather. A man would complain about it being too cold on one hand and then it being too hot with the other. Soldiers, in his experience, were accomplished masters at such dichotomy.

Tine removed the possibility of further conversation and hurried to the second vehicle. Hohn stared at the beast with appreciation. The armored personnel carriers were among the best in the galaxy, capable of delivering and receiving extreme punishment. He crossed his fingers as Tine disappeared within the bowels of the hulking machine.

Weighing over two hundred tons, the beast—as the grunts affectionately termed it—was laden with reactive armor. Twin 210mm cannons were mounted on the deck, with positions for seven additional heavy machine guns. Each company outfitted theirs differently according to individual mission mandates, but the core elements were all the same. Hohn ran a gloved hand over the pitted armor siding and closed his eyes in prayer.

Vibrations began deep within the engine well, spreading through the beast until Hohn was forced to jerk his hand away. A familiar whine followed next. The engines fired. The hum and whirl of minor systems and motor functions spinning to life whispered an end to an ordeal. The beast lurched off the ground where it hovered. A blue-white glow pulsed underneath.

Tine popped his head up. His traditional infantry helmet was gone, replaced by the internal helmets used by the crew. "We're in business!"

Hohn's heart skipped. The hardest part of the battle was over. They had a ride. A way to reach any part of the planet necessary to be rescued. Keying his helmet's comms, Hohn ordered the rest of the squad, "Drop your gear and scavenge everything useful from the other vehicles. Weapons, ammo, power cells, rations. Everything."

Whoops and cheers responded. They had finally won a victory that did not come at a price. No additional instructions were necessary. Men and women abandoned the perimeter to assist. Every useable piece of equipment was transferred to the beast as Hohn climbed up the rear boarding ramp to see what they already had. Compartments of medical supplies sat beside ammunition packs and rations. This surprised him, for the division was returning from a grueling campaign when the ship was destroyed and the survivors forced to eject. Whatever unit this beast belonged to, did a stellar job getting it back into fighting condition.

It didn't take long before the last of the salvageable equipment was stowed aboard. Hohn felt like a new man. His tiny squad had new life and the opportunity to get out of trouble faster than they got in to it. Hohn gave the outlying areas a last look before boarding his new home. Designed to fit a full platoon, the beast had plenty of room to string hammocks. The refresher even worked.

Setting his helmet on a nearby stack of ration crates, Hohn looked into the expectant eyes of his squad. Most were from different platoons, though he'd come to know them all during their time on planet. "Ladies and gents, we got a new home. Go ahead and claim your sleeping space. I want everyone washed and in clean uniforms immediately. Clean your weapons good. I have feeling we're going to need them again soon enough. After that, you rest and eat. Anyone have experience driving these beasts?"

Two hands raised. He nodded. "Good. Go see Corporal Tine and get on the driving rotation. I'm going to see where we need to go. Dismissed."

Their cheers accompanied him into the driving cockpit.

The mountains of northern Eleboran were among the most severe in the western kingdoms, regardless of the season. Mountaineers and adventurers died by the dozens when times were peaceful. Much of the mountain range remained unmapped by the government, leaving a dark spot on maps where the unknown ruled with austere authority. A land where the mountain tribes secluded themselves from a world that did not want them.

Malach sat in his cave warming his hands over a large fire. They were high in the mountains, where wind and snow were constant companions. Warriors, family and friends surrounded him, going about their business in silence. Torches lined the walls leading back into the tunnel system burrowing deep into the mountain. Endless chambers were carved and polished, enough for an entire tribe to live and grow. Ventilation shafts were bored out to bring fresh air in and smoke out. Not the most ideal living conditions, but the only ones the tribe knew.

Malach was a hard man with little room for conversation. He chewed on a strip of goat meat, listening to the runner from Delag's force as he described the actions of the traitorous off-worlders. He inspected the bone for any scraps of meat left, and once satisfied, tossed it in the fire. Malach then made a show of cleaning his lips and picking a string of meat from between his teeth. Wicked intent glowed in his eyes.

"Where are they now?" he asked. His voice was a low whisper.

"We followed them south until the government soldiers attacked," the runner answered.

Malach leaned forward. "And Delag?"

The runner's head dropped. "We think he is dead. No one has seen him since the battle."

"I want the traitor Hohn found and brought to me. His head will decorate the entrance of our caves and his body will feed our pigs. Spread the word to every tribesman in the kingdom. They will be paid handsomely for this."

The runner bowed and scurried off. His mission just beginning. Malach watched him leave before grabbing another rib. Visions of murder filled his thoughts, as a score more hurried to get outfitted, so they would spread his message. War against the government was one thing, betrayal by mercenaries sworn to serve, another. Death was too good of a reward for men like that. He briefly lamented the loss of his right hand. Delag was a capable warrior, if lacking in judgment. His name would be added to the memorial wall, where Malach would scratch it out for failing the tribes. He placed the rib to his teeth and bit deep.

TWENTY-FOUR

A moment of joy came for the worried people of Ghendis Ghadanaban. Weeks of suffering inspired by the murder of the god king threatened to snap as the time of the great peace conference neared. Emissaries from across the kingdoms were nearing the Heart Eternal, bringing the promise of the end of war and a return to normalcy for the kingdom. An empty hand some whispered, disguised to confuse the people. Regardless of rising apprehensions, dreams and nightmares were about to collide.

Larris yawned, stretched, and swung her legs out of bed. The sun was rising, cresting the eastern sand dunes. Golden rays stretched through her windows to warm her face. She was tired. Too many days and nights spent mired in meetings and suppositions left her feeling stretched, exhausted. A second yawn rippled through her and she turned to look at the sleeping man in her bed. Back to her, she took in the long curls of his black hair and muscles across his wide shoulders. Perhaps not every night was spent overseeing matters of the city.

Unable to delay longer, Larris rose and wrapped a green silk robe around her. As Overseer of the city, it was her responsibility to ensure all matters of state were conducted as flawlessly as possible. Unfortunately, that meant spending every morning locked in meetings with councilors, foreign politicians, and petitioners. A monumental waste of precious time, considering the immensity of the moment arriving.

A knock disturbed her. It was urgent, rushed. Angered at the intrusion, for her staff knew better than to approach her before the official start to the day, Larris stormed across the marble floors. Curtains whisked away at her passing. The bare flesh of the bottom of her feet slapped with each angry step.

"What?" she demanded after jerking the door open.

A young attendant swallowed her rising fear and stepped back. "Mistress, the Lord of the Prefecture has arrived. He wishes to speak with you immediately."

"Tega Ig? What reason has he given for invading my privacy?" Larris asked.

"He would not say," she answered.

Larris pursed her lips. This was unlike Tega. He was a cautious, calculating man. Any move made out of character presented potentially grave implications. "Very well, send him in."

Relief washed over her face and the attendant fled. Larris waited, choosing not to dress. She folded her arms. The rustle of silk sweeping over her flesh reminded her of simpler times, before she was elected to rule a city. Time for rumination ended immediately as Tega Ig came barreling down the corridor in full uniform. The concerned look on his face inspired worry in Larris.

"This is highly unusual, Tega. I am not to be disturbed in my private quarters. You know this," she accused.

"I do not offer apologies, Larris, for this matter I bring before you is one of utmost concern for us all," Tega said. He waited for her to step aside before entering the quarters.

Larris followed him into her sitting chamber and attempted to appear graceful as she took her seat on the cushions. "I would offer refreshments, but it is yet too early."

"It may already be too late," he said.

"Explain yourself? You know I do not abide riddles."

Tega blew his cheeks out. The scruff of a newly grown beard tickled his chin. "There is no easy way to approach the subject, so I will start at the beginning. Murders are being committed at an alarming rate, as you know."

"This is not news, Tega. You have assured me your prefects are doing everything within their power to find the killers," Larris said. She tensed, fearing what was to come.

He clasped his hands. "I have reason to believe one of the Scarlet is responsible."

Her voice caught in her throat. Such an accusation threatened to undo the foundations the city was built upon. Larris struggled to understand where this reason came from and why it was not as disappointing to hear as she might have believed.

"One of Verian's protectors?" she asked. "Impossible."

"Is it? The god king is dead. A feat that has not happened in forty-seven thousand years, Larris. Who stands to lose the most if not Verian?" Tega asked.

"The Scarlet are the very definition of justice. They have protected Ghendis Ghadanaban and the god king for millennia. What reason presents itself to allow you to believe this?" she asked.

Apprehension twisted his features, for Tega was hesitant to cast unfounded accusations about. Coming to Larris presented another set of issues, complete with unique consequences should she prove unreceptive.

"I have a witness who claims to have seen one of the Scarlet commit murder," his voice dropped low.

Her demeanor shifted. Larris leaned forward. Concern clouded the bright blue of her eyes. "A credible witness? Has she been interviewed?"

"Extensively, by several of my officers. Her story hasn't changed," Tega replied.

"This … leads us down a dark path," Larris said after a moment. "Our reliance on the Scarlet has been above reproach. Did you bring this up with Verian?"

"Would you?" he replied.

The Lord of the Scarlet was known for his short temper. Generations of leadership came and went without getting accustomed to his peculiar styles. Both Larris and Tega Ig had been in leadership positions long enough neither was willing to invoke Verian's ire.

"We must be cautious in handling this," Larris suggested. "Is it possible for me to speak with this witness? I would rather not confront Verian without verified information."

"Perhaps," was all Tega said. The risk posed by approaching Larris presented unanticipated challenges at the worst possible time. He rose and offered a curt bow. "I will be in touch the moment I have a better grasp of the situation. I am sure you and I have more than enough to keep us busy in the meantime."

Larris watched him leave, dreading the coming conference with muted conviction.

Another day passed, bringing the inevitable collision between cultures as the first envoy column came within sight. People thronged to the walls and outer fields in the hopes of catching their first glimpse of potential salvation. Rumors traveled on fleet legs, reaching every corner of the city. The black uniforms of the Mordai army stood out among the fields. Even at distances of more than a league, they could be seen marching in lock step.

Sandis watched them come through the special viewing glasses made long ago by the city's best artisans. The refractive lens magnified the approaching soldiers with unprecedented clarity. The First Prophet wondered why the inventors failed to capitalize on future profit from the invention. These lenses were now common, not only among the Heart Eternal but the rest of the kingdoms. A fortune lost.

Watching the Mordai approach robbed him of his composure. Until now, he was content with scheming with the Vizier. The reality of seeing enemy soldiers this close to his city offered both freedom and damnation. He watched for a while longer, his mind running through multitudes of scenarios playing out. The future held infinite possibilities. All he needed to do was reach out and grab them.

Satisfied, he left the balcony. Another busy day of meetings and pointless conversation about the fallen god king awaited. He'd grown tired of the regularity, of the mundanity. Life was meant for more. He was meant for more. Sandis poured a short glass of brandy and downed it, wincing at the crisp aftertaste. A man of fine quality, the First Prophet was used to delicate treats, often unavailable to all classes in the city. It was the privilege of status. Some men spent a lifetime scrabbling to get by without gaining ground. Others learned how to make the system work for them.

The Mordai marched closer.

Guards flanked him the moment he left his apartments. Additional security measures were emplaced immediately following the incident at the White Crow. Sandis kept his tongue, for he was still uncertain who the target was. Relghel Gorgal had many enemies, though most lacked the teeth to act against him. Sandis had his share of enemies as well, and most were cunning political opponents. The time for culling had dawned.

Surrounded by a squad of ill-tempered prefects, Sandis decided it was time to revisit the fallen god. The prefects argued at first, knowing that his entering the city proper added stress to an already perilous situation. His glare ended that protest. He was the First Prophet of Ghendis Ghadanaban, no part of the city was off limits to his whims.

Sandis found Relghel sitting at his usual table, perhaps rebuilt from the attack of a few days ago. The smirk on his face suggested he was expecting Sandis. A boot slid the empty chair out. Sandis accepted the invitation and gestured his prefect guards outside. Alone, he clasped his hands in front of him on the table and stared deep into Relghel's eyes. They remained that way longer than either felt comfortable with.

"Is there specific reason you come to me this day, of all days, First Prophet?" Relghel asked. His tone was irreverent.

Sandis cleared his throat, still unsure of this move. Much stood at risk. Revealing his intentions at this point might damn him. "You know the enormity of today."

"Who does not?" he spread his arms. "The Heart Eternal beats with new life yet remains stifled by fear. What is your office doing to cull such sensations?"

"I did not come to you to speak of matters of state. We are in a constant flux, now that the god king is dead. Life is not as simple as it once was."

"Life is eternal. The players come and go but the great web continues unhindered. One hundred years from now, do you think men will speak your name with reverence or disgust?" Relghel pressed.

Darkness spread across Sandis's face. "This is not why I came to you."

"I know, yet that changes nothing. You play a dangerous game," Relghel warned. "I do not think it wise that you see me for some time."

"Not even an immortal can profess to know the future," Sandis snapped. "You have no idea what is coming."

"One only needs understand the past to learn the future. Good bye, Sandis. I wish you good fortune. Remember, the end of the road may not be the end you seek," the fallen god warned.

He left Sandis sitting alone. It had been a mistake coming to the White Crow.

No sentient creatures native to the world were given the ability to fly. That was reserved for beasts and birds. Not every creature who lived was of the world, however. The Scarlet were born from a whim. Meant to serve the god kings, each cadre spent a thousand years in the service of the god king who chose them. An entire reign lasting longer than all but the strongest empires throughout the span of human history.

Skilled warriors beyond reproach, the Scarlet were masters of sword and sky. Their moral code was impeccable, an impossible standard for any mortal attempting to emulate. Winged avengers sworn to justice and equality. They were the shining beacon everyone should have looked toward. The death of the god king, under their watch, presented a chink in their perfect façade. A flaw thought impossible. They were fallible and with it, their reputation.

Those few residents bearing witness to the winged masters of the skies no longer looked upon them as saviors. Anathema surrounded their aura in many circles. Failures. Relghel ignored the abuses of the day, for his experience with mortals suggested their whims were fickle beyond comprehension. Angered to the point of riot one day and tripping over loose tongues in awe the next. Few seemed immune. It was part of the reason he fled from attaining godhood.

He hummed, hands clasped behind him as he wound up the spiral staircase, locked in darkness save for a glimpse of sunlight slipping through the cracks in the walls where the mortar had worn down. Relghel was blessed, though some argued cursed, by his unique circumstance. He, alone, was truly immortal and the thought terrified him. Up the stairs he wound, his mind coiled around them in devolving thought.

"You should not be here, *fallen one*."

Relghel jerked to a halt. He hadn't realized he had emerged from the hidden passage and was standing in the god king's empty chambers. His ultimate destination just too soon arrived. The ice in Verian's tone left little room for debate. A glance at the Scarlet's hand, draped over the ornamental hilt of his sword, was enough.

"Verian," he said. The fallen god shifted his empty hands to his front, wishing to show his intentions.

The Lord of the Scarlet remained rigid, as if ready to launch into fury at the slightest provocation. "This chamber is not meant for betrayers. Leave now."

"You should listen to what I have to say." He stood his ground.

Verian's eyes narrowed. Suspicion occupied his heart and mind. A result of the guilt gnawing at them all. "Your words are poison. Why should I waste my time, precious as it has become, bandying with you?"

"The city is changing. Matters are gaining speed. Soon it will be too late," Relghel said.

"If you are going to steal my time, at least make sense."

Relghel ran his tongue over his bottom lip. Verian was justifiably unstable in his thought processes, but continued ignorance threatened everything. "*He* has been freed."

"Impossible," Verian replied after long thought. His olive complexion paled. Blanched at the thought of what might be. "Such an event would have been noticed."

"Not if focus was elsewhere," Relghel said.

Like the death of the god king. Verian winced. Was it possible they were duped? He found the idea disturbing, if not plausible. So many odd events were occurring, it was not impossible for the Scarlet to have missed this development. If what Relghel said was accurate. "Razazel has not been a factor in generations. His power is spent."

"What if it is not? Can you explain the rise of certain nefarious powers in the city, while all eyes are on the civil war?" Relghel pressed. "This is the perfect opportunity for *him* to strike."

"Strike what target? We are exposed in all aspects," Verian said.

"The obvious threat is to your secret caravan heading to Rhorrmere."

"No one was to know of that," Verian replied.

"I may have passed on my appointment, but the secrets of your order remain open to me, Verian." Relghel paused. His case approached unfamiliar territory. "There is something else that must be addressed."

"I cannot take much more of your brand of news. We are already stretched thin," the Lord of the Scarlet admitted.

"This ... will not be easy to accept. You have a traitor in your midst."

Verian remained calm. He had suspected as much. "Who?"

The name Relghel uttered caught in his throat, while blindsiding Verian. Everything the Lord of the Scarlet once believed was proving to be a lie. The end was closer than he knew.

TWENTY-FIVE

Far from the political manipulations of the Heart Eternal, rode the fate of the free world in the small caravan of mismatched heroes. Mistrust and personal grudges divided them, yet they were the only hope Ghendis Ghadanaban had of returning a god king to the throne. A desperate gambit locked in the throes of discord. How cruel the irony of life.

The first inkling Falon got that all was not right occurred shortly after dawn, when the skies darkened. The quest was already days into the empty expanse of scrub grass and rock strewn fields, far from the cradle of civilization. With only the supplies in the wagon beds, they were forced to survive on their own. This did not worry her, for the quest was well supplied and had made detailed preparation before setting out.

Lightning striking in the near distance aroused her suspicions further. They had yet to encounter any storm of magnitude, and with the mountains looming on the horizon, this boded ill. Falon kept them moving. The storm approaching and a company of Mordai soldiers on their trail, the quest was besieged on all sides. The day was but half done when the final sign announced itself.

Caestellom tucked his wings and landed beside Falon. The impact drove a cloud of dust and pebbles into the air. His expression offered no explanation nor forgiveness. His sword was in hand. "We are under attack."

"What do you mean?" Falon asked, squinting into the sun framed behind him. "The Mordai are almost a half day's march behind and we should find refuge before that storm gains ground."

The Scarlet gestured to the mountains. "Not from that. I feel a presence. Something not of the natural world. It comes for the god king's essence."

"Nonsense. What force in this world has that power?" she asked. The certainty in his tone gave her pause. The Scarlet was taciturn by nature. For him to reveal his thoughts in such a straightforward manner, turned her stomach. *You knew this was not going to be easy, no matter what your heart desired. This might be the biggest test yet.*

"I am not certain, but it does not feel like any power natural to this world," he admitted. "We are being hunted."

Endless leagues of open terrain surrounded them. The slightest puff of dust in the distance marked the march of the Mordai. Falon figured whatever stalked them would be easily spotted, for while natural concealment was next to impossible, so too, was the ability for an opposing force to catch them unawares.

"Double the watch. Everyone on guard until this threat makes itself known or passes," she ordered. "If what you say is correct, we hold the advantages and can prepare."

The Scarlet remained unsure. He admired humans for their optimistic perspective, misplaced as it was. The truth, his truth, was laced with fear. Whatever nightmare approached would test the limits of his convictions. He stared into Falon's eyes, seeing his concern reflected back. "That will not be enough."

"What more can I do? You cannot name this threat and we are besieged by nature and the Mordai. My list of options thins," she persisted. "We continue marching the quest forward. Can you scout ahead for any natural cover or concealment?"

"Leaving the boy's side now would not be prudent," Caestellom replied.

Falon gripped her reins tighter. "Just this once, I would like you to be a member of this team. We have so far left to go."

The plea was not lost on him, though the Scarlet was aloof to the depth of human emotions. Caestellom gripped his sword tighter and launched skyward. Dust and bits of stone sliced into Falon's lower legs. The ill feeling swirling in the pit of her stomach doubled.

They continued for the remainder of the day without delay or concern. It wasn't until nightfall, when Falon ordered a brief halt to rest their mounts, that trouble found them. Silent. Oppressive. The air around them suffocating to the point of darkened vision. Caestellom reacted first. Flames wreathed his open blade, driving back the shadows and framing his hulking form. The radiance of the flames transformed his armor with hellish reflections.

"What is it?" Falon asked.

An impossible mass of darkness formed in the center of camp. Beasts roared and screamed. A wagon flipped over, sending Meone flying into a stand of scrub brush and thorns. Falon drew her sidearm but failed to lock on a discernable target. The Scarlet's armored hand shoved her aside. Angel and darkness collided. Flames showered down. Each strike offered brief glimpses of the terror besetting them.

Formless, Waujulx was created from the nightmares of a million souls. Putrid fumes, poisonous to mortals, wafted from the immense bulk. One of the moorvaan reared back, blood streaming from mouth and nostrils. It fell dead a moment later. Caestellom swung harder, slicing chunks of shadow from an ancient foe. The flames intensified. Each blow the Scarlet landed only infuriated Waujulx. Caestellom was steadily driven back, away from the wagons. Away from the god king's essence.

The prefects gathered around Falon, unsure how to react. Unwitnessed, Falon's knees trembled. Whatever confidence she might have been developing, fled in the face of raw terror. It was that moment she realized the truth of her predicament. The coward's truth that every person carrying a weapon encounters during their life. The decision to break and run or stand and fight. Falon closed her eyes and prayed for guidance.

"Sergeant, what do we do?"

Her eyes snapped open. Do? How could any of them expect her to know how best to deal with this situation? Her mind reeled, threatening to succumb to shock. The man closest doubled over and vomited. Falon watched the Scarlet being pressed back.

"Cover Caestellom. If he falls we all die," she ordered and drew a bead.

The report thundered across the empty plains. She caught the frightened cry of a boy, Aldon, before it was drowned out by the roar of rifle fire. Waujulx spun, burning sensations burrowing deep within the rot of his flesh. The Scarlet was a familiar enemy, but the sting of the mortals' weapons was new. Shadows lashed out, slender tendrils reaching for prey. Too late to react, the prefects were taken off guard, even while reloading.

Falon cried out as first one, then another of her people were lifted in the air and strangled by shadow. Their flesh dried and withered. Uniforms decayed and fluttered away. Boots and rifles thumped into the ground, a heartbeat before their skeletons. The surviving prefects broke and ran. Falon, struggling to comprehend, stood fast and emptied her sidearm into what she thought was the beast's face. Waujulx lurched for her. Each step a monstrous crunching sound. Anger radiated from the emptiness of his eyes. She knew death had finally come.

Caestellom struck from behind. Flames ran down the side of Waujulx and into his rib cage. His left side collapsed, shadows coalescing on themselves. He shrank. Invigorated by the turn, the Scarlet pressed his advantage. Confused and taking fire again, Waujulx staggered back. So did Falon. She tripped over the dead moorvaan. Her pistol skittered away. Defenseless, she flipped to hands and knees and crawled away.

Waujulx screamed. A third prefect's eardrums burst in a spray of blood and brain matter. The flaming blade pushed through the beast's back, emerging just below the throat. Molten light ran down his chest. Falon's mind threatened to snap but she found the focus to reach for her pistol and reload.

Chaos erupted around them but being on the back of the wagon prevented Tula from seeing any of it. She heard the screams and what sounded like an explosion. Her heart thundered, as she struggled to find a weapon. Anything to help the others. The Mordai were vicious warriors and outnumbered the quest twofold. How they covered so much ground was a mystery she failed to understand. Tula was about to climb from the wagon when a hand clamped around her forearm.

"Tula, don't go out there," Aldon whimpered.

Unholy roars filled the darkening skies. Aldon joined them, echoing frustration and fears of a helpless god king buried deep in his soul. Tula's heart froze. Never in her life could she imagine a sound so mournful, so wrathful. She tried to move again.

"You'll die if you go out there. Just like the others," Aldon insisted. Tears streamed down his young face, though whether his or the god king's was unknown.

"I must," Tula said and jerked free. What greeted her was unlike anything her wildest dreams might conjure.

Instead of flanks of black clad Mordai soldiers sweeping through their position, she found the skeletal remains of a pair of prefects. Fires burned across the scrub brush. Meone struggled to rise from beside the overturned wagon. Caestellom battled with a monster of illogical proportions, only he understood. Tula's preconceived notions of the world shattered under the weight of impossibility. She stared as a handful of Mascantii charged the shadow monster. Their hammer like fists thundered down before the monster shifted.

Tendrils of noxious fumes and hatred curled around the Mascantii. Roars of pain turned to screams, as he was torn apart in a cloud of gore. Tula vomited. She wiped a string of saliva from her mouth and got her first glimpse at the monster's eyes. True fear filled her soul. She failed to see how they could defeat a creature so vast.

Caestellom's flaming sword chopped across the monster's neck. Shadow and flames melted the ground where they fell. The monster roared and swung back, knocking the Scarlet off his feet. Wings snapped out, arresting Caestellom's fall. He leapt skyward until the light from his sword was lost to the night. Thinking itself freed from the nuisance, the monster turned on Tula and advanced.

She fumbled for her pistol but her fingers refused to work. Inspired terror paralyzed her as she watched death stalking her. Tula wanted to shout, to scream, anything to show defiance. Her body rebelled. The end was only a few steps away. She thought she heard Aldon cry her name. Thoughts jumbled together until they became a wasted mass. A tear escaped her eye. Then the impossible happened.

Caestellom plunged down with speed and fury. His sword plunged down between the monster's shoulder blades and ripped down the spine before piercing the ground. Scarlet and monster collided. The spell broken, Tula scrambled away and watched as the monster was split in half. Caestellom slammed into the ground and was still. The monster melted, burrowing deep gouts in the ground, where nothing green would ever grow again.

Shadows lifted and the darkness coalesced around the quest dissipated. Night returned. Tula crawled to her feet and ran back to check on Aldon. Nothing else mattered. She found him where she left him. The fear in his eyes was gone, replaced by sadness.

"Do any yet live?" he asked in a voice not his own.

Tula replied, "Some. You are not Aldon."

"I am Omoraum Dala'gharis."

Golden light filled the wagon bed before extinguishing a moment later. Tula stiffened.

Aldon gestured to the battlefield. "Danger comes. Go."

She obeyed. Weapons filled her hands, as if eager to compensate for their earlier betrayal. Tula hurried to Falon's side. Caestellom was still on the ground and the rest of the expedition was either dead or scattered. Together, the women stared off into the night. Boots marched closer. They caught the glimmer of bare steel reflecting from the fires as ranks of Mordai soldiers came into view. Broken and understrength, there was nothing Tula or Falon could do.

PART THREE

QUANTUM OF THE SOUL

TWENTY-SIX

A time of change approached. The world, as the people of Ghendis Ghadanaban understood it, was forever altered by the course of recent events. The impossible occurred and the city reeled. Panic threatened the walls, even as a handful of brave heroes traveled deeper south to find a cure. War, held at bay by the power the god king commanded, encroached upon the walls. A world of secrets swirled around both, for how could any in the Heart Eternal know the trials of those men and women chosen to save the world?

"Hands up!" a gravelly voice commanded.

Soldiers rushed forward as Tula and Falon complied. Relieving the women of their weapons and securing the rest of the scene, the Mordai soldiers were efficient. Rough hands shoved the women to their knees, jerked their hands behind their heads. A ring surrounded the fallen Scarlet, for the winged warrior was only known to those in the Heart Eternal. Few foreigners knew more than rumor.

Tula watched a thin faced man approach. He tugged his riding gloves off and tucked them inside his belt. A pencil thin moustache accented his gaunt features. Grey tainting his hair. "I am Captain Harkne. You have led my soldiers on a foul journey. Tell me, why are you running? Do you not understand the importance of curfews?"

Neither replied. Falon managed a look of defiance.

The grin Harkne offered was predatory. "You are from Ghendis Ghadanaban. That much is evident. But why are you this far from home? And in the presence of one of those … things?" He gestured toward Caestellom.

"You have no right to detain us," Falon said. "Let us go now and we can forget this happened."

Harkne surveyed the scene. "Clearly you are in distress. What sort of protector would I be to allow you to continue without aid? Think what you will of the Mordai, but we are humanitarians at heart."

"I know your kind. Your heart comes at the end of a barrel," Falon snorted.

"I expected better, though I confess to not being surprised. The ignorance of your people has long been exploited among the kingdoms," Harkne said. He began to pace, hands clasped behind him. "My commanders have established orders to arrest any suspected insurgents. Unless you provide a suitable answer stating your true purpose, I will be forced to treat you as prisoners of war. An unenviable position, you understand."

"We are on the business of the Overseer of Ghendis Ghadanaban. You have no authority over any of us," Tula interjected. "Let us go now."

"Don't I? This kingdom has fallen far from the days of glory. What are you? I don't recognize the clothing," Harkne asked. "Some sort of mercenary no doubt."

"My business is my own." Tula fell silent. She'd said enough. Nothing else was going to sway the Mordai.

His eyebrow peaked. "Indeed. You may remain silent for now, but I promise you will all beg to tell your stories once our interrogators get you." He gestured his soldiers. "Get them on their feet. Collect any other survivors and prepare to move."

Dragged to her feet, Falon managed to catch a glimpse of several soldiers attempt to lift the fallen

Scarlet. She wished he would awaken, but the battle with the shadow demon had taken a toll. Rough hands shoved her toward their surviving wagon. Panic set in when she remembered Aldon. The boy remained undiscovered, though not for long once the Mordai began loading survivors aboard. Her sole remaining prefect climbed in the back. The Mascantii were rounded up and roped together. An unconscious Meone was dumped in the wagon without regard, leaving her and Tula.

They were a step away when the ground began vibrating. Soldiers looked about, confused. Weapons were raised but without a visible target. The Mordai were caught off guard, for they had believed they were the only military force in the area. Vibrations strengthened. Nervous stares echoed back into the night. Falon expected the worst. Another monster born from nightmares far imagined. The truth was much worse.

An armored creature emerged from the night. A behemoth, it rumbled closer. Weapons and antennas bristled like spines. The thunder of twin engines roared louder than the shadow monster, forcing several soldiers to drop their weapons and cover their ears. Falon and Tula watched, mouths agape, as this new nightmare manifested. Dust and debris kicked up beneath, dispersing clouds that billowed up both sides.

A hatch popped open from the top and an armored man emerged. Face concealed by a featureless visor, he stared down on the scene in silent judgment. The Mordai commander, furious and frightened at once, stepped between his soldiers and the intruders. His legs trembled, for this was unlike anything he'd ever encountered.

"What is the meaning of this? You are interfering with an official mission by the kingdom of Mordai. Leave now and we can forget your insolence."

The words, while meant to be stern, were delivered in trembling tones. Bright lights flooded the area. A voice, amplified by external speakers placed on the chassis, barked laughter. "I don't think so, pal. We don't care too much for you local soldiers, Molie or not."

Bristling at the insult, the Mordai commander cleared his throat. "*Mordai*."

"Like I said, I don't care. What's going on here?"

"This is a private matter that does not concern you," he replied. A hand covered his face, hoping to keep the light from blinding him further.

No one knew who fired first, or why. The first shot came from a nervous soldier. A flick ricocheting from the armored beast. The reply was a hundredfold. Lances from superheated energy weapons melted weapons and flesh. Mordai soldiers fell screaming. The slaughter was total and immediate. Haze spit from the barrels as the Mordai were cut down where they stood. Only when the last man fell did the lights fade, plunging the scene into raw darkness.

Falon fell to her knees and vomited. A severed hand fell free from her shoulder. Tears streamed down her grime smeared cheeks. The unthinkable had just happened. Her nightmare continued. Tula's soft hand clutched her. A gentle reminder that all was not lost. That there were some left in the world with basic human dignity.

"Why?" she muttered. Strings of saliva hung from her lips.

Tula exhaled the heavy breath she was sure she'd been holding since being captured. "I don't know, but it's not over yet."

They looked up at the sound of boots crunching across the space between them and the beast.

"Well, what do we have here?"

Heavy winds brought the storm up from the deep south. Lightning struck down in angry lances, accompanied by the violence of thunder rippling through the clouds. Pelting rains lashed man and beast too slow to find cover in time. Cold temperatures swept in behind, driving an uncomfortable chill across the small band of travelers. They were forced to stop before long, desperate to find any shelter possible.

Valir the Tongueless stood with arms folded across his chest. The burly northerner was drenched but showed little sign of discomfort. A child of the frozen steppe, Valir endured the harshest conditions on the planet before moving south on a trader caravan. His hair was pelted to his skull. His face grim. The others huddled in a small cave behind him.

He listened to their complaints. Their miseries. Once, when he still had a tongue, Valir would have joined them. It was a soldier's right to complain. A timeless tradition dating back to the first packs of roving mercenaries on campaign. There were times when he missed the banter and camaraderie of being on campaign, but the cushioned life of working for Hean made him soft in the wrong places. This storm was the catalyst necessary to reinvent himself. A savage moment threatening to release the bonds of his inner fire. Purpose was renewed.

"Any more rain and we'll be washed away."

Thunder cracked overhead, making Hean's retainers flinch. A second voiced, "That Tongueless will see us all brought to a bad end. Mark my words."

Valir stiffened, forcing them to lower their voices.

"Quiet fool. Man's got no tongue but his ears work fine."

"I don't care," the same man replied. "I'm tired of this pointless task. We've drug our asses halfway across the world and for what? Haven't seen hide nor hair of our quarry for days. They might have turned home already."

"Ain't up to us, idiot," a third man added. "We're getting paid to do a job. Best get it done, so we can get home. I don't know about you, but I need a good drink and a warm body in my bed."

"Hands don't count as bodies."

He pointed the small dagger in his hand at his peers. "Keep talking and you'll not need either. I'm just as done with this nonsense as he is. Got to be easier money out there."

Valir covered the distance between them in two heartbeats. The bright silver of his blade reflected firelight a moment before he struck through the aggressive man's neck. It took two swings before Valir managed to decapitate him. Head and a stream of blood rolled down among the others. The northerner gave them a stern look and whipped his sword again. Ropes of dark blood flew from the blade. He sheathed the weapon and returned to his vigil.

"You heard the man. We keep hunting."

The storm passed sometime during the night and the hunt resumed at dawn. Valir drove them with renewed urgency. Leagues swept by and with them rose a growing sensation of dread. Unable to express himself in words, Valir kept a hand on the rifle holstered across his saddle. At first there was nothing to give credence to the feeling. The landscape was mostly barren, an unforgiving expanse unfit for human habitation.

Then came the heavy tracks of numerous horse prints. Weighted. Valir recognized them as belonging to soldiers. Who remained unknown. Half a day later he spied the source of his dread. Bodies, or parts of several, littered a wide area. Horse and human. Swarms of flies danced among the flocks of vultures. A jackal or two darted in around the edges, hungry for a quick meal. Valir's lips drooped at the sound of one of his companions vomiting behind him.

"What could have done this?" another whispered.

Valir drew his rifle but sensed the need was passed. Whatever slaughtered these soldiers was gone. He caught a rag of fabric, black with silver piping. Mordai. He did not lament their demise, for the Mordai were renowned for their violent manners. What he saw was fewer would-be tyrants in the world. He kept riding into the center of the engagement area. His beast drew back, unwilling to step further. Disturbed, Valir slid from the saddle.

A massive ring of darkness inspired quiet panic. No life grew within the ring. The very earth appeared scorched. A ruined waste he doubted would ever recover. Valir resisted the urge to reach down and touch the blackened soil. Instead he turned his gaze on the distant mountains, certain his quarry was almost there. Should they gain the mountains, he doubted there was much of a chance of finding them. More complications he did not need.

Valir grunted and climbed back in the saddle. He pointed toward the mountains and continued riding. The others followed but their fears were inspired. So much death could only be a bad sign. A warning of darker events yet to come.

Battered and pushed to the point of breaking, the militiamen trudged south in search of their prey. Men and women of the hill tribes, accustomed to pride and strength of determination, who were unused to losing, rode with heads hung low. Too many friends lay forgotten in several fields far behind. The slaughter reaped by a hasty attack on government lines, into a host of artillery at point blank range, reduced their numbers to but a few score. Over one hundred and fifty friends would never share the warmth of fire or spread tales of valor again.

Delag took the brunt of the remaining anger. As leader of the warband, it was his responsibility to ensure his people survived, or at least died with honor. Neither happened the night the treacherous Hohn and his off-worlders led them into a trap. Deepfelt rivers of hatred outweighed any animosity his people cast upon him. Word had already gone back to Malach and the rebel command. While Delag had few doubts to the response, he wasn't willing to wait long enough for it to reach him. Revenge trumped every desire.

The shame felt from being almost obliterated clouded his mind. Hohn was wily and in possession of incomparable weapons. Not only did he lose Malach's strongest allies, he lost the firepower that might otherwise have won the war. Regardless of what happened next, Delag and his survivors would never be allowed home. A fact prompting him to send a runner with word that he had been killed in the battle with the government forces. Their fates were set, to be earned on the hard plains of Eleboran. He led them south to whatever destiny awaited.

One of the scouts charged back late in the afternoon. Fear and wonder crossed his features. When he spoke, it was stuttered and rushed. He gestured back the way he'd just come. "We … we've found something."

Delag, in no mood for riddles, snapped, "Speak plainly. What have you found?"

"I … I do not know," the scout said.

"Show me," Delag ordered.

He followed and came upon the handful of metal vehicles of alien design. Delag immediately assumed they belonged to Hohn's arsenal. The implications inspired renewed hope, be it fleeting. He had his men scour the vehicles in hopes of learning the secrets to make them move. With such creations under his power, Delag would shift the balance of power, not only in the kingdom, but among the tribes as well. He might even grow to rival the fabled god king of Ghendis Ghadanaban.

"Sir, they are dead," the scout reported.

"Impossible. We must find the traitors. They can get these carriages working," Delag insisted.

The militiamen exchanged dubious stares. There was only so much a man could endure before reaching the breaking point. They had been pushed every step of the journey down from the mountain. What had been meant as a simple task, devolved rapidly and with poisonous symptoms. Dissent brewed. Whispers of removing Delag and finding refuge far from the war spread during the lonely hours of the night.

Delag looked upon first the vehicles and then Falahn. They had known each other since childhood, often trading broken bones from rough play when their mothers kicked them out of the house. Never true friends, it was only chance that landed Delag in command. He wondered what life might have looked like if war had never come to the tribes. Dismissing the idea as childish, Delag walked away. The dream of becoming king fading with every step.

TWENTY-SEVEN

A row of half empty beakers filled with different colored liquids stretched across the worn and stained wooden table. Alchemic formulas left noxious fumes swirling around the rafters. All failures. No matter what Hean tried in his quest for immortality, it ended in failure. The empty bottle of wine, laying on its side with a few drops of the dark red juice dripping down to the floor, was testament to his frustration.

Hean leaned back in the well worn cushions of his bench, lost in drunken stupor. Stains peppered his tunic. Expensive by every standard, Hean lost interest. Memories of the events in Lady Duema's shop left him rattled. A hollowed out caricature of his former self. Life was most cruel indeed. He wanted to laugh but only tears came.

The knocking at the door thundered in his mind. "Whaa?"

Temius Thorn slinked in. He was a gaunt man with unenviable characteristics. Others thought him sinister. Hean found only a humble servant with private motivations. He glanced at the box made of bone shoved in the corner of a desk. "Forgive me for disturbing your … work, but the Mordai delegation has arrived."

"So?" Hean blinked rapidly but his vision remained blurred.

"So, they have been rumored to have masters in arcane arts," Temius said. "Arts that might be of great interest to you, should you decide to pull your head out of the bottle."

"I'll not be sssspoken to like that," Hean slurred.

Temius offered a wry grin. "Of course not, master. I found it prudent to inform you myself. The Mordai may be the answer to your unique dilemma."

Hean's head slumped and snores soon filled the room. Temius stared after the only man in the Heart Eternal willing to hire him, while knowing his dark past. He came to the city in hopes of escaping the monster lurking in his soul but found only oppression. Hean ignored it. Every man had potential. Pulling it out took acts of greatness few managed on their own. As with everything, Hean managed to turn Temius into something else. Something more dangerous.

"Perhaps," he whispered and left.

Hean emerged from his slumber with a foul taste on his tongue and pounding hammers in his head. A belch threatened to drop him to his knees, while arousing a fresh round of lament. He was a man given to his vices, though he seldom allowed himself to become as inebriated as last night. Desperate times, he rationalized.

Temius awaited in the main office. A pitcher of ice water sat on the serving table beside a plate of fresh fruit and cheese. The slender man stood with hands behind his back, eyes silently judging. Tight lines dangled beneath his eyes, lending the appearance of his flesh falling from his thin face.

"Good morning, Master Hean," he said. His voice invoked no deference. Hean may have employed him, but he was his own man.

Hean waved him off and barely managed to make it to his desk. A foul odor trailed behind. "It's too early for nonsense, Temius."

"If you insist. I have taken the liberty of scheduling a meeting with the Mordai ambassador later today."

Hean's eyebrow arched. "Eh? Mordai?"

"Yes, sir," Temius lied. "You requested I do so last night when you were in the lab. You expressed interest in their alchemist corps. Something about them holding the key to your situation."

Dim light brightened behind his red laced eyes. Hean grasped the genius of the idea and slapped a fleshy palm on the desk—to his immediate regret. "Good. Good. Have them brought straight in. I will see them here. This could be it, Temius. An end to years of searching. Go, and have the servants fetch clean clothes and draw me a bath. One can hardly meet the ambassador to an important kingdom while stinking like a swine."

Temius bowed, leaving a tired man to convince himself that all was transpiring according to plan.

"I've waited long enough, Merrick."

Merrick took another bite from the green apple. A trickle of juice rolled down his chin. "You're not ready. The Guild will slaughter you, and me, with little effort."

Abbas scowled. "Nonsense. How much longer can I expect to remain in this room? Guild hunters already scour the city looking for me. The Crow may be a safe haven but not even Eamon can keep them from looking forever. I'm not safe here."

Merrick laughed. "You're not safe anywhere! Do you have any idea how many times I've been forced to avoid Guild members? You've become a stain on their credibility. They can't have that. The only safety you might have is leaving the city and never returning."

"I don't run from fights," Abbas replied.

He paced the room. Knuckles cracked. Nerves overpowering emotions. The longer he was secluded, the more Abbas felt the world constrict. Freedom beckoned, but with an unknown field of obstacles blocking the way, was almost impossible to gain. His mind was choked with interlocking plans. All led back to the Guild.

"Going to war with the Guild is suicide," Merrick cautioned after seeing the madness enter his friend's eyes. "We'll be slaughtered."

"Not without carving a hole in their ranks."

"That's the dumbest thing you've said yet. Neither of us have any idea how many members are in the Guild," Merrick protested.

Abbas halted and smiled. "No, but I know someone who might."

"Why do I think you're about to get me killed?"

He slapped Merrick on the shoulder. "No reward without risk, my friend. Come on. We have plans to make."

They entered the common room, only after verifying it was all but empty. Ancient Relghel sat at his usual table, prompting Abbas to wonder how old the man was and if he ever left. Curious as it was, that was a mystery for another time. The assassin caught Baradoon's attention, gesturing the big man over.

"You are very pale," Baradoon announced after sitting.

Abbas ignored the concern. "My friend. I think the time has come."

"Good. We get to crack heads."

Merrick groaned. He didn't know a soul capable of besting Baradoon in a fair fight, but they were about to take on an entire guild of professional murderers. Only a fool found joy in such matters.

"Not just yet, Baradoon," Abbas cautioned. He cast a glance toward Relghel. If the old man overheard anything, he didn't show it. "There's much groundwork we need to put in place first."

Baradoon pouted. "You said we was going to beat them at their game. You promised, Abbas."

"We are, just not quite yet. There is still much needing to be done before we can wage all out war against a powerful guild," Abbas tried calming him. Thoughts of the big man running amuck chilled his blood. They were already on dangerous ground, Baradoon might prove the catalyst to a much greater conflict.

Merrick added, "Listen to him, friend. We want revenge, but we need to be smart about it. Anything less and it's all our heads for the hangman."

Baradoon ran a thick finger across his throat, as if mimicking the sensation of being strangled. His confused look echoed the chaos tunneling through his thoughts. Not one for deep thinking, Baradoon preferred the simple life void of hard choices. Working with Eamon offered just that.

He ran the same finger up to his mouth and tickled the whiskers growing around the corner of his lips. "If we aren't going to start killing, what are we going to do? Eamon won't let me leave for long."

Abbas stiffened. "Does Eamon know?"

Baradoon shook his head. Gangly strings of hair swept across his forehead. "No. Only that I am helping you."

Merrick and Abbas exchanged dubious looks. The more people who knew what they intended, the more dangerous it became for everyone. Eamon Brisk was a standup man with a stellar reputation but even he wasn't above scrutiny when the Prefecture got involved. That sense of independence presented unwanted challenges, for all of Abbas's carefully laid plans were for naught if Eamon so much as muttered his name.

"What did you tell him, Baradoon?" Merrick asked.

"Nothing really."

Abbas's mouth went dry. "Baradoon?"

The soft scrap of a boot shifting resonated across the empty room. Baradoon hung his head, suddenly embarrassed by the admission. "Aw, it's just Eamon. He won't say nothing. I said that we was going to get revenge on the people who did you wrong. That's all. I promise."

"Are you certain?" Merrick asked.

The big man nodded.

Abbas reached across to place his hand atop Baradoon's. "You did good, friend. Go back to your job. We'll summon you when it's time." He waited until Baradoon was out of range before muttering, "That man is going to get us both killed."

Merrick couldn't have agreed more.

Due to his immense size and popularity among much of the population, Baradoon stuck out wherever he went. Normally, Abbas viewed such qualities as a drawback, but the big man provided just enough distraction no one noticed the assassin and his friend following a short distance behind. The market was packed. Hundreds of people hurrying to get supplies before tensions boiled over. All providing the perfect cover for what Abbas had in mind.

The aroma of spiced meats inspired growling stomachs. Abbas hadn't eaten since the night prior and was regretting the decision. He still hadn't recovered all his strength but getting out of the cloying room in the White Crow was what he needed. There was freedom under open skies, unparalleled by any other experience during his limited lifetime. Every smell, every sound exhilarated him.

Yet, with the reward of freedom, came danger. Any passerby might be an agent of the guild. A killer waiting to strike. Abbas resisted the urge to devolve to lament and forced each foot ahead of the next. He and Merrick spread out across the wide avenue. Each did their best to keep Baradoon in sight. Not an impossible task but one laden with challenges due to the immensity of the midday crowds.

The big man carved a path through the crowds like a knife cleaving butter. Many knew him and traded pleasantries. Others stepped aside for fear of being remembered. Baradoon commanded the scene wherever he went. That presence was the key factor Abbas hinged his plan on. They pushed deeper into the market.

Hawkers of brightly colored silk scarves and exotic jade and lapis from faraway lands blocked his progress with offers of gentle riches. He lost sight of Baradoon. Abbas pushed the merchants aside and hurried forward. Curses and obscene gestures chased him. He found Merrick waiting at the end of the block by a long empty well.

"Where did he go?" Abbas shouted.

"I don't know. I lost him when a crowd of caravans went by," Merrick answered. He continued scanning the crowds. "We'll never find him in this mess."

"There are only so many places a man his size can disappear. Come on."

They moved faster, ignoring all pretense of subterfuge in favor of speed. Crowds began thinning, giving them a better line of sight. A pair of prefects lurked nearby but appeared oblivious to the subtle dramas unfolding among the throngs of shoppers. Abbas ignored them and moved with intent. His eyes flitted across every alley and merchant stall, while his heart began to thunder in his chest.

Merrick slapped a hand on Abbas's arm. "Over there."

Crossing the street, they came upon a scene that sickened both. Abbas felt his plans unravel. Any hope of getting to the Guild began to fade. Baradoon stood over a crumpled form, fists clenched. He turned and gave them an apologetic stare, as if to suggest he knew he had done wrong. Abbas stopped in midstride, mouth agape. Merrick rushed to the fallen figure.

"Baradoon, what did you do?" Abbas whispered.

"She didn't want to come with me. I didn't mean to. I swear," Baradoon pleaded. "I only hit her once."

"She's alive," Merrick announced. "I don't know how. The side of her head is already swelling. She might not make it."

Baradoon perked up at the diagnosis. "See, I done good! We captured Ninean Foul."

Abbas stared at Ninean. Dread filled his heart. *At what cost?* "We need to get her off the streets before the prefects stick their noses here."

Ninean hefted on Baradoon's broad shoulders, the trio stole back to their room in the White Crow's cellars. The first part of the plan was complete, leaving Abbas at a loss for which direction to move next. No doubt the Guild was not going to give him much time.

TWENTY-EIGHT

Tega Ig stood with arms folded across his chest. A look of disdain soured his face. Months of preparations and he felt none of it was enough. Every corner and shadow he looked at presented new challenges. Gaping holes in what he once assumed was a cemented defense plan. Word of the waylaid Uruth delegation ruined it all. Assassinations and attacks were preventable, given appropriate intelligence. His spies scoured the undercity, even as the bulk of his forces sealed off the ambassadorial district where the peace conference was taking place.

Every precaution undertaken since the conference was announced should have calmed his nerves, for he was a consummate perfectionist. Ghendis Ghadanaban should have been a compliant, peaceful city. His instincts screamed otherwise. *What am I missing*? The question haunted him. Tega strode through the arched halls, a storm among men. He wound up where he always did when lost to brooding.

Banners of each kingdom were hung from ceiling to floor in the main conference hall. A round table, specifically created for the event by artisans from western Eleboran, was brought in sections and assembled in the center of a sea of black swirled marble tiles. Braziers were established to ensure every part of the room was lit in the event of talks lasting deep in the night. Banquet tables were positioned against the far wall and filled with fruits and glasses for water. Other perishables would come later, when opening ceremonies were complete. Flowers decorated the room, though why, was lost on him.

He found Larris directing a host of laborers placing chairs and other menial items around the room.

She seemed poised, calm under pressure. Tega envied her. Some people appeared immune to the torments of leadership. Puffing out the breath caught in his throat, Tega unfolded his arms and attended her. Few in the Heart Eternal were as dedicated and seamless as she.

"Good morning, Tega. I trust all is proceeding well with the security plan?" she asked. Her gilded voice was soothing enough to ease his troubled mind, if for a moment only.

"Not as well as I would like," Tega replied. "Refugee caravans continue to fill the city. Without more prefects, there is no way to ensure they come with fair intent. Any number of malcontents and subversives could lurk among them."

"A problem for another time," Larris said. "We must focus on the matter before us. Mordai has come. Uruth is reported to be destroyed, and Hyborlad is expected to arrive by nightfall."

"Getting them through the city unopposed is the issue. We have more refugees than anticipated. They choke the outer neighborhoods and block many of the main avenues." Tega frowned. "I will not trust the alleys to our guests' safety. Not with increased reports of the undead and other unsavory deeds arising."

Larris dismissed the others with a wave. "Has there been any additional word on the matter you came to me with?"

"How does one confront the Lord of the Scarlet without jeopardizing one's own neck?" Tega snorted. "Verian is an inarguable disciplinarian."

"He is also subject to the laws of this city," Larris countered. "Verian has been among us far longer that you or I have drawn breath. His honor should be above reproach."

"Are you willing to bring the matter to his attention?"

Her timid smile said enough. "My dear friend, I would not presume to supersede your authority in this matter. The security of Ghendis Ghadanaban is in your realm. I have every confidence in your ability to handle this, both discreetly and efficiently."

"Ever the stateswoman, Larris," Tega lied. "When can we expect to hear from Uruth? I do not like feeling powerless."

"I fear the government may delay our guests longer. Word is a new offensive is beginning soon. We may be further cut off."

Images of massed armies filling the plains before marching into the mountains inspired awe in him, for Tega always imagined himself a military man at heart. The kingdom already stood on the brink of total collapse. Another serious campaign might push it the rest of the way. Ghendis Ghadanaban would truly be alone then. A dying bastion among a sea of inhumanity.

"Just what we needed," Tega snorted. "Where is Sandis?"

"I haven't seen him yet. Odd, considering the conference is almost ready to start."

"He should be here coordinating with the other religious sects attending."

"I'm sure he is mired in endless spiritual matters," she replied.

The loss of the god king shook their foundations, perhaps Sandis's most of all. The office of the Prophets was cast in chaos. No word had reached them yet of the Rhorrmere quest. Doubters already suggested failure. How much longer could the city last before its iron spine snapped?

"There is nothing to be done for that. I will leave you to your ... decorating. Expect increased security details in position by the end of the day," Tega said.

"Where are you going, Tega?"

He started walking off. "To see our winged friend."

The time for pleasantries was ended.

The sun was low on the western horizon. The day's heat began to fade, bringing relief to those unfortunate enough to be outside all day. Sandis found little comfort in the trivial. Internal hunger for power kept him going, when all else dwindled. That primal desire stripped him of better judgment. He'd grown careless of late. The arrival of the Mordai delegation prompted him to accelerate an already fragile timeline. Tranquility was replaced with madness.

He paced, ignoring the beauty of a flight of white ibis lifting away from one of the larger forested parks to the east. There had been a time when the simplicity of life entertained him. A time for gazing into the future with hopes and dreams. Sandis was old now. His ways set. The moment for luxuries and simplistic desires had passed.

Returning to his study, Sandis laid eyes on the small envelope placed in the center of his otherwise clear desk. An envelope not there when he went to the balcony. Suspicious, he scanned the rest of his quarters and offices for sign of intrusion, even while knowing there would be none. Years of planning were now condensed into days. He felt as if he was not ready for the final stage of the great change to come. Sandis sat and opened the envelope.

He withdrew the small parchment contained within. Tired eyes scanned each word. He should have been surprised with the directness of it all, but so much was occurring, he seldom found interest in much. This presented a new set of challenges. A hastening of the timeline. Sandis snatched a match and burned the letter. There could be no evidence.

The walk across his office felt longer than normal. He despised working with the Mordai alchemists. Their arts were unnatural and against most of what man stood for. They were also, in his estimation, necessary for the advancement of his plans. Sandis opened the secret room built within the walls of his private chambers. Placing the amber stone on the woman's throat, he waited. Pale light soon poured out of her hollow eyes.

"The time is fast approaching. Is your city prepared?"

No matter how many times he endured the communication medium, Sandis could never get used to it. The abhorrent use of life went against everything he stood for. A travesty of what should have been.

"Vizier," he began. "The god king is removed and no legitimate investigation into the murder has begun. Refugee streams choke the streets, preventing the Prefecture from adequately securing the city."

"My agents have already arrived. Imperator Thrakus has been given leave to begin the next phase of this operation," the Vizier said.

Sandis blanched at how the human subject's mouth hung open, while a foreign voice burst from his throat. The promise of such fate reminded him of his place, should he not fulfill his end of the arrangements.

Sandis bobbed his head. "All is prepared. The peace conference begins in two days. Ghendis Ghadanaban will be open for your forces shortly after."

"Do not fail me, First Prophet. The future of many kingdoms rests upon your shoulders."

The light faded. The room went silent. Sandis closed the door and wondered if he had made the wrong bargain after all.

Capran Edeus gazed upon the famed Heart Eternal with awe, and more than a little mistrust. This was his first time viewing the jewel of the free world. What should have been inspiring was marred by the obvious signs of warfare ringing the outer walls. How many countless men and women languished within, while their kingdom burned down around them? A child of the open plains, Capran already felt the first trappings of claustrophobia awakening.

His midnight dark skin absorbed the fading sunlight, producing a thin sheen of sweat. Capran had spent a lifetime under oppressive heat far to the south. This northern weather paled in comparison, producing lesser people. Golden rings hung from his ears and were evenly spaced across his lower lip. Calculating eyes searched for signs of treachery, for word of the fate that had befallen the Uruth delegation had already reached him.

Capran was determined not to be caught off guard. His people were a warrior race, honed and developed over centuries. That pride of being defined him. Shoulders squared, back firm, Capran walked with his chest out and his chin defying those who might otherwise present a threat. The light fabric of his linen robes cooled him, though he preferred the boiled leather plate armor of his tribe and the wickedly curved blade that had slit a hundred throats.

Selection as Hyborlad's delegate was no coincidence. He was the second son of the king. The best warrior of his generation. Capran served in the Hyborlad Sappers, a dangerous unit of men and women with little regard for personal safety, so long as the mission was accomplished. Losses were higher than any of the regular army units. He took great pride in knowing his unit was considered the premier unit of the kingdom. Masters of the open field, Capran felt cold at the sight of so many walls. Man was not created to live in cages.

"Safri, signal our arrival," he called.

The younger Safri looked to his older brother. "But they will surely have spotted us by now. Would not doing so be pointless?"

Capran concealed his grin. Years apart, he was pleased with his brother's developing critical thinking skills. "Perhaps, but we are of Hyborlad. All who witness us should know the glory of our arrival. Sound the call."

"Yes, my *ubrik*," Safri replied, using their native word for captain.

Placing the twisted horn of the pale gazelle to his lips, Safri took a deep breath and blew. The baleful howl echoed across the final hundred meters to the Heart Eternal. Those within hearing stopped to see what produced such an alien sound. Some hurried within the gates, for the sight of a hundred or more fearsome warriors inspired fear. Capran's snarl was lustful, inspired by the thrill of marching to battle only that sound elicited.

Ghendis Ghadanaban was no conquest, however, and it took great willpower to keep from calculating how best to infiltrate the city and topple the government. He did not deny such thoughts lurked deep in his heart, for he longed for the ultimate challenge. A chance to prove his worth against the best in the world. Breaking into a wide smile, Capran whistled and gestured his delegation forward. Glory awaited.

The warriors of Hyborlad took up a traditional chant as they closed on the city. A careless person might have thought war had finally come to the sandstone walls. Those who knew better, braced for the impact of so many various entities. Perhaps war had come after all.

TWENTY-NINE

The armored personnel carrier rumbled on. Hohn rode in the commander's hatch. Helmetless, he took in the unadulterated sights around. A veteran of a dozen campaigns on as many worlds, he cared little for the local flora and fauna. Hohn was a troubled man, more so now that he'd agreed to take on a handful of refugees. The complications they presented suggested great cost to his small ten man squad, if they were going to find a way back to the fleet.

Kilometers sped by without change. He was scarcely surprised everything in sight looked the same. There was little this part of the world had to offer, whether in shelter or natural resources capable of sustaining life. Such concerns might have been an issue, if not for the good fortune of finding the carrier, aptly named *Beast* by the others. The carrier had more armor than any weapon of war he had come across and the firepower equivalent to an entire battalion. Nothing in Eleboran compared. *So why aren't I content?*

The question haunted him. Not a strong strategist, Hohn was a dedicated trigger puller. His platoon appreciated him for keeping them alive, but little else. They were most likely all dead and he was stranded with a handful of soldiers he was still trying to get used to. Only Tine provided the stability he required to keep them a cohesive fighting unit. An admirable feat, considering two of the squad had only fired their weapons in basic training before crashing here.

Given their current circumstance, Hohn figured they were in good position to ride away from the nightmare Eleboran had been and work on getting rescued. At least until they stumbled across the Mordai patrol and their new guests. Killing those soldiers sat ill with him, for it was a complete slaughter, undeserving of a warrior's honor code. Which brought him to his next, in a seemingly endless string, of problems. What to do with the people in the cargo hold. Not to mention the oversized winged freak unconscious on the deck.

The universe was vast, but he had yet to come across people with the natural ability to fly. The two women in charge were polar opposites who happened to share a bond born from duress. One was military, or so he assumed. The other left him puzzled and feeling dirty. All the more reason to remain in the cupola until he got his thoughts right. A feat nowhere near fruition.

The *Beast* rumbled on.

"We need to talk."

Falon shifted her gaze to Tula. Both women were caught off guard by the directness of the veteran standing before them. They followed him down the back ramp, careful not to step on the unconscious Caestellom on the way. Daylight was fading but it still took a moment for their eyes to adjust from the artificial interior light. The carrier was parked beside a stand of white palms, whose trunks were no bigger than a handspan wide. Mountains loomed in the near horizon. Their final destination.

"Ladies, let me properly introduce myself. I'm Hohn, sergeant of this bunch of misfits. You'll get to know the others providing you convince me to keep you aboard," he said. Hohn pointed at Falon. "You are?"

"Sergeant Falon Ruel. I am a prefect in Ghendis Ghadanaban," Falon answered. He cut her off when she made to continue.

"And you?"

Tula glared at him, defiantly crossing her arms. "Tula Gish."

He knew she was going to prove problematic. "What do you do, Tula Gish? You don't dress or act like her. Some sort of paramilitary I'm guessing."

Tula cocked her head, the term unfamiliar. "I am a Reclamator."

"You say that like it means something to me," Hohn rolled his eyes. "Let me make my position crystal clear to you both. My squad and me, we're not from this world. We were coming back from campaign when our fleet was ambushed. The ship we were on was destroyed and we crash landed on your lovely world. We're tired and want to go home. You are keeping us from doing that. Give me a good reason why."

"I belong to a guild that hunts the undead," Tula supplied. "We are a special kind of people under our own authority."

Hohn's grin stretched from ear to ear. "I like an independent spirit, but I'm still not convinced about either of you. Why were you out in the middle of nowhere? It's a long way from your city."

"Our business is our own," Falon said. The steel in her voice suggested this was nonnegotiable.

"Way I see it, you can get your ass off of my carrier right here and we part ways unless you decide to cooperate," Hohn fired back. "We camp here tonight. You and your people can sleep inside or out. I don't care which. Come dawn you either stay or go. It makes no difference to me."

He turned away, leaving them to their inevitable debate. A boot landed on the ramp when he was called back.

Got you. "Yes?"

Falon cleared her throat. Her eyes twisted in agony, from losing so many of the expedition entrusted to her and from having to seek assistance from foreigners. "I will not tell you all of what we seek, but you are entitled to know the basics. We are commissioned by the Overseer and First Prophet to bring the boy to those mountains. It is no secret the god king was slain. We are attempting to remedy that. The Mordai patrol had been tracking us for several days. They only caught us unawares after we were ambushed by a creature of shadow and death."

"A bit melodramatic, don't you think?" Hohn asked. His time on planet suggested nothing of the sort.

Tula stepped in. "I wish that were so. We were attacked by a nightmare. It killed over half of our expedition before Caestellom delivered the death blow."

"You mean the big winged fella taking up a good chunk of the deck?" he asked.

"Yes. He is a sworn protector of the god kings," Falon answered.

Hohn found the fact interesting, but little else. Until the bigger man woke, he was just luggage. "Even if I wanted to believe that, why should some monster come after you? What secrets aren't you telling?"

"I told you I would not offer up everything," Falon stood her ground.

"Fair enough," Hohn said. "This monster, do you suppose there's more lurking around?"

"Would you like the honest answer or the one that will allow you to sleep better tonight?" Tula asked.

The wind picked up just then, producing a soft howl as it rolled across the endless leagues of scrub brush and stone. Goose flesh tickled his neck and arms. Hohn's instincts made him scan the area for threats.

"I suppose you should sleep inside," he muttered without taking his eyes off the growing darkness.

Neither woman disagreed.

The storm rolled in sometime later with fury. Hail pelted the armor as winds rocked the *Beast*. Stabilizers and sound dampeners muffled most of the assault. Dull orange lights bathed the interior, suddenly less spacious with the additional personnel. Space was cleared for the four surviving humans and four Mascantii servants. Built in stoves cooked rations salvaged from the wrecked wagons.

The soldiers stared at their guests, openly wondering what could have driven them to such lengths of desperation. No one made any effort to speak to the other group. Not yet. Tine gave the sleeping giant another look before heading to the command compartment with a mug of steaming soup. He handed it to a welcoming Hohn and settled into the empty chair beside him.

"This is cozy," he said, as Hohn slurped a mouthful.

"What do you make of it?"

Tine clasped his hands behind his head and leaned back. "Honestly? I don't know. They were in a tight spot for sure, but who's to say their story is true? For all we know, they are bandits looking to slit our throats the moment we relax."

Hohn sighed. "You bring a certain happiness to this madness, Corporal."

"I do what I can," Tine replied. "Believe it or not, the only one who puts me on guard is the boy. There's something not right about him."

"Agreed, but he's part of their crew and he is just a boy," Hohn said. "I've killed plenty of people during my time in service but never a child." Leastwise not one who wasn't trying to kill me first. He drank more. Bland, but rich in nutrients, as only an army meal could be, the soup reminded him of drying blood.

Their journey was supposed to get easier after breaking ties with the militia, not more complicated. He had no idea what a god king was or why it was so important, but conviction bled through each woman's words. Hohn suspected everything revolved around the winged man and the boy, though why, he still was not sure.

"What's our next move?" Tine asked. He was as eager to get home as any of them, having grown tired of the endless conflict and political positioning they encountered in every corner of Eleboran.

"That's up to them," Hohn gestured to the main hold. We'll see what happens in the morning. I want the usual rotation tonight, plus a second watching the hold. No unnecessary chances, Tine."

"You got it, Sergeant."

They had come too far for basic mistakes. None of the new people showed any signs of hostility; if anything, they were shell shocked from the previous day's events. That did not mean treachery was negated. He settled in for the long night. Tomorrow would see what truths the survivors offered.

Falon waited for Hohn to leave the main cargo hold before sidling close to Tula. The Reclamator had her head back in the webbing of her seat, her eyes closed. Exhaustion finally overtook them. Events of the past few days, combined with the sudden loss of adrenalin, robbed them of strength.

Falon stared at Tula for a moment. Her initial feelings toward the Reclamator were softened. Admitting they were not that different was a big step for her. The quest was changed and on the verge of disaster. Falon reluctantly decided they needed to work together, at least until parting ways with the foreign soldiers, if there was any hope of getting Aldon to Rhorrmere.

"What?" Tula asked without opening her eyes.

Falon jerked in surprise. Recovering, she leaned close and whispered, "What do you think about him?"

An eye popped open. "The soldier? I don't know yet. I get the impression he is willing to help but not at any cost to his people. Can't blame him. Who in their right mind would want to tangle with the nightmare we just faced?"

"Do you think we can trust him?" Falon's reservations stemmed from the almost flippant attitude Hohn displayed. Her knowledge of the civil war was limited by Ghendis Ghadanaban's neutral position, but she had no love for the mountain tribes and their often bloodthirsty militias.

Tula stirred, wiping her eyes clear. "Until we can't. He seems like a man who just wants to go home. What do you think?"

"I think we must trust to ourselves first," Falon replied after a pause. "Getting the boy to the mountains is imperative."

Tula glanced over to the sleeping Aldon. Her heart wept for the situation thrust upon him. She tried, and failed, to imagine being cast in the center of times without any choice. "We can't let Hohn know the truth."

"No, we can't," Falon agreed.

The chance of Hohn selling them out once he learned the truth of their quest remained viable, despite his assurances of neutrality. Falon's experience outside of the city suggested there was no such thing. Trust shouldn't be given away without trial and the soldiers had yet to do more than slaughter an enemy element.

The only thing Falon knew was Aldon was the key to the future. She had no idea what was going to happen to the boy once they reached Rhorrmere, but a competent guess suggested nothing pleasant. The future of their city and perhaps the world rested in his fate. She did not envy him. Falon decided to take Tula's lead and get some sleep. There was time enough for trouble when the sun rose.

"Do you think we're going to make it?" Tula asked.

The softness of her voice betrayed the weakness she felt. Falon exhaled. "I don't want to answer that. Not yet."

Razazel marched across the face of the world as he had once done at the beginning of time. A god in his own right, he bore no equal. He did not sleep. Did not rest. Every step brought him closer to his ultimate goal. The Heart Eternal was his prize. A gift long denied him by the cursed line of god kings and their winged protectors. Pure hatred kept him alive after so many millennia. Nearly fifty thousand years passed since he last attempted to usurp the city. So long, few remembered his name.

Razazel long desired to rule the Heart Eternal, for it was the one link to raw immortality still in existence. The others were gone, lost in a forgotten war not long after the founding of the world. He cared not. Failure dogged him, even during his extended internment. But the god kings were ended, and his time was at last at hand. Murderous intent drove him on. Ever forward to that once unobtainable goal.

Lightning struck down from the empty sky, bursting upon his chest and driving him to his knees. Razazel screamed. It was a primordial sound not heard in a long, long time. Fire filled his eyes, spilling tears of molten lava. Smoke poured from his mouth and nostrils when he placed a massive palm on the cracked earth.

He immediately knew what happened. Waujulx was dead. Somehow killed by those he was sent to hunt. The how and why were unimportant. His plans were altered but not ready for abandonment just yet. One of the Orpheliac, his guardians, was dead. Two others remained. Saiatuterum was en route to Rhorrmere, a failsafe should the unthinkable occur. The third remained hidden and he feared dead.

Time now opposed him. The irony was not lost, for time was the worst prison of all. He rose on shaky legs and forced each step. Ghendis Ghadanaban was still far away and it would take all the strength he had to reach it and bring the world to its knees. Waujulx would be avenged in the blood of every man, woman, and child in the Heart Eternal.

THIRTY

The *Beast* rolled on. Despite being rigged with multiple solar powered auxiliary batteries, Hohn decided to move only during the day, giving the damaged carrier's engine core time to recover from the long trek. They moved faster than any horse or moorvaan, but it felt slow to the passengers, now their lives were slowed to near normal pace. The hotter the day grew, the more they began to notice the ground gradually slope upward.

Falon and Tula took advantage of the opportunity to ride atop the main turret behind the commander's cupola. Hohn sat beside them, casually scanning their surroundings, while attempting conversation. His time among the natives offered glimpses into their society and it was nothing he wanted to be part of. These two women, however, intrigued him, if for no other reason than the fact they were keeping secrets.

"How much further do you need to go?" he asked.

Falon answered first, hoping to keep Tula from engaging further. The relationship she shared with Aldon might prove their undoing, if Hohn pressed too hard. "That's part of the problem. Our unconscious friend was supposed to take over once we reached the base of those mountains."

"Doesn't appear like he's going to be doing that soon," Hohn replied.

They used the *Beast's* medical kits to examine Caestellom but to no avail. No remedy, indigenous or alien, had any positive effect. The Scarlet lay on the deck, unconscious and near death.

Hohn decided to press. "What's so important about him? Other than the fact he has wings."

"We'd rather not discuss that," she smiled in warning.

"Of course, you don't. That's why I asked," he smiled back. "Look, we can do this the easy way or the hard. Makes no difference to me. I'm tired of this krakking world and ready to go home. I presented you a choice last night. Time for you to live up to your end of it, or I drop you right here and say goodbye."

Falon's eyes narrowed. She was unaccustomed to being addressed in such a crass manner. "We are the same rank. I would appreciate that respect."

Her voice carried a low growl not lost on Hohn. He pushed her deliberately in an attempt at seeing how much she could stand before punching back. The one lesson learned on this world was life never went the way one thought it would. Strength was required in the wild places. The other option was far less desirable.

"Fair enough. You've earned that much, *Sergeant*. Can we stop playing games and get on with it?" Hohn asked. "The big winged fella is a problem of his own, but as long as he doesn't wake up wanting to kill everything he sees, we should be fine."

"I can't vouch for that," Falon said. Truthfully, she remained unsure if the Scarlet would awaken. "I will do my best to ensure he complies, however."

Hohn rubbed the grey stubble on his jaw. How long had it been since he last shaved? "How so?"

"We have an insurance policy in place," she replied, and immediately regretted it. At her side, Tula remained stoic.

"More secrets. How are we supposed to trust one another? I already saved your asses from some nasty folks. The least you can do is shoot me straight."

"This is a complicated matter, Hohn," she answered. "Know that we must reach those mountains and somehow find a way to wake our winged friend. What happens after that is beyond any of us."

"You are a lady of few answers that are worth a krak," Hohn snorted.

"Some answers remain to be learned."

He paused to take in a flock of geese traveling south. Feathers drifted down like rain. "Funny, isn't it? How violence can grip a land in a stranglehold but there is nothing up there suggesting so. You don't want to talk, fine. I get that. Let me tell you what I know."

The women tensed.

"My people and I saved you from imprisonment at best. Seeing all of you makes sense to me except for one. The boy. Why would he be accompanying you on a dangerous mission far from home? He's the odd shaped dice that don't roll right." Hohn stared harder, hoping to find any sign of them cracking. "Too old to be a son and not enough to be a soldier. Something tells me he is the key to all you're doing."

"He's just a boy," Tula broke in. "Leave him out of it."

Hohn leaned back and broke into laughter. Raw, pure. "I thought so. How about I go down and ask him a few questions. Might be he has a little more to say, and from a different point of view."

Tula's fists and jaw clenched. Rage contorted her face and it took all her strength to keep from launching at him. Falon reacted differently. Proud shoulders of defiance slumped, the energy lost. It became clear to her that no help was coming, and they would be left stranded with little or no possibility of success, unless one of them trusted the other.

"Very well," she said with a measured voice. "What do you know of the god kings of Ghendis Ghadanaban?"

The storm continued with hateful fury. Heavy winds knocked down trees and created mudslides from some of the taller peaks. Rains kept the combined force trapped within the *Beast* for two days without let up. Hohn ordered the carrier's refresher off limits, forcing everyone—himself included—to use the latrine outside. They had enough food, water, and warmth for the time being but some lines had to be drawn. Falon seconded him with great reluctance. Complaints increased as the storm continued.

Prophet Meone remained apart from the others. His confidence was gone. His faith shaken by the appearance of the dread creature. All he once stood for was proving to be a lie. The god king was murdered and instead of searching for the killer, the lead factions in the city were focused on a peace conference and trying to find resurrection in Rhorrmere. None of it made sense to his young mind.

He wanted to speak with Falon numerous times but the opportunity never presented itself. Natural timidity prevented him from speaking his mind. It was one in a long list of quiet laments Meone lived with. Why he was selected to join the quest was lost on him. Pushed to the point of breaking, he missed the sanctity of his former office and the limited administrative duties he was responsible for. Life in the field was not for him.

It took all the courage he could muster to strike a conversation with the foreign soldiers' second in command. So alien, so foreign. Meone found it difficult to believe how any man might be so closely akin to a lizard, yet here he stood before him. Tine, for his part, was used to the gawking by locals.

"Excuse me," Meone chirped.

Tine swiveled around in the bucket chair. He'd been monitoring weapons stocks and energy reserves. A boring job by any standard. The interruption was welcomed, if awkward. "Yes?"

"Where are you from?" Meone asked.

Tine avoided rolling his eyes. The question was one most, if not all, of the soldiers was used to taking. "Are you familiar with the Galmentu Segmentum?"

Meone shook his head. The words almost as alien as Tine. "What continent is it on?"

"Nowhere near here. What's your deal? Are you religious caste?" Tine asked.

"I am a prophet for the god king," Meone replied.

"No idea what that means. Most of these folks don't participate in religion. Too many gods and conflicts. Why are you with these others? I wouldn't have pegged you as a fighter."

I wish I knew. Doubts gnawed on him. Meone looked lost. Adrift without hope. "That is a complicated story that I have no answers for. Leastwise no legitimate answers."

"That sounds like a problem. A man should know his worth. Otherwise, what's the point?" Tine asked.

Meone wanted to ask more. To learn what could drive a man to endure a lifetime of fighting and seeing comrades fall. Soldiers made little sense to him, for his soul was dedicated to serving a higher power. But the god king was gone. Lost to an assassin's blade. Meone tried to understand.

Realization dawned a short time later, after enduring the severity of the storms, to relieve his aching bladder. The god king. All revolved around him. Meone suddenly understood he was to be the first contact with the reincarnated spirit of the god king once Caestellom brought him down from the mountain. A more noble calling there could not be. Standing there, miserable in the pouring rain, Meone decided his position in the quest was not only important, but integral in restoring what had been.

He hurried back inside the belly of the massive iron beast, shucked off his rain poncho and hurried to find Tine. Thanks were due, for he once again had purpose.

Day turned to night and then day again without the rain subsiding. Minor irritations threatened to boil over to open conflict, a fact Hohn and Falon were desperate to avoid. They managed to maneuver the *Beast* deeper into the foothills but without a true direction, further movement was pointless. Reluctant to admit it, Hohn privately accepted they were stuck.

A day later, the storm subsided. Everyone took the opportunity to exit the vehicle, making sure to leave the hatches and ramp open to air out the interior. Hohn ordered a complete maintenance check on the carrier before he and Falon went off to scout the surrounding foothills. Clothes were washed. A proper meal made. Tine oversaw the establishment of a defensive perimeter. The first Mordai patrol was removed from the board but that did not preclude others from operating in the area. Still, the overall mood of the combined group loosened.

Aldon remained within the hull. He felt out of place. His mind was increasingly fractured as the power of the god king assumed more control. This close to Rhorrmere, it was all the boy could do to keep from delving into insanity. The foreign power growing within threatened to subsume his reality. A small part of him accepted this for fact. He was selected for higher purpose. Terrified and intrigued at once.

Reservations taunted every decision. Aldon clung to the one thread of his past worth keeping: his mother.

Guilt over leaving her without a good bye gnawed his fragile psyche. Never having been without her for long periods, left him fractured far beyond anything the god king's presence inspired. Aldon sat with his legs drawn up, arms wrapped around the knees. His heart was heavy, as it was each time he thought of home.

Eager to rip his mind away from the overwhelming power consuming him, Aldon looked around the armored monster that had suddenly become home. His mind failed to comprehend how any society could envision such a creation, or the horrific amount of weaponry on display. Blocks of sunlight, still weak through the thinning veil of clouds, funneled down in a checkered pattern. A gentle reminder that simplicity yet remained, if one knew where to look for it. The smile creasing his young face was genuine and the first he had in days.

His eyes eventually fell on Caestellom. The Scarlet remained unconscious, perhaps dying. No mortals understood their physiology, rendering potential care impotent. Aldon wondered if the Scarlet felt the same pull toward Rhorrmere the god king whispered in his mind. Assumptions aside, he hoped his dilemma ended soon. He wanted his mind back. A spasm gripped his shoulders, pinching his neck.

Groaning in pain, Aldon tried to close his eyes. The god king had other ideas. It had been weeks since he last was devoured by the power in his mind. Effervescent light poured from his eyes, landing on Caestellom's chest. Aldon tried to scream but no sound came forth. Compelled, he shrank within his body. The god king dominated. He crawled forward to rest beside his stricken protector. A hand laid upon Caestellom's chest and jerked away in pain. He knew the miasmic sensation preventing the Scarlet from awakening.

Confused, the god king wondered how the anathema to his kind remained alive. Tens of thousands of years should have seen an end to that wicked breed. He knew from scrying Aldon's deepest thoughts of the battle with Waujulx, and his subsequent demise. He also recognized getting to Rhorrmere without the Scarlet was not possible. The god king summoned what powers he commanded and placed both hands on either side of Caestellom's face. Ignoring the vehement residue pulsing off the flesh, the god king funneled all he had.

Light and dark battled within the Scarlet's flesh. Some had turned necrotic. Sparks danced between his fingertips. Caestellom groaned but did not move. Refusing to be rebuked, the god king redoubled his efforts. Aldon begged from deep inside, for intense pain unlike any ever imagined racked his body. The god king did not relent. He assaulted the enemy residue, hammering it away from the Scarlet. At last he had no energy remaining and collapsed on the deck.

The rise and fall of his chest were shallow. He rasped with each inhale. Much of the skin on his arms and legs had fallen off, scorched away by hatred pure. Satisfied, the god king retreated within and Aldon returned. Tears flowed down his cheeks, cutting through the grime to stain his tunic. When at last he managed to look upon the Scarlet, he was filled with amazement. Caestellom was awake, his eyes locked on Aldon. The god king had done it.

"Caestellom?" Aldon cried. He refused to believe what his eyes showed him.

Confusion twisted his face. "My Lord?"

Aldon shook his head. "No, though the god king took control of me."

Caestellom tried moving but abandoned his efforts at once. Much of his physical strength was gone, robbed by the confrontation with the nightmare. Events replayed through his eidetic memory. Every swing and thrust. The bodies torn asunder and turned to ash. He was a creature of the unnatural, yet nothing in his existence prepared him for the encounter.

"Where are we?" he asked after absorbing his surroundings. Nothing was clear.

Aldon explained how they were saved by Hohn and his people and escorted to the base of the mountains. The quest was nearing an end but with the Scarlet unable to fulfill his destiny, they were stuck with no way forward. Caestellom absorbed all this, listening to every word for scraps of additional knowledge. When Aldon fell silent, the Scarlet managed to rise on his elbows, through great physical effort.

"We have arrived and my time has come," he reassured Aldon. "On the morrow you and I shall travel to the mountain home of the gods. The time has come to return balance to the world and free my master. Rest now, young Aldon. Tomorrow will be unlike any you have experienced. The true test of your soul is about to begin."

Aldon wanted to flee. Return to his mother and not look back. Destiny had other plans and he had a feeling he was not going to like them.

THIRTY-ONE

"Release me and I will not kill you."

Abbas Doza doubted the truth in that. His captive was not known for mercy, nor for keeping soft promises of peaceful intent. The enforcer of the Assassin Guild was one of the most tyrannical people he knew. Removing her from the board cleared the way for him getting revenge on his former masters. Long hours of deliberation were spent deciding how best to approach the matter. Never once did Abbas believe he was in the wrong, despite taking an illegal contract to murder the benevolent ruler of Ghendis Ghadanaban. It was, he decided, a matter of morality.

"Why should I believe you?" Abbas asked.

He sat across from her, one boot on a three legged stool and carving slices from a green apple with his favorite knife. Abbas recognized strength and knew he would only have a moment to react should Ninean break her bonds.

Bruised up the left side of her face from Baradoon's knuckles, Ninean winced as she tried working some of the tension out of her face. "Abbas, you swine. I should have known you were behind that ape's assault. Let me go. The Guild wants you back. Make it easy for all of us."

Abbas swallowed a piece of apple and waggled his blade at her. "Therein lies the problem. You see, I rather enjoy my head being attached to my body. You and I both know what happens if the Guild gets their hands on me again."

Ninean shrugged. "Not my problem. You're the fool who took the illegal contract. The Prefecture is already snooping around. Word is, they are pushing to shut the Guild down for good. Do you have any idea how much trouble you've created?"

"We all live with regrets," Abbas replied. "The Guild is obsolete. Sanctioned killings are reduced from last year, and the years before that. Seems people don't appreciate the idea of a proper killing. If that bear Ig gets his way, there will be no more Guild. Good riddance, I say, but that brings up one question. What happens to all of us poor assassins after?"

He waved off her attempted answer. "We become fugitives. Refugees fleeing a governmental system who wants us eliminated. How long before assassins start turning up dead in the streets or rotting in Prefecture jails? We are a dying breed, Ninean."

Her sneer spoke volumes. "Where does that leave you?"

"Where I need to be. Tega Ig and his prefects are competent enough, but they're not capable of removing a nest of murderers."

Ninean's eyes widened as his plan became clear. "You want to get on their good side by taking out your peers."

"Don't forget their payroll," he added. "None of that matters, if I have the Guild breathing down my back."

"None of this would be happening, if your greed didn't take over!" Spittle flew from her mouth in rage. "You've ruined all our lives, you hapless fool!"

Taken aback, Abbas recoiled. He hadn't expected an easy victory, nor did he think she was going to blame him for all their woes. For the first time, he began to wonder if he was wrong.

Merrick saw the danger brightening his friend's eyes and intervened. "Easy, Abbas. We can't make a move if Ninean dies today."

"That you, Merrick? I thought I smelled you hiding in the shadows," Ninean mocked. "If you're going to kill me, get on with it. I have things to do."

"No one said anything about killing you, Ninean," Merrick lied.

She snorted. "How much was it, Abbas? How much did it take to sell us out?"

"Why can't you understand? I did the impossible! I killed the god king. How much I made isn't important," he pleaded.

Ninean turned aggressive, feeling the mood shift in her favor. "It was nothing, wasn't it? You did it for glory. Fame you can never claim because to do so, would put a price on your head by every agency in the kingdom. Sad, pathetic Abbas. I should have killed you when they ordered you brought in the first time."

"I did the impossible." His voice was almost a whisper. Confidence shaken, he set the remains of the apple down. "Ninean, I'm asking for your help."

"Help?" she struggled against the heavy ropes binding her to the chair.

"Yes, help. Give me the names of the Guild Masters, so I can end this madness."

She paused, wary of a trap. Abbas was a gifted talker and a better assassin. "Cut me loose and you'll have your answer."

Ninean never saw the massive fist fly into the right side of her head.

"I expect everything is in order for the smooth facilitation of this conference, Overseer?"

The tall, slender man dressed in rich green and red silks marched down the hall with his hands clasped behind his back. The emissary of the king of Eleboran looked sickly in most regards, giving Larris an uneasy feeling in the pit of her stomach.

She replied, "Matters are progressing smoothly, Minister Quin. This city is ready."

Larris felt adding additional information was pointless. All delegations had finally arrived, including the near barbaric men and women of the hill tribes. Quin made a point of arriving last, going so far as to camp outside of the city walls until the tribesmen arrived. Larris had no use for petty politics. She always felt matters were best dealt with head on.

Quin had other ideas. A natural politician, he played angles until impossibly choreographed threads wove into the perfect tapestry. That he had any role in the atrocities engulfing the kingdom was lost on him. Quin was a hero to the crown.

"I am disappointed to find those animals are being kept in the same building as my party," he said. A thin eyebrow arched.

Larris ground her teeth before presenting her polished look. "You will understand that the steady influx of refugees has hampered our ability to separate the delegations. Safety is one of my primary concerns. The tribesmen vowed no violence, so long as the conference is taking place."

"They are subhuman in the king's eyes, Overseer. How many thousands of our citizens have been killed since this war began? We should be more cautious when applying ideals to our enemies," Quin sneered.

"Ghendis Ghadanaban is a free city, Minister. We are open to all and a neutral party to this war," Larris said.

"This city is within the borders of Eleboran. Do not forget you are all citizens of the king," he fired back.

"If the king has issues with my style of rule, he may come to relieve me himself." Larris stood her ground, recognizing a bully. Men like Quin respected power, though they might never say so. Larris knew if she rolled over now, she lost the upper hand.

Quin halted in midstride. Anger laced his face. "The king has higher priorities than *you*, Larris. Let us not forget the fact you allowed your hallowed god king to be killed, and with relative ease, I understand. Has your investigation yielded results?"

His threat conveyed without illusion. The god kings were the only beings preventing Ghendis Ghadanaban from being annexed into the kingdom proper. The Eleboran monarchy viewed this as a hindrance, denying them the riches and wealth the Heart Eternal represented.

Smug bastard. She knew the king was eager to claim the city's resources and Quin confirmed as much through his statement. A once secure position suddenly felt unstable. Larris decided playing safe—at least until the quest returned—was her best option for maintaining order with the crown.

"The head Prefect and First Prophet are working in conjunction to determine who the assassin was and who paid him," she lied. The truth was far more dismal for her liking. Nothing had been done in the weeks following Omoraum Dala'gharis's untimely demise and she was at the end of her resources.

"Indeed," Quin replied and continued walking.

Larris hurried to catch up, demonstrating the strength of her position by marching beside the arrogant man, stride for stride. The conference began in two days. She doubted she had the internal fortitude to endure Quin for that long.

Nightmares often gripped her. They were a small price to pay for placing herself at the center of the spiderweb. Lady Duema was one of the most obscure women of power in the Heart Eternal. A master of manipulation and arcane arts, she pulled her strings as needed to remain in control. Recent events rocked her, for the god king was an immortal. An untouchable force of nature beyond her ability to comprehend. His death threatened to unravel all she had striven to achieve in her long life.

That sense of self-doubt prompted her to act. Matters were moving in a twisted manner she found too concerning to ignore. Prompted by fear, Duema struck out from the sanctity of her shop in search of the one person in the city capable of providing reassurance. A man never hard to find.

She arrived without fanfare. The White Crow staff was preparing for the usual evening festivities. Heads turned her way. Some absorbed her uncanny beauty. Some quickly turned away when they perceived the dark shadows trailing her. Duema ignored them all. Her intent was focused on one man alone. She wove through the thin crowd and sat before Relghel Gorgal. True to perception, the fallen god remained stoic.

"This is a rare pleasure," he offered. "What brings you before me after so many decades, Lady Duema?"

Two hundred thirteen years she had lived and counted herself fortunate enough to have witnessed incredible events. Thankfully, her encounters with the fallen god were limited. He was the wild card she found unreadable. A danger lurking beneath her nose.

"Omoraum's assassination," she replied without pause.

"That is already old news. Much greater events are transpiring, as we speak," he said.

Placing her elbows on the table, Duema leaned forward. "What role did you play in his murder?"

Relghel betrayed no emotion. "Strong accusations. What makes you certain I had anything to do with that sad event? I turned my back on the gods and their lies long ago."

"The trickster enjoys his game," Duema answered. "No one else in this city knows you as I do, Relghel. You may fool the administration, but I know your truth."

"What truth is that?"

"That you secretly crave chaos. Thrive on it, one might say."

His cheeks twitched softly, a move barely noticeable, if she had not been looking for it. "You suspect me of having a hand in the murder?"

"Did you?" she asked.

"More the fool me, if I did," Relghel said. "I wonder what game it is you play at, lady of the dark arts. Does jealousy inspire your actions? Perhaps the opportunity to advance beyond your station?"

"My motivations are not the issue, fallen one. The assassination unbalanced the city. Dark powers have been unleashed that I suspect even you were unaware of."

It was his turn to act surprised. "What do you mean?"

I have you now. "I have witnessed events to come. An ancient foe marches on this city. He will destroy everything should he gain the walls. Your petty games have spelled our ruin." Duema rose to leave. She had heard enough.

"Lady, this enemy. Does he have a name?" Relghel asked.

"Aye, he does. Razazel."

Her dark robes swirled around her as she turned and left. The fallen god sank back in his seat and stared at the half empty mug of ale before him. His desire to drink was gone.

"Imperator Thrakus, thank you for accepting my summons," Sandis said, with a false grin. "I am sure you have much to do before the conference begins."

Thrakus looked upon the sad man representing the Order of Prophets with disdain. He knew more about Sandis than the old man assumed. Weakness had no place in the halls of leadership. A remedy Thrakus hoped to implement the moment he was given stewardship of the Heart Eternal.

"My time is valuable as you say, First Prophet. What is it you need of me?" he asked. His demeanor was harsh, befitting his command.

Sandis, unused to being challenged in his own office, balked at the insolence the Mordai showed. "I was under the impression *you* were meant to contact me upon your arrival. Perhaps I was mistaken?"

"I have my orders. What do you want?" Thrakus pushed.

"I will not be addressed so. I am First Pro…"

"You are shit to me," Thrakus interrupted. "My mission is known. There are no questions. All I need from you is to keep your lips together and do as you are told. There will be no discussion. No debate. You are a puppet, Sandis. Nothing more. Cross me and your usefulness ends. Am I clear?"

Sandis could barely nod.

"Good. Now, my initial move will occur while the delegates are about to break for their first session. I will not tell you what is going to happen and do not promise your safety. Be prepared. There are horrors in this world far beyond the scope of your pathetic imagination," Thrakus said. "Or am I mistaken in assuming this is all for your benefit of becoming the next ruler of Ghendis Ghadanaban?"

"The Vizier promised," Sandis defended.

Thrakus laughed in his face. "I am undoing that promise. This city was never going to be yours, old fool. A jewel such as the Heart Eternal is destined to be ruled by a man suited for grandeur. You may have it, of course, if you feel you have the strength to take it from me."

Sandis remained silent. Rage stewed within his soul. Thrakus left without further word, leaving the First Prophet of Ghendis Ghadanaban impotent in his seat of authority. Mind already spinning, Sandis began plotting how best to remove this unexpected thorn without implicating his own actions in the plot to overthrow the city. Tears of frustration welled up, choking him. Decades of service to the god king and his partisan band of proxies and he had nothing to show for it.

It was the curse of men for having vision beyond their ken. Sandis was a devoted son until he discovered he was being ignored. Shunned from the true decision making meetings shaping the future, he allowed his desires to get the best of him. With Thrakus making it clear he was irrelevant for the future, Sandis decided it was time to take matters into his own hands. Perhaps there was still time to mitigate the damage he had caused. The only question was what would the god king reincarnated think once he learned the truth? Sandis stewed on that thought, wondering if the quest had been removed from the board yet.

One problem at a time.

THIRTY-TWO

The deep night provided opportunity for a great many. Thieves and those bent on havoc used the natural cover to infiltrate homes and empty businesses. Men and women wishing to go unnoticed by the authorities, slunk about conducting nefarious deeds. Agents and emissaries of higher powers roamed without detection, keeping the fragile peace, when all else seemed to fade. Deeds strange and wonderful filled the deepest hours of night in the Heart Eternal.

Timeus Thorn enjoyed the long dark. He found reflection after the sun dipped below the horizon. Life had been anything but nice for him. Born to a drunkard father and promiscuous mother, Timeus was cast aside as an infant, left to die on the frozen steppes. The why and how of his survival was lost to time and faded memory, though it was never a story he willingly told.

He had done foul deeds during his youth. Crimes demanding his head in several kingdoms. All in the past now. Hean offered a new life and he eagerly accepted on the condition of behaving in the constraints of the law. Difficult, but not impossible. Timeus tried escaping the past, but every so often, it returned to haunt him.

Sitting on the edge of the roof of a three story building, he watched the night unfold. The city was abuzz with rumors and suppositions about the upcoming conference. He cared little. War and peace. Proponents for either side claimed theirs was the true way. Timeus understood one required the other to survive. So it had been since the dawn of civilization. The grey area in between was where he thrived.

The rush of wings above drew his attention. One of the Scarlet scouring the streets for villains. Or was he? Timeus peered closer. The Scarlet flew with sword drawn and a slender object clutched in his right hand. Timeus made out the curled appendages of a hand. Now that is interesting. *The Guardians of Purity aren't known for taking human life. What might that poor soul have done to warrant dismembering*?

Whispers suggested the Scarlet had been productive of late. Reports of missing people circulated. Some claimed to have witnessed the murders. Timeus discarded most as being uninformed conspiracy theorists. More than a enough people found the winged guardians disturbing and did not want them in their city. Amusing, given the relationship between the god kings and their protectors. Briefly flirting with the notion of giving chase, Timeus decided his two legs were no match for the power of wings. He pulled a handful of figs from the small satchel at his side and chewed. The night was long and strange indeed.

Lady Duema did not look up as Verian entered through the second story window she had left open. The Lord of the Scarlet marched down the stairs. Each footstep heavy, authoritative. His sword was bared. Duema's reputation had reached even his offices, and while he respected her neutrality, Verian was unwilling to test her skills. Lesser people had tried and were never seen again. He found it amusing. She ignored it all, garnering the opinion of the more people talked, the more convoluted her truth became. Reputation was about more than truth.

"Did you bring it?" she asked. Duema dropped a handful of herbs into the pot of boiling liquid.

Verian dropped the arm in front of her. "Freshly turned, as requested."

Duema glanced at the arm, annoyed at the casual interruption. The liquid sputtered, casting drops on the necrotic flesh. Foul odors collided in a greenish cloud, prompting Verian to choke. Stepping back, the Scarlet grew impatient with her.

"Is this necessary?" he asked.

She ignored him and dropped in several more dried leaves. "You wish to discover the truth behind the god king's killer do you not?"

"A foolish question. I feel I am wasting my time with this."

"That is your right. Who am I, a lowly mortal, to stop you?" Duema asked. Her disdain was forced, for she admired the Scarlet in their devotion.

"The quest should be nearing Rhorrmere. Those responsible must know by now that their deed will be undone," Verian explained. "What purpose then the assassination?"

"Greed. Jealousy. Any number of petty human emotions, though you and I both know there are other forces at work. You ask the wrong questions, Lord of the Scarlet."

Her cryptic maneuvering forced him into uncomfortable corners. Reducing his powers left him at a disadvantage. Verian knew coming to Duema presented risks, but he needed answers to a pair of dilemmas. Finding the killers was paramount. He was also convinced the rise of the dead added to the conspiracy, if little else than a distraction.

"The Prefecture looks in the wrong direction. Subterfuge is at play here. There is nothing direct about this matter," Verian said. "Larris is overwhelmed with the peace conference and the House of Prophets is all but defunct. Finding the source of the dead may lead to my prey."

Humming an old song, Duema began carving slivers of flesh and dropping them into the pot. The miasmic cloud changed from bland green to shades of ochre. Her eyes narrowed at this. Unexpected and disturbing, she became nervous.

"You must go," she said.

The urgency in her voice made him stiffen. "I do not have my answers. You struck a deal."

"That was before you brought … *this*. Your presence is a liability."

"What did you learn? What does the flesh whisper?" Verian asked. Fresh urgency motivated him.

"Dark times approach. The city will fall, if the god king is not restored," Duema said.

Verian grew impatient. "You speak in riddles."

"The only answer you may receive," she replied. "Go now. The ones you seek are much closer than you think."

Confused, the Lord of the Scarlet blinked rapidly. *Closer than I think*? The admission presented scores of names and possibilities. His quest for a fast end evaporated.

"What of our deal? Who is the source of the undead?" he demanded.

Her smile concealed, Duema waved his concern away. "A minor inconvenience, nothing more. The dead are of no consequence. That threat will dissipate on its own, but only as long as you stop the approaching storm. Please leave now. I will not ask again."

Resisting the urge to take her head, or at least attempt to, Verian unfurled his wings and lifted out of the serpent's den. The winds of change blew across the Heart Eternal, unlike any in its storied history. His place in it suddenly uncertain. Damnation or salvation. The choice yet remained. Lost in thought, Verian ignored the city as he sped back to his roost. *Those responsible are closer than I think.* That mantra played over and again. He was no closer to the truth than before entering into Duema's contract.

Ghendis Ghadanaban was unlike any other city he had ever witnessed. Towering spires and golden crowned buildings soared above the streets. Riches and wealth beyond count all but paved the streets in gold. Merchants and goods from across the world were displayed, available for the right price. It was both boon and bane to those with too much coin and weak wills.

Seedier areas of the city offered prostitution and untold carnal delights. An underground drug trade thrived amid Prefecture neglect. Thrakus found the notion intriguing, while being little more than an annoyance. He cared nothing for the underground or the established hierarchy of merchants. All would bow beneath his boot heel. The Imperator of Mordai was both prude and shallow. A man of simple passions, Thrakus took what he wanted. The city was his.

He walked with impunity through the thinning crowds as the day faded. Night presented different crowds with different intents. Caravans from Uruth passed hunter-gatherers from the cold steppes of the northern kingdoms. None paid attention to his black uniform and the glass-like polish of his boots. He repaid their ignorance in kind.

Making his way back to a private property Sandis set up before his arrival, Thrakus climbed down three flights of stairs, some of them crumbling beneath his weight. A shower of dust cascaded down before him. An unlit torch hung on the wall at the base. Thrakus produced a handheld fire starter. He doubted daylight reached this far down. Illuminated in shades of red and orange, he turned the corner and knocked on a rusted iron door at the end of a long corridor. How old this part of this city was remained hidden. The perfect place for his business.

The door creaked open. A pair of guards awaited, standing down after verifying who it was. Thrakus passed without comment. They glanced down the corridor, ensuring no one followed, before slamming the door shut behind him. The apartment was small but had three rooms. Sewage reek wafted to his nostrils. A room for the guards to rotate through shifts was off to his right. The main room had just enough space for what he needed to do.

A chair stood in the center of the room. The lone piece of furniture. Thrakus requested a spartan apartment. There was no point in anything else. He cared not for the appointments. His focus was dedicated to the man tied to the chair. Hooded and gagged, only a few knew his name, and none would remember he ever existed after tonight.

"Imperator, welcome."

Thrakus turned. Senior Alchemist Horrick emerged from the back room, wiping his hands on a stained cloth. "Horrick. Is all prepared?"

"It is, though I advise we evacuate our men before the final change overtakes him. In that state they are … unpredictable," Horrick answered.

Thrakus nodded. He ignored the alchemist and strode before the prisoner. Yanking the sack away, he found Ytel's frightened eyes glaring back at him. The former ambassador of Uruth had been his undeclared prisoner since ambushing their delegation en route to the city. The lone survivor of a militia slaughter. The discord sown into the fabric of the peace conference began long ago. It would culminate tonight.

"Good evening, Ambassador Ytel. I apologize for the severity of your treatment, but I needed you in the proper frame of mind for this to succeed," he explained.

Ytel struggled against his bonds. Spittle drooled from the corners of his mouth, as his cries of defiance were reduced to mewling.

"Calm yourself. There is no point for this. Your fate was sealed the moment you marched out from Uruth," Thrakus taunted. "Do you have any idea what is about to happen? Pain unlike any your limited imagination might conjure will wrack your body from head to foot. Bones will break. Your mind will snap. You will cease being you, as rivers of blood flush down your hide. Hair will fall out in some places. Grow wild in others. You, my dear Ytel, will become a caricature of humanity.

"Our alchemists have dedicated their lives to the transformation of, well, people. Ytel, you are about to perform a grand service for my kingdom and for that, you shall have my eternal gratitude. Tonight is your final night on this world. I wish we had more time but alas the hour of the grand reception is upon us." He removed Ytel's gag. "Scream all you wish. No one will hear."

The Imperator of Mordai nodded for Horrick to begin. The process was long and complicated. The sooner it began, the better. Despite his thirst for violence, Thrakus blanched at the sight of the unnatural talents demonstrated by the Vizier's alchemists. Theirs was an acquired taste he never developed. Best to let Horrick work without being watched. Some matters required the seclusion of silence.

Thrakus emerged into the cool evening and breathed deep. Nothing prevented the grin from filling his face. He wondered if anyone in the city realized what was about to occur. That their lives were about to change forever. That singular idea inspired great glee to a man with a twisted heart. Ghendis Ghadanaban stood upon the precipice. Soon it would fall and Thrakus would rise. The time of tyrants was at last at hand.

THIRTY-THREE

Hohn and Tine conversed with Falon and Tula a short distance from the *Beast*. A full day of good weather improved moods and afforded all the opportunity to change out of soiled clothes. The Mascantii found a nearby creek and took the uniforms down to be washed, thankful to be away from the cloistered humans. Loyal servants, their patience extended but so far. The opportunity to spread out was appreciated by all.

"That still leaves us with no way clear of these foothills. I think we shou…"

Hohn's mouth dropped open at the sight emerging from the carrier's hold. His hand edged down to his sidearm. The others followed his line of sight. Tine jerked back, surprised at seeing the giant man with wings. Visible relief washed over the women. The ruination of their quest now appeared undone. Hope was rekindled.

Caestellom strode down the back ramp, ignoring the stares of the foreign soldiers, as he marched toward Falon. His face a stoic mask, the Scarlet ached from long days of inactivity. Fresh scars lined his exposed flesh, marring the once god-like features. He offered a clipped nod to Tula and halted a meter away.

"Prefect, I have recovered," he stated. "Is the creature destroyed?"

"Yes, you killed it, Caestellom," Falon confirmed. "Are you well?"

"Enough to complete my purpose. How close are we to Rhorrmere?"

"That question is best asked of you. Our new friends guided us this far, but we have nothing to base our knowledge off," Tula answered. "How did you recover?"

His squarish head turned to her. "The boy. His powers are manifesting. It is almost time."

"Time for what?" Hohn asked. Curiosity got the better of discretion.

"I do not recognize you," the Scarlet replied.

Falon interrupted before the potential for disagreement arose. "This is Sergeant Hohn. His people rescued us from a Mordai patrol."

"Nice to meet you," Hohn smirked.

Caestellom ignored him. "We are nearly there. A few leagues distant is the path into the mountains. We should leave as soon as possible. The attack by the Orpheliac was the beginning. Our enemies are massing. Linger too long and we risk secondary attacks by forces well beyond your comprehension."

"Monsters, eh?" Hohn asked. His hand remained on his sidearm, despite the familiarity exhibited by the women. Their stances suggested unspoken tension.

"Nightmares."

Hohn's lips pursed. "I've run across my share."

"Nothing like this," Caestellom replied. He returned his attention to Falon. "We must keep moving. The path is near."

"Can you guide where we need to go?" she asked. Her confidence was shaken, threatening to shatter after the trauma of days past.

"I can. Must we ride upon the metal beast?" The Scarlet mistrusted what he did not know, that meant Hohn and the *Beast*.

Hohn's grin was false. "Just point me in the right direction."

The *Beast* rolled on, working down the draw back to the flatlands where it could traverse the terrain with relative ease. Falon, growing comfortable with both the concept and the conditions, rode beside Hohn. The open air slapped her face gently as the leagues rolled by. Dusk was settling across the horizon when they pulled into an occupied oasis. Guns ready, Hohn ordered a halt. He and Falon went to barter their safe passage. Better to make friends instead of enemies.

They returned moments later with good news. Engines powered down and the crew and passengers disembarked to make the best of the coming night. A merchant caravan occupied the oasis. Seven wagons, two stories high, were parked in twin lines. Their moorvaan were unhooked and placed in a large paddock. Torches lined the perimeter for this was no pleasant part of the world.

The merchants were from distant Golun and pleasant enough. Meats and fresh fruits were shared, for a price, as well as flagons of wine and chilled ale. Hohn's soldiers bonded with the caravan guards. Camaraderie was often the most important aspect of service. Nothing brought people together like the shared labor of hardships in the field.

"'Ware my friends, rumor has it there are bandits in the area," Merchant Weflen said, between a swig of wine and a deep, chest hurting belch.

Hohn tore a strip of roasted meat off the skewer and chewed thoughtfully. Distinct with a spiced flavor, he knew better than to ask what it was. "Bandits don't concern me too much. I don't suppose you've seen any of the hill tribes down this way though?"

"They do not reach so far south. Most of the tribesmen have joined the militia and the wars with Eleboran," Weflen confirmed. "Bandits here are from the desert tribes. They owe no allegiance to any kingdom and are violent men. You would be wise to heed my warning. Stay clear of them, if possible."

Hohn reasoned it explanation enough for the high security and large amount of guards positioned around the wagons. The added firepower of the *Beast* offered better protection than any single round black powder rifle could muster. He did notice the lack of cannons, for which he felt immediate relief. Too many barrages while fighting in the north left him rattled and in no hurry to relive.

Falon finished her mug of ale. It was a guilty pleasure she seldom indulged in. Foam painted her upper lip. "Have they been spotted near here?"

"None by my lookouts but do not let that lull you in complacency. They are wily foes who strike with little warning," Weflen said.

"Thank you for the information, Merchant. We shall be careful the rest of our journey," Falon said.

They finished their meal discussing trivial matters, careful to avoid the truth of their presence. Some time after the mid of night, both parties retired. Hohn stumbled into the turret where he'd strung a hammock. His eyes burned, and his belly was full. Stripping down to undershirt and trousers, he slipped into his bed, eager for the promise of a good night's sleep. It was the first since landing on this world.

He awoke to the thunder of *Beast's* main weapons ripping into the night. "Krak!" he flipped down, tugged his boots on and thumbed the heads up display screen. Multiple hostiles appeared as red blips. Close to thirty slinking along the perimeter. Bandits. His already foul mood darkened when he realized they were spread out enough to keep his heavy arsenal ineffective.

"Looks like we do this the hard way," he muttered and reached for his rifle. "Tine!"

The smaller corporal was already armored up and waiting for commands. Others were gearing up, ready to take the battle to the enemy. Months of constant action left them on the razor's edge. Downtime was needed to recover strength and peace of mind but was the one gift Hohn was unable to promise. They stacked on Hohn as he passed.

"What can we do?" Falon asked. Her rifle was in hand. The single shot weapon was no match for the space soldier's superior firepower, though it was even with every other native weapon.

Hohn approved of her tenacity to fight. "Maintain the perimeter around *Beast*. We'll have this cleared up in short order. Anyone gets through us, put a round between their eyes."

"What about prisoners?" she asked.

The question affirmed his belief that none of the locals were prepared for the violence about to be unleashed. "We don't need them."

Dressed in armor from helmet to boot, the soldiers marched into the night, fanning into a wide triangle. Facemasks displayed the area with precision, leaving all targets in full view. He almost wished the odds were closer to being even. Slaughter approached. Inner peace settled over the soldiers, for this was what they were trained for. Men and women whose sole dedication was to the killing of others. Hohn almost pitied the bandits.

The squad splintered off in two man teams. Their advance was silent. Professional. Hohn stalked through the meter high weeds surrounding the oasis, using intermittent palm trees for cover. Three bandits approached with weapons leveled. They were heading for the wagons. Face locked in concealed grimace, Hohn raised his rifle and fired. Blinding lances of energy sliced across the air to strike the bandits in the chest and head. All three fell in lifeless clumps of flesh. Steam billowed from the wounds as the soldiers passed.

The crack of return fire echoed over the field. Hohn ducked reflexively. Local bullets could still kill if they struck the right spot. "Where's the shooter?"

He and his partner split five meters apart and crawled through the brush. Heavy ground vegetation masked the enemy heat signature, leveling the field. For the time being. Hohn was an experienced warrior who knew his job well. A stream of data scrolled across the right sight of his visor but there was no information on the shooter. He advanced to the edge of the brush and kneeled. Only the barrel of his rifle was exposed.

Another shot blazed overhead, striking the tree a meter to his right. *Whoever this sniper is, he has talent.* Hohn approved. He'd been without a worthy fight since crash landing several months ago. Further exposing himself was an invitation to a lucky shot. One he wasn't keen on taking without greater intelligence.

Nothing of the bandit was exposed. Hohn caught flickers of body heat behind a stand of three palms. Nothing he could shoot at and hit, however. Bullets and energy beams crisscrossed throughout the oasis. Branches and bits of bark fell. The body count rose as Hohn's people stalked across the area with ruthless intent.

"Sergeant, five enemy coming in fast from the west. They appear to be mounted," Tine's voice commed over the helmets.

Hohn grimaced. Dismounted forces were simple to counter and eliminate. Mounted was another matter, even with his available firepower. He shifted left and charged across the semi-open terrain, leaping over corpses and fallen trees. A wounded caravanner lay screaming with both hands clutching his lower leg to stop the blood flow. A growing pool darkened the sand and dirt beneath him.

Thermal optics picked up the incoming bandits. They were moving too fast to target with his standard rifle. Cursing, Hohn pushed harder to get into a firing position offering stability and cover, limited as it might be. Boots kicked up dust in passing. His heartbeat pounded in his head. Breathing elevated, Hohn allowed the battle rage to take control. Training and instinct took over.

He slammed into the trunk of a young palm and brought his rifle up. Heavy breathing altered the rise and fall of his chest, forcing him to adjust his aim. He blinked rapidly to clear his vision. Augmented sensors adjusted to his new field of fire and conveyed target acquisitions to his weapon. Useful, but he had come to rely on his senses just as much. Sliding the tip of his finger into the trigger guard, Hohn took slow and steady breaths.

The lead rider came into view but Hohn held his fire. Announcing his presence too soon exposed him to being run down by the other four. He was good, but not enough to escape unscathed. Fortunately, the bandits were unversed in tactics and rode in single file. He drew a bead on the middle rider and fired.

White hot energy lanced across the space separating them and struck the bandit in the center of his chest. Rider pitched back, dead before hitting the ground. Horses whinnied in sudden fright. The bandits milled, confused. Hohn fired again and again. Two more fell, though the second was only wounded. He pressed his luck and lost. The bandits spotted the small cloud of supercharged air hovering around him and trained their rifles in his direction.

Hohn dove to the ground before bullets cracked around him. Schematics showed no damage to his armor but his position was compromised and he was outgunned. Horses bore down on him. Handguns and sabers drawn, they aimed to kill him slowly. Hohn rolled to his back and fired off a few blasts. None hit but the effect was enough to drive the horses away. Allowed a few moments, he got to his knees and took aim again. This time he took the lead rider between the eyes. The others broke off, sudden understanding that they were in the more vulnerable position.

"Mounted element disengaging. Numbers reduced," he commed. "All teams report status."

One by one they called in. He was relieved there were no casualties, not that he expected many from the outset, but battles seldom went the way they were planned. His displays showed only a handful of moving targets, prompting the order to regroup in the center of the wagons. Beaten so, the bandits lost the will to fight and were retreating. Another time he might have ordered the total extermination to prevent word from reaching back to their camp. This one time, he decided allowing a few survivors better served his objective of remaining untouched for the duration of his time on this world.

He reached the wagons, stopping to check the bodies to ensure they were dead and not lying in wait. Those found alive were dispatched, for prisoners held no value. Several caravanners were dead and one of the wagons back axel destroyed but they escaped the firefight relatively unscathed. Hohn finally relaxed and removed his helmet. Sweat dampened his forehead, matting his silver flecked hair to flesh.

Tine arrived a moment later and clapped his sergeant on the shoulder pauldron. "The area is as clear as it is going to be, Sergeant. What's next?"

"I wish I knew. It seems every time we have this krakking place figured out, another rock gets thrown at us," Hohn replied.

"All part of the job. At least we don't have to deal with the militia, "Tine said. "They smelled bad."

Hohn laughed. The first genuine laugh he'd had in weeks. "I suppose we need to get a detail together and bury those bodies before the sun comes up. The last thing we need is a host of carrion eaters. Have those caravan guards start digging and then rotate a small guard schedule."

"You think they will return?" Tine asked.

"No, but I'm old enough to not take chances."

The explosion tore through the last wagon in line. Debris and flames flew like deadly shrapnel into the exposed caravanners. Men and women fell screaming. The shockwave threw the soldiers to the ground. Hohn swallowed a mouthful of dirt before snatching his helmet from the ground and slamming it on.

Krak! Now what? He should have remembered one of the first lessons from basic training. Don't ask questions you aren't ready for the answer to.

THIRTY-FOUR

Valir halted his group in the spot of his prey's last bivouac. He left the others to rest and eat while he surveyed the ground. Many of the prints he found were what he expected, but many were foreign. Boots of an unknown type marred the area, and plenty of them. Curious, he placed a palm in the nearest print and pushed. The soil was soft, recently disturbed. Satisfied, Valir rose and followed the tracks until he was positive of both the direction and the identities of his prey. Confident the quest from Ghendis Ghadanaban had linked up with a foreign body of soldiers and was heading southwest, Valir signaled for the rest to follow.

The going was easy compared to the expanse of desert crossed some weeks ago. What bothered him most was the often lack of a trail. Whatever transport the quest now used, it left no physical treads, forcing him to rely on finding the debris patterns left behind. Puzzled, he knew only that it bore immense weight to disturb the ground so. What beast could have made such ruin in passing was beyond his knowledge. Not even the snow dragons of distant Erekuul Reach were known to leave such signs. Nerves on edge, Valir decided to be cautious.

Valir's team pushed forward with ruthless intent, determined to catch the quest and steal what Hean demanded. Why the merchant needed a mere boy was beyond him, but he was never a great thinker. Following orders calmed him. Filled him with a sense of greater purpose. His time in the northern army was among the best of his life. There was no reason to think, just act. Training and obedience took over, making the detachment to regular life easier. He missed those days but had made his bed that fateful day that led to his tongue being cut out.

They continued for the next day and into the night, ever heading toward the mountains. Valir's knowledge of this area was limited, practically nothing, but he was no fool. The quest sought their prize among the dark peaks. Fresh urgency arose. He knew there was little chance of catching them once they gained the valleys and draws. He spurred his beast on, heedless of the gathering darkness.

The sun was lost over the far horizon when his efforts were rewarded. Firelight echoed across the mountain walls. Maps showed an oasis nearby. It was the logical destination for any party traveling cross country. His grin revealed a row of dull and broken teeth. He had them at last. Invigorated, Valir dug his heels into his moorvaan and charged.

It was only when the sounds of gunfire crackled around them, amplified by the nearby mountain walls, that he slowed. The others tensed, looking to him for guidance. None were brave or foolish, choosing to linger in the grey area in between. Hean chose his minions wisely. Valir thought them useless and would have dispatched the lot, if not for perceived complications in abducting the boy and escaping undetected.

Using confusion for cover, they snuck upon the oasis. Valir heard rustling among the reeds and sapling palms, combined with the rush of horses. Bandits. He saw opportunity and decided not to wait. Signaling the others to dismount, the Tongueless snatched his rifle and a small satchel of explosives from his saddlebags. One man remained back with the mounts, as the others shuffled into the undergrowth. They were not going to get a better chance to complete their mission.

Leaves slapped his face and slid around his shoulders. Valir ignored the vegetation and crept closer.

Strange bolts of light sizzled nearby, giving him pause. Raw energy laced the air. He sniffed and recoiled from the stench. It reeked of burned flesh. The foreign boot prints. The strange form of weaponry. Valir added them up and concluded he was not prepared to engage with such hostile forces.

Bandits whooped desert war cries. Valir knew this was the only chance he would get to steal the child. Once the battle ended and the bandits fled, if any survived, nothing he and his handful of men possessed was enough to counter this new threat. He bade the others stay put and lurched ahead as fast as he could. His right shoulder slammed into the body of the rear wagon. Valir searched the night and found only corpses nearby.

The Tongueless drew a deep breath to calm his rising nerves. Placing the satchel behind the rear wheel, Valir struck his flint, sparking the long line of fuses tied together. A dozen sticks of explosives were wired together, enough to destroy the wagon several times over. He tucked the fuses in as much cover as was available and ran for his life. The merchant wagon exploded in a hail of flames and shrapnel. Flaming slivers of wood tore through the surrounding area.

The concussion left ringing in his ears. Valir growled, knowing better but time was against him. He pushed off the sand and debris and began his hunt. The others would be doing the same from various points around the oasis, unless they fled in terror. He vowed to hunt them down and slaughter them all for their cowardice. If he escaped. Moving with haste, he threw back the flaps on each wagon in turn. None yielded results.

"Movement! Twenty meters out and closing slow."

The voice sounded artificial, as if it came from no human. Valir kept searching, unaware of the level of reprisal heading for him. Footsteps ranged around him. A riderless horse ambled close by. Tiny red beams of light crisscrossed the area. More bolts of energy flashed. They reminded him of storms on the high steppes. Then he spied a creation that should not have been possible. A metal beast larger than any flesh and bone animal he had ever encountered. Dark and ominous, weapons protruded from all angles. This was a thing for killing.

Impressed by the bulk before him, Valir forgot his hunters and approached. Reasoning suggested the boy would be located within the most secure area of the oasis. This metal beast was surely that. He crept closer, mesmerized by the lethality demonstrated at every angle. Thoughts of what he might have accomplished before being banished south buoyed his spirit with distraction. This, he decided, was worthy of a true warrior. Valir stretched a hand forth and laid his palm upon the cold flank.

A red dot flared on the back of his hand. His breath caught in his throat. A second dot joined the first. Then a third. The sound of rifles being cocked was too familiar. Cursing his ignorance, Valir the Tongueless froze.

"Easy now, big man. Get those hands up. No sudden movement."

Valir did as instructed.

"Good boy. Now turn around slow."

Angered at being taken without a fight, he took in his captors for the first time. Some were human. Prefect and Reclamator from Ghendis Ghadanaban. The others were profoundly disturbing. Armored aliens with hidden faces behind metal plates. Their weapons were similar to the beast behind him.

"What about the others?" the leader asked.

A smaller soldier standing to his right replied. "Neutralized. This is the last one. We rounded up their mounts and supplies."

The leader nodded. "Maybe we can sell them to the merchants. No point in letting this desolate area claim them."

"What are we going to do with him?" the prefect intervened.

Valir knew her to be deadly. Small yet stocky, the prefect had stern eyes suggesting she had been through a great deal. To his surprise, the Reclamator bore the same haggard look. The soldiers may have presented imminent threat, but these women concerned him more.

The leader adjusted his aim to the center of Valir's chest. "I suppose we need to find out who you are and why you are attacking us. Speak up. This is your one chance."

Valir grinned and opened his mouth wide. The stump of his tongue waggled at them.

Shoulders slumped, the leader removed his helmet and scowled. "Well, krak."

"I know his markings," Tula insisted. "He works for Hean."

"The trade company master?" Meone chimed in. Awkward and feeling out of place, the prophet was slowly coming out of his imposed shell. Weeks away from the First Prophet, Meone's experiences on the quest fundamentally changed him.

"Is this guy important?" Hohn asked. He ran a fingertip over his stubble, rubbing the hair the wrong way.

Tula took a swallow of water before replying. "Enough, in the right circles. I didn't think he was a player in this game."

"Could be he was here to raid the caravan," Falon suggested.

The comment felt flat on her tongue. Her heart knew the truth but her mind refused to accept what her eyes saw. There was no viable reason for any agents to be this far from the city and the opportunity for coincidence was far too small.

"You and I both know that isn't true. You're being hunted," Hohn said with a straight face. "I bet it has everything to do with that boy."

"What would Hean want with Aldon?" Tula asked. She was under the impression no one outside of their quest and the officials of the highest offices knew of the quest. The Arax Trading Company was already the wealthiest in the western kingdoms. Hean stood to gain nothing from stopping them. She winced. *Except unparalleled power. With Aldon in his hands, he will be able to control the entire city.*

Caestellom emerged from the night. The tips of his wings poked up behind his shoulders. Blood painted the right side of his face. "He seeks to claim the boy for his own and yield him to gain unfettered power. Our enemies multiply and confront us on many levels. Time is almost up. I must get the boy to Rhorrmere."

"What's so special about this place?" Hohn asked. The information gleaned from Tula and Falon left many holes in his understanding. Their winged friend was reluctant to say more than a few words. His taciturn nature placed them all in jeopardy. The only certainty was this kingdom was far more complex than any he had fought in before.

All expected little in return of answers. Caestellom surprised them. "It is the birthday of the god kings. The one link between immortality and this existence. Only there can the line of god kings be restored."

Tula narrowed her eyes with suspicion. "What will happen to Aldon once he arrives?"

The Scarlet jut his chin forward. "His apotheosis."

Silence dominated the gathering. Furtive looks were exchanged. Hohn absorbed their reactions before impatience took over. Blowing out an exasperated breath, he asked, "Anyone care to explain what the krak that means?"

"He will ascend to godhood." Caestellom folded his arms and waited for the inevitable argument to begin. Until now, none knew the truth of their task. He doubted any would have signed on to willingly be a part of ending the life of an innocent boy, so that Omoraum Dala'gharis could be reborn. Sacrifice was not a mortal trait.

Tula dropped her head. Their quest to save Aldon and the Heart Eternal was in vain. "Aldon was never meant to survive."

"Not as you know him. He has been chosen. The god king's essence fled his dying form and found Aldon Cay. There is an unspoken level of purity in him. He will make a fine host," Caestellom answered.

"We've been lied to this entire time," Meone whispered.

"Misdirected. It is the way of things, Prophet Meone," the Scarlet said. His matter of fact responses were without emotion.

Hohn saw the conversation devolving and stepped in. "What happens if this apotheosis doesn't happen?"

Caestellom fixed him with a withering glare. "All life on this world dies."

"Sums it up good enough for me," Hohn said. "I don't know about the rest of you, but I don't feel like dying anytime soon. Let's get this kid to the mountain, so we can go back to our normal lives."

He laughed inside. *As if anything would ever be normal again.*

The breaking dawn scattered night in streaks of pink, orange, and pale blue. The few Mascantii survivors viewed this as a bad omen and refused to go any further. Nothing Tula or Falon said made any difference. Frustrated, the women abandoned their efforts in favor of preparing for their final push to Rhorrmere. Aldon had been left out of the deliberations at Caestellom's behest. The less the boy knew of his fate, the better.

Tula tried to put the negative thoughts that had been manifesting throughout the night out of her mind, for there was more of the god king inside him than his true self. She didn't know how any of this would play out but was certain she was never going to see Aldon again. Any kinship felt between them was lost to the vagaries of fate. She felt sorrow deep within. A misery unlike any ever experienced.

"Tula, it is time," Falon said.

Reluctant to begin, Tula followed the prefect to the oasis shore where the others were assembled. Mournful stares and hardened glances welcomed the Reclamator. Oh, how she wished to return to the normalcy of her life, if hunting the risen dead was considered normal. Tula sighed. She was not prepared for anything to come.

"Morning," Hohn called with a cheerful wave. His rifle was trained on Valir's head. The northern giant knelt beside him. "On your feet, big boy."

"Are we certain this is the right course of action?" Falon asked. No matter which path her thoughts led, all whispered letting Hean's stooge go was wrong.

"He's no good to any of us. The rest of his people are eliminated. He's alone and can't speak a krakking word to what happened," Hohn reiterated their conversation from the night before. "Setting him loose with his tail between his legs will send the right message. His threat is gone. Best cut ties and move on."

Against the will of the group, Falon bit her tongue. Best not to rock the boat without certainty of positive results. She backed down.

Tine came up to cut Valir's ties. The Tongueless glared at the smaller man, disgusted and amazed at his near lizard-like appearance. He turned to Hohn and offered a clipped bow of respect. A warrior deserved no less. Climbing onto his moorvaan, Valir offered a strangled laugh and dug his heels in. Beast and rider fled. Back to Ghendis Ghadanaban. Back to the misery of servitude.

Hohn watched until they were out of sight. Satisfied no additional ambush was about to spring, he turned and said, "Now that we're finished with that madness, how about we get this boy to his mountain. I've never seen a god before."

A single tear, unnoticed by all, spilled from Tula's eye.

THIRTY-FIVE

Months of preparations were reaching fruition. Delegates and emissaries from every sect and kingdom involved in the long Eleboran civil war had arrived, with the notable exception of the waylaid envoy from Uruth, and were beginning to file into the conference chamber. Hundreds of servants shuffled about tasks, both important and menial. This was their one time to show the world the value of the citizens of the Heart Eternal. A great and secret show played out before a handful of nobles, lords, and generals.

Overseer Larris knew she should have felt relief, any sort of gratitude her endless planning and preparations were amounting to the single most important conference of world leaders in generations. Ghendis Ghadanaban held a lofty reputation among both elite and common born. It was a city of hope. Of promise. There was no other place in any civilization. For all that, she felt far from satisfied.

Rumors of a nightmare stalking the dark places of her city reached her. A terrible monster with an endless thirst for blood and raw flesh. The people were scared, and it was rising. A tide was coming in, crashing against the pillars of society. Doors and windows were now locked in the daylight. Markets and bazaars stood mostly empty. Trade was slowly grinding to a halt, for none were willing to risk being slaughtered for the sake of a handful of coins. Time was running out and she did not know where to turn for help.

Frustrated, Larris considered her limited options. Tega Ig was off on his private crusade to find the god king's assassin. He was her closest ally but his obsession with righting a grievous wrong committed under his nose threatened to unbalance him. Pushing him on was the suddenly unstable First Prophet. Larris did not know what game Sandis was playing but felt it went contrary to the good will of the city. She had not gotten to the point of placing him under observation yet. His behavior during the conference would go far in telling her where he stood. And on what side.

Of them all, only Verian appeared consistent. The Lord of the Scarlet was a volatile creation under the best of circumstances. The matter consuming the city robbed him of his foresight. He was as blinded as she in seeing how events might play out. The uncertainty of losing the god king mere weeks before the peace conference left them all rattled, while stealing a measure of power that might otherwise be claimed. Failure today meant unending years of violence and bloodshed, as more of the kingdom's citizens died.

Larris felt trapped, for it had fallen onto her shoulders, as Overseer, to lead the conference and find peace. That weight threatened to rob her strength. Already weak with indecision, Larris wanted to crawl into a hole and hide. The best days were behind. What dawn remained, the Heart Eternal might be marred with the promise of blood. Some matters were beyond a single woman, regardless of what strength Larris relied upon.

"Overseer? They are ready and waiting for you to begin."

She winced, knowing the words were inevitable. A call to action she could no longer avoid, all while dreading what must be done. The conclusion of a grand act in which she was not designed to perform the ultimate role. Larris never desired to rise this far in the social power scheme. She was a simple woman at heart, though those days had long since fled. Lost among the hierarchal struggle few commoners experienced, she was resigned to confront the inevitable.

"Thank you, Daurei," she replied and gave her retainer a warm a smile. The desert woman had been at her side for many years. A priceless accompaniment, guiding her through the storm. "You may retire for the morning."

"Mistress, there may be …"

Larris waved off her concern. "I don't imagine any great emergency occurring before the noon meal. Go, enjoy your time with your daughter. There will be need of you soon enough."

"Thank you, Mistress," Daurei bowed and scurried down the hall.

Alone, much like the entirety of her life, Larris strode forth into the unknown. It was a position she was far too accustomed to. Still, this was a momentous time for the Heart Eternal and this region. Any misstep might prove disastrous. A pair of guards opened the doors and she strode in with as much authority as she could muster. History waited for no one.

Abbas Doza was a man with purpose. Dressed in skin tight trousers and tunic, he swept through the near empty streets along the western market. Each step measured by the flow of his black cape trailing behind. An array of blades was tucked in bandoliers crisscrossing his chest. Another was tucked into a boot. He was the vision of death. 'Ware all who stumbled upon his path, for the Heart Eternal would weep this night.

Information gained from Ninean Foul, if accurate, offered an array of targets. Men and women he had met outside of the Guild constraints without knowing. Anonymity meant a great deal among their kind. A fact he once appreciated. Now it served to hinder his progression. The only way for Abbas to remain alive, was by eliminating all potential threats. That meant those responsible for placing a bounty on his life after he escaped their torture for breaking Guild rules.

He hardly thought his role in this was innocent. The opportunity to kill the one being in the entire world that was previously thought untouchable, the fabled god king of Ghendis Ghadanaban, was too much to pass. Abbas wanted, needed, to make his mark on the world, even if no one would ever know he was responsible. The irony was not lost. The Guild Masters made their position clear. He was an outcast, wanted for murder. Excommunicated from all he once knew, the former assassin sought to level the playing board.

The first lead Ninean provided was a middle-aged man he had met several times at the White Crow. Jaum Zev was an enigmatic sort who kept to himself. Wealthy to a degree, he maintained a sizeable manor two streets off from the market district. Abbas cared little for social status. What concerned him was the size of Zev's staff. Over a score of house guards and servants, no doubt capable killers in their own regard, shuffled about their daily duties.

No fool, Abbas and Merrick spent days scouting routes of travel, daily activities, and meal times. Entry points were marked, along with potential escape routes Zev might take should he feel threatened. The task was daunting. Zev's mansion looked lavishly normal to passersby, but Abbas knew it was a small fortress. Even should they get in undetected, the chances of getting out unscathed were low.

He slid into the midday shadows on the corner across the street. Merrick was already there. "What do you think?"

Merrick snorted. "I think we are both fools for doing this."

"I never pretended to be otherwise," Abbas replied. False confidence was better than none. A sharp pain tickled his ribs, fast and passing in a not so subtle reminder he had yet to heal fully.

"You do know there is a real chance Ninean gave us the wrong information? We might be taking out an opponent rather than one of the Guild Masters," Merrick questioned.

The possibility was high and was something Abbas might have done likewise, if their roles were reversed. Traitors and deceit were aplenty in the underworld of the Heart Eternal.

Abbas disagreed. "No. She's loyal but won't jeopardize her son. This is the right house."

Merrick still found it difficult to accept a brute like Ninean Foul was capable of producing offspring, much less function as a loving mother, willing to do anything for her child. This was a city of wonders, he surmised.

"Enough talk," Abbas said. "We strike now."

Merrick blew out a pensive breath, tickling the hair drooping over his eyebrows. Kill and move. That was the plan. Adrenalin overpowering his rising fear, he followed Abbas across the street. They split up. One moving down the road to swing around the back. Abbas made for the front door, reckoning to take the house off guard enough they would not have time to recover.

A servant answered the door and received a dagger through the throat. Abbas was in no position to assume anyone was innocent. He ripped the blade free, a rope of bright blood spewing after, and stepped through the partially opened door. Two guards moved from behind a pair of pillars flanking the entry. Short swords flashed. Abbas ducked forward and rolled, rising on one knee. He slashed the first guard across the stomach and spun on the second. Caught unaware by the speed of assault, the guard could only blink when Abbas's blade punched up into his sternum. A sword fell. The first guard stopped writhing and lay still in a spreading pool of blood and intestines. Abbas slashed the second guard's throat and kept moving.

Crashing from the rear of the house suggested Merrick was enacting his part. The distraction drew several staff and guards, opening a lane for Abbas to gain the alabaster staircase. He took the steps two at a time. Movement behind and below drew his attention, forcing him to stop and confront a trio of attackers. A gaunt man, far older than any who should be playing at violence, led them. A slender rapier wavered in his hand.

Abbas spied the fear in his eyes. This man was no fighter. A housecarl then. The trio of blades whipped across the distance between them. The first caught the old man between the eyes. He toppled lifeless down the stairs, his blood leaving obscene streaks on the marble. The second clipped a guard in the shoulder. He jerked back with a grunt.

The third missed and the guard was on him a heartbeat later. They exchanged furious blows. A curtain of sparks showered down each time. Abbas was outmatched. The guard was bigger and stronger. His assault pushed the assassin up the stairs. A lucky swipe caught Abbas on the forearm. The red line showed through his torn sleeve. Angered, Abbas made a feint for the guard's head, and after the man committed to defending his throat, slipped right and drove his dagger up under the armpit and into the guard's unarmored heart.

Choosing to ignore the wounded guard nursing his broken shoulder, Abbas bounded the final few steps and came face to face with Jaum Zev. The master assassin was dressed in a pair of loose linen trousers and nothing else. He glared at Abbas with a steeled gaze. Muscles rippled across his chest and shoulders. Zev was every ounce the predator.

"Enough of this. You came here for me," Zev said. His voice reminded Abbas of steel scraping granite.

Breathing hard, Abbas pointed his dagger at Zev. The older assassin offered a feral grin and dropped into his fighting stance. Abbas leaned forward and waited. Zev took the bait and attacked. Fleshy footsteps slapped down the hall. His every focus was bent on murdering the intruder. He never got the chance. Abbas reached behind and withdrew the small pistol hidden in his waistband.

The shot rumbled like thunder through the mansion. Zev jerked to a halt, blinking rapidly with his face twisted in confusion. He stared at the smoke pouring from the barrel and dropped to his knees. Red blossomed across his upper chest. His heart pumping precious blood and life out. Mouth agape, Zev failed to speak. Every heartbeat brought death closer. The light behind his eyes began to fade. He toppled over and lay staring up.

Abbas stood over the dying Zev. "You should have killed me when you had the chance."

Tucking the pistol away, the assassin drew a serrated blade. There was yet work to be done and precious little time to finish. He knelt and began to cut.

"This is nonsense. We're wasting our time."

Polux gave his partner a sidelong glare, tired of listening to him gripe. Their shift began at sundown and now, close to midnight, Ulit had yet to let up. The prefects were reassigned from their normal duties to hunt down reports and rumors of a new terror stalking the streets. Seventeen bodies had been discovered within the last two days. Concerns mounted over the Prefecture's inability to maintain order and security during the peace conference. Already hungry for claiming Ghendis Ghadanaban for itself, the ruling body of Eleboran only needed the right excuse.

Neither Polux nor Ulit knew or cared for the politics behind their reassignment. They were part of over one hundred prefects diverted from customary positions. Tega Ig had cast a wide net to catch the beast responsible, despite no credible witnesses having come forward. Compounded with the recent rise in murders, the city stood on the edge of panic. All Polux and Ulit knew was they were not getting any bonus pay and their hours shifted from day to night. Not the best conditions under any circumstance.

Ulit stifled a yawn. He had yet to get used to the changing shifts. "It's just a job, Polux. Tega knows what he's doing, else he wouldn't be in his position."

"Does he?" Polux stopped in the middle of the street. "Seems to me like we are hunting a ghost. Dead bodies indeed! Have you seen any of them? Me neither!"

Ulit was about to reply, when a strange sound drew his attention to the nearest alley. "Did you hear that?"

"What?"

Frantic scratching, as if someone or something was trying to escape a cage erupted from the shadows before them. Ulit froze, unsure how to proceed. Months of training offered no relatable experiences for him to draw from. Ultimately, he drew his pistol and edged closer. Graphic images of conjured nightmares flashed in his mind. A terror unparalleled from song or story. He swallowed his fear, trusting to his training. He barely registered Polux's bootsteps echoing behind.

The prefect halted at the edge of light and shadow. His heart thundered between his ears. Shadows moved. The scratching stopped. Ulit exhaled slowly and raised his pistol. The attack was so fast he had no time to react. Claws reached from the darkness to latch onto his upper torso. Ulit fired, but the shot went wild. A mass of putrid flesh burst from cover and tackled him. They rolled twice before Ulit felt his lungs ripped from his chest. Unable to breath, the prefect lived his final moments babbling for his mother with blood stained lips.

A second shot clipped the creature in the chest without effect. Polux staggered back and tried to reload, as the creature dropped the now dead Ulit and turned on Polux. He had time for one scream before being ripped apart.

THIRTY-SIX

"It is time," Caestellom announced.

His wings were unfurled, absorbing the morning sunlight. None of the quest had paid attention to their majesty until now, for he truly looked like the servant of a god. Resplendent armor reflected the first light of dawn. A long sword was strapped to his hip and a pair of battle axes poked up from behind his head. The straps of his sandals rose to mid-calf, accented by the pleats of his alabaster chiton.

Tula choked back her sob, for she was about to lose the one person she felt closeness with. Aldon was a brave boy, but nothing he could say or do was able to change what was about to happen. Falon urged that this was for the best, both for the city and the boy. No one deserved to live with the essence of a god, lest they succumb to madness. Tula reluctantly agreed and offered to escort Aldon to his waiting guardian.

Every step was akin to a knife plunging into her. Every heartbeat an eternity unlived. She wished there was another way. Anything to spare them the mental anguish of knowing it was through their deeds that Aldon would cease to be. Caestellom was wise not to have mentioned this before reaching the base of the mountains.

For his part, Aldon was mostly gone. Retreated into his mind while the god-king dominated. The act was nearly complete. All that remained was to get him to Rhorrmere and begin the transformation process. When pressed, the Scarlet assured them Aldon would feel no pain. He was to be the forty-eighth person to undergo the change. A worthier calling there was not. Tula remained dubious, for the words of immortals carried little weight with her. She gave Aldon a final squeeze on the shoulder after leaving him beside the Scarlet and turning away. The golden light flickering from Aldon's eyes followed her.

She was almost back with the others when a cry spun her around.

"Tula, wait!" Aldon broke free or was let free in a final act of kindness before Omoraum Dala'gharis took over.

Tula braced as Aldon crashed into her with the fiercest hug she'd ever received. Unable to control them any longer, her tears broke free and left tracks through the stains on her cheeks.

"You were my best friend throughout this," he whispered into her ear. "Don't cry for me. I will be all right. I promise."

Aldon released her and returned to his place beside Caestellom, where he looked up to the giant and said, "I am ready."

The Scarlet's gaze lingered on Tula, barely able to stand in her grief, despite the warm smile creasing her face. He did not profess to understand human emotions, often viewing them as manifested frailty, but the bond between the new god king and his protector threatened to question everything he knew.

"Hold on tightly," he said and wrapped his arms around Aldon's chest.

The boy obeyed, and they launched into the sky as fast as a bullet. The quest tracked them until they were lost to the clouds and the domain of the god kings beyond. None of them spied the elongated figure wreathed in feathers and scales detach from the mountain face in pursuit.

"Now what?" Hohn asked.

The boy and his winged protector had been gone for the better part of the day, leaving the others mired with indecision. They'd been given instructions to return to the Heart Eternal. That their task was fulfilled, and no further oaths bound them. The women viewed this as a form of failure, despite having done all they could to ensure Aldon survived the arduous journey south. Mission complete, they no longer had any quest to guide them. That lack of purpose threatened to consume them.

Falon chewed thoughtfully on the piece of dried meat. Rations were restocked, thanks to the grateful caravaners. Fresh food and water, including a healthy assortment of fruits and vegetables, were now aplenty but she found it odd and was content with her dried field rations.

"We should return to the city and make our final reports," she suggested.

Hohn barked a laugh. "I don't expect your leaders would take kindly to *Beast* here rolling through their gates unannounced. We're as likely to start a war as be welcomed."

"You will be rewarded for all you have done for us," Meone said. His tone was matter of fact, despite the growing unease in his mind. Now that their purpose was fulfilled, the prophet found himself wondering if Hohn and his foreigners should be regarded as threats. Nothing in the arsenal of Ghendis Ghadanaban compared to the raw firepower these alien soldiers displayed.

"Think so, huh?" Hohn countered.

He'd been through similar situations and all ended poorly. Here he was little better than a mercenary. An expendable tool discarded after doing what it needed to. Hohn neglected to entertain the notion of returning with the quest's survivors. He fancied having his head attached to his shoulders too much. That and what was sure to be a bounty on their heads for their betrayal of the militia would have spread throughout the kingdom already.

"You are suggesting I am lying?" the prophet balked.

"No, I'm suggesting you *think* that's the truth. I've been around long enough to know people don't react the way you think they will," Hohn replied. "You think this way because you were in the middle of it with us. None of your leaders back in that city spent one day or night out here. They have no idea what you've seen or done. Regardless of how you view it, they'll see my people as threats."

"He's right," Tula interrupted. She'd been silent since Aldon left. A piece of her left with him, hollowing her out. "They acted the same way with me. No one wants to work with a Reclamator but are happy touting our deeds to others, while we keep them safe."

"Where will you go?" Falon asked. She did not dispute Tula's claims, for she had been one of those against including the Reclamator in the quest.

"All we've wanted to do since crash landing was get home," he said. The admission took more out of him than he imagined.

Weeks and months of struggling culminated in an impossible situation far from where it began. The militia was no doubt still hunting them but lacked any serious threat now Hohn had the *Beast*. Only one fact was clear. They could not go near civilization, lest they risk being caught in the webs of a similar situation. A chance none of them were willing to take.

He licked his lips. "I've always believed that this squad can't be the only ones who survived the landing. Our cruiser carried over seven thousand soldiers, marines, and sailors. Chances are there are more of us on this planet. We need to find them and call for help."

"Do you think such possible? After all you've been through?" Falon asked. She began to wonder what traveling among the stars was like. The lure tugged at her heart.

He shrugged. "We have to try."

Tula bit into a fruit with purple skin and sweet, yellow meat. Juices dribbled down her chin, reminding her of a guiltless childhood. How she missed those days. If only life remained so simple. Perhaps they might not be in this position, cast away from all she knew and bewildered by the sudden loss of the only comfort she had.

Tine dropped down beside Hohn, offering the sergeant a canteen. Ignoring the doldrum looks souring their faces, he asked, "What do you suppose is happening up there? I've never seen a god before."

Thunder rumbled across the skies as if on cue. Gazes lifted to see lightning slashing through the thick cloud banks concealing Rhorrmere. Tula winced. Her mind raced through innumerable possibilities, all of them bad.

They landed atop a wide plateau jutting over the precipice several thousand feet above ground level. The air was thin, but breathable for Scarlet and Aldon's god king enhanced physiology. Lost far below lay the world and its mortal concerns. Windswept platforms and buildings stretched back into the heart of the mountain, for it was there the connection to the planet was born. A connection every celestial power emanated from.

Aldon stared at the impossible serenity laid out before him. Pristine marble floors ran a hundred meters before leading up to a pair of twenty foot doors made of copper and etched with figures born of legend. Statues of creatures not witnessed by man in thousands of centuries lined the path, glaring down on him in silent judgment. Aldon shivered from their stares.

Archways were carved from the living stone. Torches flickered from some, where darkness claimed others. Rhorrmere. Birth place of gods. A flight of yellow ibis huddled atop the main doorway. They provided the only spark of color suggesting anything close to natural. Soft vibrations tickled his feet. The very mountain was alive with raw, unfiltered power.

"Come. We must not delay," Caestellom said.

The Scarlet forged ahead, eager to complete his task and reclaim the throne of Ghendis Ghadanaban for his master once again. Authority rang with each footstep. Lingering behind, the part of Aldon allowed to bear witness to the majesty, was filled with thoughts of turning back. Fleeing to his past life and his ill mother. Terrible thoughts antagonized him. Was she dead? Had his father buried her and moved on, selling their home and leaving the city like they often whispered about when they thought he wasn't listening. A comforting fantasy, if little else.

"I don't want this," he whispered.

There is no choice. You have been chosen. So it has been since the dawn of time.

Aldon halted. The voice came from inside his head, deep within the recesses of his fractured mind. An impossibility under any other circumstance.

"This isn't what I am meant for. Get out of my mind."

Seldom do great men choose their fates. This is the highest honor we might achieve.

"We?" Aldon asked.

Soft laughter rattled around his mind. *I was once mortal, like you. I, too, was chosen to become more than my mortal flesh offered.*

Aldon shook his head, hoping to dislodge the voice. "You never gave me a choice!"

No, and for that you have my apologies. There was nothing else to be done. The city must have a god king, else the entire world folds into nightmare and death. The time has come for you to rise above your limitations.

"What of my parents?" Aldon asked. They were the lone aspect tethering him to his old life. Spending eternity without them, was a dire prospect.

They will be cared for. There is nothing more. It is time for your ascension.

The voice faded, leaving Aldon alone with the jumbled reconciliation of thoughts and presences in his mind. Through clouded eyes he saw the Scarlet waiting for him. The main doors to Rhorrmere were open, beckoning. Aldon placed his right foot forward and stepped onto an irreversible path.

"You chose wisely," Caestellom said with quiet approval as Aldon passed him.

They continued in silence. Aldon's eyes were wide with wonder as the glory of Rhorrmere was opened to him. Carved pillars twenty meters tall stretched to the vaulted ceilings. Vines and plants of every species decorated alcoves and outcroppings on all sides. Twin waterfalls, on opposite sides of the mountain hall, splashed over a kilometer into the ground. Golden light shined down through hundreds of windows carved into the roof of the mountain. Aldon's breath caught in his throat.

"Impressive is it not? Caestellom asked. "Long have I desired to look upon my ancient home. It fills me with hope again."

"You do not return?" Aldon asked.

"It is forbidden for the duration of our duty to the god king. Only when his reign is passed on to the successor are we given the opportunity to return home."

"But I see no one else," Aldon said.

"Nor shall you," Caestellom confirmed. "This is a gateway. A portal between this world and the realm my kind originate from. The chamber is this way."

He led Aldon down impossible corridors laden with more refined beauty than any place in the known world. The decadence of it embarrassed Aldon, for he had grown up poor, struggling to earn the food on their table. The vast wealth of Rhorrmere went unknown by all but a few. Curiosity snagged his attention and he began to wonder what opulence lay behind the veil of realms.

Caestellom stopped before a singular wooden door. The wood was ancient, sanded to a smooth finish and creamy from origin tree. It smelled of honey. "I can go no further. Inside this chamber you will experience apotheosis."

"Will it hurt?" Aldon swallowed his fear.

The Scarlet regarded him with cocked head. This was his first experience escorting an initiate to the source of power. Nothing in his training or instructions from Verian prepared him for the intimacy of watching a companion, even a mere mortal, struggle to comprehend the altering transformation about to occur. He never doubted the importance of his mission, for his kind was not prone to questioning orders, but a mild kinship had formed over the course of their quest. Caestellom was left wondering what those below were going through. Was it similar to what he felt when the god king was assassinated?

"Perhaps a moment," he replied, against his better judgment.

Aldon hung his head. "And when I am … changed? What will happen to my soul?"

"Even I am not privileged to all the answers," Caestellom answered.

"I'm scared," Aldon admitted.

The Scarlet knew there were no words of comfort or condolence available to provide the boy with the confidence required to undergo the change. Aldon was a simple creature and the god king seemed to toy with him by allowing his consciousness free during these final moments. Life was not fair, for anyone.

"Summon the wells of your courage. A moment only and the future will be yours for seven hundred years, young Aldon," he finally said.

An explosion rocked Rhorrmere. Chunks of ceiling containing millennia old frescos crashed around them. Raw power sizzled the air, electrifying it. Aldon's knees weakened, and he retched from the heavy acidic stench permeating the corridor. Caestellom drew his sword on impulse and faced the mountain entry. A serpentine figure writhed among the tons of debris where it had shattered the main doors. Dust and smoke curled around it.

"Wha…?" Aldon struggled to ask.

Caestellom gripped his sword with both hands. "Quickly, Aldon! Into the chamber! This foe is beyond you. Hurry!"

Without waiting, the Scarlet leapt into the air and sped to meet the invader. Horror had come to Rhorrmere for the first time in generations.

THIRTY-SEVEN

Aldon watched as the Scarlet and nightmare collided. He was reminded of the creature slain several days ago and his stomach rebelled again. Blinking away the tears, he was able to get his first glimpse of the creature. Massive wings of feathers and scales stretched the width of the entry. A hideously elongated body covered in mottled feather twisted to get free. Armor-like scales ran the length of its body. Two sets of short arms ended with claws as long as Aldon was tall. The wicked tail slashed into ancient stone, further ruining the glory Rhorrmere once was.

Unable to look away, Aldon watched as his protector collided with the creature. Sparks flew from both, each intent on murdering the other. His heart quickened, for he had only been on the outskirts of battle before now. The savage fury on display before him was akin to madness. Aldon winced with each blow. Cries of pain threatened to burst his eardrums. He dropped to his knees and covered his ears, oblivious to the tiny trickle of blood leaking from each.

Caestellom was a proven warrior, having dispatched the last nightmare, but he was barely recovered from that ordeal. Weakened, the Scarlet had every chance of falling. Aldon jerked up when the floor vibrations, subtle until now, strengthened. His immediate fear was the mountain was collapsing and they were all going to die. A soft groan, almost like a whispered kiss breathing down the back of his neck, drew his attention. Turning, Aldon saw the door to the apotheosis chamber had opened.

His heart was ready to collapse. Part of him wanted to help the Scarlet, even knowing that doing so meant unavoidable death. He was no fighter. No great soldier from ancient ballads. His life had been filled with peace until the night the god king's essence discovered him weeping in the alley. Yet what he lacked in martial prowess, Aldon made up for with courage. He knew the only true way to help Caestellom was by entering the chamber and gaining the powers of a god. Nothing for it, Aldon Cay pulled himself from the floor and entered the chamber.

The door closed behind him, leaving the battle of titanic foes to their fates.

Instincts took over the moment he recognized the threat. Caestellom pushed his sword before him, meaning to plunge it into the creature's heart and sever the lifeblood before getting involved in a protracted engagement. His wounds from fighting Waujulx had yet to heal, leaving his strength depleted. The first of the Orpheliac proved more than a match for the Scarlet. His cursory look at the second threatened to undo him.

Saiatuterum disengaged from the piles of rubble in time to see the winged guardian speeding toward him. How alike they both were. Each assigned the unenviable task of preventing the other from succeeding. It could end in only one way. One of them needed to die. Saiatuterum had felt his brother's death and knew it could only have come at the hands of the Scarlet preparing to attack. With the promise of vengeance in the air, he attacked.

They collided above the once pristine halls of Rhorrmere. Shockwaves assaulted the mountain upon impact. Sword and claw hacked and slashed. Feathers fell, sprinkled with the first light drops of blood. Saiatuterum experienced pain for the first time since his imprisonment when the sword tip plunged into his ribcage. He slashed, catching the Scarlet across his unprotected face. The blow was fierce enough to send his attacker crashing to the ground. Going for the kill, Saiatuterum flew to the roof and struck down straight as an arrow.

Caestellom shook the fog from his head and looked up in time to see the creature plunging down on him with claws bared He rolled left before the impact and heard a satisfying crunch of bones as the creature slammed into the floor. Risking a look away, the Scarlet was relieved to see Aldon slip into the apotheosis chamber. It was the last time they would ever see one another.

Wicked claws curled around his throat. Caestellom struggled to remove them before his head snapped off. Using every ounce of strength, the Scarlet managed to drive one hand away but the other clutched harder. He brought his sword up, seeking to cut the hand free. Unwilling to abandon his promised bounty, Saiatuterum flung the Scarlet away. Caestellom flipped over and back down the hall and into the open sky. The Orpheliac followed at speed.

Their battle reengaged among the clouds, where beast and protector first came into being. Lightning wreathed the area. Superheated bolts of energy charged the atmosphere. Caestellom regained control moments before crashing into a series of jagged cliffs. Wings flapping to alter course, he turned on his foe. They clashed again, unwitnessed by all. This time the Scarlet managed to slice through Saiatuterum's right wing. Enraged, the winged monster slammed into Caestellom. They plummeted in loose spirals, unable to untangle.

Down through the clouds they battled. A fist punched. Claws raked deep gouges through armor and flesh. Strength faded in both. Caestellom roared as dagger-like fangs bore down into his shoulder, crunching bone and flesh. He pushed a thumb in the creature's eye and didn't stop until he felt a satisfying pop. Ichor painted his hand. Saiatuterum's fangs bit harder. Angel and demon, they continued to fall.

They heard the thunderclap before seeing what caused it. Hohn and Falon were the first to react. Each snatched rifles from nearby and scanned skyward. Helmetless, Hohn was just as blind as Falon. He growled at being caught unprepared but recognized the situation did not call for full defensive measures. The caravan was gone, leaving the mixed band of soldiers and questers alone at the oasis. No immediate threats present, Hohn had ordered a partial stand down. He regretted that decision.

Plunging down from the skies above came two beings out of legend. Hohn's mouth fell open as he recognized the Scarlet, or what was left of him.

"Full defense! Guns up!" he bellowed. "Tine, get on those AA guns!"

"What's going on?" his corporal called after poking his head from *Beast's* main roof hatch.

Hohn spat and reached for his helmet. "We're about to be krakked!"

The camp broke into action. Hohn's soldiers performed with well drilled precision. Falon and the others attempted to follow their lead by arming themselves. Only the Mascantii porters appeared ready for a fight. They brandished clubs and readied. Falon admired their steadfastness but doubted what a piece of wood might do against the monster falling to the ground. Panic rose in her chest, urging her to break and run.

Caestellom and the creature separated a hundred meters from the ground. The monster wobbled away, one wing dangling limply as the Scarlet hovered in place. He bled from a score of cuts, including deep gouges circling his throat. The tip of his sword was gone. Red stains painted his armor and chiton. Once impeccable feathers were in disrepair, leaving him with a disheveled appearance. His face was tight. Eyes focused.

Falon could tell he was at the ends of his strength. Whatever foul manifestation of hate the Scarlet combated, was his match in every regard. She wanted to weep, knowing there was little a lone woman with a single shot rifle could accomplish. Memories of her failure during the first attack haunted her, threatening to render her immobile.

"Falon … Sergeant! Get your people inside. You can't fight this," Hohn shouted.

Stunned into action, Falon ran for the *Beast's* back ramp, and presumed safety. She was relieved to find Tula doing the same. Meone was already cowering among the webbed seats, whispering prayers to the god king. Only the Mascantii chose to remain behind. Loyal unto death. She wished she had their conviction.

The ramp raised after she boarded. Safe for the moment, Falon took in the chaotic scene. Soldiers manned each of the heavy weapons bolted into the frame. Hohn was already in the turret, strapped in to the command chair. *Beast* hummed to life. The turret spun a moment before the entire vehicle rocked as Hohn tripped the air defense cannons. Energy bolts shredded the sky around the flying monster.

Saiatuterum dodged the incoming rounds. The Scarlet was his true foe, but this armored threat proved a greater challenge. One he could ultimately flee. Deciding he needed to kill the god king protector, the Orpheliac made one final attack. Not to be outdone, the Scarlet responded in kind. Claws ripped deep into Caestellom's abdomen, as his sword punched through Saiatuterum's sternum and out his spine. Bones shattered in the collision. Ripping his claws free, Saiatuterum cast his enemy to the ground and turned to flee.

Anti-aircraft rounds from twin cannons found their targets, shredding the flying nightmare. Saiatuterum banked left, desperate to escape the unexpected onslaught. The vile bolts of light tracked him, ever a heartbeat behind. He knew his foe was not yet dead. Getting to him was a different matter. The mortals were defending their fallen comrade, though Saiatuterum could not fathom why. Surely they had to know he was going to kill them all once the Scarlet was dead?

One wing broken and the other shredded, Saiatuterum crashed into the ground. Soft sand splashed over him. Smoke wafted from his wounds. He was hurt, badly. Worse, the human bearing the god king's essence had escaped him. The transformation would be occurring now, regardless of the conflict on the ground below. There was nothing for it now. He had failed Razazel and would pay for it when the moment arose.

It was a struggle to rise. To take each agonizing step toward the metal beast assaulting him. Saiatuterum recognized the taste of death far better than any of his opponents. It burned his nostrils and soured his stomach. The Orpheliac had enough strength for one final assault. A last chance to kill his ancient enemy. He spied the Scarlet rise to his hands and knees. Angered, Saiatuterum attacked.

Energy rounds slashed through the air, striking him in the chest and limbs. Chunks of flesh were obliterated. He pushed harder, desperate to claim his prize before darkness claimed him. A string of rounds stitched across his shoulders before zeroing on his head. Brains, blood, and bone burst apart. What remained slapped into the sand with sickening thuds. Blood dropped like rain, burning deep holes wherever it touched. An immense wave of sorrow swept across the battlefield. As if the world could at least weep in relief. Weapons powered down.

"Keep those crew served up. I don't want anything catching off guard again. Tine, stay in the turret until I give the all clear," Hohn ordered.

Tine trained his weapon on the corpse remains. "You're not going out there?"

"Might as well. I have nothing else to do," Hohn replied. He slapped the button to lower the rear hatch and stormed out. Soft bootsteps behind told him Falon followed.

"I need to see this for myself," she defended and pushed past him.

He didn't judge her for it. He would want to know, too. There was little to see of the winged creature but a ruined corpse. Falon's stomach soured from the putrefying stench. Maggots crawled through the dead flesh, born upon the moment of death. Bile rose in her throat, forcing Falon to cover her mouth and nose with her sleeve.

"Nasty bugger, isn't it?" Hohn asked. He wished again for his helmet to filter out the poisoned oxygen. "This one like the other that attacked you?"

She nodded. "Yes, but different. The first didn't fly."

He pointed at the corpse with his rifle. "This one isn't anymore. I wonder how many more of these things are out there."

Any answer was delayed by Caestellom staggering into view. Hohn gasped uncharacteristically.

How the Scarlet remained on his feet was beyond his ability to comprehend. Wounds capable of killing a man several times over covered him. The light in his eyes dimmed. Gone was his haughty demeanor. He took three steps before collapsing.

Hohn turned back to the *Beast* and shouted, "Medic! Bring up the aid packs!"

He and Falon ran to Caestellom's side. A cursory glance told them he was not going to rise again. Blood flowed down his limbs. One arm was broken. Puncture wounds in his torso tunneled through his back. How he had lived this long was beyond either mortal. Still, he struggled to sit up.

"Relax, Caestellom," Falon urged. Sorrow laced her tone. "Help is coming."

"There is … no need," he said through bloodstained teeth. "Is it … dead?"

"Blasted it to shreds," Hohn confirmed. "Where's the boy?"

Caestellom's head struck the sand and he closed his eyes. "Gone. He … even now be … comes the god king."

"You did it," Falon grasped his hand and squeezed.

"My task … is complete," the Scarlet said.

He exhaled a final breath and was no more. Death had come to the Scarlet, though it did not matter. The boy was undergoing the transformation and would return to Ghendis Ghadanaban before the ancient enemy arrived. Neither Falon nor Hohn knew any of this. They were wracked with grief. Falon dropped to her knees and wept upon seeing Caestellom's peaceful look. She imagined him happy and longed for the day when she might achieve the same.

Hohn stared down on the impossible man with regret. For his faults, Caestellom was a grand warrior deserving better. The medic arrived with Tula and Meone a step behind. "You're not going to need that."

"Is he?" Tula asked.

"Yes."

Mixed emotions clashed within her. Tula never felt affinity for the Scarlet, especially after learning his true purpose on the quest. Stealing Aldon, regardless of the higher purpose, stirred deep resentment. None of her protests or feelings negated his loss, however. The Scarlet were less of an organization with Caestellom gone.

"What should we do with him?" she asked.

"Do his people have any customs?" Hohn asked. "It doesn't seem right burying him in the middle of nowhere."

"The Scarlet are a private organization. Their dealings with the city are contained to the senior leadership," Falon managed after regaining control of her emotions. "This is the first time one of them has died among us, at least that I am aware of."

Their argument ended when brilliant heat began pulsing off the body. They were forced to step back to avoid being burned. White light, blinding with its effervescence, bathed the oasis. All feelings of anger or sorrow fled. Tranquility rushed in, calming beast and man. When the light faded and the world returned to normal, Caestellom's body was gone.

Tula gazed skyward, following the last vestige of light as it retreated to the mountains. Back to Rhorrmere. Her heart wept with joy. She wished Aldon found the same sense of peace. He deserved no less.

"I'll be damned," Hohn muttered.

"He's been called home," Tula said.

"Brings me back to my earlier point," Hohn said. "What do we do now?"

No one had answers.

THIRTY-EIGHT

They finished packing the excess crates of supplies left by the caravanners throughout the remainder of the day. Thoughts lingered on the events of the past few days. On the impossibility of Aldon becoming a god. The loss of Caestellom to monsters spawned from forgotten nightmares of earliest civilization. There was a lack of sense linking these events. Few of the surviving questers spoke. Their minds were fogged by the sudden lack of purpose. Aldon had arrived in Rhorrmere. Their task was complete.

Falon found Tula sitting on a small boulder overlooking the water. Her feet dangled as a child's might, having first discovered the unadulterated joy of the beauty of nature. Water bugs danced across the surface, ignorant of the trials of man.

"There is nothing like this in the city," Falon said.

Tula shuffled to one side of the rock and gestured for Falon to join her. "No. Though I doubt I will be able to look upon the streets the same again. This quest has changed me."

"It is our nature to change with our experiences," Falon sat beside her. The urge to tug her boots off awakened. The promise of an empty childhood.

"No one should endure what we were forced to, Falon," she replied.

"No, I don't suppose they should."

Tula took the stone in her hand and skipped it across the water. "Do you think Aldon suffered?"

"Hard to know but I like to think he didn't. He is …"

Tula wheeled on her, finger jabbing at her face. "Don't you dare try and tell me he's in a better place or he's been called to a higher purpose. It's all rubbish!"

"I was going to say that he is beyond our concern," Falon swallowed the surge of anger coloring her face. "We do not always get to choose our fates. Whatever reason the god king found him is above our reckoning, Tula. Stop being hard on yourself. There was no way to know what would happen once we delivered him to Rhorrmere."

No, but we should have guessed. Caestellom had always been taciturn when dealing with them. Tula figured it was due to his secret. The possibility of the quest turning against him should they discover the truth of what Aldon was to become was too high to entrust to a bunch of strangers. Perhaps not even the Overseer or First Prophet knew. The Scarlet were cautious allies prone to remaining segregated from human society.

"I feel empty, Falon," Tula said.

The admission caught her off guard, though Falon was guilty of feeling the same. "Resuming our daily routines will prove difficult after this, but what else can we do? We have lives to return to, Tula. This was but a small task."

Tula skipped a second rock, watching each bounce until it plunged into the water. "We should get back. No doubt Hohn will be eager to depart."

Falon grinned. "I don't think he is as eager to return to civilization as we are."

Sharing a laugh, Tula said, "That man does need more friends. He's been trapped with those soldiers for too long."

Side by side, they made their way back to the *Beast*. Neither were in a hurry.

The digital map project across a wide screen dominating one wall of the interior. Topographic relays from deployed sensors showed them the world as it was, rather than a traditional one-dimensional map. The women were amazed, for such technology was unheard of. Hohn was amused by their sense of wonder. Such tools were taken for granted by his people.

"We've been amassing data since we first gained access to her," he said with a loving pat of the carrier's wall. "Every scrap of plottable terrain for almost two hundred klicks. What I don't have is coordinates for your city or how long it will take to reach it."

"You mean to take us home?" Tula asked.

"I mean to get you close enough without arousing suspicion," he corrected. "I'm still not going to risk taking my people too close. That being said, I think you've earned a ride home, especially considering your wagons and transportation have been destroyed."

Falon studied the map. Some of the terrain was familiar, for their two paths merged several days ago. "We must travel back to here," she pointed to the edge of the desolate terrain south of the desert, "and head north."

"How far?" Hohn asked.

Falon glanced at Tula. The Reclamator spoke up. "It took us almost two full weeks from Ghendis Ghadanaban to that point, including crossing the desert."

"I hate sand," Tine chimed in.

Hohn ignored him. "That whole thing is your city's name? There's a mouthful." He folded his arms, studying the map. "I figure it will take maybe a third of that to get you within walking distance."

"That would be most appreciated, Sergeant," Falon said.

"Like I said, the least we can do," Hohn replied. "Besides, it's about time we started moving again. I don't like being cooped up in one place for too long." *Especially when we still have bounties on our heads.*

    The Beast cruised across the broken terrain leading up to the river. Kilometers sped by without incident. A welcome relief for all. They passed the scene of the Mordai ambush and were not surprised to find the bodies stripped of all useful items. Nomads were known to raid battlefields. Carrion eaters flocked by the hundreds. Some of the dead were already reduced to glimmering white bones. Falon absorbed the scene, taking special notice of how the land was dead for a hundred meters where they killed the first monster. She thought she heard a whisper of agony on the winds as they drove by.

    Night was no impediment to the armored personnel carrier but the journey was halted by human limitations. A full day's ride left them aching to get out and stretch their legs, despite having more room than was both necessary and imaginable inside the main hull. Hatches were cast open to refresh the stagnant air. Details were assigned to fill empty water cans and dig a slit trench for waste. Hohn relented in allowing a cookfire. The *Beast's* resources were only going to last for so long before it became an armored fixture. Conservation was vital, at least until he secured a ride home.

    The Mascantii returned from a fast foraging expedition with several ringed pheasants, a sack of tubers, and pears from a patch of desert cactus. Laughter joined the aroma of roasting game bird. Much of the tension left them. Rhorrmere was a day's trek away and with it the bitter sting of memories best unremembered. Food was shared. Tales of deeds both daring and quizzical spread. Hohn and his squad dazzled them with stories from distant worlds far beyond the limits of imagination.

Hohn plunked down beside Tula and passed a small green bottle. "You look like a woman with a lot on her mind. Nothing a little of this won't fix."

"I don't drink," she replied. Her knees were drawn, arms wrapped around them.

Hohn snorted. "I don't either, but I know when I need a release. You're screwed tight. Most likely with guilt. Let it go, Tula. Otherwise, it's going to devour you whole."

She stared at him with tear filled eyes. "How can I? Aldon was just a boy. He didn't deserve this."

"Who are we to say who deserves what? From what I gathered, and its not much mind you, he still has another six or seven hundred years left in his time as this god king of yours. I don't know about you, but that's a damned sight longer than I plan on being around," he said.

Tula struggled to imagine seven hundred years. In her late twenties, she figured she had another good six decades before time caught up and won its battle with her. Until Hohn brought up the duration of the god king's reign, she felt eighty was almost too long.

"Hundreds of years without friends, family, or confidants," she mused.

Hohn gestured with the bottle again. "I imagine he's going to have a few more of those winged fellows to protect him."

Tula finally laughed. She accepted the bottle and took a long swig. Fire trailed down her throat to boil deep within her stomach. Tula gagged and passed the bottle back. "Are you trying to kill me?"

She missed his wink. "Why would I want to do that? Drink enough of this and you won't be thinking about too much. That I promise."

"Where do you come from, Hohn?" she asked after the nauseous feeling faded.

He took another drink. "That is a long story."

"We have time," she replied.

"Aye, that we do. That we do," Hohn settled in for what promised to be a long night.

They crossed the river and charged headlong into the desert. Kilometers sped by and the quest to save Ghendis Ghadanaban drew closer to home. Many of the soldiers were envious, for there was no guarantee of them finding a way off world. The prospect of being stranded here for the rest of their lives was daunting, almost frightening, but they were soldiers and used to adverse environments and situations. *Beast* was cresting a large dune when an impact jarred the vehicle. The subsequent explosion made ears rings.

"What the krak was that?" Hohn shouted.

A second detonation brought them to a halt. Soldiers rushed to battle stations, while the questors worried another monster was attacking. Hohn knew better. He had been in the army long enough to know the sound of anti-armor rocket fire. This was a war he could fight and fight well. Swinging out of his hammock, Hohn snatched his armor and helmet and hurried to the command cupola.

"Where's it coming from?" he demanded.

A young tech private with dull orange skin and webbed hands ran the main gun tracking. Her first campaign had just ended before the carrier ship was destroyed and the survivors stranded. She had never been in a direct fire situation before and her heart hammered with the possibility of being killed by their own weapons.

"Three mark eighteen," she answered. "Two hundred meters out. Lone gunman."

"We missed a weapon," Hohn cursed. The mistake might kill them all. "Magnify. I want to see who this bastard is."

Tech Private Illei obeyed. "Yes, Sergeant."

Hohn leaned forward, devouring the image on the heads-up display. Two men in ragged clothing reloading the rocket. The image intensified. Hohn caught his first glimpse of their attackers faces. "I'll be damned. The little weasel survived."

"Sergeant?" Illei asked.

"Nothing. Back us out of sight," Hohn said.

"We're not going to use the main guns?" Tine asked after crawling up to take the empty third seat.

"Waste of ammo," Hohn replied. "Delag is cunning. Once he sees us locking on, he'll fade back into the desert."

"What are you going to do?"

Hohn grabbed his helmet and a rifle. "I'm going to end this for good. I want all defensive measures manned. Expect incoming from anywhere. These militia boys don't prefer stand up fights."

"You need backup?" Tine asked.

Hohn didn't answer.

"Traitor! Come out and die like a man," Delag bellowed.

His good fortune at finding alien weapons, albeit a single rocket launcher with a handful of rounds, made him momentarily as powerful as the mercenaries. Killing them would not only allow him to go home with his honor, but gain command of a new, stronger unit. Delag only needed to claim Hohn's head. His wait was short.

Hohn crested the same dune the *Beast* retreated from sight. The urge to kill Delag without pause was strong, but Hohn wanted the man to see who was robbing him of his life. Justice demanded more but time was limited. He hated deserts.

"You're supposed to be dead," Hohn replied.

Three more militia popped up beside their leader. *Five to one. Not the odds I prefer*. Still, killing promised to be only slightly difficult. He held the advantages of firepower and purpose. Single shot rifles were like flies against his armor and energy weapon.

Delag sneered. "I've been wanting to kill you for a long time, scum."

Hohn slowly raised his hands. "You should be careful with that. It's not a toy. Better men than you have been hurt because they didn't know what they were doing."

The anti-armor rocket leveled on him. A warhead poked from the end, dangerous if Delag's trigger finger slipped. "You talk too much."

"Don't say I didn't warn you," Hohn shrugged. His fingers curled around the grip of the smaller assault rifle strapped to his back.

Faster and with the advantage of catching the militia unaware, Hohn whipped the rifle up and over his head. He dropped into a kneeling firing position simultaneously and opened fire. The man beside Delag dropped with a gapping hole burning in his chest. The rocket fired, the missile going wide and detonating in a sand dune. Sand and sizzling fragments of metal whistled through the air.

Hohn fired again and again. Bullets danced off his armor, hardly powerful enough to rock him. He was a precision marksman. Every shot was accountable. Bodies dropped until only Delag remained. Stunned, the militiaman took a step back. Hohn rose, his weapon trained on Delag's chest. A heartbeat passed between them before Hohn fired. He turned before the body hit the sand, slung his rifle and headed back to the *Beast*.

Tula waited for him by the back ramp. The look on her face was a mixture of awe and revulsion. "You make friends wherever you go, don't you?"

"Perks of the job," he replied and kept walking past her.

Tine waited for him just inside the hull.

"You, too?" Hohn asked.

A veteran of nearly as many campaigns, the corporal shook his head. "You know me better than that. Looks like we got the last of them. No additional heat signatures on the radar. Delag the last one?"

"Bastard got what he had coming. He never should have double crossed us," Hohn said.

Tine agreed but kept his opinion silent. There were times a warrior needed to get lost within his thoughts. "What now?"

Hohn glanced at the few survivors of the god king quest. He'd given his word, the only thing of worth he had left. Abandoning them now meant almost certain death, if they made it to the desert. Honor demanded one course of action. "We head to this Ghendo Ghabababable of theirs and figure it out from there."

"Ghendis Ghadanaban," Tula countered as she slipped past.

Hohn offered look of false hurt. "That's what I said."

Tine's snicker was barely audible. "When do you want to leave?"

"I figure we've earned a rest. Establish a perimeter and bed down for the night. One more day isn't going to hurt anything," he said.

"You got it, Sergeant," Tine gave a halfhearted salute and hurried into the belly of the *Beast*. This adventure might be ended, but he was betting on another about to begin. Their time on world suggested nothing else.

THIRTY-NINE

Deliberations had been ongoing for two days and were officially stalled. Every effort officials from Ghendis Ghadanaban made to further communications and smooth bruised egos, ended in failure. Months of planning were wasted, as parties refused to see past petty grievances and a false sense of entitlement. Heated words dominated the hall, replete with accusatory fingers and angry gestures. Prefects were brought in as a precaution. Bloodshed would not be permitted, despite the decreasing levels of civility.

Overseer Larris had never felt more helpless. She had dedicated countless hours to ensuring all was prepared for the delegates. It was all for naught. Hostilities threatened to ruin everything and it was all she could do to keep them from each other's throats. Frustrated, Larris slipped away when the others were occupied.

There was no succor in the hall, nor any in the small chambers dedicated to individual consultations during breaks. Golden rays of sunlight streamed down through two story windows, bathing the hall with grandness unparalleled by all but the palace of the god king. She felt the warmth strike her cheeks and closed her eyes. If only each day proved as delicate as the subtle moments of tranquility.

"Overseer Larris, I have news."

She frowned at the disturbance. *Not one moment of peace.* Larris opened her eyes and was not surprised to find a prefect captain standing at attention before her. "What is it?"

"There has been a development, ma'am. Master Tega Ig has requested your presence," the captain answered.

Larris sucked in a deep breath. "Has this to do with the conference?"

"I am not permitted to say," he told her. "Master Ig insists it is most urgent, however."

Raised voices behind the closed doors made her mind up. A break was needed if there was any hope of saving the conference and her kingdom. "Lead the way."

She followed the captain to a seldom used part of the building and found Tega Ig waiting. He was not alone. Standing behind him, almost lost among the multicolored curtains, was a woman she had never seen. Exotic, with dark eyes and flowing black hair, the woman stared at her.

"Ah, Larris, you came," Tega said. A look of genuine relief flashed across his face. "I wasn't certain if you would."

"What is going on, Tega? They need me at the conference," she replied. "Who is this?"

"This is Lady Duema and she has brought most dire news," he said.

Larris took the empty chair closest to the door. "I can't afford any ill news today, Tega. The conference is ready to dissolve, and the war will go on. It has all been in vain."

"What she tells me goes far beyond this peace conference," he cautioned. "We have been betrayed."

Larris jerked up. "Betrayed? By whom?"

"The First Prophet has had illicit dealings with many dark powers, not the least of which a rogue assassin and the envoy from Mordai," Duema interjected. Her tone was severe, marking the seriousness of her message.

"You cannot be serious," Larris scoffed. The quiet part of her mind knew Sandis had been acting odd of late, but she refused to accept his complicity in deicide. "Sandis has served our city for decades."

"Larris, I believe her," Tega added. "Regardless, we are going to raid his quarters now. While he sits in the conference."

She was torn. Torn between coming to the aid of an old friend and standing with her city, her people in defense of righteousness. Duty beat loyalty, for the moment. "Very well, I shall join you. This matter is too delicate to be left to one faction, Tega. I will not accept no."

"I wasn't going to stop you," he said.

They found the emaciated slave from Mordai on accident. A prefect knocked over a vase, spilling water across the marble floor as it shattered. Larris spied the water disappear under what appeared a normal wall. Prefects broke through to find a concealed door and the slave within. Horrified, Larris stumbled back as the woman was brought into the light. She stared at the jewel affixed to her throat and the crimes committed against her body. Her stomach rebelled.

"Bring Sandis to my office. Arrest him immediately," she said with throaty breath.

"He may resist," Tega said.

Her silence told his all he needed to know. "Seal these quarters. No one enters. Use force, if necessary. I want this ... creature brought to the medical center. There must be some way to remove that stone without killing her."

The rustle of armed men and women filled the once serene halls of the offices of the First Prophet. Tega caught up to Larris as they descended the grand staircase leading to the conference. He insisted she not follow him in and this time she agreed. It would not do for the

Overseer of Ghendis Ghadanaban to play her cards so openly in front of potential enemies. She knew the Mordai were foes, but it was concern over Minister Quin that worried her most. The king was looking for any excuse to annex the city. Larris refused to cave.

She waited in a hidden alcove off the main hall for Tega and his prefects to do their work. Built with vantage points, Larris watched everything. Prefects marched in with weapons drawn and surrounded Sandis. The old man blustered and fumed with indignation, but she saw through the façade. He had every look of a man who knew his game was ended. It wasn't until he rose to be escorted from the hall, that the violence erupted around them.

Thrakus sprang to his feet immediately upon seeing the stream of prefects march in. "What is the meaning of this? We are under diplomatic protection."

"This does not concern you, Ambassador Thrakus," Tega growled. His impulse was to arrest them both and be done with the foul mess at once. Larris cautioned otherwise.

Quin took his cue and rose as well. "He is not wrong, Prefect Ig. Has the hospitality of your famed independent city lessened of late?"

"Minister, this concerns Ghendis Ghadanaban and nothing else," Tega replied.

"You forget this city stands in the kingdom of Eleboran," Quin countered, without raising his voice. "Why are you arresting your First Prophet?"

Others at the table chimed in, eager to learn the cause of such disruption. Tega fumed and could stand it no longer. "He is accused of treason and heresy against the god king."

"Nonsense," Thrakus spoke up, too quickly for coincidence.

Tega wheeled on him. "In conspiracy with your kingdom, Ambassador."

That was all the provocation Thrakus needed. He thumbed the communication stone in his trouser pocket, knowing his soldiers were listening. "Thank you for saying that. I grew tired of this charade long ago."

Doors burst open and Mordai soldiers rushed in. Stunned, the nearest prefect raised her pistol and was about to order them to halt, when she was shot between the eyes. Gunfire erupted on both sides of the hall. Minister Quin was caught in the crossfire and died instantly, an unfortunate circumstance, lost among the chaos. Mordai and prefects fell, dead or wounded. Delegates took cover behind flimsy chairs in the hopes of surviving the day. Thrakus stood tall amidst it all. A force of his own among the tides of the storm. Drawing the concealed pistol from within his robes, he took aim at Sandis and fired. The shot went wide, striking a tapestry on the wall behind him. Growling, Thrakus adjusted his aim, but Sandis was already moving.

No hero, Sandis scurried through the melee and rising clouds of gunpowder smoke to slip through a side door and down a small tunnel leading to the opposite side of the building. From there he inched into the empty hallway and crept to an abandoned stairwell. The distraction of growing battle in the conference hall pulled guards from across the building, giving him freedom to move unhindered.

Common sense suggested his quarters were being watched, forcing him to make a drastic move. How or why Tega Ig and Larris discovered his treason remained a mystery, one he figured he would never come to learn given his current circumstance. Hampered by his robes, his movement was slowed. It didn't take long before he heard the rush of boots and panicked cries of discovery from behind. He had been found.

Sandis hurried as fast as his old legs could carry him, but the sounds drew closer. He slipped into a hidden passage and began the long climb. Heart pounded, lungs burning, Sandis climbed for his life. Minutes dragged on and he began to fear he was going to die on the stairs. When at last he gained the top floor, he was winded and shaking from exertion. Cool winds blew across the open roof to kiss his face.

Fresh energy filled his body. Sandis wept, for the sun was dropping across the horizon. The sky was ablaze with red and pink hues. Such beauty. Resolve ignited, the First Prophet of Ghendis Ghadanaban strode to the edge and looked across his beloved city one final time. There had been a time when it meant everything. A shining beacon of what life might be like for all. Then greed crept into his heart and twisted it with poison. Years of scheming resulted in failure. The hourglass was nearly empty. A flock of speckled ibis flitted across the nearest rooftops, unconcerned for the travesty of man. Emboldened by their freedom, Sandis stepped onto the edge.

"Sandis wait!" Tega shouted after gaining the rooftop. A squad of prefects stood puffing at his back.

Sandis kept looking forward. A sad smile creased his face. Closing his eyes, he leaned forward and pitched over. The fall took longer than he imagined.

The Mordai moved swiftly in a coordinated assault. Platoons rushed to secure the gates and main arteries leading in and out of the city. Others, funneled through seldom used paths in the sewer system, surrounded the administration buildings. Without the power of the god king to protect them, the people of

Ghendis Ghadanaban were helpless to resist. Those with presence of mind to grab a weapon and try were beaten into submission or killed on the spot. Mordai discipline was as ruthless as it was efficient.

Thrakus secured the conference hall, taking those few who survived prisoner. Pushed from the center of the city, the prefects struggled to find any way to circumvent the Mordai before their stranglehold on the city was complete. Tega Ig rallied almost one hundred men and women to his side and formed the core of the resistance. Fighting soon raged street by street. The Mordai were able to strike unexpected, forcing the defenders to collapse and react to their aggressions.

High above, oblivious to the trials of man in the night, Lord Verian and his Scarlet waited. He cared little for the humans. They were trivial at best but were sworn into his protection. Even with his winged soldiers, there was little he could do to stem the tide of violence flooding through the streets. The Mordai had been preparing for this moment for months, if not longer. His resources were already depleted with Caestellom gone and the god king dead. Tega Ig and his prefects would be forced to deal with the usurpers. He had other matters to attend.

"You are not to leave this building," he ordered his faithful. "Do not engage with the Mordai unless they attempt to enter."

"Master, are we to leave this city to ruin and depredation?" a Scarlet asked.

"The god king may return at any moment," Verian replied. *If Caestellom was successful.* There had been no word from the quest for weeks. "I shall return shortly. Let none pass."

They saluted as one. The thump of fists slapping armor echoing across the room. Verian strode to the open archway overlooking the city and spread his wings. He was airborne a moment later and soaring over Ghendis Ghadanaban in search of his prey. It did not take long. Far from the fighting, lost to the moment, was the nightmare creature responsible for killing over a score of people. A useful distraction, he mused, for the Mordai dogs.

Verian drew his sword and tucked his wings in for a dive. The beast that was once Ambassador Ytel of Uruth rampaged through the streets. Fresh blood dripped from razor sharp claws and teeth. Covered with pustules and reeking of death, Ytel tore in to any unfortunate enough to cross his path. He had evaded Verian every night, until now. Destiny brought them together in what promised to be a clash of nightmares. Skilled as he was in combat, the Lord of the Scarlet was unused to monsters.

The Ytel creature glanced up a moment before Verian struck. Feathers fell as the two powerful entities clashed. Steel met claw in a shower of sparks. Each was match for the other in raw strength. Verian was pressed to find an opening to deliver the killing blow. As fast as he was, the Ytel creature was faster and filled with hate. Ducking back to avoid a decapitating blow, the creature slashed under Verian's exposed side. Nails scraped bone. Verian yelped in pain and leapt back.

He failed to recall the last time he saw his own blood and it enraged him. The creature jumped to attack and Verian slashed with all his strength. Steel caught flesh under the armpit. Verian twisted and ripped the blade free. An arm dropped at his feet. The creature flew past Verian and crashed into the wall of the nearest building. A cloud of dust erupted, occluding much of the area.

Invigorated, Verian pressed his attack. Despite being sorely wounded, the Ytel creature continued fending off blows, yet more continued to strike, as his strength wore down from blood loss. Rivers of black blood decorated the cobblestones. Verian ignored everything but the killing blow. He attacked with unmitigated fury. A slash opened the creature's stomach. Gore and entrails spilled, splashing across Verian's sandals. The Scarlet stepped back, and with the creature pinned against the wall, plunged his sword through the soft throat tissue and into the brain.

Verian stepped back as the creature slid to the ground. The light in its eyes dimmed but Verian swore he spied a smile before it faded completely. It confirmed his suspicions that the creature was once human and paid for his sins by becoming a nightmare. No one deserved such fate. Disgusted, Verian whipped his sword down. Blood and ichor dripped away. It was not until he wiped the rest clean with a rag, that he realized how easy the conquest had been. Questions entertained him during his flight back. Was the creature a distraction until the Mordai attacked or was it glad to finally meet its demise, so that it could be released from endless torment and misery? Questions he knew no answer would suffice. The Lord of the Scarlet returned to his quarters with much on his mind.

FORTY

Tega Ig scowled at the medic tying the stained bandage around his arm to stop the bleeding. A Mordai bullet struck him shortly before dawn, narrowly missing his chest. Fighting had raged throughout the remainder of the night and threatened to consume the city for a second day. Word reached him of fresh Mordai reinforcements from battle hardened regiments preparing to enter the city through the eastern gates. Unless his prefects and civil defense militia managed to regain control to the entry point, and get the gates shut, there was little doubt in his mind the city would fall.

"You should keep pressure on it and find a place to sit down," the medic cautioned before packing her supplies and moving on to the next casualty.

Tega watched her go. There was no question of ignoring her. He had a battle to fight and sitting on the side, while good men and women died, was not an option. Exhausted, the Master of Prefects worried his tenure was going to end in failure. His name cursed for generations. Grimacing, he rose and went to collect a new weapon. His last pistol was lost during the retreat from the conference hall. A large stack lay on the nearby table. Many had bloodstains. Despair awakened and Tega lamented the loss of so many.

"Head up, lad. We're still in this fight," he said, after spying a young prefect with his head hung. Dirt and grime stained his face and hands. His uniform was torn from a frantic night of fighting for his life. Defeat lingered in his eyes. A boy forced to become a man.

"Yes, sir," he replied. Buoyed by Tega's personal attention, he reached for a box of bullets.

Tega clapped him on the shoulder. There was fight yet left in him. Close to a hundred others crowded the small warehouse. Everyone from veterans to rookies fresh from the academy. Those closest overheard him and pepped up. Tega knew what he must do and began making his way through the crowd. Prefects reached out to him. Their hands grasping at his uniform, as if that would grant them strength. He soaked it in, knowing there was still hope. Reaching the center of the room, he raised his hands for silence.

"Friends, we are beset by enemies on all sides. Let that not trouble you, for we are all that stand between the oppression of those Mordai dogs and freedom," he began. Heads bobbed. "Your homes, your families, your loved ones all depend on you to withstand the storm! Dig deep into your resolve and find the courage, the strength, the raw determination to save them and this city. Cast these dogs back to the desert with their tails between their legs! Are you with me?"

The roar knocked dust from the rafters.

The beleaguered prefects of Ghendis Ghadanaban took care of their wounds, ate what rations as were available, and replenished weapons and ammunition. A sleepless night left them weary. Raw determination to defend their people kept them on their feet. Bolstered by Tega Ig, the prefects slipped from cover as dawn broke. Teams of three to five rushed into the dying night and toward Mordai emplacements. Caught unawares in several instances, the Mordai soldiers were slaughtered where they stood.

The streets ran red with blood. Bodies littered the city of god kings. Men and women, and more than a few unfortunate children. The villainy of Mordai appeared limitless. Vengeance propelled the prefect defenders to fight harder, yet for each victory, defeat followed. Ambushes were traded across the eastern districts. Every firefight left the prefecture depleted a little more. Block by block, the defense shrank.

Tega ignored the advice, and no little insistence, of his senior officers and sergeants and led the campaign from the streets. They argued he was too valuable to lose in the fighting but it fell on deaf ears. Determined to reap a terrible count, the Master of Prefects strode forth to confront death. An hour later and he was drenched in sweat and blood. His rifle was gone, ruined when a Mordai bullet struck just above the trigger housing. Down to a pair of pistols and a now well-used sword, Tega led his team down a side alley off the main market avenue.

Word reached him of the Mordai attempting to establish a massive counter checkpoint at the crossroads. If successful, they would freeze traffic for the entire city and control one of the lifelines leading to the gates. A target that big would require many soldiers. Tega pushed as hard as his tired legs would take him. Less than twenty prefects were at his back. He knew no less than a platoon of Mordai awaited. Chances of survival were slim and he was without immediate reinforcements.

The prefect assault force edged closer to the end of the alley and halted. Many were panting, hands on their knees. Tega applauded their efforts, for they were never meant to fight a war. Pistol drawn, he peered around the corner and was dismayed. Fifty soldiers busied building sandbag barricades surrounding a massive bunker constructed in the center of the intersection. He spied the barrel of a cannon jutting from behind a pile of boards and it soured his stomach. There was no way he could hope to defeat an active artillery piece with so many infantry in support.

"We must move quickly," he told the others. Explaining the situation, Tega described the cannon positioning and what they faced.

Undaunted, the prefects were too invigorated to back down. They split into two groups and struck out in parallel routes. Tega ordered them to attack as soon as the first group got into position. If anything, their slaughter would provide a useful distraction for the second team to assault the cannon. Heart hammering in his chest, the Master of Prefects hurried to what he knew was certain doom. Gunfire erupted from across the street. The others arrived first.

Sounds of pain followed. Men and women from both sides screaming as battle joined. Already outnumbered, Tega urged his group faster. Pistols cocked and swords drawn, they attacked. He took aim at the back of the nearest Mordai and fired. Blood fountained across his back and the man fell with a strangled cry. Tega let momentum carry him on. Other shots followed and more Mordai fell. Pinched on both sides, the Mordai infantrymen were caught off guard. Tega's group had a clear run to the cannon.

A spray of bullets dropped three of his group and forced the others to jerk to a halt. The cannon crew emerged from cover with bayonets fixed. They advanced on the prefects in step. Enraged, Tega fired at the section leader. The bullet caught him in the throat. Both lines met with sword and blade. Bodies slammed into each other. Flesh was cut. Life lost. Wounded from the night prior, Tega took a slash across his upper thigh and stumbled. There was nothing he could do beside stare in resignation as death plunged down.

The explosion threw bodies aside in a hail of shrapnel and razor-sharp slivers of wood. Those caught nearest the blast were shredded. Pink mist floated in their wake. Secondary explosions rocked the battlefield. Smoke and flames erupted to a chorus of screams. Hands dragged Tega to his feet and away from the impact area, despite his protests. Thick, black smoke clouded the field. Figures in dark cloaks rushed past him. Tega thought they wore masks but was unable to make anything out in the haze. He struggled to break free and rejoin the fight. Rough hands tightened their grip and held him in place.

"That would be most unwise," a thin voice whispered in his ear. "We must be away before others come."

Tega ignored the man. His people were dying. They needed him. Still, his rescuers refused to let him go. They dragged him back farther. Several people in black cloaks hurried his way. Many bore prefects on their backs or under a shoulder. More than Tega hoped, yet far less than he wished. He was shoved around the corner a moment before a massive explosion rocked the area. The second floor of the nearest building collapsed under the force of impact.

Only when the cloud of dust and debris rolled past, was he allowed up on his own. Tega wheeled on the man who had spoken to him. "What was that? My people were still engaged back there!"

"Those prefects who yet lived were retrieved before the cannon was destroyed," the man replied, "Though I suspect it would have proven beneficial to recover the weapon than destroy it."

Tega's faced darkened with rage. "Who are you?"

"Timeus Thorn, at your service," he answered.

Eyes narrowed with suspicion, Tega pressed for more answers, heedless of the potential of being discovered by Mordai. "I've never seen you. Who do you work for and who are these others?"

"They are members of the Reclamator Guild. Men and women with special alchemical knowledge necessary to eliminate large targets," Timeous said. "As for who I am, well, that is a matter my master would best have left to another time, matters being what they are."

"Reclamators? When did they join the fight?" Tega asked. He winced as fresh jets of pain ran up his leg.

"About the same time the Assassin Guild decided to. The Mordai are many but so are the underlying hazards in this city. We are not as helpless as our foes believe. A fact they are discovering across the city. The god king may be gone but the Heart Eternal yet beats proud," Timeous said.

Reluctant to accept the gesture, Tega extended his hand in friendship. "My thanks, Master Thorn. I would like to invite you to continue the fight with us. Your timing was impeccable."

"If only I could, Tega Ig, but my talents are best used elsewhere," Timeous replied. "See to your wounded. The Mordai will not be stunned for long. Seize whatever advantages you can."

Timeous and his Reclamator squad disappeared into the smoke, heading back to the scene of their slaughter. Their departure weakened Tega's position but earned his respect. The city might stand, if others like Timeous Thorn were scouring the streets. Shaking off the nostalgia, Tega looked to those men and women still with him. Their fight was far from over.

The onslaught of violence rocked the Heart Eternal. Citizens without any notion of what was unfolding were caught in the middle. Prisoner numbers rose. The streets were no longer safe. So it was Abbas Doza and his small group of friends found themselves cast from their quest and thrown into an unexpected war.

Already a trail of bodies lay in their wake. Determined as he was, Abbas refused to become mired in pointless struggle, while his true targets remained. He argued this was the opportune moment to lift the price on his head and become a free man. Not even the Guild Masters would expect his brazen attack in the midst of such raw chaos.

They struck like vipers. Always unexpected and always with brutal lethality. Guild Masters were killed where they were caught. Abbas had no pretensions of trial or assigning quilt. His sole purpose was the recovery of his name. Freedom to operate under license again beckoned and he would not stop until he achieved that.

Explosions detonated across the city. Mordai cannons were smuggled into the city and being employed to repulse defenders. Abbas used them as cover as he slipped through the side entrance to his second to last target. Guild Master Euni Sequa awaited him in the main hallway. Her slender arms were folded. Blood stained the trim of her sleeves. A single lock of silver hair hung out of place on her otherwise perfect head.

"I assumed it was you," she said with a sneer. "You are as a bug needing to be squashed, lest your brood overrun us all."

"You talk too much," Abbas growled.

"Did you truly believe you could get away with it? Murder the god king? Fool. Your name was cursed the moment you took the job," Euni continued undeterred.

"None of that matters after you die here."

Her face remained placid. "There are larger matters at stake than your vanity. The day fast approaches when our kind will no longer be required. What then will you do? When the glory fades and you are forced to live on the run?"

"What are talking about? Speak plainly before I sever your head from your shoulders," he pressed.

Euni bit off a crisp laugh. "Fool, the god king is reborn. Your glory has already collapsed. No legend of Abbas Doza for future generations. No one shall remember your name."

"That makes two of us then," Abbas ground out and launched into his attack.

It was not until the sun broke the veil of night, that the battle tides shifted. Golden light blossomed across Ghendis Ghadanaban with unparalleled radiance. Warmth stole the chill as it penetrated every door and open window. The sonic boom knocked those caught unaware to the ground. Noses bled. Ears rang. Slowly, first a handful then others, began gazing up at the tower where the god king dwelt. Unnatural light, brilliant in every regard, flowed from the balconies. People fell to their knees in prayer as word spread. The god king was returned.

Fighting ground to a halt. Both sides struggled to comprehend what was happening. A sense of tranquility swept over the city. Weapons were laid down. Forgotten were the hatreds of the moment. Those nearest would claim unto their deathbeds that they were the first to view the god king reborn. A point of pride for entire families. Others wept and covered their faces lest the radiance melt their skin.

Through the light strode the figure of Omoraum Dala'gharis, reborn in new flesh. All that remained of Aldon Cay was locked away in the depths of distant memory. Invigorated by the rebirth, the god king looked down upon his city in turmoil and wept. So much hatred and destruction plagued them since his death. How many hundreds of his loyal flock no longer drew breath for the fraction of greed encroaching upon their dreams? Omoraum sniffed the morning wind. His enemies, those great betrayers, yet remained in the city walls. Those he would deal with later. First Ghendis Ghadanaban required cleansing.

The god king cast his arms to his sides and tilted his head back. When he sang, it was the voice of the heavens. Mordai soldiers fell dead. Their minds boiling at the foreign sound. Others ran screaming, only to be slaughtered by vengeful citizens and a small army of prefects led by the twice wounded Tega Ig. Battalions of Mordai fled Ghendis Ghadanaban. Officers and soldiers alike ran for their lives, for the power of the god king was too strong.

FORTY-ONE

Abbas Doza ran for his life. Golden light followed, tracking every turn and misdirect. He was covered in sweat and nearing exhaustion. Fear propelled him, though such raw emotion only went so far. When his legs finally gave out, Abbas turned to face his pursuer. He had been so close to his goal. One Guild Master remained. The man capable of pardoning and reinstating him. So close.

The light faded, leaving him with spots dancing in his eyes. His vision was blurred with tears as the figure took shape. Only once had he experienced such sights. The night he murdered the god king. Abbas marveled how life tended to come in circles. The assassin laid his weapons on the ground at his feet and waited.

"I have no regrets. Do you hear me? I took a job and performed it to the best of my ability. No one in history can claim to have killed a god king. Only me. Only Abbas Doza! Do what you must, for I have no shame in my deeds."

"You are forgiven," Omoraum said.

The god king's hand extended and a blast of pure light bathed Abbas. When it faded, the assassin was nothing more than a pile of ash, already blowing away in the quick breeze.

"Most of the fighting is ended. We have retaken all but one of the gates. Mordai sappers destroyed the hinges on the eastern gate during their assault and rigged them with some sort of bastardized cannon rounds," Tega reported.

Overseer Larris absorbed the reports from all field commanders. Most of the delegates, those still alive, were absconded to safehouses far from the fighting. Only now was she able to send recovery teams to collect the dead. Much to her dismay, Imperator Thrakus was nowhere to be found. She knew, as did Tega, the battle for Ghendis Ghadanaban would not end until he was found and brought to trial for his crimes.

"You have another problem," rumbled the deep bass of Capran Edeus. "With your Minister of State dead, the king of Eleboran will expect answers. Word has not reached your capital of the god king's return, magnificent as it was. I fear your trials are just beginning, Overseer Larris."

She regarded him a moment, absorbing the purity of his dark flesh. So different from her own. The emissary of Hyborlad, replete with golden rings and baubles, proved a staunch ally during the fighting. He had no love for the Mordai and suspected the truth behind the missing Uruth delegation. Not adverse to killing, Capran spent the better part of the night dispatching Mordai soldiers to the afterlife.

"One matter at a time, Ambassador," she said with a sigh. Thoughts of the king were the farthest from her mind. "We must re-secure the city and get the gates fixed before the Mordai decide to counterattack."

Capran balked. "Do you believe such is possible after the near annihilation of their best forces? I think you overestimate their prowess."

"At this point, I am unwilling to take anything for granted," she replied.

Capran bowed in response. "Perhaps then it is best your god king has resurrected. Are the reports of him walking the streets true?"

Larris paused. Until now, she'd failed to consider many implications of the quest's success. There was no doubt the god king had returned, but in what capacity? She prayed for guidance but received only silence among the roar of chaos as the Heart Eternal struggled to right itself. *How much a city can change in the span of but a day.*

"Ambassador, the god king is free to do as he pleases. This city was created by his kind and meant to serve as a bastion of hope and freedom," Larris chose her words carefully. "That he again walks the living world is a miracle to be sure, but we must not overlook the fact we have always been left to our own devices, except in the direst of circumstances."

"I can think of little more dire than usurpation," Capran replied.

"Overseer! We are getting reports of an unknown hostile approaching from the east," a runner shouted.

Conversations ceased as heads turned her way. Embarrassed by the sudden attention, the runner snapped to attention before Tega Ig and handed him the parchment.

"Thank you, corporal," Tega said. Larris and Capran edged closer, while he read the missive. "No word on what this thing is? Not some machination of the Mordai?"

"They say it is as if pure hatred stalks the lands," she replied. "Some claim to have spied fire and smoke rising from it as it moves nearer."

"This is no time for hearsay," Tega snapped. His frustrations already high, the Master of Prefects needed concrete facts, not supposition. "Larris, I am taking my staff and heading to the walls. I wish to see this calamity with my own eyes."

"We should depart now, before the beast gets too close," Larris answered.

He started to protest before recalling a similar defiance committed earlier in the day. Ghendis Ghadanaban was in good hands with a leader like Larris. "Very well. I shall have a carriage brought around."

Larris laid a gentle hand on his forearm. "I already have one waiting."

She slipped away to the bemusement of Capran. The Hyborlad Ambassador would never admit such in public, but he found the fire in the woman enticing. Hands tucked into his belt, he followed. They gained the central guard center on the eastern wall in no time. Prefects closed the roads, allowing her group to travel at speed, without concern over trampling citizens. Field glasses were prepared for them. Captains and militia leaders milled behind, as the city leaders crowded each other to get the better view.

"That is not human," Tega muttered. "I've never seen the like."

"We cannot defeat a creature like that with our weapons," Larris seconded. "What is it?"

A down draft announced the arrival of Lord Verian. He looked rejuvenated and ready for battle. "A demon from the beginning of the world. Razazel. The god kings once fought a terrible war against that foul race. Just like Omoraum, Razazel is the last of his kind. The others were killed over the span of millennia."

"Why has it come?" Larris asked, already guessing the answer.

"It must have sensed the god king's demise," Verian theorized. "It has come to finish the job. We must not allow that to pass. He will plunge the world into eternal darkness. My Scarlet are prepared to fight for you."

About damned time. Your winged heroes were absent during the fighting for the city. Tega folded his arms, his judgments private. His eyes were fixed on Razazel. Each step closer made the demon appear larger than life. He thought he spied elements of smoke and flame echoing in every footstep. Despair filled his heart. All he had fought for the previous night was now in jeopardy of being in vain.

The beat of many wings succeeded in drawing his attention away from approaching death. Tega Ig was amazed for the second time in as many moments, as ninety-eight Scarlet landed atop the wall. They represented the entire compliment. A more powerful force he could not imagine. Still, Tega harbored doubt that even they were enough to stop Razazel. Resplendent in their golden armor, the Scarlet awaited word from their Lord to attack. They were unafraid of death. Tega wished he had that power at his disposal.

A clarion blew wild notes across the city. As one, the Scarlet dropped to one knee and bowed their heads. Tega and the others glanced around for the source. Mouths fell open at the sight of the god king marching up the nearest stairwell to stand among his flock. Bodies obeying of their own, Tega found himself on his knees as well. So great was the power of the god king, they were forced to obey.

"Rise, my children," Omoraum ordered.

The Scarlet rose and drew their swords. Verian bowed his head with reverence before presenting himself before the god king. "My lord, Razazel approaches. There is no sign of his Orpheliac."

"Two have been destroyed. The third is yet to be awakened," Omoraum stated. "Your Scarlet will remain airborne while I meet this foe."

"But you are only returned to the world. Surely your powers have not manifested enough to defeat the demon," Verian protested.

An eyebrow arched. "You question my will?"

Rebuked, Verian backed down. "No. My concern is for your safety only. I have failed you once already and should be relieved of my duties for it. We cannot afford a second such loss."

Omoraum laid a hand on Verian's shoulder and the Lord of the Scarlet was buoyed with renewed confidence. "There will be no repeat, Verian. We shall speak on this later. For now, there is a battle to win."

The god king lifted into the afternoon sky, surrounded by pure golden light. The Scarlet rose around him. Vengeance lingered in their eyes. Now was the hour to cleanse their failings and return their order to glory. Close to one hundred thousand citizens waited behind the walls of Ghendis Ghadanaban, without knowing how close the end was. The Scarlet would fight and die for them and for the god king. They sped forward to war and destiny.

Omoraum landed without sound twenty meters before the approaching Razazel. Shock twisted the demon's features, for he assumed his minions were successful in preventing the resurrection. Undeterred by the change of facts, the demon halted and drew a curved black claw, dripping poisons.

"This city belongs to me, god king," he rasped.

Omoraum replied, "Not so long as a god king survives. You have broken the pact. Such crimes demand retribution."

"Countless millennia have I waited to claim my due. You will not delay me," Razazel despaired. Endless imprisonment spurred his actions. He was driven to the point of madness.

He sprinted forward and the battle of light and darkness resumed after so very long. Blades clashed. Golden rays of light burned against a shield of darkness. The ground withered and died beneath them as the demon siphoned strength from the soul of the world. Neither gained ground at first, for they were evenly matched. A wall of Scarlet hovered just out of range, ready to dive down on Razazel, should the god king require it. None were as transfixed by the ferocity of the fighting as Verian.

His desire to avenge his failures nearly consumed him. It took every ounce of will to obey the god king's last order. Flames burst from a fresh fissure as Omoraum missed with what was meant to be a death blow. Razazel struck in the same motion. Claws raked the god king's armor. Sparks and dark ichor flashed before the light burned them away. Off balance, Omoraum reeled back before his foe decapitated him.

Razazel committed his first tactical mistake by thinking victory was at hand. He pursued the god king, abandoning all pretense of defense. The move proved almost fatal. Omoraum used the deceit to whip the tip of his sword through Razazel's sword wrist. Foulness marred the ground where the demon's blood splattered. Instead of pressing the assault, Omoraum retreated from the viscous material. His sword pointed to the demon's chest.

"This ends now, blight," Omoraum decreed.

He jammed his sword into the ground. Light so pure, it blinded the demon. The god king watched as Razazel, panicked by the sudden turn of events, stared down at his legs. True fear filled his body. Hair and lesions burned away, as the light crawled up his legs to his waist. He screamed when it reached his chest. A clawed hand reached for the god king, but he was frozen in place. His sword disintegrated as the light devoured it. The demon's mouth opened for a final scream, as the light crawled over his head and into his mouth.

Razazel collapsed, yet still breathing. Omoraum stood over the demon, a conqueror with a benevolent streak. Summoning his Scarlet, the god king knelt beside his ancient enemy. Alive, the demon was unable to move, speak, or escape.

"You should kill him and be done with it, Lord," Verian suggested. The sight of Razazel filled him with loathing.

"No, there must be balance in the world. We are the last of our kinds, Verian. Killing either gives the other unlimited power," Omoraum said. "He is to be returned to his prison and left to rot in darkness. Do not think to disobey me on this," he added, after seeing the look of hate in Verian's eyes.

"It will be done," the Lord of the Scarlet assured.

Omoraum stood back so his Scarlet could sweep in and secure the demon. Once finished, they prepared for the long flight to the Nameless Mountain. The god king stopped them. "Verian, know that Caestellom acquitted himself with honor. Though he gave his life for my sake, his name will be etched in the halls of glory for all to remember. Your Scarlet remain in great esteem. Go now, lest the demon awakens and renews our battle so soon."

Omoraum Dala'gharis stood alone for some time after that. He sensed the approaching armored personnel carrier rumbling across the distant horizon. It would be days yet before the quest survivors and their alien comrades arrived. They were his last great secret. A separate game yet to be played. For now, the Heart Eternal needed rebuilding. Major positions in several of the ruling bodies were depleted. Those were human affairs, and though Sandis contracted his assassination, the god king was resigned to let them play out. He had other business to attend. At a table in the White Crow sat an old friend with whom he needed to have a word.

It was two days later when a bedraggled Imperator Thrakus was discovered by a squad of prefects. Dressed in rags and stinking of human filth, the Mordai pretended to be a citizen but his face was too well known. He was detained and kept on the side of the street until Tega Ig arrived to confirm his identity. The Master of Prefects wasted little time acknowledging the prisoner as Imperator Thrakus.
With those words, Thrakus was said to have stood taller with lost pride and demanded to be treated according to the peace treaties signed by the major kingdoms. Tega Ig, acting as supreme justice authority in the city, executed him on the spot with a single pistol shot and left his body for all to see. Just another casualty in a long list of atrocities still being uncovered. There was no grave marker or proper burial for the man responsible for so much pain and death. With Thrakus dead, some semblance of order began to return to the Heart Eternal.

FORTY-TWO

Days turned into weeks as the Heart Eternal slowly recovered from the nightmares of invasion. The stain of Mordai occupation, remarkably higher than any imagined for such short tenure, was washed away like so much filth. Once more, the Scarlet patrolled the night skies. Reports of the risen dead, fell. The city was able to breathe again. A wave of fresh recruits, eager to prevent another insurrection, flowed into prefect recruiting stations. Depleted ranks were ready to be filled.

So it was one late afternoon that no one paid attention to the three travelers entering the south gate. A prefect, Reclamator, and prophet returning from their perilous quest to the deep south. A quest none would ever learn the truth of, nor know of. Their glory was etched in the annals of Ghendis Ghadanaban. They would never want again. Larris saw to that. She vowed their deeds great enough to earn full pensions with bonus.

Tula and Falon stood alone in an empty chamber. Delegates were long gone. Meone had been whisked away to his Order. His part in the tale ended with anonymity. No one would know his name. Time offered little healing for his shattered mind. Meone struggled to the end of his days, trying to understand all he had seen and done. Others praised him a hero. It was praise he felt he did not deserve. By his own admission, his actions during the quest were limited and mired by indecision. It would not be until many decades passed before his services were called on again. This time, there was no simple solution. It would take all his will just to survive.

"We have come a long way, Tula," Falon said. Her emotions remained mixed. The prefect still despised the Reclamator Guild, but Tula had proven her worth a hundred times over. "It saddens me to part after so much."

"This is not that large of a city, Falon. We might run in to each other again," Tula replied. Her tone was warm, for she had come to form a bond with the once rigid sergeant.

Falon dreaded the return to duty. With the city in its current state, there seemed little opportunity in the future for familiar pleasantries. Their unspoken bond was strong but filled with missed chances. Falon was a woman of few friends, choosing to dedicate her life to her job and the city. Tula's friendship changed that.

"There is much left to be done," Falon said. "I can make no promises."

Tula shrugged, a gesture she did not feel. "There is always the White Crow. Eamon Brisk is a good man, with the best drinks in town."

"We deserve some after what we've been through," Falon agreed. Her mind already worked through tomorrow, hoping to find a way to make that happen. The shadow of prefect captain edging into the doorway drew her attention. "My time has come. I wish you the very best in this life, Tula Gish. You are a true hero and a champion worthy of such title."

She extended her hand. Tears forming, Tula leaned forward to embrace her former foe. They hugged for long minutes before either was able to break free. Raw emotions spilled over. They parted ways sobbing, not from sadness but from the release of bitter memories. It was a cleansing of sorts. One neither was familiar or comfortable with. Falon reluctantly disengaged and went back to work.

Her story would continue for years, seeing her rise to the position of Master of Prefects. Already at an old age, Falon Ruel was one of the most beloved leaders in city history. Her battles were many and varying in severity, but she used each experience to craft her career and reputation. She and Tula remained friends until the end of her days.

Tula stood alone for longer than she knew. Events of their quest flashed by, presenting her with challenges and issues she struggled to comprehend. Her tears continued until sundown. By then, she was sore and exhausted. Head down on the nearest table, she failed to hear the soft slippers enter and halt beside her.

"This is no state for one of Ghendis Ghadanaban's greatest living heroes."

Tula jerked up and wiped the grime away. "Overseer Larris. Forgive my appearance."

"Nonsense. We are all entitled to rare fits of emotion. You most of all," Larris sat beside her. "I have need of your continued service. The Guild leaders have been notified. You will be compensated for your time and efforts."

"What is it I must do?" Tula asked.

Larris laid soft fingers on her sleeve. "Come to my office in the morning. You and I are about to start a lengthy relationship. I wish you to serve me directly. This experience has shown me our weaknesses and I will not be taken unaware again."

She saw the doubt lingering behind Tula's eyes. "Take the night to think on it. Healing will come naturally. You cannot force it. Thank you for all you have done for us, Tula. You truly saved the city."

Not trusting her voice, Tula hung her head. A fresh wave of tears approached.

Halfway across the city, deep in his private laboratory, Hean drummed his fingers on the aged cherry desk. Every effort at recreating eternal life met with dismal failure. Dozens of specimens were cast away, turned into the risen dead. The bright spot in that was, he helped keep the Reclamators in business. A shame really, but the consequences of failure. He wrote off the losses in trade value. The Arax Trading Company moved in swiftly after the debacle of the Mordai incursion. Fresh contracts were created with all the neighboring kingdoms, Eleboran notwithstanding. All efforts to communicate with the king were shunned. Apparently the loss of his favored minister left the man with an ill taste regarding the Heart Eternal.

The door creaked open and Timeus Thorn slipped in. Hean considered the man before him, expecting ill news. Instead, Timeus offered a wry grin. "Good evening, Master Hean."

"What this time, Timeus? I am in no mood tonight," Hean dismissed him.

Timeus sat without being offered. "You should be interested to hear this."

Knowing there was no escape from the conversation, Hean leaned back and poured a glass of brandy. "Go on."

"As you know, I offered my services to several factors during the night of fighting," Timeus began. "Ignoring certain deeds, I have raised your standing in important eyes. The Lord of the Scarlet is most appreciative."

"Unless he is willing to offer contract for your deeds, that fails to interest me," Hean warned.

"Not that I am aware, but that is not the point of this conversation. During my exploits, I managed to find a most interesting character wandering through the depths of violence. I believe you are interested in Valir the Tongueless?"

"He lives?" Hean spit his brandy out. The return of the god king left him with the realization of his favored servant meeting an untimely demise far from the city. Learning the northerner lived was news, indeed. It also prompted fresh suspicion of betrayal.

"And reaped a terrible toll among the Mordai. It appears he has issues to work out with the conclusion of his last assignment," Timeus admitted. "Fortunately, for you I managed to convince him to return home. He should be arriving shortly."

"How many survived?" Hean asked.

"Just Valir. The man is most resilient."

Hean resisted the urge to place his face in a palm. The gross incompetence of his staff pushed him closer to the edge of insanity. What he would give for one moment of brilliance. "Have him report to me immediately. There is much I wish to discuss with our northern friend."

"Of course," Timeus said and rose. "If there is nothing else?"

Disturbed, Hean waved him away and returned to his drink. There was still much to be accomplished before he could rest. Immortality awaited. It belonged to him. Hean was left alone, with only the odd bone box to keep him occupied.

Efforts to elect a replacement for the late Sandis Vartan stalled through arguments and discontent. Rife with betrayal and concern, the Order of Prophets struggled to establish dominance in the new regime. Suspicion mocked them, for word had spread through anonymous sources of the First Prophet's role in the god king's assassination. The people were unforgiving and unwilling to forget. Overseer Larris attempted placing oversights on the secretive Order until a suitable replacement was emplaced but the Scarlet intervened.

Only the god king commanded the Prophets and his wrath was severe.

Tega Ig cared little for their self-induced turmoil. His prefect corps was rebuilding, with slight emphasis on military training. Tega vowed never to be caught with his pants around his ankles again. It took many months but he recovered from his wounds. Many would suffer with the guilt of murdering Thrakus in the streets but he found the memory kept him warm during those cold nights. Hardest for him was resisting the urge to turn Ghendis Ghadanaban into a police state. The will of the people would never tolerate such intrusions.

Content with his position, Tega remained on duty for many years. A day of reckoning would come when Mordai assassins, harboring deep thoughts of vengeance, stole into the city and found him alone one night. The statue erected in his honor stood proudly outside of the prefect headquarters. As was often, heroes became martyrs in a world at war.

The kingdom of Eleboran failed to find a peaceful solution with the militia. Malach and his tribes continued their war for many years, each side trying to eliminate the other. King J'hquar passed without seeing an end to civil war. Foreign soldiers occupied his kingdom for over a decade until a council of peers attempted to carve Eleboran into small enclaves. The future in peril, the civil war turned in a new direction.

None of this affected Relghel Gorgal. The fallen god enjoyed his days and nights in the comforts of the White Crow. No one bothered him. His confederates were dead. Their roles played out to the end. None but the god king would ever learn the truth behind his actions. Their relationship proved difficult, for eternals had long memories.

"That's the look of a man with much on his mind," Eamon announced, as he arrived with a fresh pitcher of ale.

Relghel grinned, the act so slight, it almost went unnoticed. "We live in interesting times, my friend. Please, sit."

Eamon did. Silence dominated them for long moments. "Is it over?"

"No. This was but the beginning," Relghel replied without pause. "There are powers at work in the world that even I fail to comprehend. Omoraum needed to die. It was the only way to flush out Razazel."

"I fail to see the logic behind that," Eamon said after swallowing a mouthful of ale. "What can be worse than an ancient demon come to conquer us?"

"Do you truly wish to know, or shall we continue to live out our lives in blissful ignorance?" the fallen god asked. "Razazel is the threat we knew. Both Omoraum and I have sensed the coming of something far more powerful, more sinister. Our world will be in jeopardy. By removing one nightmare from the board, I was able to buy us time."

"By sacrificing Sandis and Abbas?" Eamon asked.

"Their losses will be felt for some time but were necessary. Both men were consumed with greed and power," Relghel admitted. "They would have acted in similar fashion without my interference."

"You allowed the god king to die," Eamon pointed out. He looked around conspiratorially. "That alone should see you at the bottom of a prefect prison."

"What is it you fear, Eamon Brisk?"

"I'm still trying to work that out. Are you a threat to the Crow?" he asked.

Relghel sighed. He wished he had a better answer. "I do not know."

They drank in silence for some time, content to let the future sort itself.

"It sure is a sight," Tine exhaled.

Since dropping the quest survivors off less than a day's walk from the Heart Eternal, the squad remained in place. Too many military units were in play throughout the kingdom, making it impossible for *Beast* to rumble away undetected. They parked in a large grove of iron trees, the twisted trunks spiraling high. It was the first time since crash landing, the beleaguered squad found down time.

"A sight to behold," Hohn agreed. "You thinking about going in?"

"We have been on our own for a long time now," the corporal replied. "I could use a bit of companionship and real food and drink again."

"We all could but it's not safe right now. We get anywhere close to that mess and there's no chance of getting home," Hohn cautioned.

Tine lowered his eyes. Whispers circled the squad. Home was lost. They were stranded on this world. Alone. Hopeless. No one was willing to say it aloud, for superstitions ran high among soldiers.

"What are we going to do next?" Tine asked, eager to change the subject.

Hohn wished he had a better answer. Anything to keep their spirits high. The cold reality was he had no actionable plan. Driving around the world in search of a potential escape plan was nothing more than sleight of hand. His worth was in combat, whether space or ground. Leading a small team of reluctant warriors across an alien landscape presented more challenges than the sergeant could fathom.

"We can't give up," Hohn finally said. "There must be other survivors from the ship."

"We should have heard something by now," Tine countered.

"What are the odds of the ten of us being the sole survivors from a ship carrying over ten thousand?" he asked. "There are more out there. Perhaps scattered across the planet. We owe it to ourselves, and them, to find as many as we can. The vehicles survived intact. Odds are more equipment did."

"You're hoping some of it is long range comms?"

Hohn nodded. "Hope is a powerful tool, Tine. We still have the militia to deal with. They may be tribal savages but Malach is a man of his word. It won't be long before he learns what happened to Delag, and us."

"We have the firepower to negate the tribes," Tine said.

"Kill the entire population? What would that make us? No, our best option is to lay low and keep our heads down. One day I would like to see home again." *Even if it is the austere corridors of a space station.*

Tine stretched and yawned. "What's our move?"

Hohn returned his gaze to the Heart Eternal. Longing conflicted with emotion, leaving him in an odd place. "There's no harm in staying here for a few more days. Hell, I might just be convinced to let the squad check out the city. It's a brand-new world for us, Tine. I don't know what tomorrow holds, but all we can do is meet it head on."

Corporal and sergeant sat atop *Beast* and wondered what the future held.

EPILOGUE

Jorrus Cay awoke to the sound of footsteps creaking across his common room floor. Careful, deliberate and uncomfortably familiar, his heart thudded. The older man slipped from the bed and reached for the rifle he kept against the wall. Not every district in the Heart Eternal promised peace. Jorrus slipped into a light tunic and offered a prayer to the god king. Heart in his throat, he went in search of the intruder.

The house was empty. Windows were shuttered. Door locked. Jorrus had grown more cautious since Aldon disappeared. With his wife on death's door, he struggled with trying to find reason behind life. He felt alone. Abandoned by everyone he loved. Steeling his mind against the inevitable, he spent his days trying to forget the bad times. Madness awaited otherwise. Satisfied no intruder lurked, Jorrus poured a small cup of water before going back to bed. Nights with his wife were fleeting, coming to an end much sooner than either wanted. He did not want to miss a single moment.

Thus, it was he failed to spy the soft golden light slipping from beneath the bedroom door. Eyes sore from exhaustion, he pushed open the door and gazed upon a wonder. Bathed in golden light, the god king stood over his wife's sleeping figure. The look on her face was complete serenity. The god king reached down to place a golden hand on her brow. She sighed as waves of energy pulsed into her fragile body.

When it was done, the god king stepped back and turned to Jorrus. "There is no need of that with me, Jorrus Cay. I did not come to harm you."

Redness burned his face as he noticed the rifle was aimed at the god king's chest. "S'sorry."

"She is healed. The two of you will live long, meaningful lives," the god king explained without prompt. "Love her. She needs you more than you imagine."

Jorrus blinked away the tears and when he could see again, the god king was gone. He stood alone in his bedroom. A soft groan drew his attention. Jorrus looked down to see his wife smiling back at him.

"I feel wonderful. Oh Jorrus, what happened?" she asked. Her voice was strong. Healthy like he remembered.

Jorrus laid his rifle down and sat beside her. "I honestly don't know."

They embraced and wept as only lovers could.

Night continued to pass across the Heart Eternal. It was a time of wonders for those who had already given up hope. The god king had returned, and all was right with the world once again.

END

Return to the Heart Eternal in:

DOWN DARK ROADS BEST FORGOTTEN

COMING SOON!

Check out these other great reads by
Christian Warren Freed

DREAMS OF WINTER
A FORGOTTEN GODS TALE
CHRISTIAN WARREN FREED

It is a troubled time, for the old gods are returning and they want the universe back...

Under the rigid guidance of the Conclave, the seven hundred known worlds carve out a new empire with the compassion and wisdom the gods once offered. But a terrible secret, known only to the most powerful, threatens to undo three millennia of progress. The gods are not dead at all. They merely sleep. And they are being hunted.

Senior Inquisitor Tolde Breed is sent to the planet Crimeat to investigate the escape of one of the deadliest beings in the history of the universe: Amongeratix, one of the fabled THREE, sons of the god-king. Tolde arrives on a world where heresy breeds insurrection and war is only a matter of time. Aided by Sister Abigail of the Order of Blood Witches, and a company of Prekhauten Guards, Tolde hurries to find Amongeratix and return him to Conclave custody before he can restart his reign of terror.

What he doesn't know is that the Three are already operating on Crimeat.

WHERE HAVE ALL THE ELVES GONE?

CHRISTIAN WARREN FREED

Everyone knows Elves don't exist. Or do they?

Daniel Thomas spent years making a career of turning his imagination into the reality of bestselling fantasy novels. But times are tough. No one wants to read about elves and dragons anymore. Daniel learns this firsthand when his agent flatly says no to his latest and, what he deems, to be greatest novel yet. Dissatisfied with the turn to zombies and vampire lovers, he takes his manuscript and heads out to confront his agent.

His world changes when he finds his agent dying on the floor of her office. Too late to help, he watches as her dead body disintegrates into a pile of ash and dust. Daniel doesn't have time to ponder what just happened as a band of assassins breaks in, forcing him to flee to the Citadel and the home of the king of the high elves in order to survive. Daniel soon discovers that all the creatures he once thought he imagined actually exist and are living among us. His revelation comes at a price however, as he is drawn into a murder-mystery that will push him to the edge of sanity and show him things no human has witnessed in centuries.

the Dragon Hunters

CHRISTIAN WARREN FREED

The Mage Wars are a fading memory. The kingdoms of Malweir focus on rebuilding what was lost and moving beyond the vast amounts of death and devastation. For some it is easy, others far worse. Some men are made in battle. Grelic of Thrae is one. A seasoned veteran of numerous campaigns and raids, Grelic is a warrior without a war. He languishes under mugs of ale and poor choices that eventually find him locked in the dungeons of King Rentor. His only chance at redemption is an offer tantamount to suicide: travel north with a misfit band of adventurers and learn the truth of what happened in the village of Gend.

Grelic, suddenly tired of his life, reluctantly agrees and meets the only survivor of the horrible massacre: Fitch Iane. Broken, mentally and physically, Fitch babbles about demons stalking through the mists and a terrible monster prowling the skies, breathing fire and death.

What begins as a simple reconnaissance mission quickly turns into a quest to stop Sidian, the Silver Mage from accomplishing his goals in the Deadlands. The last of the dark mages seeks to recover the four shards of the crystal of Tol Shere and open the gateway to release the dark gods from their eternal prison.

Grelic and his team are sorely outnumbered and ill prepared to deal with the combined threats of a dark mage and one of the great dragons from the west. Not even the might of the Aeldruin, high elf mercenaries, and Dakeb, the last of the mages, promises to be enough to stop evil and restore peace to Thrae.

BIO

Christian W. Freed was born in Buffalo, N.Y. more years ago than he would like to remember. After spending more than 20 years in the active duty US Army he has turned his talents to writing. Since retiring, he has gone on to publish more than 20 science fiction and fantasy novels as well as his combat memoirs from his time in Iraq and Afghanistan. His first book, Hammers in the Wind, has been the #1 free book on Kindle 4 times and he holds a fancy certificate from the L Ron Hubbard Writers of the Future Contest.

Passionate about history, he combines his knowledge of the past with modern military tactics to create an engaging, quasi-realistic world for the readers. He graduated from Campbell University with a degree in history and a Masters of Arts degree in Digital Communications from the University of North Carolina at Chapel Hill. He currently lives outside of Raleigh, N.C. and devotes his time to writing, his family, and their two Bernese Mountain Dogs. If you drive by you might just find him on the porch with a cigar in one hand and a pen in the other. You can find out more about his work by clicking on any one of the social media icons listed below. You can find out more about his work by following him on:

Facebook: @https://www.facebook.com/ChristianFreed
Twitter: @ChristianWFreed
Instagram: @ christianwarrenfreed

Like what you read? Let him know with an email or review.

warfighterbooks@gmail.com

CPSIA information can be obtained
at www.ICGtesting.com
Printed in the USA
BVHW031109300422
635802BV00017B/707